some
friendships
just end...

CRIMSON FADED

...others
come back
to bite you.

CAERYS CALLAGHAN

CRANTHORPE
—MILLNER—
PUBLISHERS

First published by Cranthorpe Millner Publishers (2025)

ISBN 978-1-80378-317-8 (Paperback)

www.cranthorpemillner.com

Cranthorpe Millner Publishers

For those who grew up obsessed with vampires,
here's something to dig your teeth into.

PROLOGUE

Thorn Manor

Ten years ago

Hazel Bridget stared up at the looming double doors of Thorn Manor. She knew they were a wealthy family – her best friend Ophelia Thorn had proven that with her expensive dress taste – so, as Hazel stood there, pulling at the slightly frayed hem of her T-shirt, she couldn't help but feel out of place compared to the grandness of it all.

A fountain sat in the driveway, buzzing in the otherwise quiet air as water sprayed out from a fish statue in the centre. There was an engraving on the marble of the fountain in a foreign language that Hazel couldn't decipher.

The manor house itself was a sight for sore eyes. Ivory white bricks were coated in vines and rose bushes ran up to the second floor windows. Despite the unlikely possibility of window washers willing to travel out this far, the glass was glistening and spotless in the faint spring sunlight.

Thorn Manor wasn't exactly part of Aramoor Bridge, Hazel's hometown. It was on the outskirts, up in the forest that overlooked the small town. The woods stretched out for miles, and the Thorn estate took advantage of the natural concealment, hiding away from the rest of the town.

Hazel had been met with the black iron gates surrounding the manor and immediately took them as a challenge. Sure, her hands were raw and her knees hurt from the jump, but her determination outweighed anything else.

The giant timber door seemed to swallow her melodic knocking, and she took a step back to wait for it to open. After a moment of silence, she frowned.

Hazel fumbled with her sleeves, blowing out an awkward breath as she let her head roll onto her shoulders to study her surroundings a little more. The pathway leading to the front door was adorned with pebbles, each one carefully arranged to highlight the shape of the glossy black driveway on which sat an outdated, but very expensive-looking car.

They had agreed on noon; it was now almost two. Hazel was losing patience. This wasn't the first time her headstrong best friend had been late. The girl was probably redoing her pigtails or changing her outfit for the fifth time – Ophelia Thorn was pretty high maintenance for an eight-year-old. This was, however, the first time Hazel had been impatient enough to actually come to her best friend's house.

It was odd. There was an elegance to the manor, but at the same time it made Hazel uneasy. It was almost too perfect. They didn't seem open to visitors, as the locked gate suggested, but it was more than that; she felt like she was being watched, and the feeling caused the hairs on the back of her neck to stand up. She turned and, for a second, she almost left, though the door opened before she could.

Hazel turned back to the front door to see Caleb Thorn standing in front of her, a mixture of amusement and confusion coating his face.

She jumped slightly, biting back the small squeal that threatened to escape her lips as she scrunched her nose at the blond boy, making him chuckle under his breath.

Caleb was Ophelia's older brother. Even though he was barely a year older than his sister and only a few months older than Hazel, he rarely hung out with them, mainly because the Thorns avoided each other like the plague at school, as siblings usually did.

"Dominique?" he asked with a sweet smile, holding the giant oak door close to his chest and subsequently blocking Hazel's view of the hallway inside.

"It's Hazel. Dominique's just my name on the register at school, it's not my real name," she replied with a raise of her shoulders.

Caleb leaned his head onto the doorframe and let out a soft hum. "It's not your real name? Are you undercover? Like a spy?"

She blinked at him in return.

"Are you here for information?" He bent forwards with a smirk before his expression fell. "Wait, *are you* here for information?"

Hazel pouted. "No! I just don't like my first name! My middle name is better. Even my mum calls me Hazel."

Caleb snickered. "Hazel suits you more. It's a nice colour, brown and green, just like your hair," he said, pointing at the bunched-up ponytail at the top of her head before reaching over and picking out a leaf.

"Huh? Oh," Hazel blurted, widening her eyes at the leaf in his palm. It must have tangled into her hair during her climb.

Caleb let his head fall back against the side of the door as he crossed his arms. "So, *Hazel*, what are you doing here?"

Hazel straightened out her face and let the remaining leaves fall out of her hair with a shuffle. "Ophelia was supposed to meet me at the park hours ago. My mum already dropped me off and I got bored waiting," she explained, looking over Caleb's shoulder and into the house.

Caleb followed her line of sight, then subtly pulled the door closer to his chest. Hazel frowned and opened her mouth to speak, but he got there first. "Oh, well, I'm not that surprised. If she were on time, the world would implode." He blew out an over-enthusiastic breath, mimicking an explosion as she stared, blinking at him, then he pointed behind her. "Climbed the gate?" he asked, although the humoured look on his face suggested he already knew the answer.

Hazel nodded, and Caleb let out another pleased sound that grew into a curious hum.

"How did you find us? I mean, no one ever knows where we live."

She shrugged and pointed towards the road leading into the forest. "Well, Ophelia always gets us to drop her off up the road there, so I followed it. This is the only house around."

Caleb raised an eyebrow. "You followed it? Up from the road? All this way?"

With a nod, Hazel pointed to her sticker-covered bike that she'd left leaning against the other side of the gate. "I don't know how Ophelia walks all that way. It took me ages to ride here. Almost burst a tire." She shrugged.

Caleb smirked, leaning closer to speak again when his smile suddenly faded.

Hazel narrowed her eyes as he glanced behind the door, whispered to someone on the other side, and then peered back over, looking past her, something like alarm in his eyes. He was looking at the ground a few feet away from where she was standing, his face pale. He gulped, moving back between the doors again.

The wind screeched through the trees, bleeding into the buzzing of the water fountain as Hazel slowly turned, trying to see what Caleb had seen, but nervous too, because what could possibly have caused this reaction in him? She caught the briefest glimpses of the splash of something red, but her best friend's cheery voice grabbed her attention before she could properly make out what it was.

"Hazy! So sorry I'm late. Come on, let's go before anyone takes our swings!" Ophelia trilled, almost knocking her brother over as she skipped past him, grabbing onto Hazel's arm.

"Wait, what about Cal—" As Hazel spun back around, she realised the door was now closed and Caleb was gone. She blinked at the speed of it all and let out a confused breath, but before she could question it any further, Ophelia pulled at her arm, dragging her away from the manor.

As her friend guided her toward the gate – quite roughly at that – Hazel snuck another glance at the spot Caleb had been staring at. Now she could clearly see there was a dark stain on the pebbles leading to the front door; sunlight glistened off the trail, almost as if the pebbles were wet. Nearby was a small clear plastic bag. It was torn down the middle with some sort of sticker on the front. She never got to read the writing on it, or question the puddle it left, before she was dragged out through the black iron gates.

CHAPTER ONE

Mundane

Leaves flew around Hazel's bare feet as she ran through the forest. Her heart was beating fast, thumping out of her chest with the urge to *get away*, though she didn't know what exactly she was running from, or who.

It was just getting dark out. The moon provided a dim light on the uneven forest grounds surrounding her, while shadows bounced off the copper-coloured leaves, making them look like fireflies as they fell.

A branch snapped from somewhere up ahead and Hazel's heart sank, plummeting deeper as she lifted her gaze toward the towering trees where a dark, hooded figure was waiting for her, looming ominously. An ambush.

It was difficult for Hazel to see in the faded light – everything seemed dreary and blurred – but she could make out the messy, dark brown hair peeking out from under the figure's raised hood.

The figure stepped forward, revealing a ragged-edged dagger, which should have been her cue to run again. However, she was completely bewildered, unable to move, until a crow startled her, swooping down and throwing off her balance.

As she regained her composure, Hazel had a sudden realisation – she was only a few metres away from the unmistakable black iron gate that led to her ex-best friend's house.

Nervously, Hazel swallowed and made an effort to move closer to the safety of the manor when her feet slipped, and she tumbled into the mud. A sharp sting shot up her back, winding her, and she frowned, coughing up a dark red substance. The metallic taste clung to her lips, causing her to stumble and grasp at branches for stability.

With her other hand, Hazel reached behind her back and felt the warmth of blood flowing over her fingers, followed by the feeling of icy metal against her skin.

She gasped, grabbing the dagger and craning her neck over her shoulder. This seemed to lure the crow back to her as it flew past her head into the dark forest behind, straight towards the hooded figure whose mouth fell open as his gaze dropped onto Hazel, mumbled words falling from his lips.

She thought any sane person would be running as fast as they could in the opposite direction, but something about the boy didn't ignite that natural fear inside of her. Instead, she felt a dawning obligation to get closer.

Hazel tried to stand, pushing up on her arms, but the pain was too overbearing and she slipped further into the thick mud, mixing it into her blood like some sort of cursed soup. She shuddered at the gunk, trying not to gag as she glanced upwards.

The cloaked figure's voice grew louder, echoing around the misty trees in an eerie cadence, and for some unknown, probably idiotic reason, she just *had* to know what he was saying.

Despite her own cries of pain, Hazel dragged herself forward. Her eyes watered in the mist that filled the air, blowing her matted hair into her face as she squinted, trying to see better. From what she could make out – which wasn't much – the figure had brown eyes, a stark golden colour that fell between the lines of light and dark. His face, which was otherwise indistinguishable, was highlighted by chiselled cheekbones and faint dimples that were hidden beneath his scornful expression.

As Hazel approached him, he suddenly started screaming, his mouth stretching wide like a scene from a horror movie. Hazel pulled a face, shielding her ears from the unbearable screeching, until she couldn't bear it anymore and clamped her eyes closed.

Out of nowhere, the boy yelled her name. Not the one she had grown accustomed to, Hazel Bridget, but the one she had tried to erase from her memory, her legal name.

"Dominique Valdez!"

Hazel's eyes snapped open, hand reaching for the wound on her back as an alarm blared through the room.

With a sigh of relief after finding nothing, she dropped her hand from her back and grabbed her phone, shielding her eyes from the glare of sunlight that filtered through her curtain as she snoozed her alarm.

It was barely seven in the morning and classes didn't start until nine, so she twisted around in her sheets, letting herself fall face first into the pillow with a grumble.

Hazel was a second-year sixth form student at Aramoor Academy, the local – and only – secondary school situated in her little town of Aramoor Bridge. It was a mundane school in a fairly quiet town, not much happened apart from the odd supermarket shoplifting scandal, though that was a given being far out in the remote English countryside.

The nightmare replayed itself in Hazel's mind, prompting

her to reach to her back again just to be sure. Thankfully, it was still blood free, no wound, no dagger, no physical harm. Just a bad dream. This was at least the fourth time she'd had it. Her dreams were set on a constant loop, always replaying the same scene and consisting of the same cast – the crow, the hooded guy, Thorn Manor.

She'd brought the dream up to her mother, Nina. Nina had toyed with Hazel's idea of night terrors but eventually brushed it off as stress and an overactive imagination. She even went as far as to suggest, in a firmly disapproving tone, that it was an, "*Unconscious way of wondering about your father.*" And that put an uneasy but firm end to the conversation.

Valdez was Hazel's father's surname. And the name Dominique must be linked to him in some way as well, because after he left them, her name had changed from Dominique Valdez to Hazel Bridget, Bridget being her mother's maiden name. The original name still appeared on her old birth certificate and other personal documents though, so no matter what her mother did to distance Hazel from the father she barely knew, she couldn't ignore the fact that she'd once shared a name with the man who had abandoned them.

There were only three things Hazel knew about her father. The first, his name was Alden Valdez, the second, he was Puerto Rican, and the third, he was demon-spawn; a man that her mother refused to talk about.

Hazel sighed. There were so many things her mother *didn't like* to talk about, no matter how many questions Hazel had.

As always, she focused on letting the dream subside from her consciousness, convincing herself that her dream paranoia was just that – paranoia – before relaxing on her phone until she had to shower.

Guitar solos, gritty electric ballads, and shirtless guys in

Scream masks populated her Instagram feed along with some makeup pages she liked to take inspiration from – despite mostly just wearing eyeliner. Sometimes she'd draw tiny stars in the outer corners of her eyes, but she usually wiped them off before she left.

While scrolling, she stumbled upon the unrealistically flawless face of her former best friend, who had posted an unnecessary number of pictures. Trying to escape, Hazel scrolled away, but the blonde's influencer-like posts continued to flood her feed. They showed the girl twirling her bleached curls around her finger with an angelic smile, masking the true malevolence lurking under her glittery eyeshadow.

Hazel had first crossed paths with Ophelia Thorn at five years old, a lifetime ago, on their first ever day at school, forming a bond over their mutual fear of unfamiliarity and sticking to each other like glue. That friendship didn't last for long. Eventually Ophelia decided Hazel wasn't good enough for her. Like her father, she had swiftly disappeared from Hazel's life, just as everyone seemed to.

Due to her own insecurities, Hazel may have overreacted. She'd told everyone she knew to watch out for the bleach blonde backstabber and insisted Ophelia would set anyone on fire if it meant she could stare at herself in the flames – along with a few other *not very nice* things.

Rumours spread from that, and soon enough, Ophelia became Aramoor Bridge's *It* girl. Everyone feared her, never really daring to get close, all the while brimming with an overwhelming desire to befriend her. They were in awe of her, her beauty, her sharp tongue, watching her like she was some sort of predator behind the glass at a zoo and, weirdly enough, Ophelia seemed to love it, the attention of it all, probably the power that came from it, too. Hazel almost felt justified for what she had done because of that.

Ophelia had ripped the plaster off, but Hazel had poured salt into the wound, wedging a point between them that could never be bridged.

Maybe that was the reason her dream bothered her so much. Why did the most horrifying part take place at Ophelia's home? What was her subconscious trying to tell her?

Following a quick breakfast, Hazel waited on the pavement outside her house, picking at her faded nail polish until a familiar car pulled into the driveway.

"There she is, the light of my life!" a cheery voice called from the open window of a small, egg-shaped car.

Shielding her eyes from the sun, Hazel sighed at the expectant look she'd received. "Apple of my eye," she replied, earning a gleeful smile in return.

"Fruit of my loin!" the other girl chirruped in her east London accent, plopping both arms out of the window.

With a bemused expression, Hazel shook her head, walking around to the passenger side of the car. "Grim. I want nothing to do with your loins," she protested playfully, slumping into her seat.

Dramatically, her friend placed a hand on her heart and let out an exasperated huff. "Oi, you'd be lucky for a slither of my loins. My lovely, lavish, lusciously divine loins." She over-enunciated each word, revelling in Hazel's distaste.

Hazel pulled the seatbelt over herself with a pleading look. "Oh god, stop, please. It's too early for you to be going on about your loins."

Amber placed her hands on the wheel and clicked her flowery nails onto it as she started the car back up. "Fine," she said, elongating the vowel. "Finished your assignment, then?"

Amber Surley had a heart of gold and could get along with anyone, though she decided to spend most of her time with Hazel, despite her lack of popularity. It wasn't her fault exactly, she was nice enough to her classmates, just a little socially awkward in certain situations. They'd been inseparable since they were fifteen, when Amber moved to her father's hometown and Ophelia became a living embodiment of *Jennifer's Body*.

Amber was always described as being as pretty as a picture – mostly by pensioners in the nursing home she volunteered at and her father, who, after losing his wife, coddled his daughter like there was no tomorrow. She had warm brown eyes and rich dark skin, always complemented by soft pastel colours and paisley sweaters.

"We have another one of those?" Hazel mumbled, wrinkling her nose while she picked at the fraying holes in her jeans.

Amber tutted under her breath, pulling away from the cul-de-sac and onto the main road. "Yeah, they tend to be a common occurrence, surprisingly. The one for Mr Hardington's class? The one he gave you an extension for. You still haven't done it?"

Hazel shrugged her shoulders defensively. "I… started it… and then took a break and then had a breakdown, so took another break, and that break lasted a… long time."

With a sigh, Amber shook her head. "This is the third assignment you've missed. He's going to lose it."

Instead of replying, Hazel gave her friend a small, forced smile and stared out the window as the car filled up with a mixture of pop and country music.

Dozens of trees passed by them in a blur, and Hazel's eyes wandered to where they always did, up the hill on the far side of town and into the forest. All she could see was green, but she knew there was something more beyond that: the home of her nightmares. Thorn Manor.

After lunch, the girls strolled down the colourless school corridors, making their way to their lockers. They were already running late to class due to an unfortunate incident with a juice carton, leaving them alone in the corridor.

Hazel aggressively wiped at her favourite leather jacket, trying to rid it of the smell of orange juice. Beside her, Amber was studying a piece of paper, one that had a cheesy cartoon sun in the corner.

"*La clima se ve buena hoy,*" Hazel read, glancing at the page with a raise of her eyebrow. She looked towards the wide panelled window to their left, noting the grey fog outside, and crinkled her lip with a small snort. "The weather is looking good today, my arse."

Amber glanced up from her page, snickering, before leaning back against her locker with a teasing swoon. "It's so sexy when you talk Spanish, do it again."

"*El olor de este jugo de naranja me está enfermando,*" Hazel said, still wiping unenthusiastically at her stained jacket.

Amber giggled and stuffed the piece of paper into her tote bag, looking up proudly. "The smell of this orange juice is knocking me sick?"

Hazel nodded, impressed. "Yeah. Hey, that Spanish class is really working."

"Good. I knew it was worth taking on the extra workload," Amber replied, pulling a pack of makeup wipes from her locker and offering them out.

"Why?" Hazel mumbled, grabbing a wipe gratefully.

The other girl shrugged, with a gentle smile on her face. "My best friend speaks the language. It made sense for me to take the class."

"Well, you picked it up fast."

On her father's side, Hazel was half Puerto Rican, and British on her mother's side, although she didn't know where exactly her mother had grown up, only that it was somewhere up north, on the border. When Hazel was younger, she'd been determined to learn Spanish, since that was the language spoken in Puerto Rico and she wanted to feel in some small way close to her father. Even if Nina hated him, he was still her dad; his blood was her blood. She was Puerto Rican too.

She didn't use it much nowadays, but it had come in handy for her Spanish GCSE at least.

Amber's attention was quickly pulled away by a buzz. A small, strained noise escaped the girl's throat as she read the notification from her phone. "Another person's gone missing from Henley Mar. That's only a few towns over." She frowned, holding her phone out.

Hazel pushed the device down and gave her friend a sympathetic look. "It's probably nothing. People gossip about these things and they get out of hand."

Amber gave her an unsure expression and shifted her attention back to her phone.

As she continued cleaning her jacket, Hazel's shoulders grew tense. A chilling sensation ran over her, sending a static-like feeling through her fingertips as her mind blurred with a strange sense of déjà-vu. She glanced up, accidentally slamming her locker shut and received a strange look from her friend, but before Amber could speak, Hazel noticed a dark hooded figure moving almost like a shadow in the dim corridor.

"Who is that?" she whispered.

The figure made his way towards an empty classroom, reaching for the handle, only to discover it was locked. His dark, messy hair was poking through the side of his hoodie, and as Hazel watched him push his body weight into the door as quietly as he could, another sickly wave washed over her.

The boy wore his hood up, likely under the impression it would cover his face, but Hazel could still see some distinguishable features as he glanced around the corridor.

His face was slightly grimy, as though he had been wandering the forest for days. Even with the thick material concealing his body, he was quite visibly muscular, and his eyes, the most standout characteristic from this distance, had a colour like sunlit tree bark.

With one last strike, the door opened, and as he vanished into the room, they exchanged a fleeting look.

"Huh? Who?" Amber muttered, still fixated on her phone.

Hazel blinked, peering down the hallway. "Never mind. I'll meet you in class, just got to do something first."

With a contemplative look, Amber nodded, before making her way down the opposing hall, pulling a pen to her mouth as she continued to stare at her phone.

As she got to the classroom door, Hazel's hand hovered over the handle, hesitant about whether to open it or not.

"Your whole hypnotic psychosis thing is freaking me out. Are you high?" a tauntingly bittersweet voice asked from behind.

When Hazel turned, she was met with Ophelia Thorn's

suspicious stare, her piercing blue eyes locked on her, as if *she* was the one that had just appeared out of thin air. The rich girl wore a black suede skirt and a cutoff jumper that showed off the tattoo on her ribcage, just below her right breast. A small crimson rose, its stem covered in thorns, just like her last name.

"I… no! Someone went in there," Hazel grumbled, reluctant to speak to the snarky blonde. She pushed through the door, ignoring the other girl's piercing gaze, only to find an empty room.

"Oh, great, I always knew you would lose it," Ophelia snickered, walking in behind her. "Just didn't think it would happen so soon."

"I'm not crazy! I saw him walk in here, it looked like he'd wandered in from the forest."

Ophelia laughed, leaning against a nearby desk. "Is *he* in the room with us right now?"

Hazel smiled sarcastically and turned toward the open window, feeling the cold breeze tugging at her skin. "Why would he climb out of the window?" she mumbled, more to herself.

With an annoyed breath, Ophelia moved from the desk and stepped closer. She stopped in front of the windowsill, her expression widening as she reached out to touch something on the ledge – an ashy, dark lilac substance that instantly had her recoiling.

Hazel watched the girl's cautious face, quirking an eyebrow at her peculiar reaction. "You never seen tobacco before?" she asked, holding back a snort as Ophelia's head snapped toward her.

"Do I look like someone who would involve myself in such disgusting habits? Wouldn't want the smell to overpower my Chanel."

Hazel grimaced in response. "I don't even know how to respond to that."

"Exactly," Ophelia replied, giving her a snide look before stepping past, shoving into her shoulder as she did so.

With a tired sigh, Hazel spun around, driven by the force of the movement. "What do you want? Why did you follow me in here?"

Ophelia shrugged. "Mr Hardington was asking for you because you were late, and I volunteered to come get you as an excuse to leave that god-awful room for five minutes. If I were you, I wouldn't bother going. He didn't look happy with you." A smirk replaced her snarl. "In fact, you might have a better chance of survival if you skipped town."

Exasperated, Hazel walked out of the room, leaving Ophelia alone to gaze out the window, probably planning her next verbal attack.

The moment Hazel stepped into class, the room was filled with overlapping conversations.

At the table beside the door, a couple of people were whispering about a girl from the year above who had disappeared. Before Hazel could hear any more, Mr Hardington tapped her shoulder. He was a short, stubby man, older than most of the teachers, with thinning grey hair that mainly clumped to one side of his head.

"Fifteen minutes late, Miss Bridget," he lectured, spitting a line of saliva with the words.

With a stoic expression, Hazel stepped past him, wiping her hand across her face and offering a feigned apologetic smile. "Don't start, don't start, don't start, don't start," she muttered under her breath like a mantra as she went, unsure if it was aimed at the grumpy old man or herself.

Over the course of the year, Mr Hardington had pretty much become the most significant obstacle in Hazel's life. At first, she'd ignored him, taken his words with a pinch of salt, but after a whole term of snide comments and dirty looks, she was beginning to lose her patience.

From their shared desk at the back, Amber looked up, clearly trying to show with her eyes that it was better to ignore him, though Hazel quickly averted her gaze.

"What was that?" Hardington demanded.

Hazel was aware of the entire class watching her now. They loved it whenever someone spoke back because it only took the slightest of things to set their teacher off.

"Nothing," she muttered, hoping he'd drop it, but that would be wishful thinking.

"Really, Miss Bridget? I'm sure you said something. For your sake, I'm hoping it was, 'yes, Mr Hardington, here is my essay', because if you've come into my classroom empty-handed again, then my ever-winding patience is going to run out!" His tone was harsh, blending into the sound of snickers. At the back of the room, Amber sighed and leaned onto her forearms.

Hazel risked a glance at the saliva-spitting man, letting out a sigh at the enraged look on his face. "I don't have it," she admitted, trying not to look around at the eager, vulture-like eyes watching them.

Hardington stared at her, and she tilted her head, cringing as he gazed down the bridge of his nose. "You better start writing! In fact, why don't you take the stage and give us all a live viewing? I want to hear your rendition of the reading loud and clear." He sat down heavily at his desk and gestured towards the front. A dozen pairs of eyes shifted between the two of them.

Without saying a word, Hazel spun around stiffly and headed toward the door.

"Wrong way, Miss Bridget! Come up here and show everyone what happens when you don't do your work in my class! You step out of that door, and you'll be back in this classroom every day this week after hours!"

Hazel kept walking, letting her boots scrape along the linoleum flooring. She wasn't even sure if sixth form students could get detention, since they were technically no longer part of the secondary school.

That hadn't really stopped Hardington before, however.

Upon reaching the door, she cast a final glance at him, blinked wildly, and turned away. As Hazel spun around, she collided with Ophelia, who was unfortunately just returning to the classroom.

They crashed into each other and Ophelia screeched. "What the f—"

Her words were abruptly cut off by Hardington. "Sit down!" he bellowed.

Ophelia narrowed her gaze. "Really? She bumped into me!"

He watched her for a second, enraged at the sudden outburst. "You too? You want a detention, girl?"

With an innocent look, Ophelia opened her mouth to speak, only to be cut off again.

"Just sit down!"

Icy blue eyes pierced into Hazel's as she slipped into her seat, tapping her acrylic nails against the wooden desk furiously.

Hazel furrowed her brow as she slipped out of the doorway, picking up her pace to get away before Hardington could plod after her. However, as she turned the corner, she crashed into someone else. She cursed under her breath and looked up as sturdy arms steadied her.

"Woah. You scared of missing the bus or something?" It was Caleb Thorn, smirking down at her. She recognised the breezy tone of his voice instantly, matched with a cheesy grin. He brushed a hand through his dirty-blond hair and chuckled softly, amused at her frustration.

"No. My English teacher's just an arsehole." Hazel sighed, glancing back over her shoulder with a frown.

After a moment, Caleb released her shoulders and offered a friendly smile. "Oh, Mr Hardington? Yeah. He can be a right dick, the trick is to hide his glasses in his desk before class starts. Can't pester you if he can't see you," Caleb mused, with a subtle wink.

Hazel looked up at him bemusedly. It was strange really, how different he was from his sister. Good strange. Even when they were kids Caleb had always been lovely. In the early years of secondary school, he used to sit and chat with her after school while she waited for Ophelia's dance or singing lessons to be over. They didn't see each other much now that they were older, but he still smiled at her in the corridors. Clearly, she'd picked the wrong sibling to befriend. "Thanks… I'll give it a try."

"No problem. Just don't get caught. I've heard he has a special room under the school for misbehaving students."

A small snort slipped through Hazel's lips and she shook her head. "Wouldn't surprise me."

"Apparently there's a blender down there, too, so I'd be careful, wouldn't want to get caught in that *mix-up*," he added, his eyes dancing with mischief.

Hazel cocked a brow. "Okay, bye, Caleb," she said, stepping away with a bewildered smile.

He waved as she disappeared behind the corner, moving towards the double doors that led out of the building.

CHAPTER TWO

Nightmare Reality

Hazel lifted the pendant of her necklace to her mouth. She'd already waited twenty minutes for the bus, and now it had started to rain. The water was only coming down in spurts, but it was still unpredictable, just like the town's public transport.

The bus stop had no seats, no windows, not even a roof. It was just a post and a board. Hazel didn't fancy standing in the rain for who knows how long, so she decided to think through her other options. There was, however, only one, and the thought of it alone made her want to chew right through her necklace.

There was a path that connected the back of the woods to the school, leading directly into the town centre. It wasn't that far, and it wasn't uphill like parts of the forest were further in land. Spread out around the countryside that linked the surrounding towns together were small grassy cliffsides, riddled with spiky pine trees.

It was pretty to look at, but it was a trek to get to. Thankfully this portion of the woods was all flat land. Hazel had opted for this route many times in the past. Sometimes Amber would drag her out for a jog, promising a trip to the nearest coffee shop for a hot chocolate at the end. But now, the forest seemed darker. A weird thickness danced in the air because of the rain, and Hazel was filled with an overwhelming sense of dread.

But what other choice did she have? She set off into the woods, telling herself she was just feeling unsettled by the dream and the appearance of the hooded stranger at school. There was something about him that resembled her dream so realistically, bringing a fragment of it to life, but she told herself that was just a coincidence. She wasn't psychic, she knew it was just a dream, a continuous nightmare of a dream, yes, but just a dream nonetheless.

As Hazel walked further into the woods, the path beneath her feet started to disappear, blending into muddy overgrowth and years of desire paths that split off in different directions. It would be so easy to get lost out here if she hadn't practically grown up in these woods. She dreaded to think what the forest would be like at night, with hardly any light to lead the way. There were signs, of course, to keep people on track, guiding them toward the centre of Aramoor Bridge, but even those wouldn't be visible in the dark.

Hazel took in her surroundings as she walked, breathing in the fresh air and musky smell of the autumn leaves crunching beneath her feet. She usually felt calm in the forest, with the wind blowing leaves in her path and the chirp of birds in the air, singing their funny little melodies.

Today was not one of those calm days.

The wind sounded like eerie whispers and the leaves were dark, grimy, and slippery. Hazel had to grab onto the nearest tree a few times to keep from falling.

The birds were the worst part. They sat in the trees above her and stared down soundlessly, just watching, as if they knew something she didn't.

The creepiness of it all had her mind rounding back on itself, pushing logic further and further out of the window, *like her hooded friend.*

Who was he, and did he even go to her sixth form? Why did he resemble the lead star of her dreams? Was he even real, or was he a figment of her imagination? Surely he hadn't actually climbed out the window? Amber hadn't seen him, and neither had Ophelia. Was he ever there at all, or was the snarky blonde right and Hazel was losing her mind?

If he were real and an actual human person, he would have gone this exact way. This was the only path, unless he was wandering the forest mindlessly.

As absurd as it sounded, it almost gave Hazel a sense of hope: maybe if she did come across him, her questions would be answered and she could prove that she was very much sane. On the other hand, there was also the risk of potential death if her dreams *did* turn out to be visions of the future.

She was almost at the edge of town when she heard leaves crunch behind her, but when she turned around, she was met with nothing. She continued walking, speeding up a little.

After a few minutes, the same thing happened again. She narrowed her eyes, glancing at the barely visible path. Light blurred from a pub in the distance, the one through the graffitied concrete passageway that led out of the woods. It was only a few feet away, but something was urging her to hide. Usually she ignored her gut, as it always seemed to work against her, but right now she couldn't help but agree.

Hazel moved towards a tree a few paces back and crouched beside it, feeling like an absolute idiot for at least a whole minute. Although, to her surprise, her gut was right for once.

The hooded figure suddenly emerged from the forest, drifting onto the path. In his hand was a dagger, a very sharp, pocket-sized blade. Its handle had carvings, spiral-like patterns that looked like tree vines.

An itchy feeling crawled up Hazel's spine as the guy tangled through the trees. The wind blew his hood off, revealing a snippet of his face before he pulled it back up and she knew for sure then that it was the same boy she had seen at school. He had the same golden, but dark brown eyes, the same almost black hair, and his lips were twisted into a similar frown. The dream aside, he was familiar, almost as if Hazel could place him somewhere in the back of her mind.

She held her breath as he began to speak, half-expecting him to call her name.

"Where are you…? I know you're out here."

Hazel clamped a hand to her mouth, hoping he wouldn't hear her staggered breathing.

"You can't hide forever. Eventually you'll have to eat again."

Hazel stayed silent and hidden behind the tree for what felt like a lifetime before another voice called out from within the trees, a feminine voice with a northern twang. "Lucas! Where are you? I told you to wait for me, you lousy git!"

The boy grumbled under his breath as he scanned the area. His gaze landed on the tree Hazel was crouched behind, and she lowered herself to the ground, trying to shrink in size. Luckily, the rain was getting heavier, pouring down his face and making it harder to see.

"Luke! Come on! The rain's only going to get worse! We'll track it when it's over. My incense is getting wet!"

Hazel furrowed her brow at the voice, almost smiling at the light-hearted tone. She watched as Lucas threw his head back with a grunt and turned around.

Once he was out of sight, Hazel removed her hand from her mouth and breathed a sigh of relief.

The image of the shimmering dagger was scorched into her memory.

A couple of hours after she got home, Hazel fiddled with her phone, debating whether or not to call the police. What would she tell them? A guy who stabbed her in a dream was wandering around the forest with a fancy dagger? It was too absurd, too unbelievable, even for herself. There were animals in those woods: deer, foxes, and badgers, and although it was prohibited, there had been cases of unlicensed hunters in the past, and the boy was definitely hunting something.

Hazel sat in her room, plucking at strings. It had been too quiet, and so, instinctively, she'd reached for her guitar. The gentle sound of her playing drifted from a soft melodic tune into something a little more ominous, echoing in a minor key across the inky bedroom walls.

Images flashed in her mind every time her fingers plucked one of the strings – the wind blowing through the guy's dark-tangled curls and the dangerous glint in his eyes.

Her hand grazed the curves of the guitar, running over the trailing indents she'd carved into it when she was younger: a long spirally shape that travelled along the rim of the wood. She peered down at it, feeling a crackle of static hit her fingertips as another image flashed in her mind – the dagger handle covered in carvings, long and spiralling, like vines from a tree.

The room fell silent once more and her palm slipped from her guitar. Hazel closed her eyes, exhaling deeply to push away the tight feeling in her throat, and soon enough, the silence in the room melted away to the gentle strumming beneath her fingertips.

CHAPTER THREE

Hunting Grounds

Lucas strode into camp, which sat in a large and very much hidden clearing in the woods engulfing Aramoor Bridge. It was just before the incline of a grassy hilltop, giving them a glimpse into the small, old market town behind the cover of tall pine trees.

A dozen tents were scattered around long, wispy trees that overlooked the sky at a perfect angle, something Lucas took advantage of when he couldn't sleep.

Around the centre of the clearing was an open fire pit where they would eat and share stories, or ramble animatedly like a murder of crows. The people here weren't his real family, and he hardly liked most of them – they were brutal, angry, and kind of cult-like – but he'd been with them since he was a baby. His parents had died and he'd been forced to grow up around strangers and learn to defend against the very things that had killed them.

Lucas's group was only a tiny section of a much bigger organisation. They engulfed the country, fighting and protecting. Strong, but still human.

As he strolled through the camp, he passed a group of kids. They weren't exactly kids, like him, most of them were about to enter their early twenties, but in terms of camp status, that's where they stood.

There was Claudia and Liam Knowles, brother and sister.

It was rare for people here to have actual family members - in fact it was rare for people to even have surnames; most came from foster homes and care systems. Lucas kept his own surname to himself, it was one of the only things that really felt like his anyway. The younger of the two, Liam, was a good kid. He was only thirteen and probably the most bearable of them all, definitely more so than his sister, who was a bit of a live wire. Lucas avoided her entirely.

Then there was Hollie, a snobby-faced girl with a lip piercing who he'd never actually seen smile before. He was convinced she simply couldn't at this point. Sitting beside her was Miles. Stubble painted his chin, giving him the illusion of looking older and wiser – but he was still just as nervous and unsure as he'd always been.

Lucas had been friends with him once. Miles wasn't like the others. He was kind, sweet, and so unbelievably soft it pained Lucas sometimes. However, he was easily led. As soon as the others stepped into the picture, that was it for their friendship. Lucas couldn't bear the loud-mouthed boy or the girl with the glare so eventually he'd taken a step back, opting to keep his own company. It was better that way.

Lucas tried to sneak past the group, but Jamie Chandra, the loud-mouthed boy in question, stood up with a sly grin.

Jamie and Hollie had joined the group together, from the same children's home, one that was taken under the arms of their organisation – that's how they built up their numbers, training abandoned children, turning them into warriors, and giving them a purpose.

"Luco!" Jamie cheered, with the hint of something evil behind his bronze eyes. Lucas couldn't stand him, they'd practically been in competition since the day they met. Everything Lucas did and everywhere he went, Jamie was one step behind, trying to steal the limelight.

Lucas turned to face the boy with an unamused expression, his gaze darting down to the silver scar painting the side of Jamie's neck. It was a matching scar to the one on Lucas's face. They'd got it the same day, trying to prove who had the better skillset. The scar was a punishment for getting distracted, that's what Chris – their group leader – had said, but, of course, Jamie's scar was better-looking. *Egotistical prat.*

"I've heard you messed up your patrol. I told Chris he should have kept you in the training tent," Jamie teased, grinning at his snickering friends.

Lucas furrowed his brow, letting out a deep breath. "What are you talking about?"

Jamie laughed, placing his legs on Claudia's lap. "Chris is looking for you. Good luck. Oh, and tell Hippy to stop leaving her stones outside my tent, I keep *almost* tripping on them!"

Lucas pulled a face, turning to the sliver of trees lining the campsite. He decided to take the quiet route that would take him round the back of the camp rather than through the middle, since he could already hear some of the other hunters training or, more accurately, getting beaten up by Sandy, Chris's second in command.

Sandy had served in the army. The only thing harsher than her personality was the stubble on top of her head. Hair could be pulled and so that, along with her patience, was always cut short. Her crew were pretty much carbon copies of each other: clean cut, straight-backed, with robot-like attitudes. Lucas did have to admit, however, that her and her soldiers were a lot better than the slimy, greasy-haired barbarians Chris had invited into the group last summer. They were messy, loud and obnoxious, always drinking around the fire pit and making everyone uncomfortable.

The camp used to be smaller. Lucas used to know everyone by name. There were still some good ones, but the majority were strangers. No one really stuck around for too long.

The faint scent of incense filled the air as he got closer to his tent, though he came to a sudden stop as the hair on the back of his neck stood up. A prickle ran through his fingertips, like pins and needles, and he turned, swinging his elbow down toward his attacker, but the figure shifted at the last minute, dropping the nightshade-laced weapon they were holding, and grabbing Lucas's wrist, twisting it upside down.

Lucas bit down on his tongue to stop a wince and glanced up to meet the camp leader's mossy green eyes.

"Got to be quicker than that, son," Chris said, bending down to pick up his fallen dagger and Lucas stood a little straighter. Christopher Leonard had pretty much brought Lucas up, though he was more of a sergeant than a father. The older man studied him with a sly smile. "So, you're back. Happy hunting?"

Lucas rubbed at his wrist, avoiding the man's eyes. They had lost track of what they were hunting hours ago and spent most of the day trying to catch up to it again.

Christopher uncharacteristically shrugged it off. "That's okay. I have another job for you, a crucial one," he said. Lucas swallowed tightly.

"I want you to join the local sixth form in Aramoor Bridge, the one we sent you to today."

Not that, anything but that. Lucas looked up with wide, pleading eyes. "We searched the school. It's clear. Don't send me, send Jamie, he'd love it."

Chris gripped his shoulder. "Don't whine! It makes you look desperate, and…"

"Desperation is a weakness."

Chris nodded. "We don't have time for weakness, you know that. Jamie is a little too… confident, but you'll fit right in. We need someone to just lurk in the background. Besides, you did *not* search that school thoroughly enough."

Lucas sighed. "I went around the perimeter a couple of times but couldn't see anything out of the ordinary. I got called out before I could finish."

Chris held his gaze, sternly. "There are trails of something else lurking in this town, some of which lead to the school. You see anything, you report back to me. Got that?"

Lucas nodded and waited for Chris to move away before he allowed his shoulders to slump in defeat. He stormed into his tent, throwing his stuff on the floor.

Something came barrelling through the air but he turned and caught it before it hit him. It was a practice knife, one they used to train the younger children back in the Barracks – their training grounds in the city, where most hunters learn to fight. Lucas glanced up at the auburn-haired girl who had thrown it with an exasperated look. "Farah, what are you doing?"

She grabbed the knife from him with a smirk and stepped past. "Just making sure you are staying sharp on your feet. I told you to come back with me till the rain stopped, you're gonna tire yourself out."

"Chris is making me go to school," Lucas said, ignoring her worries and jumping straight into ranting.

Farah widened her honey-coloured eyes and let out an amused breath. "Aren't you a bit old for school?"

He gave her a blank look. "It has a sixth form. Which is probably worse. It'll have even more teenagers."

"Luke, we're teenagers."

Lucas sat on one of the camping beds, picking up a drawing he'd left on her pillow earlier that day. It was of a frog, sitting in the middle of a pond with a striped umbrella hat on its head. Farah liked it when he left her his sketches.

She sat down beside him. "Oh, no. How will you possibly survive?"

He dropped the sketch and gave her a pointed look, frowning as she let out a laugh.

"C'mon, you'll be fine. There might be some cute girls or guys for you to silently gawk over."

Lucas huffed. "I don't gawk."

"Adam Kelley from that group merge last year," Farah started, counting on her fingers, "that blonde girl who left to go to the Barracks, you used to talk about her non-stop but never actually spoke *to* her. What about the girl with the glasses from—"

"Shut up," Lucas grumbled, turning away from her with reddened cheeks. "I didn't silently gawk. I just saw no reason to talk to them since they wouldn't be staying long, just like we won't be staying here. I'd rather jump into a river full of sirens than go to that hellhole of a school."

Farah grabbed his shoulders, manoeuvring him back towards her. "You can survive a couple of days."

He shook his head, bending down to pick up his backpack, reaching for a notebook, and turning it to an open page.

Lucas liked drawing, but his real passion had always been writing. He felt like the pages could melt him away if he let himself get lost in it, which happened the second a pen was in his hand, the same way he could fade into battle with a dagger, like it was an extended part of him. Mostly he wrote survival notes and strategies; whatever came to him, he put it on a page.

Lucas had grown up entranced by stories. Greek mythology was his favourite, the tales of the gods, all with different attributes, battle strategies, and monsters. It wasn't that different from the world around him, maybe a little tamer if anything. When he was younger, he'd imagined he was like Hercules, fighting for his place amongst the Olympians. It made the realities of the world a little less terrifying. If he was part god, then he couldn't get hurt. Though eventually he grew out of relying on fantasy, striving towards strategy and technique instead. If he lived in his head, believing he was invincible like the gods, then he would definitely fly too close to the sun.

"Chris thinks there may be something else in the town, in the school. Something that's managed to stay hidden. He wants me to scope it out," Lucas explained, looking at his best friend.

As expected, Farah's face dropped. "Not everything is a threat. Some of them can be quite good company… if they're hidden in this town, then maybe we should leave them be."

Lucas rolled his eyes, turning his attention to the smelly floral candle in the corner. He stood up and blew it out, suddenly unable to stand it. "You know we can't do that," he mumbled, wafting the air. "These things always turn out dangerous. That's why you're here, remember?"

Farah stared at him as if she had something to say, but it faded like the smoke in the air and she looked down at the floor.

Lucas sighed. He grabbed another candle labelled *sunflower whispers* and lit the wicker, letting the musty smell coat the room as he sat beside the auburn-haired girl again, deciding, for once, not to mention how stupid the candle name was. Even though it was irrevocably stupid. How could a sunflower whisper? "Sorry," he said instead.

She peered up, smiling softly as he rolled his eyes and opened his arms, letting her sink into his side as the candle flickered ahead of them.

"Jamie said you keep leaving stones outside his tent," Lucas mumbled.

Farah's face lit up with a mischievous glint and he furrowed his brow curiously.

"They're stabilising gems, cleansing, re-shaping. I'm trying to make him less nasty and irritable."

Lucas snorted. "Well, he keeps tripping over them."

"Yeah, that was part of my reasoning too."

As Farah lay fast asleep, Lucas stared up at the ceiling, wide awake and stony-faced.

He'd never gone to school before. Well, not one with a real education system and nursery rhymes at least. His classes had consisted of learning which bones can be broken at certain angles and how to sharpen blades with the hilt of another.

Despite knowing he needed it, Lucas didn't want to sleep, because whenever he closed his eyes, he'd always have the same dream.

It started with him wandering around the forest in the dark, then, after a few strange things in between, ended with him stabbing a girl in the back. A human girl.

Lucas didn't remember much about her, just some minor details: her sad brown eyes, her dark, wavy hair, and the dimples on her cheeks. She looked young, around his age, and had a familiarity about her he couldn't quite explain. All he could do in the dream was watch as the girl started to bleed out. Then, just before she'd die, she'd open her mouth and scream his name, causing him to wake up in a cold sweat.

CHAPTER FOUR

Crazy Uncle Ernie

Thursday went by quickly and surprisingly peacefully, mainly because Hazel didn't have English.

She was able to avoid Mr Hardington for most of the day by lingering behind corners and waiting for him to enter his classroom. It wasn't that difficult, really, the grumpy old man was mostly preoccupied with catching students vaping in the bathrooms. She did, however, have a hard time focusing on pretty much anything the entire day.

Hazel tried to convince herself that what she saw yesterday wasn't real. Maybe the hooded stranger was simply robbing the science class of its Bunsen burners, or she'd gotten contact high from the kids smoking weed behind the school's car park.

At lunch, she'd meant to meet Amber outside the canteen, but instead, Hazel found herself nestled in the corner of the library, clicking through webpages on an ancient computer.

"What are we reading?" Amber sang from above her.

Spinning around to face her friend, Hazel bumped her leg on the desk, letting out a strained noise.

"Er, nothing, just something for History," she lied, rubbing her ankle. "Sorry, I forgot we were supposed to meet."

Amber brushed it off with a wave of her hand and sat down. "It's fine. Something for History?"

Hazel was researching armed hunters. It seemed illegal

enough for people to run around the woods with daggers, so she thought maybe there would be a news article or something, but her search had only led to dead ends. Without saying a word, she tried to turn to the computer again, only for Amber to intervene, placing her heel on her chair leg.

"Strike one," the curly-haired girl said, in an accusatory tone.

Hazel raised her hands in an awkward surrender.

"What are you really doing?" Amber asked.

Hazel nervously chewed her cheek and then rotated the computer towards her friend, whose face crumbled with confusion.

"What is that? Wait, is this like when people dress up and go into the woods to fake fight each other? Like roleplay?" Amber asked.

Hazel hesitated, her expression blank, before reluctantly nodding.

"Is there... do you... is this like..." Amber cleared her throat, looking about before lowering her voice. "A knife thing...? Because some stuff I can understand, but, Haze, that's a bit extreme."

There was a brief pause as Hazel stared at her friend in mild alarm. "What? No! Of course not! I was just... I was searching for something I'd seen online!" She buried her face in her hands and glanced over her shoulder to ensure no one had overheard their conversation.

Breathing a sigh of relief, Amber slapped her hand to her chest. "Oh, thank god," she said. "Not that I'm shaming or anything, but that would have been a lot to unpack."

Laughing bashfully, Hazel rotated the screen out of sight, shutting down the browser. "Lunch?"

When Hazel got to detention, because apparently sixth form students *could* be given detention, Ophelia was already there, twirling her curls as she took endless photos of herself. A few desks down, another student was lounging in his seat, flicking a lighter on and off. Hazel could see the singed edges of his maths book withering away in his open backpack. Still, he seemed less bothersome than Ophelia, who snarled up at Hazel as soon as she stepped through the door.

Eventually, after a painfully strenuous lecture, Hardington left the room, leaving them all to read over some work.

The other student, the arsonist, put headphones in, while Hazel grabbed her phone, using the time to delve deeper into her 'research'. She swallowed roughly as a series of menacing blades filled her screen.

"What are you doing?"

Hazel jumped, caught off guard, as Ophelia peered over her at the screen, arms folded over her chest.

She didn't reply, glancing back at her phone and trying to swipe off the browser. Unfortunately, the other girl got to it first, snatching the device. Ophelia's snarky look faded away as the screen came back to life, showcasing a variety of mediaeval daggers.

As Ophelia gasped in surprise, Hazel couldn't help but notice a flash of crimson in her eyes before they settled back to blue.

"What's wrong with your eyes? Did you get contacts?" Hazel asked. "I didn't know they made ones like that."

Ophelia took a step back and dropped the phone on the desk. "No… Oh… yeah, contacts. You wouldn't know because they're expensive," she replied, before moving the conversation along with a suspicious tone. "Why are you looking at knives?"

Hazel blinked and reached for her phone. "I don't know… thought I saw one like that in the woods. Have you ever seen one like that?" she asked, returning the accusing look.

With a dismissive scoff, Ophelia swept her hair over her shoulder and made her way back to her seat, barely glancing back as she spoke. "Nah, I have a social life, don't spend my time roaming the woods like a weirdo."

Hazel opened her mouth to speak but let it fall closed as Ophelia plopped back down in her seat. Clearly, it wasn't worth either of their time. Still, she couldn't help but wonder about what she'd seen in her eyes.

By the time detention ended, it was already dark out, and no cars were left outside.

"I thought you were picking me up," Ophelia spat into her phone. Hazel watched from a few paces behind as they stepped out from the entryway doors.

"Well, tell Dad he'll have to wait, Caleb! I'm not getting the bus! Forget it, I'll walk home," she growled, hanging up.

Hazel curled an eyebrow. "You're going to walk all the way through town and then through the woods? That'll take hours."

Ophelia's head snapped toward her. "I don't remember asking for your opinion," she seethed, storming away in the opposite direction.

Frustrated, Hazel leaned against the bus stop post, popping in earbuds. She remembered sitting at bus stops like this with Ophelia back in year seven, waiting for the bus together, listening to the same music, laughing and joking around. There was a time when Ophelia almost didn't seem evil. Hazel sometimes missed that.

The bus journey was quiet apart from the music playing in her ears, and Hazel started to doze off, until an image of a dagger followed by a pair of flashing red eyes snapped her back to reality, causing her to jump up and press the stop button.

She slunk into her seat, gulping as the driver turned towards the next stop – the centre of town. She'd have to get off now and walk the rest of the way home, save herself the embarrassment of pressing the button and staying put. Hazel gripped her bag, getting ready to leave, before she caught sight of a girl heading towards the park through an alleyway. A blonde girl, with a dainty white jacket and stern strut. Ophelia.

Hazel's brows knitted together, wondering how she had beaten her to the town centre, before she narrowed her eyes at something in the shadows.

Engrossed in her phone, Ophelia seemed unaware of the menacing figure trailing behind her.

The bus came to a stop and Hazel made her way into the cold, autumn night. She could have gone the other way, right through the middle of the high street, the safer path home, but she wasn't about to let Ophelia get attacked or murdered. Did she debate it? Of course, but she wouldn't actually let it happen.

When she finally caught up to her, the blonde swiftly turned. "Stop following me, stalker."

Hazel took a step back, scanning the area frantically. "I'm not following you. I…" she trailed off. "Well, I am, but… where'd he go?"

Annoyed, Ophelia uncrossed her arms and began walking away, but Hazel hurried to catch up with her. "A guy followed you in here, so I came to make sure you were okay," she explained.

Ophelia laughed. "I don't need you to save me."

Hazel kicked at a stone beneath her feet. "Okay, I'll leave you to be murdered, then," she muttered, turning around, though the hesitance in her movements wouldn't actually let her leave. "Sorry for interrupting—"

Before she could finish that thought, she was pushed face first into a large, horrid-smelling rubbish bin. Hazel cursed, hearing a sharp shushing sound from above. "Are you taking the piss?!"

"Just trust me. Be quiet and don't move," Ophelia shot back, banging on the metal lid above her.

An orange glow from the streetlight outside crept in through a crack in the top as Hazel pushed upwards, trying to open the lid.

Someone was holding it down.

Hazel grunted, contemplating various murder methods when Ophelia began to speak again, only it was not directed to her this time.

"You can't be here," she said. "Look, this territory is taken already. So why don't you just turn around and piss off?"

Hazel peered through the cracks, squinting to catch a glimpse of who Ophelia was talking to. It was a middle-aged guy who looked a little, well, a lot, worse for wear. He was covered in dark crimson streaks that tore through his clothes, coating him in a sticky sheen. The only thing clean about him was his teeth. He stared at Ophelia with a grin, and Hazel could see the moonlight flicker off his pearly whites, making them seem sharper. His right arm bore a noticeable gash, like a bite from an animal that had left a mark.

Ophelia seemed to notice this too. She glanced towards it and covered her nose with her palm, turning away in disgust. "Okay, so you're new to this and disgusting. Well, you can't be here. You have to go somewhere else."

A tense silence filled the air. Ophelia let out a sigh and then turned to face the man once more. Hazel couldn't see what she was doing, but whatever it was, it made the man's smirk turn into a scowl. He huffed and began to leave.

As Hazel leaned forward, gripping the edge of the bin to hold herself up enough to see, her hand slipped and sliced on the metal. She let out a startled yelp.

Ophelia cursed, spinning around as the man suddenly grabbed her by the throat and lifted her off the ground, growling through bared teeth. Hazel instinctively covered her mouth with her hand, forgetting about the blood running down her arm as she watched in horror. She wanted to scream, intervene, do *something,* but she was paralysed as she watched the man tighten his grip around Ophelia's neck.

Suddenly, Ophelia swung her legs out and kneed him in the stomach. It was almost unnatural, the grace of the action, like some sort of strange ballet move. The force of the blow caused the man to release her and clutch his stomach.

Ophelia landed, crouched on the ground, then pinned him down. "I mean it this time. You need to go."

They exchanged sneers, then their attention shifted to the rubbish bin as the lid shot open. Hazel inhaled sharply, instantly regretting opening it.

The man quickly stood up and tried to move past Ophelia, heading straight towards Hazel until the blonde grabbed his arm.

She hissed in his face, and in retaliation he bit her arm,

digging his teeth in before shoving her backwards into the metal container.

As Ophelia slammed against the dirty frame, her now bleeding arm collided directly into Hazel's face, knocking her backwards.

While the other girl gasped, and stood up, kicking the stranger in the stomach, Hazel peeled herself from the cardboard beneath her, bringing her hand to her mouth, then recoiled with a grimace when she saw the droplets of red covering it. Not her own blood, but Ophelia's that had smeared over her at their connection. She let out a gag.

At this point, Hazel had seen more than enough. As their fight raged on, she darted into a nearby alley, desperate to create some distance between herself and *whatever the hell* was going on over there.

Part of her felt guilty for abandoning Ophelia, while the other half was just very confused. She would call the police to ensure her safety, but she wanted no further part in the situation.

Hazel stopped to grab her phone and glanced down at her arm. Blood was dripping from a pretty nasty gash near her inner elbow. With a wince, she took off her slightly torn jacket and tried to stem the bleeding until her shoulders tensed at the sound of footsteps echoing behind her.

"I have a weapon!" Hazel grunted, lifting her small, star shaped bag up.

"Oh yeah? What is it, your *impeccable* dress sense?" Ophelia snickered, and Hazel dropped her bag, frowning.

She stared at Ophelia wildly and the girl cleared her throat. "Look, I… er, I knew him. He's my crazy uncle Ernie. He isn't supposed to be out alone."

Hazel pulled a face. "Why would you fight him?"

The blonde smiled, straining, with a sarcastic undertone. "Uncle Ernie loves to wrestle."

Hazel blinked, stumbling backwards as Ophelia grabbed her arm to inspect the injury. "Do you have any self-awareness?"

Ignoring the snide comment, Hazel stared up, narrowing her eyes. "I don't believe you," she muttered.

Ophelia applied pressure to the wound in response, causing Hazel to jump a little. "Well, you should."

Both of them stared, neither willing to break their accusatory gaze, until Hazel felt something cold slither down her arm, burning into her wound like a blast of acid. She looked down to see blood still pooling from Ophelia's wrist. It dripped onto Hazel's leather jacket bandage and the skin beneath it, causing a shiver to run down her body at the connection. She pulled away, casting a disgusted frown, although Ophelia didn't seem to notice as she scanned the area. Her eyes were sharp and focused, slitted like a predator.

"I could walk you home," Ophelia offered off-handedly, still staring into the alleyway as Hazel moved into the neighbouring streetlight.

"No, thanks."

Ophelia scoffed and followed behind, glancing over her shoulder as if waiting for another attack. "Suit yourself. I'm only trying to help."

"Okay, then tell me what actually happened," Hazel retorted, spinning around and forcing the other girl to stop.

Ophelia shifted her stance to one hip. "I already did. Not my fault if you don't believe me. You've always been hysterical."

Hazel gripped her own arm tightly, squeezing the leather-bandage in a fit of frustration. She winced as her wound stung, an icy shiver running up her arm. "Look, something is going on here. I saw something… Contact lenses can't change like that."

"You don't know what you saw," Ophelia spat, flicking her hair onto her other shoulder as she walked past Hazel, bumping into her harshly and leaving her in the alley.

CHAPTER FIVE

Under the Weather

Hazel found herself back in the forest. The dream played out how it usually did. However, this time, when it got to the part where she was stabbed in the back, she spun around and caught the dagger in mid-air. Surprised, she let it fall and gazed into the forest ahead.

A body lay on the floor. The hooded boy.

The colour had been drained from his face, but that wasn't the only thing that seemed to be drained. Hazel caught sight of a deep gash on the right side of his neck: puncture wounds.

A drop of blood dripped onto him from above as she looked, pooling into the masses of red that clung to his greying skin. Hazel reached up to where it had come from, wiping across her mouth. More blood was covering her lips. Her breath caught in her throat.

The crow appeared then, flying past and turning her attention to the manor ahead.

Something was different this time. As Hazel looked up into the windows, she saw lights, dark red lights. She narrowed her eyes, then realised they weren't lights, but glowing eyes.

The hooded figure's body jolted suddenly, and he sat up and yelled her name.

Hazel gasped as she woke up, feeling a hoarseness in the back of her throat. She rubbed at her lips. No blood. It was just a weird new version of her dream.

The sun was blazing furiously through the curtains. Hazel lifted her hand to shield her eyes, then crawled towards the bottom of her bed, yanking the blinds shut to help soothe the pressure building in her head. She clutched her forehead and stared up at her ceiling, watching dust particles float around the room, so vibrant and grainy it made her dizzy.

She didn't want to go back to sleep and risk another horrific dream. So instead, she pulled herself out of bed and slumped onto her desk chair.

"Hey Petal."

With her head in her hands, Hazel glanced up from her laptop screen. "Hm?" she asked, looking up at her mother with heavy eyes. She hadn't even noticed her enter the room.

Nina leaned against the desk, her gentle green eyes roaming over her daughter's face as she slowly closed the laptop over. "I've got a late shift tonight. So come home straight after school, okay? Another person went missing last night."

Hazel nodded and raised the computer screen again. Her mother was a receptionist at the local hospital; she was always on the late shift.

"Are you okay? You look a bit pale," Nina asked, placing her hand on Hazel's forehead, which she quickly shook off.

"I'm fine, Mum," Hazel said. "Just a little tired."

Nina didn't look convinced.

"Really, I'm fine," she urged, but Hazel wasn't sure if she even believed it herself.

After a horrendous first lesson, Hazel could barely keep her eyes open. She felt like the earth was pulling her into the ground. *Maybe it was.* The teacher was yammering on about something or other, and Hazel couldn't bear it anymore. It was only the second lesson of the day, but she was so overwhelmingly tired and achy, she was fighting to stay awake.

She crossed her arms on her desk, making a pillow, and leaned her head down.

Amber hummed playfully. "You're gonna miss all the maths."

"I'm still listening, just with my eyes closed," Hazel grimaced.

Amber scoffed, then opened a workbook, placing it in front of them as a cover.

Almost immediately, Hazel fell into a deep sleep. As she expected, her dream began to play out, the same way it had this morning: the woods, the hooded guy, the blood running down her lips…

The chair beside her skidded, followed by a whispering voice. "Haze, wake up. Lawton's starting to notice."

"Dominique Valdez!" a voice screamed suddenly, and Hazel opened her eyes, almost tumbling from her chair as she regained consciousness. A few heads turned towards her and she steadied herself, putting the workbook barricade she'd knocked over back up in order to block them out.

"Are you okay? You look ill," Amber whispered, leaning in.

A strange thumping sound echoed in Hazel's ears as her friend got closer, prompting her to stumble out of her seat.

"Hey. Where are you going?" Amber asked, worry filling her tone.

Hazel stared at her blankly. There was a tightness in her

chest, and she was very aware of the people watching her. It made the muscles in her arms tense, feeling heavy as bile rose up her throat. Suddenly, she felt too hot, too exposed, like she was backed into a corner.

"Hazel, do you want me to come with—"

"Can you just back off?" Hazel snapped, clamping a hand to her forehead. Amber widened her eyes at the outburst, but before she could say anything, Hazel glanced at Miss Lawton. "I need some air."

The teacher nodded, busy trying to calm the class down, and Hazel darted out of the room.

She staggered down the hallway until she got to the girls' toilets, where she clutched onto the sink and splashed water on her face. Her eyes were hypersensitive and heavy. Hazel rummaged through her bag, plucking out the pair of sunglasses she'd borrowed from Amber's 'emergency hangover kit' for her headache, and fumbled to place them over her face.

"God, you look awful," exclaimed the person Hazel wanted to see least in the world, Ophelia Thorn.

Hazel peered into the mirror, clutching the sink as she gazed into the taller girl's eyes, searching for any sign of a crimson glare.

With a bewildered expression, Ophelia turned and walked away.

"Wait," Hazel breathed, turning to face the blonde stiffly. "What happened last night? And no rubbish about your *Uncle Eddie*."

Ophelia studied her for a moment. "Uncle *Ernie*," she corrected. "He's just a bit strange. Look, what you saw… I think you might be a bit confused. That honestly was just my uncle. He shouldn't have been out, he's not very well, but it's okay, I sorted it."

"I'm not confused," Hazel said, sloppily pushing the sunglasses above her head.

The other girl let out a pleased hum. "Good. Finally, we're on the same—"

"I know what I saw, and I know you're hiding something."

Ophelia narrowed her eyes, lifting one eyebrow snidely and turned around, leaving Hazel to stare after her, even more unconvinced.

She turned back to the sink, splashing more water on her face. It wasn't long before another girl entered the bathroom.

In an attempt to look casual, Hazel pulled out her earbuds, filling the awkward silence with music. She'd pulled the sunglasses back down now, thankful for the shade against the harsh bathroom light, but a strange sensation hit the back of her throat.

She glanced up to see the girl was having a nosebleed, stuffing toilet paper up her nose. "Can you grab me some more loo roll, please?" the girl asked, leaning over the running sink, her blood mixing into the water.

Hazel stared. There was something so profound about the vibrant colour against the porcelain white.

"Hello?" the girl said, looking at her strangely through the mirror.

Feeling slightly embarrassed, Hazel grabbed the girl some toilet roll before turning towards the exit.

As she moved through the busy halls, her head pounded, thumping like every heart near her was beating directly in her ears. She stumbled, and an acid-like sensation built up in her throat, causing her to close her eyes.

Then it stopped, bleeding away in the tone of a steady, smooth voice.

"Didn't know you could walk so slow," Caleb murmured, his playful voice beckoning Hazel to open her eyes. "You're usually in such a rush."

She smiled softly, silently grateful that someone had broken her from the dizzy spell. "Yeah, well, why are you never in class? Do you just roam the halls hoping to run into girls?" The pain was still there, just dull, flushing back and forth in her mind like the rocking of a boat.

Caleb grinned. "Oh, I'm not actually here. I'm just part of your imagination, I'm your consciousness reminding you not to crash into another unsuspecting victim." The bangles on his arm jittered as he moved. Some were beaded, rather badly at that, with brown and sapphire balls, while others were a strange, knitted texture, less expensive-looking than the fancy watch on his other wrist. Hazel hummed teasingly in response.

"Free period. I was heading to the library to play on my Switch," Caleb explained, nudging her in the shoulder as they started to walk beside each other. "So, where are you off to today? Another runaway?"

"No. I don't always do that." She sighed. "Just had to get out of class. Everything's so loud, and my eyes and gums have been hurting like mad."

Caleb shot her a knowing look. "If you drink a whole jug of water before you go to sleep, it's supposed to help with *this* the next morning."

She laughed dryly. "I'm not hungover, Caleb. I just feel off. How's your sister? She got the worst of it," Hazel asked, looking up at his confused face. "That creepy guy?" she added. "Your *uncle*. She fought him off when he tried to attack us in the middle of town last night... I didn't know she was so... well, skilled, I guess."

Caleb stared off into the distance, clearly thinking hard until Hazel softly nudged his arm.

"Caleb?"

He cleared his throat. "Oh, yeah, she's taken up… kicking."

Hazel frowned. "You mean kick boxing?"

Caleb brushed a hand through his hair. "Yeah, sure," he said, turning to walk in the opposite direction, but not before glancing back with a kind smile. "I hope you feel better soon, Hazel."

As she watched Caleb walk away, she became aware of a mop of curly black hair trying to dodge discreetly past her. She sighed, feeling guilty, and called out, "Amber, wait."

Amber gave a grumpy sniffle. "Listen, if you wanted space, you could have just asked, you didn't need to go all ballistic on me back there. I'm sorry if I was bothering you, but—"

Hazel placed a hand to her forehead to rub away some tension. "No, *I'm* sorry. You were only trying to help. I shouldn't have snapped."

Amber studied her for a second then dropped the frown from her face and let out a breath of relief. "Well, thank god for that, I thought I was gonna pass out from all the negativity. Anyway, now that we're friends again, have you seen the new guy? I wanna lick his face."

Hazel snorted. "Bloody hell, keep it in your pants."

The other girl hummed in debate and linked their arms together, pulling Hazel towards their dreaded English lesson.

Hushed whispers filled the room, particularly from the girls, as the new kid stepped into class.

"Everyone, quiet!"

The noise simmered down as Mr Hardington addressed the class. "Good. Now, everyone, we have a new student today. Lucas… Wal—"

"It's—"

"Doesn't matter," Hardington said, glaring at the boy for interrupting. "Take a seat."

At the mention of the name, Hazel's head snapped up. She recognised the boy instantly, with his sunlit irises and twisted frown. A chill ran down her spine and she glanced at her desk, but when she braved to look up again, Hazel realised his eyes had been locked with someone else's. Ophelia Thorn's.

When class ended, Ophelia stood quicker than anyone else and paced down the hallway, heading straight towards her older brother.

She grabbed him by the arm and he let out a sigh, tilting his head to the side. "What? Is this about what Hazel saw? If we just talk to her—"

"There's one here," Ophelia interrupted.

Caleb's eyes widened, and the muscles in his jaw clenched slightly.

"Here? Now?" he whispered warily, then his features softened, and he squinted. "Are you sure?" he asked, ignoring the murderous look he received in return. "Because you— Oi, ow!" he whined as Ophelia smacked his arm.

"I'm sure, dickhead!"

Caleb frowned at her. "Okay fine, chill. Go on." He gestured for her to continue, rubbing his arm.

"A boy in my class, the new kid. He reeked of nightshade

and kept looking at me." Ophelia's words came out sharp, venomous.

Caleb chewed at his lip then nodded, grabbing her arm to pull her outside.

So caught up in whatever drug *nightshade* was, neither of them spotted Hazel, who had heard every word.

By lunchtime, Hazel felt like she was a hiccup away from vomiting violently into the rubbish bin beside her table. She placed a hand on her stomach and sucked in a breath to refrain from doing so.

The stench of paint from the recent cafeteria renovation didn't help much. It had really needed it though. For a long time now, there had been a giant scorch mark left in the centre of the room. Why it was there? Hazel didn't know, teenagers were weird and liked to set fires sometimes.

"So, what are we eating?" Amber asked, sitting down at the table with her lunch tray. Hazel shrugged, pointing at a lonely banana and her friend frowned.

"Hey, bananas are good for the brain. I've got a lot of thinking to do lately," Hazel said in defence of her pathetic lunch.

Amber raised an eyebrow. "What does that mean?"

An awkward breath slipped through Hazel's lips. "We've got a bunch of exams coming up after Christmas."

"Well, I've got exactly what you need," Amber said as she dived into her floral tote bag and pulled out a box of brownies. "These are good, if not better, for your brain." She grinned, biting into one.

Hazel attempted to hide her shudder, focusing on not

gagging. She liked brownies, just not right now.

"Don't worry too much about the exams," Amber muttered through bites. "We've got that study group, remember? I signed us up for it like a month ago."

With a wince, Hazel nodded. For obvious reasons, she was falling behind in English, so Amber had signed them both up for the class, which unfortunately fell on a Sunday. Hardington loved to make students miserable.

"Why did it have to be Sunday? Couldn't it have been after school?" Hazel complained. "Plus, we're going out tomorrow night, if I have to deal with that man hungover, I'm either going to die or end up in jail."

Amber shrugged, taking another brownie. "Come on, we can have a social life *and* good marks. It's not that hard."

"Isn't it?" Hazel grumbled, with an unamused look on her face as a hooded figure crept past their table.

"You know it isn't raining inside. You can take that off," Amber called out, luring the boy's attention. He didn't take down his hood, but he did glance their way, making Hazel silently curse her friend under her breath.

"It's Lucas, isn't it?" Amber asked, stretching out her hand for him to shake. Reluctantly, he accepted it, raising an eyebrow as she shook his hand a little too enthusiastically. "I'm Amber, and this is Hazel."

Lucas looked at Hazel, and for a second, he squinted, his brow furrowing.

Hazel quickly glanced away, feeling a little too familiar with his stare.

"Don't worry, she doesn't bite." Amber smiled at him.

"Hope not," he mumbled, mustering what looked like a pained attempt at a smile. Amber pulled him down onto a chair beside her, offering him a brownie as a disconcerted expression flashed on his face.

Under his right eye, a faint white line staggered down his cheek, splitting off at a point. Hazel couldn't help but wonder if it came from one of those daggers.

"Hazel?"

Startled by the sound of her name, she looked up and coughed uncomfortably, unintentionally squishing her banana.

"Have we met before?" Lucas asked, peering at her suspiciously, while at the same time pulling a face as she wiped banana mush from her fingers.

Hazel studied him for a second, then bit the inside of her cheek. "Yes, I saw you here the other day. You broke into a classroom and snuck out of the window," she said as nonchalantly as she could.

Amber looked between them both and mumbled some indistinguishable merry tune to break the tension. It didn't work.

They both gave her a strange look and she smiled, opening her mouth to speak.

"Why were you breaking and entering? Is that what the hoodie is for? Trying to hide your identity?" Hazel cut in before Amber had the chance to say anything.

Lucas creased his brows. "I was checking the place out." He turned his gaze back to Amber, who again tried to speak, but couldn't get a word in. "You never know who you'll come into contact with. I thought it would be better to scope the place out first."

Amber nodded sweetly, waiting for one of them to intercept again before speaking. "I mean, you probably could have just called up and booked a viewing, but, you know, gotta do what you gotta do." She smiled. Hazel blinked at her.

Lucas's phone started to ring before he could answer. He offered a semi-forced smile between them and excused himself, stepping away.

"Well, I like him. He seems nice," Amber offered, going back to her brownie.

Hazel didn't respond. She just watched him walk away, narrowing her eyes as he pushed out of the doorway.

CHAPTER SIX

Master of Distractions

Caleb frowned at his sister. She was sitting in his passenger seat, complaining about how slow he was driving. "I'm going the speed limit."

"We can literally run faster than this," Ophelia grumbled, throwing her heeled feet onto the dashboard.

"Yeah, I know, but you know what Mum says. We have to at least try to act human," Caleb argued, pushing her feet back to the floor.

Ophelia groaned, crossing her arms against her stomach like a toddler. "Why do you always do what Mum says, have you not got your own mind?"

A small, offended laugh fell from Caleb's lips. "Oh, come on, like you don't do the same thing."

"Only so I don't get my phone taken from me again. You just do what she asks because you want to, her little second in command."

Ophelia's phone buzzed, distracting her just as Caleb was about to reply. A message from their mum. She read it out loud: "'I'm on my way. Meet me south of the woods, no messing around, we're just going to scope out their camp.'"

A few minutes later, Caleb pulled his car up next to his mother, who was standing beside the forest with her arms crossed.

"Get in, I'll circle around," he said, opening his window.

"No, we go by foot. We don't want them to know we're watching them. I want some better insight so that we are prepared for anything," she shot back, sternly.

Caleb nodded in agreement as Ophelia leapt out of the car. "Let's go, then, I almost fell asleep in there. Caleb's driving is worse than his awful jokes." She yawned, moving for the woods, but their mother pulled her back.

"One of you needs to take the car back. I'm taking Caleb with me," she said.

Flaring her nostrils in frustration, Ophelia freed her arm from her mother's grip. "Make him do it." She motioned to her brother. "I can track down the hunter's scent. He had a really cheap-smelling aftershave that only I caught, not Caleb, so it makes more sense for me to go."

Their mother exhaled sharply. "Caleb's more trained for this. He has better focus."

"I can focus!" Ophelia whined, and the older woman raised an eyebrow in response.

Caleb leaned out of the window, giving his mother a reassuring look. "She can do it, Mum. Without her we'd just be wandering the woods blindly with no scent to follow."

With a smug smile, Ophelia glanced at her brother, immediately regaining her composure as the woman turned towards her. After a loud sigh, she agreed.

"Caleb, take the car home. Go into town first, down the long road. We can't risk one of them seeing it back here and tracking it to the manor."

Caleb nodded. "Okay, I'll just catch up to you afterwards," he insisted. However, his mother's grey eyes sharpened.

"No, I need you to stay home," she explained, as Ophelia let out a little victory laugh. "In case this goes south, you know how we do it. Your father's at his shop and one of us needs to stay behind. If there's a fight, we could use the element of surprise. Besides, someone has to keep an eye on dinner, I have the slow cooker on."

Ophelia's lips dropped into a disgusted frown.

"But—" he tried, only to be cut off with a wave of his mother's hand. He knew that look; the decision was final. He watched as his mother turned and began walking into the woods.

Ophelia coughed into her hand and gave her brother a purposeful look. "Get rid of whatever crap is in the slow cooker," she whispered, then followed after their mother.

Caleb stared after them for a few seconds before starting his car.

There was a pit in Hazel's stomach, an emptiness her lunch was not filling. It clawed deep into her core and overlapped her senses. Everything was loud as she stepped down the corridor: the creaking of lockers, the shrill snapping of voices, and the overbearing pressure of a dozen heartbeats. She stopped walking, causing Amber to collide into her.

Hazel closed her eyes and took in a few deep breaths.

Somewhere in the back of her mind, she could hear Amber calling out to her, but the words didn't register through the rhythmic beating of the girl's heart. It pounded in her ears, like the patter of rain, soft and velvety, thick and crimson red—

With a sudden jolt, Hazel pushed away from her friend, placing a hand out in front of her as she took a step back.

Amber frowned; Hazel snapped at her to stay put. She wasn't even sure why, there was an urgency inside of her, a nauseous feeling that got worse the closer she got.

"Just go to class," Hazel said through gritted teeth, trying not to take another breath. "I'll go to the nurse, then go home early. Please, you're gonna be late." Amber pulled a face, shaking her head in confusion, but Hazel gave her a pleading look. "I'll call you… I just… I don't want to throw up on you," she lied.

Hazel finally blew out the breath she'd been holding as Amber headed down the corridor. Once she was out of sight, she turned away and walked straight past the nurse's office.

The bus wasn't due for another hour at least, so she opted to take the road instead. She didn't want to take the forest pathway again and risk bumping into *Lucas* and his unremovable hoodie.

The further Hazel got from sixth form, the better she felt. No strange sounds or overwhelming smells, just peaceful forest air, perfect silence, that was until she heard the sound of an engine.

"Hey, stranger, need a ride?" Caleb asked, reaching over to open his passenger side door.

Hazel debated whether or not to keep walking. Every time she'd been near anyone today, her whole body felt like it was on fire, but for some reason something about Caleb didn't have that effect as she peered up at the warm-hearted smile on his face.

Hazel got into the car and he pulled back onto the tree lined road. Already she was thankful to be sitting down, still knackered. The tension trickled out of her bones and settled in the fumes left behind by the exhaust pipe.

"That's dangerous, you know," she muttered.

With a jovial look, he glanced at her before refocusing on the road. "What is?"

"Offering strangers a lift, haven't you seen any horror movies?" she teased, fastening her seat belt.

He shook his head. "You're not really a stranger, and you seem pretty harmless. I think I'm safe."

She hummed in debate, securing the belt in place. "I wouldn't be so sure, Caleb. I could eat you alive."

He chuckled under his breath at that, and she glanced at him with a peculiar expression. "What are you doing in this part of town? Aren't you supposed to be in school?"

"Family emergency, but it's all good. I was just passing by on my way home," Caleb replied, before grinning at her. "I could say the same for you. Aren't you supposed to be in class? Or do you just not do that anymore?"

Hazel let out a soft, entertained breath and looked out the window, watching the blurring trees fade together. "I'm still not feeling well."

Caleb clicked his tongue, then returned his attention to the road. "That's what someone who wanted to skive lessons would say."

Hazel wrinkled her nose. "If I wanted to skive, then I would have come up with a better plan. Faked my death, or fainted or something."

The blue-eyed boy jutted out his lip in consideration. "Personally, I'd go with faking your death, the fainting thing is a little overdone, and there's a lot more wriggle room with a false death… Fell down the stairs, or maybe got eaten by a shark, that's a fun one, why don't you go with that?"

"I would, but where would we get the shark?" Hazel sighed, feigning a sad look.

Turning a corner, Caleb glanced at her mischievously. "There's an aquarium we could break into a few towns over, we'll stop off for ski masks on the way."

Hazel snorted, toying with her sleeves. The hem of her t-shirt had a lacy fabric and she liked how it felt under her fingertips. "Yeah, because I'm sure a goldfish-sized shark could do the job."

They stopped at a red light, and he flicked his head toward her, placing a hand on the gear stick. "Oi, it definitely could. Don't underestimate the little guys, size doesn't matter." He smirked, then dropped his head onto the steering wheel with a pitiful groan. Hazel laughed, pulling her hand toward her mouth. "Not what I meant," he muffled through the wheel.

She chuckled, sending him an amused, raillery grin. "Well, you've said it now."

"Can I unsay it? I wanna unsay it."

Hazel shook her head, and he pouted as the light turned green.

As they drove, Hazel pointed through the trees to the left. "Don't you live up there?" she asked as he continued to drive in the opposite direction.

Caleb brushed a hand through his hair, keeping the other on the wheel. "Yeah, but I'm taking the scenic route. It helps clear my mind."

She knew he was holding something back, but she didn't want to push him. "Fair enough. I could do with a bit of mind clearing myself," she said, and when he looked at her, all the silliness from their conversation before seemed to evaporate.

"Wanna talk about it?" he asked, glancing back and forth between her and the road.

She sighed. "Nah, it'll only bring the mood down."

His hand outstretched towards the car's touch screen radio, lowering the music as Hazel focused on the lace pattern on her sleeves.

"It won't bring the mood down," Caleb tried. "If it helps,

you could tell me something that's bothering you, and in return, I'll tell you something that's bothering me?"

Hazel lay her head on the window, grunting at the sweet smile on his face. "Okay, fine. I sort of… don't laugh, but I feel like I'm losing my mind. I've been feeling weird all day. I don't know what's going on, but I think maybe it has something to do with my father. I've been having these dreams, sometimes they seem so real. I don't know… they're strange." She sank into the seat and picked at the fading black nail varnish on her fingertips, feeling rather embarrassed.

"I don't think you're losing your mind, Hazel. I mean, you're not the most level-headed person I've ever met." Caleb smirked, and she gave him a pointed frown. "Dreaming about lost family members isn't weird. Trust me. It's okay to want to know where they are, even if you feel like you shouldn't. That doesn't make you crazy, it just makes you human."

"Thank you, but from what I've heard, he doesn't sound like the type of dad I should miss… Anyway, your turn." She exhaled, watching as rain started to fall on the windshield.

Caleb contemplated his words before grinning. "Right, so, there's this tough level in this game I've been playing—"

"An actual problem, Caleb, not a game problem."

After a light-hearted chuckle, he nodded and switched on the window wiper. "Okay… so, I have this idea of what I want to do when I leave sixth form, right? Take a dabble at university maybe, but I don't think my parents would let me. Especially not for graphic design or video game development, something I'm actually interested in. They want me to be some sort of stony-faced councilman like my uncle. It's been my mother's plan ever since I could walk."

Most sixth forms only have a two-year course, but there were certain students, like Caleb, that stayed on an extra

year, either for a BTEC or higher education reasons — or
just because they aren't ready to move on yet. Hazel wasn't
sure what that reason was for Caleb, but she guessed this had
something to do with it.

She scrunched up her nose, staring at him strangely. "I
can't imagine you as a politician."

"Neither can I!" Caleb laughed, sticking his tongue
between his teeth. "It's too serious, and I honestly just can't
be bothered. It's like my whole future is planned ahead of me,
and I don't really have a choice in the matter. I know there are
risks, but my mum's always saying how capable I am, so surely
she could trust me enough to handle myself for a few years
before I eventually give in and do what she wants."

"Risks?"

Caleb tapped his fingers against the steering wheel in a
whimsical pattern. "You know, er… kidnappers, criminals…
other university guys. I'm just a lanky British rich kid. They'd
eat me alive."

Hazel let out a laugh, knitting her eyebrows together.
Despite the fact Caleb kept to himself a lot, he was funny,
openly warm as well, it was a wonder he didn't have more
friends. Plus, he wasn't *lanky* per se, he was slim, yeah, but
that was more a factor of his height. He was actually quite
athletic-looking, which was strange, because he wasn't on any
of the sports teams or anything, nor had he ever been to her
knowledge.

"Hey, this isn't a laughing matter. Look at me and tell me
they wouldn't duct tape me to a wall and flip my dorm room
upside down," he quipped, looking between her and the road.

"I think you've watched too many movies, Caleb. Even if
they were all arseholes, you're smarter and wittier. And you
don't have to do what your parents want you to do. Screw

that. It's your life, not theirs."

Caleb looked out at the road, his lips lifting at the corners.

"Besides, you could always just hide the duct tape," Hazel added and he chuckled.

"I could, yeah."

As they approached the road to Hazel's house, Caleb rubbed a hand through his hair again. "If you ever... if the dreams keep you up, you could text me... if you want to. I'm always up late anyway, and I'm a master of distractions."

Hazel smiled to herself. "Master of distractions?"

"I can talk a lot about a lot of things. You want a distraction, and I'll take you on a deep dive of how inaccurate the dinosaurs from Jurassic Park really are," he offered, pulling the car up onto the side of the road.

As she grabbed her bag, Hazel let out a humoured sniff. "Oh, great, I've always wondered about that."

"Yeah, it's wild. The raptors weren't that big, they were tiny, like ankle biter size, and not all the dinosaurs were even from the Jurassic era... I could go on, but I don't wanna get ahead of myself. I love that movie. I could talk about it for hours, trust me."

Hazel raised an eyebrow, then reached into her leather jacket for her phone. "Clearly. Give me your number then, dino boy," she said, handing her phone to him. "In fact, set your name as Dino Boy. That way I know who I'm talking to."

Caleb laughed, typing the digits in as he shook his head. "Is that name stuck or is there any flexibility?"

"Master of distractions?"

"I'll stick with Dino Boy."

She chuckled softly, pulling her sleeves down her wrists. "Thanks for the ride... and the talk. I appreciate it. Dinosaur facts and all."

"No problem. Any time you want to talk, you know where to reach me." Caleb handed Hazel her phone with a warm smile.

There was an underlying feeling creeping back into Hazel's stomach once she was alone in her room, but she pushed it away, trying to focus on the comforting smell of her home and the feeling of the blanket wrapped around her shoulders.

A slight buzzing came from her pocket and Hazel grabbed her phone, seeing a message from Amber. It was a photo of her leaving school with a question mark caption. She was about to reply when she caught a glimpse of Lucas in the background of the photo, heading into the woods.

A pinch of irritation hit her, festering in her mind.

She didn't believe in psychics, prophecies, or any of that stuff, Lucas was obviously some sort of damaged loner who wore his hood as a protective shield and frown as a weapon, another moody, predictable, pretentious arsehole to add to the ever-growing list, hunting animals to make himself seem tougher. The fact that he had to do that with a black hoodie over his face to resemble her subconscious arch nemesis was just a kick in the teeth, like some sort of cruel joke. But either way, if he really was out there hurting innocent animals, then surely something should be done about it.

She couldn't go to the police, not if she didn't have evidence, but Hazel had a rough idea of where he lurked from watching him in the woods the other day. She could get evidence, use her phone to capture him with the dagger in his hand. Or, if she was wrong about him, and it really was some sort of live action roleplay in the woods, then there would be no harm done, *probably.*

Maybe if she just got the chance to speak to him, and properly talk, not like in the cafeteria, then she'd realise he was nothing like her dream. Because that was just a dream, it couldn't hurt her. Right?

Hazel stood up and grabbed her coat.

It was highly unlikely she'd even find him, but she had to try. She had to do something except sit inside twiddling her thumbs.

As Hazel reached the treeline, everything seemed to come to life. Birds chirped loudly from above, and the smell and sound of the crunchy leaves flooded her senses, making her eyes water. She felt overwhelmed, but in a good way – everything was so vibrant.

As she got deeper into the woods, a strange smell filled her nose. It was like something she'd never smelt before, something she could've never imagined. A euphoric feeling clouded her thoughts and propelled itself to the front of her mind like it was the upmost important thing in the world.

It led her to an oak tree in the middle of a clearing, just past the old, abandoned stone bridge that sat vacant in the forest, tucked under a shelter of moss and crumbling gravel. It used to stand over a canal, but that was filled in decades ago, leaving the bridge behind with nothing but a bunch of tree roots for company.

Some kids thought the bridge was cursed, and that's why it was so eerie. Hazel didn't believe in curses, but something sure felt off as she stalked toward the large, inviting oak tree.

There was something on it, glistening in the sunlight and the part of her brain that usually saw red flags seemed to have gone dormant.

Hazel glanced up, reaching out to touch the tree, until a screech of metal came flying through the air, landing in the wood above her.

An arrow.

All at once, her senses returned, and she ran without looking back.

She was fast, faster than she'd ever been before, but that didn't mean she was graceful. Hazel clumsily dipped through the trees, grabbing onto branches to stop herself from tripping, and she didn't stop until she reached a road she recognised, one that she knew led to Thorn Manor.

Once she'd made it the rest of the way, she slammed her fists into the door as hard as she could. After a second, Caleb opened the door, confusion evident on his face before he met her fearful gaze and let her in, closing the door behind them.

His eyes were wide as he watched her. "Your—"

"I think someone was chasing me... this was the closest place I could think of, and I thought you'd be home by now," Hazel interrupted as she caught her breath against the huge double door.

Caleb stepped closer to her, studying her face. "How... how?"

She frowned, her panic increasing at his expression. "What?"

Caleb's hand delicately cradled her chin, tilting her face towards him. "Your eyes are red."

CHAPTER SEVEN

Bear Hunt

As Lucas ventured further into the forest, mist and fog trailed behind him, winding through the trees like a flowing stream of vapour. He'd always liked being out here, with the trees, the leaves. There was a sense of comfort in the smell of the rain. In some strange way, he felt connected to the forest, the earth, the way the air filled his lungs. It always gave him a spurt of raw energy.

As Lucas walked, he noticed a thin line of rope tied from one tree to another. With a smirk, he grabbed his dagger from his belt and tossed it towards the ground, slicing the rope in half. He rubbed his hands together and bent down to pick up the blade, but as he got back to his feet, something hit him.

Lucas glanced upwards to find Farah perched in a tree, wearing a grin and holding a handful of rocks. "You underestimated me again!" she sang, jumping down and playfully punching him in the arm.

"What are you doing here?" he asked, with a grumpy expression that was difficult to maintain as she beamed at him.

"You said on the phone that you were going to search the forest after school. I thought you could use some backup," she replied, readjusting the crossbow slung over her shoulder.

Lucas scoffed. "Thanks. If I need to hide from a bear, I'll call you."

"We don't even have bears in this country, but c'mon, Luke, if we did, you know I'd win that fight," Farah said, winking as she skipped ahead.

When they reached an open space, Lucas clapped his hands together and made his way to the large oak tree in the centre of the clearing. It was bigger than the surrounding trees and left a trail of tangling roots that had breached the surface, but as soon as he'd seen it, he'd known he was in the right place. "Okay, so, I thought we could leave a trap, then wait to see if any of them catch the scent and lead us back to their base." He pulled out his dagger, holding his palm out and hovering the sharp edge over his thumb, before lowering it.

Farah leaned against a tree, watching him hesitate with a humoured look. "Just—"

"I've got it, thanks," Lucas spat, and she threw her arms up in surrender.

"Just let me do it. It's okay, loads of people are scared of needles and stuff."

Lucas frowned. "I'm not scared! I've been hit with sharp things plenty of times."

"Yeah, but never purposely. You always use the decoy blood instead of your own," Farah replied, walking towards him and taking the blade with a gentle look. "Just let me do it, it doesn't bother me."

"It doesn't bother me either!" Lucas protested, while making no effort to take the dagger back from her. "It's just that whenever I use my own, it never seems to catch their attention long enough, probably because of the nightshade. I overdo it sometimes."

"Or," Farah teased, cutting a line into her thumb. Lucas tried not to wince. "They can sense the hostility in the blood, like acid." She pressed her thumb to the tree, spreading the blood, then smiled jovially. "I hope my blood tastes sweet, like nectarines and strawberries," she said, not at all bothered by the judgemental look she was receiving. Farah sucked on her thumb then cocked her head to the side as Lucas reached into his bag for some rope. "I don't know why we're trying to trap them, we could at least try talking first." She sighed. "How many times do I have to tell you we don't have to hate them? Not all of them, at least."

Lucas shook his head stubbornly, unravelling his rope. "That's not what I was taught, and even though we can't kill the cleaner ones, it doesn't mean they're not a threat. Don't be so naïve, Far."

He stood up, rubbing his hands on his jeans before stepping past her, not missing the way her eyes followed him with a solemn expression.

"In my old group—"

"In my old group, I was friends with the monsters, and we played UNO and braided each other's hair," Lucas mocked, tying the rope to the bottom of the tree.

Farah frowned. "Lucas, c'mon, you know what happened. I'm only alive because Lisha helped me escape that attack."

"How do you know she wasn't planning on killing you herself?"

Farah sighed. "Because she wasn't like that, Lucas, she was my first love. You know, you can't just assume they're all monsters just because a rogue one *supposedly* killed your mother."

Lucas spun around, dropping the rope before he could secure it properly. He peered at her in disbelief.

It grew quiet for a second, then Farah widened her eyes apologetically and stepped toward him. "Wait, I'm sorry, I didn't mean it to come out like that."

Lucas grabbed his bag, pulling it over his shoulder bitterly. "*Supposedly*? Look, I get that you have some weird attraction to these things, but don't bring Shelley into your nonsense." He stormed past, snaking around her into the cover of the trees as Farah trailed behind him.

"Chris is a maniac. He manipulates people all the time. I've seen it. Some of the stories he's told, he mixes them up or exaggerates them to make them sound worse. I've heard the story of that night, and I'm sorry, but not everything adds up. The born ones don't just ambush people in broad daylight, especially not trained hunters. Lucas, please, I know you see it too sometimes, the way he is."

Lucas huffed and spun around to face her, but his attention was steered by the rope moving in his hand. He hadn't managed to finish his trap, but someone must have trampled over it anyway. He grabbed Farah's arm and guided her behind a tree. They could hear someone getting closer to the blood. Lucas couldn't make out who it was, but that didn't matter. They didn't have to see it, his plan was to follow it home.

He reached for his dagger, but Farah pushed his arm down, grabbing the bow from her back instead. Lucas rolled his eyes as she placed an arrow into it and aimed for the tree. Once it hit its mark and the *thing* fled, he jumped up, following it.

While the creature would be faster than them, their training enabled them to track it through footprints and crushed leaves. Midway through their run, Farah grabbed Lucas's arm, stopping him and directing his attention through the trees ahead of them.

Past the acres of land stretching deep into the forest and enclosed by a towering black iron gate stood a massive Manor house, coated with rose bushes, or really, *thorn* bushes.

A dark glint took over Lucas's features. "Let's go tell Chris," he said, as Farah widened her eyes.

"What, no! We don't even know if they're a threat yet, let's hang about for a bit and—"

Lucas blew out a frustrated breath, storming away from her. "This is why he sent me to that dreadful school and not you. Because I know they're *always* a threat."

Lucas looked up at his adoptive mother with pleading eyes.

"Just two more minutes, please, Shelley," he asked, pouting.

Shelley swallowed back a breath, failing to hide the warm grin forming on her lips as he blinked up at her. She had taken care of Lucas since he joined the camp. He was only a baby back then, dropped off at the Barracks in London without so much as an explanation with him, and Shelley had been the one to find him. She had fought to convince Chris to let her take him with her instead of leaving him with the other children in the Barracks.

See, Chris and Shelley had never gotten along. Something to do with his late wife, Lily Anne who was Shelley's best friend. Lily Anne died, tracking some rogue bitten ones across Manchester, a clean one was masked within the group and she'd sacrificed herself to take them down.

Things were apparently never the same after that. Shelley and Chris couldn't get along without Lily Anne, though Lucas didn't really understand all of that.

"You've been playing out here all day. I want you to come inside and work on your numbers, love." Shelley chuckled as Lucas toyed with the practice dagger in his hand, flipping it back and forth.

"Please!" he begged.

She sighed and tousled his hair, nodding as he bounced on his feet. "Thirty minutes, then come straight home, okay? Don't go too far. I have a meeting and I want you to stay within shouting range!"

Their camp was set up in an old, demolished neighbourhood. All the houses were deserted, getting ready to be knocked down and made into apartment buildings.

Lucas didn't stay within shouting range.

He set off, strolling down the road until he reached an old playground. Its colours, once energetic and playful, had faded and become washed out, but Lucas didn't care. He hadn't ever been in a playground before, and he was ecstatic to have one all to himself. He moved towards a rusty swing set, giving it a test push. When it didn't crumble completely, he grinned and hopped on.

Overgrown flowers shifted in the wind below him and he chuckled as they reached up and brushed against his ankles, tickling his dangling feet.

It wasn't long before the sound of the breeze pulled his attention, and he slowly turned to see a teenage boy.

He had rusty blond hair that fell to his shoulders, and a worried look on his face. "Hey, you should head home, kid. It's not safe here," he said, from the edge of the overgrown grass.

Lucas watched him with narrow eyes. "I can protect myself," he replied, jumping from the swings and into a fighting pose.

The flowers at his feet stood tall, some of them swaying toward Lucas like his own personal soldiers.

The teenager smiled. "Oh, clearly, but for my sake, let's go somewhere a little less scary. How about I take you to your parents?"

Lucas deflated a little and the older boy softened his expression. As he went to speak again, something moved in the bushes outside of the park. The teenager spun to confront the sound, and Lucas caught a glimpse of the red tint in his irises.

"You're one of them!" he said, pulling out his dagger with a frightened gasp.

Once the bush settled again, the teenager turned around with a shy smile, his gaze lingering on the small dagger in Lucas's hand.

"It's okay, not bitten, you're not in danger. I'm just passing by on my way home. I come out here to read," he explained, holding up a worn leather satchel overflowing with books.

Lucas narrowed his eyes. "Chris told me your kind are all the same."

"He is mistaken. I'm not going to hurt you. My name is Eli," he said, holding his hand out to Lucas, who carefully shook it, eyeing the books with a newfound interest.

"I'm Lucas," he replied after a moment.

Eli smiled, pulling one of the books from his bag and handing it to him. "Let me take you home, Lucas. It's not safe out here."

As they passed the giant trucks lined up on the outskirts of the camp, a grumbling voice yelled down to them from above.

"Stop where you are and let go of the boy!"

Eli nervously looked up. "Just dropping him off, found him back there with…" he trailed off, smiling at Lucas before glancing back at the armed man. "Just stay alert, it could have followed us back. I just wanted to make sure he was safe before I left."

As he turned to leave, an arrow struck his path, causing him to take a step back. Eli peered up in alarm as the hunter reloaded his bow.

"Don't take another step or the next one is going between your eyes."

Lucas let out an angry grunt, stepping in front of Eli. "Wait!

He's my friend!" he cried. Eli gripped his shoulder, trying to subtly nudge him out of the way, but Lucas wouldn't budge. "You leave him alone!"

The man on top of the truck eyed them condescendingly, then turned, picking up a walkie talkie. "You might wanna come out here, Chris. The kid's brought one with him."

After a moment, Chris burst out of a partly demolished house, followed by Sandy, who grabbed Lucas while Christopher stalked right toward the teenager behind him.

"He brought me home because of the noises, so that I was safe!" Lucas yelled, kicking out from the woman's arms.

"Shut it, kid, this is adult business," Sandy spat, sending him a scowl.

Lucas glared at the stony-faced woman.

Soon enough, another figure came running out from the house. Shelley. She widened her eyes and scowled deeply at Sandy, pulling out her dagger. "Let him go!"

As both women scowled at each other, Lucas wriggled free and ran into Shelley's arms. "Shelley! Tell him to let my friend go!"

Chris clasped a hand around the teenager's throat and Eli let out a choked noise.

"Let him go, Chris. Look at him. He's not a threat. He helped Lucas. You know the rules, he's obviously not a bitten," Shelley tried, pushing Lucas behind her.

From behind them, Sandy scoffed, causing Shelley to turn around with sharp eyes.

"Wouldn't want me to call the council, would you?"

Chris gritted his teeth, then threw Eli forward, letting him hit the ground.

"Take him in for questioning," he ordered, looking at Sandy, who stalked forward and yanked the teenager by his arm. Eli gulped.

Lucas cried as he watched Eli get dragged into the house. Eli's book bag had been abandoned on the floor, the contents pouring onto the damp grass.

Chris glared at Lucas, storming over and pulling him from Shelley's grasp before she could stop him. "They are not our friends. They are evil, bloodthirsty monsters! Don't you ever forget that!"

"You do not need to scream at him, Chris. He's seven years old!" Shelley hissed.

"Whatever you're teaching that boy, you need to stop. He brought that thing here… He needs to know that we hunt them, we kill them, we don't befriend them. Even if they seem harmless, they never are, you kill or you get killed."

Lucas heard Shelley release a sigh from where he stood, burying his face into the back of her jumper. "Lily Anne wouldn't want this."

There was silence for a second.

"That thing? Chris, that's just a boy, he can't be older than seventeen. Let him go, he was protecting Lucas… I bet the real threat is out there now. You know the Arcane council wouldn't agree with how you do things. If word got back to base, you know what they'd say."

Chris growled. "You're sticking up for it? This thing over your own people? You'd threaten us! Threaten me? And for what? Some soulless adolescent. You're pathetic. He's a monster and Lucas needs to know that."

Shelley didn't yell back, in fact, when she spoke again, she did so with a little sadness in her voice. "You never used to be like this. You know what Lily Anne would say, she believed in the peace."

Chris huffed. "I believed in the peace. That's why she's dead."

Later on, Lucas sat on his bed, twirling his dagger around his fingers. It was his first one.

He had carved tree vine shapes into the handle to make it his own. He didn't like the simpleness of it before, and for his first blade, he wanted it to be special.

Shelley moved toward him and took the blade from his hands, tucking him into the blankets.

"Why does Chris hate Eli? He didn't hurt me," Lucas said.

Shelley smiled softly. "Because, love, sometimes people hate those that they don't understand."

"But can't we just make him understand," Lucas huffed, pouting his lip. Shelley moved her hand into his hair, threading it backwards.

"Not everyone is willing, but that doesn't mean you can't try. Chris is right about a lot of things, a lot of Eli's kind are dangerous, monsters even, but some of them are just like us, and they need protecting just as much as the rest of us. I'm proud of you for trying, but leave it to me, I'll help your friend," she whispered, leaning down to kiss his forehead.

Lucas woke up to someone shaking him. It was Chris, with a panicked look as he pulled him out of bed.

"I need your help! Your friend, he got angry and attacked everyone at the lookout house!"

A choked noise lodged into the bottom of Lucas's throat. "But... but, Shelley said."

"She's out there now, trying to stop him, but he won't listen!" Christopher interrupted, his expression dark. "If he's really your friend, then he'll listen to you."

As they reached the lookout point where Eli was being held, Chris grabbed Lucas by the shoulder. "You go first, son. Try to reason with him, but if your friend can't control his instincts... you shout for me and I'll come running."

Lucas nodded and stepped into the dark, empty house. He stood in the hallway hopelessly for a minute, jumping as the door slammed closed, then tore his hands away from his eyes and stepped forward. He was beyond scared, but he had to be strong for Shelley, and surely, surely, Eli wouldn't hurt her. This was a mistake, Chris was being silly, Lucas would find them both and they'd be okay, and Chris wouldn't be angry because he'd finally understand.

The top of the corridor was dark, the only light coming from under a door on the far end. He pulled his dagger out from its holster and stepped towards it. There was a small sob coming from the inside. Lucas let out a timid breath, and then pushed the door open.

Red. Everything was red. It was the first thing Lucas could see, then his eyes adjusted to the light and a whimper slipped from his lips.

Shelley lay on the carpet, her hair tangled over her face as blood flowed from a large gash on her neck. The air around Lucas grew thin, and the world got weird and small all of a sudden.

"Shelley?"

She didn't respond. The knot growing in Lucas's chest got tighter. He didn't even know when he'd started moving, but suddenly he was kneeling beside her, brushing the hair from her face so she could open her eyes.

"Shelley, come on. Get up, we have to leave now."

Again, nothing.

The buzzing in his ears got louder, and Lucas soon realised there were small sobs coming from the corner.

"We have to get out of here. They let in a wolf… the one that's been stalking this town. It killed her. It'll kill us, too," Eli cried. He too was covered in blood, though his skin was unnaturally clear of wounds beneath his ripped T-shirt.

Lucas tilted his head up with teary, hateful eyes. "You did this!"

"No! It wasn't me! He's lying, Lucas! Did he say it was me? It was the wolf!" Eli pleaded.

Lucas studied him, the blood on his lips, the red in his eyes, and then he looked back down at the gash on his mother's neck.

Something clicked in his mind.

"Please, Lucas, you have to believe me. Those are claw marks, not fangs… Please, listen to me."

Lucas couldn't take his eyes off his mother's motionless body, unsure what to believe. He could feel the full moon's glow from the window, shining into the room and shimmering in the pool of blood that lay ahead of him.

"See, Lucas, they kill and they lie. They can't be our friends. Do you see that we must kill them, even the born ones? Once they've taken a life or turned someone, the silly little law can't stop us." Chris was standing in the doorway now.

Lucas's head shot up, his eyes wrestling with uncertainty. as he peered between them both.

Christopher grabbed his face, turning it towards Shelley. "This is what they do! You led him here, and this is what he's done!"

Eli stood to his feet, stumbling slightly. His wrists were restraint free but they were stained a sickly purple colour. "Don't listen to him. This is not your fault, Lucas," he said breathlessly, glaring at the older hunter.

Chris laughed. "Pathetic." He stepped past Lucas, who was frozen on the spot, then grabbed the teenager by the throat. Eli bared his teeth and growled weakly.

"See, Lucas, liars, all of them," Chris grumbled, staring at Eli once more, before kneeing him in the stomach.

The teenager crumbled to the ground after that.

"I'm sorry, I'm sorry—" Lucas sobbed into Christopher's shoulder as he was picked up, his eyes fixed on Shelley's unmoving body as he was carried out of the room.

Farah stormed to the tent as Lucas rolled his eyes and slumped down on one of the wooden log benches outside.

"What's wrong with your friend?" Chris asked, watching Farah with a condescending look.

Lucas shrugged his shoulders. He didn't want to get Farah in trouble, but he also knew getting her on board would be a lost cause.

Chris gripped him by the shoulder. "Come on now, son, you know better than to keep things from me." His grip felt like a vice, tightening and tightening until eventually Lucas snapped.

"We found out where the born ones are based. They have a manor house in the south of the woods… Farah didn't want you to know yet," he mumbled, feeling slightly guilty for selling out his friend, but he didn't want to protect the monsters.

Christopher's jaw clenched. "Still wanting to save them?" he spat. "Don't you listen to her, you know what they are. They killed your family. You have to hold their kind responsible… You will not let your guard down around them ever! Do you understand?" Lucas barely got the chance to nod before Chris started mumbling like a mad man. "I haven't spent all these years training you for you to go behind my back, keeping things from me. These creatures, these monsters, killed everyone you love. If you let your guard down and listen to her, then I promise you that you and that red-haired friend of yours will be dead too."

Lucas swallowed tightly.

"They kill us, so we kill them, and if you can't kill them… then you're done for. We have to stand strong. You did well finding the base. Don't let her convince you to keep things from me again, okay?" It almost felt like a threat, like something bad would happen to Farah if he didn't oblige, but it couldn't have been. Chris was a little over the top sometimes, but he wouldn't take it that far.

Lucas nodded.

He knew he couldn't trust these creatures; he didn't need to be reminded. It irked him a little actually, he'd already had Farah all the way home rambling on about how the council strives for peace and they should give the *monsters* the benefit of the doubt.

Blah, blah, blah, blah.

And now Chris was going off on a tangent, too. Was Lucas not allowed to have his own thoughts and opinions?

After the leader walked away, Lucas headed back into the woods, moving uphill toward one of the small cliffsides that overlooked Aramoor Bridge. He could see it all from this angle, the mixture of pine and oak trees that covered the ground, the long spirally road that led into town and the white and black panelling on a few buildings within it.

Sitting down on the hard floor, Lucas took out a photograph from his pocket, one of himself as a baby, being held by a smiling green-eyed woman. She looked kind, happy even as she glanced down at him, despite the fact his chubby baby hands were reaching for one of her earrings. Both earrings were in the shape of leaves, a line of them like a tree vine, painted in gold and dangling. Just like the charm on his necklace.

It was the only thing he had from his birth parents, that golden leaf charm, along with the photograph, which by the name written on the back of it must have been meant for his father. The front read, *'Our baby boy! Lucas. I can't believe he's a month old already. This one likes the camera a little more.'* The photograph was dated in the corner. If it wasn't for that, he probably wouldn't have known when his real birthday was, or his name.

With a sigh, Lucas moved the picture onto his lap and took a deep breath, taking in the fresh musty air.

He trusted Farah more than anyone, but she was too kind. He agreed with her that Chris was nuts, but the older hunter had taught him how to survive, and surviving was all Lucas knew how to do. It's true, he'd never left this group, but they were only a tiny fraction of a bigger organisation, the Nosferatu Warriors.

There were other hunters, of course, with different names, regions, but the Nosferatu Warriors were known as some of the best. They were the only humans to have a seat on the Arcane Council.

Lucas had seen firsthand what happens when a monster is given the benefit of the doubt. He looked down at the photo again, contemplating what he wanted to be. Someone who sided with the very thing that killed Shelley, killed his parents, or someone that would put an end to them. After a second, he'd made up his mind, and put the photo away, replacing it with the cold comfort of his dagger.

CHAPTER EIGHT
Reflection

"What?" Hazel breathed, on the verge of vomiting. She barely had a chance to register that she was actually inside Thorn Manor.

The hallway had a classy feel, with slick dark wood flooring that led up the staircase at the centre of the room. The walls, a light beige, were adorned with intricate patterns, and there were little trinkets everywhere, hidden away on shelf corners. There was a faded stone statue of a woman by the stairs; she was covering her face with one concrete hand as the other pointed towards the front door. In the hand covering the statue's face, there was a rose, as if she was some sort of extravagant plant pot.

A self-moving vacuum collided into Hazel's feet, and she nudged it softly in the opposite direction. It turned back around, however, coming at her again and she narrowed her eyes.

With an amused look, Caleb sent the device flying across the hall and guided Hazel into the living room. There was no wall between the previous room and the living room, only an archway. In the middle was an L-shaped settee on a fancy rug, in front of it a large mirror sat atop a sleek stone fireplace.

As soon as Hazel spotted the mirror, she stumbled towards it. Just as Caleb had said, her eyes were a dark crimson colour, like Ophelia's had been. She stared at herself in shock, using a finger to pull at the skin under her eye.

"Who bit you?" Caleb asked.

"No one bit me, what are you talking about?" she replied, rubbing at her eyes frantically. It felt like she was looking at something else – some weird, unrecognisable version of herself. "What's wrong with me?"

Caleb moved closer and carefully turned her around. "Nothing… nothing's wrong with you, it's just…" He rubbed a hand over the back of his neck, chewing his lip as his words faded away. Hazel widened her eyes in an impatient way and he let out an unsteady breath. "Ah, shit, it must have… the other night, in the park."

"What?" she asked, fear and confusion blending into her tone.

Caleb's eyes met hers, and he swallowed deeply. "You had to have been bitten the other night. Bitten and then… fed."

Hazel stared at him with a mixture of silent fury and undeniable confusion as he checked her over, using his hand to tilt her head to either side of her neck. "Nothing. Bit. Me." She gritted her teeth, her expression turning into a glare as he continued to tilt her head from side to side. She caught his wrist. "Talk, Caleb, you're freaking me out."

He stilled and looked back up at her face, studying it as her nostrils flared. With every breath, she could almost feel the redness deepen, a strange tingling sensation behind her eyes.

"Okay… okay, just breathe. You need to stay calm or you'll lose control," Caleb whispered.

Her eyes narrowed in response. "Stay calm? Me? Stay bloody calm? Really? How about you stay calm!"

Caleb backed away, leaning against the wall. He folded his arms over and brushed at his chin, tilting his neck with a silent debate. Then he clicked his tongue. "You're a vampire."

An impetuous huff fell from Hazel's lips. She threw her head backwards and turned away from him, looking back in the mirror, while grumbling something unintelligible under her breath.

"Well, I don't know what any of that meant, but by the tone I'm guessing it was along the lines of 'is this a joke, you can't be serious', to which my answer would be I *can* be serious and I *am*. Please, turn around," Caleb continued, the sweetness of his voice embedded with a certain franticness.

Hazel closed her eyes and forced herself to take a long hard breath. When she opened them again, she was met with Caleb's reflection, the same redness in his eyes that shone in her own. She took a step back in shock.

"See, not joking, I know because we're the same. My whole family are vampires," he explained as his eyes slowly melted back to their soft azure colour.

Caleb pushed away from the wall and moved closer, but Hazel shook her head stubbornly. "No," she said, sending him an uncertain expression, and he stayed put. "Either you're wearing some sort of wildly expensive contacts or we have some strange illness... Oh, for god's sake—" Her eyes widened, and she glanced down at her arm, pulling the sleeve back, her wound was still covered by a plaster.

Caleb tilted his head curiously. She stared back at him with a nervously irked expression.

"I cut my arm in the alley, on some metal, and Ophelia grabbed it to look it over... but she was bleeding too. Her blood... I remember pulling back because of how cold it was. That must be..."

"How it happened," Caleb finished for her, looking down at the ground in consideration. He had a look in his eye now, as if he'd just heard the confirmation he was looking for.

Hazel nodded, before creasing her eyebrows. "Yeah, that's how she infected me with whatever weird blood disease you guys have!" Her breathing began to get heavier, and she started to pant. "That's why her eyes changed too, right? I'm pretty sure we should all go get checked out."

"Hazel."

She dropped her hands onto her knees and crouched over, feeling the air leave her lungs in heaves.

A pair of arms pulled her upright and Caleb curled a finger under her chin, forcing her to look up at him. "Breathe," he instructed gently, scanning her face as he let out an example breath.

Hazel did as he asked, breathing in deep and slow, battling her body for oxygen and losing tremendously. A whimper settled in the back of her throat.

Caleb brushed his finger over the skin of her chin, guiding her to take another steady exhale. One in, one out, and again.

She kept breathing until, eventually, the red faded from her irises, the reflection in the mirror returning to normal.

He moved his hand to her shoulder, holding her steady. Their eyes remained fixed on each other, Hazel's sceptical expression softening under his warm gaze.

Breathing normally now, she blinked at him, knitting her brows together. "Vampires don't exist. I… I must have caught something from her, some sort of…"

Caleb brushed a hand through his sandy hair. "Yes, you caught something, but it's not a disease. Well, not in the technical term anyway, it enhances, not weakens. It's like a backwards illness," he joked as she stared at him in disbelief. "Hazel, I'm telling you the truth," he tried, but she shook her head.

"This isn't funny, Caleb."

He sighed, sucking at his gums and then opened his mouth. His front two canines had sharpened into points.

"Explain this?" Caleb implored, with his mouth still open.

Hazel scoffed, glancing away. "It's just been Halloween, they sell those in pretty much every shop on the high street."

"Touch them then."

"I'd rather not stick my fingers in your mouth, thanks."

Caleb shrugged, then casually sped around her and landed on the sofa with his legs crossed. He'd moved at an inhuman speed, a blast of air whooshing past Hazel's face as he went.

"That's… that doesn't prove anything." She frowned, feeling less confident.

He arched an eyebrow and sped to her side. "Doesn't it?" he mused, disappearing again.

Hazel felt a breeze from his fast movements and whipped her head around to follow him, but he was nowhere to be found. She let out an unsteady breath, then swivelled around and headed towards the door, muttering "nope," under her breath. However, much to her surprise, the blue-eyed boy was standing right in front of her with a stupid grin on his face.

She furrowed her brow, watching him for a second before swallowing back a bated breath. "Okay, prove it," she whispered, peering up with a peculiar expression.

Caleb bit back a laugh. "Have you not been watching? I just did."

"With what? Fake fangs and a living room beep test? I told you this isn't funny, Caleb." Her lips lifted slightly as he gave her a feigned pout.

"They're not fake…"

She took another step closer to him. He was around six feet, and at her *big* height of five foot two, there was quite a gap between them, but it seemed to vanish as she stepped into his space.

"Prove it then."

With a smirk, he took her hand. She curved an eyebrow immediately but allowed him to guide her toward the front garden.

Caleb seated her on the water fountain and retreated a few steps, standing in front of the manor house. It sat behind him like a perfect picture. Hazel was sure she could snap a shot, and it could be used on the cover of a magazine: Caleb Thorn's smirking figure modelled in front of the fine white brick. All it was missing was a pair of sunglasses and a Lamborghini.

"Okay, time me," he said, looking up at the building with a confident shrug.

Hazel pulled a face. "Time you doing what?" she asked, but he only winked in response. With an exasperated sigh, she threw her arms up in a 'fine' motion. "One," she muttered impatiently, there was no way he was going to convince her of this, it was just absolutely absurd—

Before her lips had even parted to form the number two, Caleb had shot forward and scaled up the front of the manor, climbing the building as if it was a tree.

"Five…" Hazel breathed, as he got halfway up. He grabbed a vine from the hanging greenery with one hand and jumped to grab another, hanging off it and swinging his body effortlessly.

He was practically just a blur of movement.

"… Seven."

Caleb slowed his movements for a few seconds to look over his shoulder and smirk at Hazel, who did nothing but blink at him.

"Eleven…"

Then he was off again, grabbing onto the brick and ascending so quickly it almost gave her whiplash.

He reached the top of the building and disappeared onto the roof.

"Fourteen— okay… Just… Come back down," she grumbled, pulling her jacket sleeves down and looking away.

A few seconds later there was a thud, and Hazel glanced up to see Caleb casually brushing gravel from his hands as he walked back over to her.

He slumped down onto the fountain and nudged her shoulder. "Believe me now?"

"Did you just jump?!" she croaked.

Caleb laughed and leaned back on his palms. "Yeah," he said indifferently. "You could too if you tried."

She shook her head. "No, I really couldn't. I'm… I'm not like you."

Caleb leaned back further to look at the sun. "You ran here, you said so yourself… explain to me then how you got here so fast. I barely dropped you off three quarters of an hour ago, it takes a couple at least to walk all this way."

Hazel stammered for an answer. When she couldn't find one, Caleb made a smug sound in the back of his throat.

"But Ophelia didn't bite me," Hazel whispered, frowning and peering down at her arm. "Neither did the weird guy in the alley."

"Well, there are two types of vampires: those who are born into it, and those who are bitten."

"You think I might have been born like this?" she asked. Caleb moved his head around a little in consideration.

"If you were bitten, you'd have already lost your mind and tried to kill me, so I think our odds are looking pretty good. Do you want to kill me?"

Hazel looked at him, squinting, then shrugged. "No, not right now."

"I'd say that's a good sign." Caleb smiled. "My family and I are born vampires, or pure vampires, as Ophelia likes to say." He beamed, but Hazel didn't return the enthusiasm.

"Ophelia's a vampire... that's... oh, god." She gasped, the genuine concern in her features making Caleb laugh.

"Born vampires aren't like what you see in movies, we can go out in sunlight." He gestured to the way the sun shone down on them, then pulled his sleeves up to his elbows. "We eat normal food, we even age up until a certain point."

His long-sleeved T-shirt was now scrunched up, leaving his arms bare. As he leaned back again, Hazel could see a flash of scarlet up his left forearm. Sneaking another glimpse, she spotted the outline of a red rose, its stem layered in thorns. She thought back to Ophelia's rose on her ribcage.

"We are more enhanced morally and physically than the bitten. Bitten vampires are the real threat. They kill for sport, not caring whose blood gets spilled. They really are monsters. Most don't even remember their past lives. So technically, Ophelia is harmless. Just don't piss her off," he joked.

The water sprayed melodically behind them, and Hazel let the sound fade into her thoughts as she tried to process it all.

As they sat there basking in the sunlight, Caleb wrinkled his nose in confusion and leaned into Hazel. He held her hair back and pulled himself closer to her neck. "What are you doing? You're not going to bite me, right?" she murmured, watching him. Her heart started to beat faster, matching the rhythmic tempo of the water fountain. "Vampires don't bite each other."

Caleb pulled away from her. "No," he assured her, holding back a chuckle. "You're safe. It's just... I should have been able to tell you were one of us by smell, but I can't." He peered into her eyes carefully, like he was searching for something. From the angle, Hazel could see small flecks of silver in his eyes, mixed into the cool ocean blue like tiny crashing waves.

She stared back and slowly twisted her head. "Sounds more like a you problem than a me problem," she said, more as a question than a statement.

Caleb breathed out a laugh and smiled, pulling away to give her some space. "Maybe."

"Do you… do we, I guess, drink blood?" Her face twisted with disgust, already guessing the answer from his abashed reaction.

"Yeah, but we have to, and we do it humanely. We drink animal blood, but it's not as… how can I put this without sounding insane? It's like feeding a tiger straight veg. Sure, it would probably fill it up, but it hasn't got all the supplements the tiger needs to survive. Animal blood hasn't got all the nutrients our bodies need. If we live off just that for too long, we grow weaker. So now and then we have to…"

Hazel's eyes widened fearfully, and she almost bit through her lip, but Caleb shook his head.

"Not that, never that. My parents set up their own blood drive donation at the back of my dad's antiques store, so we're fully stocked. It's what we call 'watered down blood'," he explained, giving her a gentle look. "It's filtered so it's not as intense, and filled with some supplements to last longer. Most of us do that because it helps with the whole bloodlust thing. If you can't taste the real stuff, you can't want it." Caleb didn't sound so sure of that statement. It seemed more like something he'd been told rather than something he believed.

"People just willingly give their blood?" she asked.

Caleb shrugged. "It's like a charity. It's for a good cause."

He wriggled his brows.

Hazel winced, burying her face in her knee, and Caleb frowned.

"Look, we aren't monsters. I mean it. We only drink the watered-down stuff when the animal blood isn't cutting it. I'd never drink it from the source, I don't want to hurt anyone, and I don't want to be something that I'm not. If we drank from a human, tasted the blood while it's warm… especially at our age, then that feral inhuman part of us — those killer instincts that we try to bury – could take over. We'd become more like the bitten." Caleb sighed. "We encounter them from time to time, like that one Ophelia saved you from."

It made a lot more sense now. Ophelia was protecting her from that man, God knows why, but that must have been why she'd been acting so strange.

"He must have been recently turned because Ophelia could see his bite marks. He's still around here, hunting at night."

Hazel gulped. "That's why Lucas is here, he's hunting the weird guy."

"Well yeah, I was getting to that," Caleb said, a little taken aback. "That guy is a Nosferatu Warrior. They hunt dangerous supernaturals, mostly bitten vampires. Their rules state that they can't harm born vampires, though that doesn't stop them from hating us. How did you know about that?" he asked, before his eyes flashed with resignation. "Was he the one chasing you in the woods?"

"I don't know. If it was, I don't think he knew it was me. He never saw me, I was too fast."

"Still, we'll have to be careful. They're bloody sneaky, but they won't lay a finger on you, I promise."

Eventually they ended up back inside the manor, perched on the settee in the living room.

Hazel turned her attention to a dusty old book on the coffee table. Reaching over and turning the page, she saw there was an image of a bitten vampire covered in blood, looking far past human. She shivered and closed the book. "Well, I don't understand how I was born like this. My mother is definitely human," she said, laying back on the couch.

Caleb stood up and sped unnaturally towards the fireplace, leaning against it as if the action were completely normal. Hazel blinked, flicking her head over to him with a stammer in her breath. Each time he did that she found herself feeling motion sick.

He grabbed one of the photos from the fireplace. There were three in total, family pictures. One was of a pretty blonde woman in a 1920's style wedding dress. There was a man with circular glasses kissing her shoulder from behind. He looked a lot like Alexander Thorn, Caleb's father. The man was well known around the town for his old antique store on the high street.

Hazel didn't know Caleb's mother as much, she'd only met the woman a few times in passing.

"Maybe your mother chose to stay human," Caleb suggested, walking back over.

Hazel furrowed her brow. "You can choose that?"

He nodded, turning the next photograph around so she could see it. "Born vampires have to mix their blood with another vampire to transition."

In the photo, Caleb's father was smiling, wrapping an arm around his wife but her expression remained dim, as if she were unimpressed. Hazel then saw the reason why. Just below, standing in front of them, were Caleb and Ophelia. They couldn't have been older than nine and ten. Little Caleb was facing Ophelia, wincing and pushing her as she smiled cunningly. She had her foot on his, as if she'd purposely stomped on it seconds before the photo was taken.

Standing next to Ophelia was a girl who looked around her mid-teens. She was very petite, with fair sandy hair and wore a Spider-Man T-shirt.

"That's my older sister, Rosemary."

Hazel's eyes widened. How had she never known they had an older sister? "Where is she?" she asked.

Caleb's smile dropped slightly. He chewed his lip. "I don't know. She left a long time ago when she chose to stay human."

"Fully human?" Hazel asked, still looking at the teenage girl. She looked sad, out of place, apart from everyone else in the photo. The only thing proving that wrong was the way her hand sat on Caleb's shoulder, comforting him as he frowned at their younger sister.

"Well, when we are born, we're somewhat human, but we've always had enhancements. Better agility, a better sense of smell and hearing. We hardly ever even get sick."

Hazel thought back through her life. There were things that shouldn't have made sense, times she should have broken bones or caught colds and bugs from people who were ill, but never did.

"At a certain age, we have to choose whether to become a vampire fully. My mother calls it *the ceremony*," he said mockingly, before carrying on. "When we are ready, the head of the clan, in my case my mother, will cut their hand with a ceremonial blade and let the blood fall into a cup. You use the same blade to cut your own hand and pour the fully-grown vampire's blood into it…"

Hazel's nose scrunched and she faked a gag.

Caleb pulled a face in agreement. "The blood mixes together, blending with a gene already in our DNA. You could also drink it, but I don't know, the thought grossed me out."

She let out a soft, playful breath. "The thought of drinking blood grossed out the vampire?"

"I was still human then. I didn't like the thought of blood, never mind drinking it," he chuckled. "It just has to get into the bloodstream. It doesn't happen straight away. The blood travels through the body until it reaches every artery and organ, that's when you change. And not every born vampire wants the change. Rosemary didn't. She wouldn't do it, so Mum was forced to send her away."

Hazel was lost for words. "Send her away? Why?"

"It's the rules. If you choose to stay human, then you're choosing to leave everything you've ever known behind. It's for safety reasons. Not to mention family dignity. Even vampires have laws," he finished glumly, facing the fireplace.

Hazel took a tentative step forward before awkwardly slinking her arms around Caleb's torso. He stiffened beneath her at first, then tilted his head to raise an eyebrow at her.

She pushed his face away before he could meet her gaze. "Shut up and let me comfort you."

His shoulders bounced as he let out a small, amused sound, but it fizzled out as another voice cut through the air.

"What in the living nightmare hell is this?" Ophelia yelled, standing in the archway of the room.

There was complete silence for at least five seconds.

The blonde glared at the pair, storming over. "You know we can't have people here, never mind this *bitch*." Ophelia yanked Hazel by the arm, ignoring the yelp that slipped from her lips as she was dragged out of the room.

Caleb sped unnaturally into the hallway to block her path, and Ophelia's jaw almost hit the floor.

"Walk normally, you idiot!" she hissed, motioning to Hazel with her eyes.

Hazel pulled her arm free from the girl's grasp. "Look, I know, okay. I know everything."

Ophelia's eyes filled with a ruby glare, and she stepped forward with an unpredictable look, only to be cut off by her brother, who stepped between them.

"Back off," he scolded, letting his own eyes bleed in warning as Ophelia bared her teeth, two of which had sharpened into points.

They glared at each other and a bitter snarl formed on Ophelia's lips. "She knows? You told her? Have you completely lost your mind?"

"Back off, Lia." Caleb sighed. "You don't even know what's happening, stop jumping to conclusions."

Ophelia laughed shrilly and pushed an acrylic nail into his chest. "Oh, you idiotic, absurd—"

"Knock it off, now!" a woman yelled from the front doorway, appearing out of nowhere with an impatient expression plastered on her face. "What's going on? Who is this?"

Julianna Thorn looked no older than thirty-five, with sharp pinched features and solid cheekbones.

Caleb pushed Hazel back an inch and she let him, happy to be hidden away from the intense eyes of the goddess woman standing at the doorway.

Ophelia spoke first. "She knows about us," she sneered, throwing a harsh look in Hazel's direction.

Julianna's jaw slackened, and she took a step forward, but Caleb moved first – he was quicker, it seemed. "She's one of us," he insisted.

Julianna raised an eyebrow, then stole a glance at Hazel over his shoulder, and peered back at her son. "She is?"

Caleb nodded. "She's born, not bitten. I've checked her for bites."

"Is that what they're calling it now, *checking for bites*?" Ophelia scoffed.

The older woman shushed her, and, like a child, she pouted and crossed her arms.

Julianna motioned for Caleb to move out of the way, which he did reluctantly, giving Hazel a reassuring look. "It was Ophelia's blood that turned her. An accident," he explained.

Hazel didn't miss the way Ophelia's eyebrows knitted together in both horror and perplexity.

Julianna nodded, sending a scornful look to her daughter before turning her unforgiving eyes on Hazel, watching, studying. Then, with a smile that looked odd on her harsh features, she reached out her hand.

Hazel blinked, accepting her proffered hand, aware suddenly of how sweaty her palms were.

Julianna did not shake her hand, which was fine, great even, as the thought of an awkward handshake would have haunted Hazel for hours. Instead, the woman grabbed her wrist and jabbed her nail into Hazel's skin, drawing blood.

She pulled her arm back with a horrified look and Caleb returned to her side, rubbing the blood away and showing her that the wound had already begun to heal. Another thing she would have to get used to, she assumed.

"You're right. She is one of us. I'm surprised we couldn't

smell it on you. Dominique, isn't it? I remember you."

Hazel wanted to correct her with the name, but didn't dare, so nodded a little too enthusiastically.

"Her name is Hazel," Ophelia mocked. "What do we do about her?"

Julianna glared at her daughter. "We help her. Especially if it was your blood that turned her! How many times have I warned you about your reckless behaviour? Now look what you've done." Julianna cleared her throat, turning to Hazel. "You will stay here as long as you need."

Hazel looked down at her boots, surprised and a little ashamed at how the icy woman had her trembling. "Oh, thanks, but I need to go home. It's getting late and my mother wanted me home already."

There was an awkward silence before Julianna spoke again. "It takes time to gain control. You aren't going anywhere. Ophelia will show you to your room," she said sternly.

"Why do I have to? She's Caleb's friend, not mine," Ophelia grumbled.

"Caleb is not to go to her room. You may be creatures of the night, but you're still teenagers living under my roof. Now, Ophelia, play nice," Julianna hissed, turning towards the stairs.

Hazel gulped and watched as the woman disappeared.

Ophelia huffed and grabbed Hazel by the arm, pulling her up the stairs roughly, but before she could be dragged away, she risked a glance at Caleb, who rolled his head with a sympathetic upside-down smile.

CHAPTER NINE

Growing Pains

"Here you go. The Wi-Fi password is Thorn28, there's an en-suite in your room, and if you need anything, ask Caleb. His room is that way." Ophelia pointed down the hallway, and Hazel followed her finger with astonishment as she staggered behind. The corridors felt never ending, especially with the wide windows that lined them, revealing the expansive forest. "And don't bother me."

They were now standing outside a large oak door.

Ophelia pushed it open and held her hand out passive aggressively, waiting for Hazel to step inside.

Hazel peered into the room. It was lighter than the hallways, with ivory walls and a queen-sized bed in the centre. There were no paintings on the walls or trinkets of any sort, in fact, the room was bland, and clearly unlived in. She lingered in the doorway and Ophelia clipped her in the ankle, forcing her to stumble inside.

"Ow!" Hazel grabbed onto the side of the wall to steady herself, turning back as Ophelia waved sarcastically and went to walk away. Before she could get too far, Hazel grabbed her by the arm. "I have questions."

Ophelia rolled her eyes and yanked her arm free. "Ask my *brother.* You two seemed frighteningly cosy before, I'm sure he'd be glad to help."

There was a threat in there somewhere. Hazel just couldn't

place where exactly.

"Please."

Releasing a fitful huff, Ophelia shoved past, moving to sit on the bed. "Make it quick."

Hazel let out a breath and followed her into the room.

"So, the other night, that guy, who obviously wasn't your uncle, was going to kill me, right? But if I have vampire blood, why would he try to attack me?"

Ophelia closed her eyes impatiently. "You weren't a vampire yet, you were still human. Blood stays partially human, just slightly enhanced, until it's mixed, then it changes. Like, your DNA physically changes. Still, blood tastes different from humans with the gene, so the bitten tend not to attack them, you can tell the difference by smell." She eyed Hazel suspiciously and jutted her lip. "Usually."

Hazel folded her arms around herself. She didn't know how to feel about that. Why couldn't they smell her? Was something wrong with her?

"Your blood got into my bloodstream. I felt it."

"Yeah, that ugly creep bit me," Ophelia sneered, glancing down at her healed arm. Her blue eyes darkened, and Hazel thought she heard a pitiful laugh under the girl's breath. "It'll fade from your bloodstream, it's not like a sire situation or anything."

"Thank god."

"Oh, please, like I'd want you following me around. You'd be a crap personal assistant anyway."

"What happens now?" Hazel sighed, lying down on the bed.

"You'll be taught control, likely by my parents. They'll teach you how not to kill your friends, or rather, *friend*, seeing as you only have the one. Then you'll learn how to understand your abilities, how to use them and contain them, and not set yourself or anyone else on fire."

Hazel's eyes lit up in a bizarre mix of fear and fascination.

"Stay away from the warrior freak kid, I'm pretty sure he knows about my family, but not you, so it's better it stays that way. Hunters are tricky." Ophelia lay back on the bed, next to Hazel.

There was a familiarity in the air, in the shape of how their bodies mirrored each other, like muscle memory.

"I'm going to ignore the friend thing. Thanks for that," Hazel said, and Ophelia smirked from beside her. "But... abilities? Fire? We can set things on fire?"

The other girl nodded, looking uninterested. Hazel blinked. "What else can we do? Can we fly, too?"

Ophelia sat up on her elbow. "Can we fly? Are you messing? What do you think this is?"

Hazel shrugged, frowning. "So, we can't fly?"

"Obviously not. Look, you'll get more answers tomorrow. Just sleep. It's going to be a long day, and I'm sure my mother will rope me in somehow. Thanks for spoiling my Saturday plans," Ophelia grumbled, sitting up from the bed.

Hazel pulled her knees into her stomach. "You said the hunters are tricky. Lucas chased me through the woods. That's how I got here."

Ophelia's features sharpened. "He saw you?"

"No, I don't think so."

Ophelia's mouth puckered. "You don't think so?"

Hazel frowned at the girl's bitter tone and moved to the edge of the bed. "I was too fast, there was no way he would have. I didn't even see him. I'm just guessing it was him because he seems to be everywhere I don't want him to be."

Ophelia didn't respond, she just stared as if contemplating murder.

Hazel narrowed her eyes. "What—"

"These are trained hunters. It's their job to hunt and kill our kind. We are a confirmed family of born vampires, they know about us and aren't permitted to hunt us. They don't know about you! Without proof that you are of pure blood, they'll assume you are bitten. You can't be casual about this, or you'll die! He wouldn't hesitate to kill you. You can't let him find out about you."

Hazel raised an eyebrow. "Why don't they hunt born vampires?"

"Because it's against the rules. They know we are not a threat, but if they think we've killed or turned a human, they can and *will* hunt us. It's not just you that this could affect."

After that, Ophelia left and Hazel thought back to her mother, who was probably sitting at the table, waiting for a response to her dozen text messages.

Hazel had meant to reply to them, she really had. But what was she supposed to say? *Mum, why didn't you tell me I was a vampire? Do you happen to have a really specific gene that can turn someone's whole life around? If so, did you know you'd passed it to me? Or was that a parting gift from my father?*

There were also a few missed calls from Amber. *Sorry, Amber, I can't talk right now, I'm busy spending the night at Ophelia Thorn's house.*

She was supposed to be staying at Amber's tomorrow night anyway, after the bar, so she could just tell her mother they decided to make it a two-night thing. Although Hazel doubted they'd be going out at all now.

She'd have to call Amber back at some point to say she wasn't feeling up to it… but as she stared at her friend's name in her contacts, she just couldn't bring herself to do it. Amber would know something was up, she always did, and Hazel didn't have much of an explanation right now.

As she guiltily scrolled away from Amber's contact to find her mother's, Ophelia briefly came back, slumping some pyjamas and a sad-looking sandwich on the bed.

It was strange, being around Ophelia again. Hazel thought back to when they drifted apart. Year nine, about a week before summer. Some of it made sense now, in some odd, not so comforting way. It was strange to think that if she'd known the truth all those years ago, maybe they'd still be friends.

Or maybe not.

There wasn't much they had in common. They were complete opposites; they weren't the same kids they used to be, when that stuff never used to matter. They never would be those kids again.

Sometimes, people just outgrow each other.

Hazel and Ophelia spent their lunch break relaxing on the grass, ignoring the raucous game being played by their classmates on the nearby football field. It looked like a violent, amplified version of tag, using the old, worn ball near the white nets as a weapon.

Ophelia scoffed at the scene, pulling a face of disgust as more and more students scrambled through the muddy field.

"Don't worry, they'll get bored and go back inside eventually," Hazel said, holding her hand up to stop the glare of the sun from blinding her.

"Not soon enough," Ophelia mused. "You'd think they'd have grown up by now, matured a little, at least."

"At fourteen? Nah, they've still got a few years left in them, I bet."

"Until they change?"

Hazel shrugged, pulling at some daisies, while Ophelia lay back.

"What if… what if one day we change?" Ophelia wondered aloud.

"We're not the ones rolling around in the mud," Hazel replied. "I don't think we have as much maturing to do."

"I don't mean maturing," Ophelia said hesitantly. "I mean, what if everything around us changes, what if we change? Like, everything we've ever known just one day becomes something else."

"Is this a riddle? Am I supposed to answer that?"

Ophelia sighed. "No, it doesn't matter." She sat up, staring across the pitch as the other students began to move their game indoors. The sun was now blocked by the clouds.

Hazel furrowed her brows. "Well, it clearly does. Where is this coming from? What's changing?"

Still staring at the muddy field, Ophelia let out a hollow breath. "Nothing yet."

As the clouds above swept over them, Hazel picked up the dead flowers she'd been toying with and showed off the daisy chain bracelets she'd created. "Change just happens, Lia. We can't control it, but not every change has to be bad," Hazel assured her, reaching over to tie the daisy chain onto the girl's wrist. "And it doesn't matter what happens to us. We're always going to be connected, like the daisies."

Ophelia smiled sadly, staring down at the matching daisy chain on Hazel's wrist.

It didn't take very long for those daisy chains to wither and die.

Caleb was in the basement, where they stored their blood bags. Selecting one at random, he ripped it open and slumped down onto the sofa to gush it down. He thought back to his own transition, two years ago, a couple of months after he'd turned sixteen. That's when his mother had decided he was ready. His parents were so proud, even if Caleb was a little unsure at the time, though he kept that to himself.

The ceremony itself was easy, what came next was the hard part. The hunger was overwhelming and unpredictable, just like the mood swings. Plus, waves of pain trickled over his body in spurts, especially in his gums.

Once he'd had his first sip of blood, however, that was it. The power coursed through his veins like gasoline. It was unlike anything he'd ever felt before. Which, as he'd come to find out, was a very dangerous feeling.

Caleb had broken free from the basement where he'd been kept and strolled right into his secondary school in a pair of sunglasses and a partly torn T-shirt. Luckily, Ophelia came across him before any trouble was caused.

That was two days after his transition, and the weight of it all had been too much to control. Although that didn't seem to be the case for Hazel.

"Disgusting," Ophelia complained, judging her brother from the doorway. He ignored her and kept drinking. "Stress eating?" she taunted.

He hummed sarcastically.

"What happened to the vines in the front? Dad's outside in the gardens sulking over it."

Caleb guiltily rubbed at his neck.

Ophelia let out a disapproving laugh. "What did you do?"

He took another swig of his drink. "Hazel didn't believe me at first. So… I… kinda climbed the house. Might have pulled a little too hard on the vines."

She raised an eyebrow. "Let's evaluate your actions. You let her into our house, you told her we were vampires, and then you paraded yourself around like a dancing monkey," she said, listing off her fingers.

Caleb's lips tilted proudly in the corners of his mouth, and he pulled the red liquid back to his lips. "Well, I didn't dance, but I did swing around on a bunch of vines, so that's actually a pretty accurate metaphor," he mused.

She rolled her eyes. "That's not something to be proud about."

He shrugged, grinning through bloody teeth.

"That girl's gonna get us all killed," Ophelia groaned, swiping a wine glass and a blood bag and sitting next to her brother.

"No she's not, we've got this under control."

"Have we?" Ophelia spat sarcastically, glancing up at him with knitted brows.

Caleb nodded his head. "Do you remember how hard the first couple of months were after we turned?"

"Pretty sure the chains are still in here somewhere. I always hated those."

"Yeah, exactly," he replied. "Lia, we couldn't be around humans, we couldn't control it, but Hazel has been around people all day and pretty much managed it."

"Pretty much?" she asked doubtfully.

"Well, there was a moment in the bathroom, a girl had a nosebleed. Hazel said she felt herself slipping but kept it under control. Do you know what this means?"

"She's easily distracted?" Ophelia smirked, cruelly.

"It means we could prove she is of full blood. Bitten vampires don't have this much control. *We* didn't even have this much control." He smiled to himself, but Ophelia quickly discouraged him.

"Don't jump to conclusions. It's only been a day. Could just be beginner's luck."

Caleb gave her a tired look and she raised her arms defensively. "I agree she's not bitten, but we still have no proof of her being a born vampire either. This isn't going to be easy with the Nosferatu Warriors. Mum and I couldn't find them in the woods, they're sneaky, and you know they'll bring us down at any chance they get," she said, grabbing the blood bag from his hand and chugging the rest of it down neatly.

Caleb let out a sigh, rubbing a hand over his chin as he stared out into the darkness of the cellar. "They won't get a chance."

Ophelia laughed dryly. "You sound like Mum," she mused, standing up from the couch.

"That's not a bad thing," he said. "She always knows what she's doing."

Ophelia hummed, looking down at her shimmery pink nails. "No, she just likes to act like she does. You know it doesn't really matter what you do or say, no one can really please her. She'll always be disappointed at something or other."

Caleb glanced away from his sister, his grin faltering a little. "Stop it. She wants to help. You're just sorry you're getting roped into it."

Ophelia shrugged in agreement, before walking away, leaving him alone in the basement.

CHAPTER TEN

Stars

Alexander Thorn was still mending the vines outside the manor when Caleb strolled outside.

"Need a hand?"

The man jumped down and rubbed at his palms, looking back up to admire his work, before grabbing his son's shoulder and leading him toward the back garden.

"No, I'll finish it up tomorrow, stupid crows."

Caleb rubbed at the back of his neck. "Yeah, those damned birds."

As they reached the gate, Alexander held a hand out to let his son pass by first and Caleb smiled apologetically. "It was me. I didn't mean to pull them too roughly, I'm sorry."

Alexander chuckled. "I know, I was just pulling your leg, I needed to re-root them anyway."

He clapped the younger boy on the back and led him toward the greenhouse. "While you're here, we'll grab the lavender you need for tomorrow."

Caleb raised his brow curiously.

"For the blood, so your friend can't smell it when you take her out for training. Your mother told me about her."

The greenhouse was quite big inside. On one side lay a line of multicoloured plants and bushes, exotic and slightly scary-looking. On the other, a bunch of shelving and storage, with tools and frilly aprons hung up on the wall.

There was an empty space where a row of nightshade used to sit. Alexander had got rid of those when his children became of age, but the dirt was still tinged lilac.

Nightshade was deadly to vampires, born or bitten. The beautiful amethyst flowers burned their skin and poisoned them from the inside out if kept in their bodies for too long. Many vampires believed that, because the plant grew in the dead of night, witches propagated it as a mockery. They were, by nature, nocturnal creatures, so it was a cruel joke that something so similar could be the very thing that killed them.

Nosferatu Warriors were notorious for growing and cultivating the plant. They were probably more linked with it than *witches,* seeing as the latter didn't really exist. It was just a rumour, a scary story to make little vampire born children behave.

Alexander, however, had always said it was just a plant. A beautiful deadly plant that lingered wherever it grew. He was a collector at the end of the day, and they'd just been part of his collection. Caleb was glad his father had got rid of it now, with the hunters circling in on them. It would be pretty silly if they got murdered by use of their own plants.

"Why aren't you and Mum training Hazel?" Caleb asked. "I mean, I've only been doing this for two years. You've got centuries on me."

"Oi, century singular. I'm barely over a hundred, you little git." Alexander grinned, placing a bunch of lavender in Caleb's hand. "We want you to train her. It'll be good experience for your future."

Caleb twisted his nose at the strong scent as his father added more lavender onto the pile. "But—"

"We trust you, Cal, and you won't be alone. Take your sister with you. Your mother thinks she could do with learning a bit of responsibility."

Caleb snorted. "Yeah, that's gonna go down well when you tell her."

"Oh no, your first job as mentor is to tell her yourself." Alexander laughed, looking up at his son with a brisk smile, before fixing the ends of his glasses. Medically, he didn't need them to see, but he liked the old, oval-shape of them.

"Great." Caleb sighed, looking down at the pile of plants in his arms in resignation.

It felt like the walls were closing in on her.

Hazel didn't like feeling trapped at the best of times – who did? – but this was intolerable. It was late, she should be tired, but her body was buzzing with energy and trepidation. I mean, she was in *Thorn Manor*. How could she be expected to just… sleep?

She moved to the door soundlessly but as she went to try the handle, she heard voices coming towards her down the corridor.

"I don't give a shit about responsibility, Caleb, we've been vampires for less than three years. They've had decades on us. Why don't they train her?"

"You know they're busy, the store, the hunters, the bloody Arcane Council. I was a little unsure at first myself, but we can do it," Caleb responded. "I taught you some things, remember, and back then I'd only been a vampire for a couple of months. We pick up things quickly. Come on, can you help me out with this… please?"

Hazel couldn't see her but she could sense Ophelia's selfish pout. "Okay, fine, but I'm gonna complain every second."

"Oh, I'm betting on that," Caleb muttered, earning a snarl in response.

Hazel heard a door opening.

"Lia! wait, one more thing."

Slowly the door crept open again and there was a dramatic yawn, followed by a whiny, "What now?"

"I… I've been thinking. And, look, don't tell Mum and Dad this time, but I think I've found where Rosemary could be. She has a new job, and I'm not exactly sure if it's her, but if we—"

Ophelia cut him off. "Caleb, you have to let it go, she doesn't want to be found. The more you look for her, the more you're just disappointed. She chose her path. Let her take it."

There was a slam of a door, then a distinctive sigh. After a moment Hazel heard Caleb walk away.

Once she was sure he was gone, she tried the handle, half expecting it to be locked, but it yielded, and she grinned. She couldn't help herself. She was in a *vampire's mansion*. There was no way she could simply sit still.

She had barely gone two steps though before she was grabbed from behind. She yelped, but no noise came out as a hand quickly covered her mouth.

"Just me," Caleb whispered. Hazel turned to face him with an irked expression, shoving him away as he laughed quietly. "So, Indiana Jones, where are you off too? Got any crystal skulls to find?""

"You really are a secret nerd in disguise, aren't you?" she mumbled, avoiding his eyes.

Caleb smirked. "It's not a secret, I'm just a nerd. Stop stalling."

"I'm not stalling," she said, scrunching her lip.

"Oh? Then what are you doing?"

Hazel straightened her back, swallowing awkwardly. "I was looking for the bathroom."

A smug look fell onto his face. "Your room has an en-suite."

Hazel groaned. "Okay, fine. I couldn't sleep. I don't like feeling like a prisoner."

Caleb gave her a sympathetic look, pulling her along the corridor. "You're not a prisoner, Hazel, you're just not in full control yet, and you could hurt someone. My mother is trying to help. She does it in an obliviously scary way, but she means well."

"I got through the whole day without hurting anyone, so I think I've got it covered," Hazel mumbled, stepping back into the guest room.

Caleb smiled. "You're pretty stubborn, you know."

She let out an accusatory snort in response. "You're pretty annoying, *you know*."

"Hey, all I heard was that I'm pretty."

Hazel grabbed a throw pillow from the bed's overflowing collection and flung it at him. He caught it effortlessly, grinning as she sighed and sat at the foot of the bed.

Caleb leaned on an empty set of drawers. "Try to get some sleep, we'll be up early tomorrow," he said. "Do you need anything? More blankets, some water?"

Hazel shook her head, pulling the quilt around her shoulders. She hoped the building anxiety in her stomach wasn't showing on her face, but she doubted that with the way her fingers clung to the blanket.

Caleb softened his expression. "A distraction?" She looked up at him and nodded. "Okay," he said. "Tell me something about yourself that I don't already know."

"You're supposed to be distracting me, not the other way around."

Caleb laughed. "This is a distraction for you. It's much more distracting when it's something you're interested in. Go on, what don't I know?"

She shrugged. "My birthday is the fourteenth of October."

"Nah, I already knew that. I was at most of your childhood birthday parties, remember?" he said, propping the pillow behind himself. "Remember that year the bouncy castle got cancelled because of the rain, so your mum put on that makeshift magic show?"

Hazel brought the blanket up over her face. "Oh god, I was hoping everyone had forgotten about that."

"Was pretty good actually, I'm still wondering how she did that disappearing apple thing." Caleb chuckled, glancing toward the window. The curtains were open, letting in the orange glow of the lamps outside that lined the elegant drive. "Want me to shut the curtain? Sometimes it gets a little bright in the morning."

Hazel popped her head out of the blanket and shook it. "Leave it open, I like looking at the stars."

An amused smile formed on Caleb's lips. "Yeah?"

"Yeah," she replied. "They're always there, even when they're not."

"Makes sense," he mocked, and she grabbed another pillow playfully.

He raised his hands in surrender. "Please elaborate before you resort to violence."

Hazel dropped the pillow on the sheets and looked towards the stars with a shrug. "They're always there, day in, day out, even if we can't see them. We're the ones that move while the earth spins. The stars are constant, while we're ever changing."

"Stars die out, though, they aren't always there. Not forever," Caleb retorted, following her gaze toward the glowing sky.

"Yeah, but even if a star burns out a trillion light-years away, we can still see it shining just as bright as it used to. In a way, they're immortal."

Caleb chuckled under his breath, and Hazel turned towards him dubiously. "Immortal? Was that on purpose?" he asked.

A shy smile crept onto her face. "No, I didn't think about it like that." She gulped. "Are we really immortal?"

"Pretty much. We won't reach full maturity until at least our late twenties," he said, rubbing at his jaw. "But after that, well I don't know… there are vampires out there that are in their eight hundreds, so we don't really have an expiration date. That doesn't mean we're indestructible though, vampires still die."

"Stars still burn out," Hazel added.

Caleb smiled sweetly and let out an amused breath. "I guess it makes sense. Stars are frozen in time, just like us, and if you got close enough to them, you'd probably burn."

"Deadly."

"But mesmerising to look at," he added with a wink. "I wonder what kind of star I am? Maybe a shooting star because they're so fast."

Hazel snorted as Caleb sped from the wooden drawers to the window at full pelt, making a show of his speed before sitting cross-legged.

"See?" He smirked, glancing back at her.

Hazel moved off the bed to join him on the floor. "Nah,

you're not a star."

Caleb turned to her with a playfully offended look, pouting his lip.

She chuckled softly, pulling the blanket around her again. "You'd be the sun."

His eyes lit up at that and he leaned back on his elbows. "Because I shine the brightest?"

"Because you're big-headed."

"Okay, that's fair," he conceded, shrugging.

"And sometimes when I look at you, it hurts my eyes because of your hyper energy," she continued, pulling her knees up under her chin as the quilt tumbled from her shoulders. It wasn't really cold; it was more of a support bubble if anything. She didn't mind that it had slipped away.

He grinned. "Well, that must make you the moon, then."

"Because I'm gloomy?"

"Well, I was going to say you're full of gloom and that rhymes with moon, but you ruined my joke," he teased, nudging his knee into hers. "You'd be the moon because it's mysterious, kinda quiet, introverted."

Hazel laughed.

"No, really, it's intriguing, I think. Darker on one side, but lighter when you've seen more of it," Caleb elaborated, peering over at her. "Stubborn too. It never moves, guess you could say that's where you differentiate seeing as you're always on the go."

Hazel sniffed good-humouredly, turning to look back at the constellations. She thought back to the conversation she had overheard. She looked at him, noticing the faraway look in his eyes. "Caleb?" she asked, drawing his attention. "Have you looked for Rosemary before?"

He sat up straight and clasped his hands, toying with his

fingers. "Yeah, a couple times. First was a few years ago, before I turned," he replied. "But my mother found out and shut me down. I think she was afraid I'd join Rosemary and stay human. Then after I turned, I tried again. I found a picture of her on a university website. I tried to go, but Ophelia found out, and she didn't really share my enthusiasm," he trailed off. "I know our world is dangerous, but I just want to know that she's okay. Sometimes I worry something will find her, link her to being a Thorn. We're a well-known family in our community. My uncle is on the Arcane Council."

Hazel gave him a confused look.

"The Council is built up of other supernatural factions, including the Nosferatu Warriors. They decide the laws, punishments, all of the legal stuff. It's a little like law and order, but with more pizzazz," Caleb mused, chuckling as she blinked at him. "What I mean is, I just want to see her, even if from a distance. To know she's safe and happy."

He turned back towards the window and Hazel frowned. "I could help you find her," she whispered, watching his expression as he turned toward her.

"Yeah?"

"Yeah."

They sat for a while, watching the stars, until he stood up. "Right, I best be off. Goodnight, I hope the sun doesn't wake you up in the morning with its big head."

Hazel watched him go with a soft grin, then looked back to the stars.

CHAPTER ELEVEN

Through the Flames

Hazel rubbed at the sleep in her eyes and glanced tiredly at Caleb. "Did we have to do this so early?"

"It's past seven." He shrugged. "The earlier we start the better, if you want to be done with this sooner."

Hazel frowned, yawning, and he jabbed her in the side playfully, chuckling as she glared at him. "I'm trying to wake you up," he mused, grinning as he went to jab her again.

Hazel leaned away from him and let out a sharp laugh.

"Okay, first things first, you need to control yourself," Ophelia huffed, turning to face them both with an irritated expression.

They'd reached a clearing in the woods outside the house, somewhere close enough to the manor that the hunters shouldn't bother them, but far enough to give them the space they needed.

Caleb shoved his sister out of the way, disregarding the hiss she gave him. "What Lia means is that you need to learn control." He pointed to a tree for Ophelia to sit by.

"How do I do that? How do I even know when I'm not in control?" Hazel asked, tugging at the sleeves of her jacket.

"You feel it in your bones, like something taking over you," Caleb answered, pulling his blue backpack over his shoulder. "Kinda feels like you're being hypnotised."

"Okay, I think I've felt that before," Hazel responded uncomfortably.

"That's good, so you can recognise the feeling, now we just have to push it away," he said. "I want you to close your eyes."

Hazel pulled a face, then did as he asked.

"When you feel that hypnotic feeling, you have to open your other senses," he continued. "Feel the earth around you, let it pull you back. Listen to the sounds, the different smells, anything you can find to focus on hard enough." There was a shuffling sound, like he was rummaging in his backpack. "Just concentrate. Tell me what you smell."

A strong scent filled Hazel's nostrils. It was a sweet smell, floral, and a bit herbal. "Lavender?" she whispered, furrowing her eyebrows.

"Yeah! That's good! Just like that, keep homing in on those senses."

Caleb slowly started to unwrap something; Hazel could hear the sound of rope tearing through his fingers.

Then her back stiffened. She could taste something metallic in the air, it tingled up her skin, leaving a trail of goosebumps. The burning came next, up her throat like a boiling, stagnant pain. She pulled a hand up to her neck and rubbed at it.

"Caleb…" Hazel exhaled, hearing a hoarseness in her voice that wasn't there before.

After his name left her lips, she took a breath in, which was a big mistake. A potent scent washed over her, filling every sense, every nerve ending in her body with need. At the sound of tearing plastic, Hazel opened her eyes to see Caleb studying her. His teeth were pointed, visible through his parted lips. Her attention moved down to the little plastic bag in his hand. The liquid inside swirled like a tiny red ocean, spilling over the sides and onto Caleb's fingers.

Hazel glanced up, meeting his daring blue eyes, and he licked his lips mischievously.

"You want it, don't you?" he whispered, bringing the bloodied edge of his hand to his lips.

A growl left Hazel's throat involuntarily. The burning was growing more intense by the second, mixing with the blaring white noise in her mind. The sight of the blood trickling down his fingers had her mouth hanging open, sharp teeth pinching into her own lips.

"Cal," Ophelia warned from under the tree.

Hazel narrowed her eyes as Caleb rubbed more blood over his lips with the tip of his thumb, tasting it for himself while keeping her gaze.

"Stop taunting her!" Ophelia hissed. "Are you insane? She's going to attack you."

Caleb didn't move, instead, he kept his gaze on Hazel, letting the blood bag drop to the floor. "She has to lose control to gain control. I know what I'm doing." His hands were stained scarlet as he held them up towards her, beckoning her closer. "That's it," he whispered. "Come get me."

"Caleb!" Ophelia spat, but he shushed her with his pointer finger, never taking his eyes off Hazel.

He was a threat. Every inch of Hazel screamed to attack, to claw at him, rip him apart before he could steal more blood for himself. She staggered forwards in a frenzy, only to be pushed back by Ophelia, who dashed between them.

"I told you this was a bad idea," she complained.

"Hazel, focus on the birds above us. You can hear them singing, home in on it, try to only focus on the birds," Caleb encouraged her, ignoring his sister. The teasing tone was gone from his voice.

He kept his focus on her, pointing up with one hand as he used the other to hold his sister back.

Hazel's eyes followed his movements. There was a flutter of motion above, her eyes trailed it for a second before her attention dropped back down to Caleb and she snarled.

Ophelia tried to push her brother's arm away, but he wouldn't budge. "Let me go!" she yelled.

He ignored her and watched as Hazel's head flickered up again at the sound of birds chirping. "That's it, just like that."

She could just about decipher the soft whisper of his words through the thick blur in her mind.

"Close your eyes, Hazel."

Hazel hesitated. All she could think about was the blood bag, the liquid squelching around it, the smell so potent it stung at her nose. She ripped her attention away from the smell.

The birds chirped sweetly, singing through the trees. The more attention Hazel paid to the melodies, the more she could focus on them, allowing her heart rate to slow as she controlled her breathing.

It seemed like forever had gone by before she opened her eyes to see Caleb smiling at her.

Ophelia clapped slowly from behind him, taunting both of them with a sarcastic glare. "Okay, not bad, but if that were a real person, you'd have lost it, so let's go again."

With most of the blood bags spilled on either Caleb, Ophelia, or the forest floor, they decided to call it a day.

"You did well, you know, better than most," Caleb said

after he changed out of his blood-stained shirt.

"Yeah, not good enough, though." Hazel sighed, holding a palm over her nose. Even though he'd changed his clothing, some of the liquid had still stuck to the bare skin underneath it. Apparently, she'd been more composed than he'd expected, even after tasting the blood, but that didn't mean it was easy. Her throat felt raw, her bones ached with every step, and there was a sickly feeling in her stomach.

"That's an understatement. What a waste of a day," Ophelia scoffed, peering back snidely before marching ahead.

Hazel frowned, until Caleb got closer to her, whispering while they walked. "Don't listen to her, she wasn't so perfect at it herself. Remember a couple of years ago when Lia was off school for a while?"

Hazel nodded, staring down at his chest where the T-shirt stuck to his torso. Caleb noticed her wandering eyes and snickered, causing her head to snap up. She coughed and pulled at her sleeves, motioning for him to continue.

"She could barely leave the house. We had to lock her in her room. I thought she was going to murder me at one point."

Over the transitional period, Ophelia would scream the house down and belittle everyone as much as possible through the small gap under her door. Caleb tried to avoid her as best he could until the day finally came for her to return to school.

A month had passed, and her parents had decided she needed to be around humans to get used to them. With Caleb being of full blood now, they trusted him to watch over her.

The fateful day came and Ophelia bounced down the stairs,

hair flowing onto her shoulder as she smiled sweetly at her brother.

"Ready, Cal?" She grinned, squeezing him on the shoulder as she propelled herself out of the doorway towards the car he'd got for his birthday, a sleek silver Jaguar – the same car she'd tried to key in a jealous fit when he'd first received it.

Caleb gulped and glanced frightfully at his mother. She ignored him, calling out to Ophelia about keeping a level head. Caleb wanted to laugh. He didn't.

The entire journey there, he kept glancing at his sister, not trusting her unusual cheery demeanour as she applied lipstick using the passenger side mirror.

"It's gonna be a bit overwhelming at first. Come find me if it gets too much or if you need anything. Don't hold it all in, okay? That'll just make it worse," Caleb whispered, daring a final glance at her as they pulled into the car park.

Ophelia let out a harsh snicker, rolling her eyes in a light-hearted manner as she swivelled towards him. "You worry too much," she said, pointing a shiny pink nail in his direction. "I'm fine. Relax. I can handle it. I'm not the one who broke out of the basement, am I?"

Caleb sighed, slumping in his seat as Ophelia strutted over to her friends with open arms, not even breaking a sweat. She seemed completely fine, overly enthusiastic, in fact, but he knew his sister, and she could hide things well.

The morning seemed to go by incident free, to the point Caleb almost started to relax, but as he was about to head to his third class, he noticed a broken hair clip on the floor. A hot pink one that had been thrown at him many times over the past month.

He cursed under his breath and sped around the empty halls until he heard a familiar bittersweet voice coming from the cafeteria.

"Piss off!"

"You've been acting so weird today, what's wrong with you?" one of Ophelia's friends said, a snobby-looking redhead.

Ophelia visibly stiffened, pushing the girl back with a snarl.

"That girl was right about you, you're crazy!" another one cackled.

Ophelia spun around to face her friend, and for a second Caleb noticed a red tinge blur into her irises.

He burst into the room. "Shouldn't you lot be terrorising a substitute teacher or something?" he said, pulling Ophelia behind his back.

Some of the girls blushed and giggled, whispering to each other.

"Hi Caleb," one of them swooned, smiling flirtatiously. "We were just talking, messing around." She glanced over his shoulder, but he steered her attention away from his sister.

"Oh, come on, Ophelia, tell him we were just joking," the redhead butted in.

Caleb felt Ophelia tense behind him and placed a hand onto her arm. She was shaking, vibrating with furious energy.

He turned toward her snide friend and flicked his head to the side with irritation. "Well, sorry to be the one to tell you, but your jokes really aren't funny. If you have to try this hard to impress other people that's just rather sad. Now piss off, will you?" he asked charmingly. The other girls giggled again, moving for the door.

After watching the redhead huff and storm away, Caleb spun around to see Ophelia slump down onto a blue bench. There were tears forming in her eyes as she clutched a palm to her throat.

Caleb crouched in front of her, frowning as she twisted her face up. "It's okay, Lia, just breathe," he whispered.

She looked up at him and mumbled something incoherent.

"What was that?" he asked.

Her lips scrunched up as she let out a low, animalistic breath. "I should have torn their heads off."

Caleb gulped and peered up at her, knitting his brows together. "Ah, let's hope that was metaphorical."

Ophelia dropped her head into her hands. "It hurts, Caleb. I feel like I'm on fire." She winced; her voice was gravelly.

He reached an arm out to her shoulder. "I know, but it will get better, I promise. Let's go home," he tried. "We can always try again tomorrow."

She let out a pained sob, gripping her throat again. "I can't… I can't move, I can't…" Ophelia tried to stand up, stumbling over her own feet and almost crashing to the ground.

He grabbed onto her forearms, feeling the heat radiating from her, and ducked down to her level. "Hey, look at me. You're okay, let's just get out of here," he said, scanning her face.

Her breathing was staggered and unsteady as she shook her head frantically, then all of a sudden Ophelia squeezed her eyes shut, stumbling into his arms with a gut-wrenching cry.

The entire cafeteria erupted into flames around them and Ophelia crumbled to the floor.

Caleb wrapped his arms around her, falling with her, and peered around the room as the fire pinched at his skin. "Lia, open your eyes! It will stop the flames!"

Ophelia clutched her head tighter, ignoring him, and he let out a frantic noise. The fire crackled around them in a perfect circle. Smoke rose into the air, creating shadows and blocking the sunlight from the windows.

"Okay, shit… Just listen to me." He winced, pulling them both backwards. Caleb's eyes watered from the smoke, he squinted them and softened his tone. "I know it's scary, everything's too much. Too loud, too fast," he said, pulling his little sister into his chest. "But it's going to get easier, I promise. I'm right here, okay?

And I will be, day by day, step by step. You can do that, right? Take it step by step?"

Through her quivering, Ophelia nodded slowly.

"Okay, great. The first one's an easy one, all I want you to do is open your eyes."

Ophelia whimpered and closed them tighter in response.

The fire stood tall, towering over them, almost hitting the ceiling.

"Lia," Caleb coughed, using an elbow to shield them from the smoke. They couldn't choke on it, or die from it filling their lungs, but it still wouldn't be a pleasant experience.

The fire rose behind him, trickling up his back, and he couldn't help the pained noise that escaped his lips.

A gasp left Ophelia's throat and her eyes tore open, red blurring into blue as the flames burnt out.

After a few minutes, Caleb stood and moved towards the fire alarm, dodging the hot, burned floor. Water poured down from the sprinklers on the ceiling, slightly delayed, before he finally triggered the alarm.

Ophelia looked up and the water blended into her tears, washing them away with her running mascara. She let out a raspy laugh watching as her brother staggered back over to her and crouched by her side.

He helped her up, then let out a relieved chuckle himself as the water sizzled against the singed flooring.

Soon enough, they were standing in the middle of the charred circle, laughing fitfully as cold water poured down around them, soaking them both entirely.

Caleb took the fall, telling everyone he'd accidentally dropped a cigarette on his maths homework. That didn't explain the charcoaled mark on the floor or the fact that he and Ophelia were found manically laughing in the downpour, or even the way the

As the trio stepped through the doors to the manor, there was a heavy crashing sound from somewhere within.

Hazel widened her eyes, but the other two just sighed in a familiar exasperation. Caleb sped forward. In his absence, Hazel glanced at Ophelia, who yawned and followed after her brother, leaving Hazel to reluctantly trail behind her.

Alexander's voice came from the dining room. "We have to go out and find him, the longer he's here, the longer the hunters will be too."

The dining table had been flipped on its side, sending a bunch of centrepieces crashing to the ground as well.

Julianna paced back and forth. Her husband was sitting on a now table-less dining chair, rubbing a hand across his lips. "Now I have to buy a new table."

"Oh, don't," Julianna grumbled.

Caleb was standing in the doorway, confusion written on his face as he peered between his parents. "What's wrong?" he asked.

His mother gave him a guilty look, then looked over at Alexander, completely brushing over her son's question. "If we go out, we are putting ourselves, our *children*, at risk of being seen with the bitten, perhaps mistaken for it. Let the warriors handle it. That's why they're here."

"These are innocent people, Julie, it's not right," Alexander argued, gripping a newspaper. Julianna let out a loud, tense breath and glanced over at the broken dining table.

Mr Thorn stood from his seat and walked towards the doorway. "I'm going to go order a table."

"What's going on?" Caleb asked, more frustrated now. His father stepped past him, gently slapping the newspaper article to his chest before speeding away.

Julianna sighed and rubbed at the crease in her forehead. "Another body has been found drained of blood, but this time it was in Aramoor Bridge."

"The longer this bitten stray stays here, the more at risk we are. They could find out about her," Ophelia muttered, gesturing in Hazel's direction as she walked into the room and lounged on one of the chairs. "Or orchestrate an attack on us, bitten vampires hate us. He could find other bitten and ambush us. Daddy's right, maybe we should be looking for him."

"She's right, Mum. We can't just do nothing, not when people are dying," Caleb cut in delicately, walking over and slotting into a seat beside his sister, who kicked her shoes off and let them plop to the ground.

Julianna sharpened her gaze and Ophelia huffed, bending down to pick up her shoes from the carpet, something which Hazel thought was a bit pointless, seeing as the carpet was also covered in candle sticks and *table*.

"This is not up for discussion! You will not look for him! It's not our job, it's not a risk we have to take," Julianna snapped, letting her eyes linger on Caleb, who glanced down at the floor.

The older woman then kicked at the broken table with a frustrated grunt and stormed down the hallway.

"Alexander, put that catalogue down!"

Caleb rubbed at his forehead. "What now? We can't go against her."

"Oh, don't be absurd! What's she gonna do? Ground us? I'm quaking," Ophelia spat, letting her leg flop down and purposefully kicking her brother in the stomach.

Caleb pushed at her feet, causing her to almost tumble from the chair. "She'll never trust us again if we go against her word, you saw that look on her face. Maybe we could get her on board," he tried.

Ophelia crossed her arms with a scoff. "That'll never happen, and if you think otherwise, you're just delusional. It doesn't matter if you're her *favourite*. She's still not gonna listen to anything you have to say."

"I'm not her favourite—"

"Oh, come off it. We both know you are."

Hazel, who had been deathly quiet up until that moment, strolled over and grabbed the newspaper from Caleb, studying it. "Amber is going out tonight, to that part of town," she whispered, realising she'd forgotten to cancel those plans.

Caleb glanced up at her, chewing the corner of his lip nervously, while Ophelia rolled her eyes. "So?"

Hazel blinked, wildly. "So? What do you mean, so? I can't let her go alone, it's dangerous!"

"Then convince her not to go," Ophelia complained, resuming her position from before, with her feet dangling over the edge of the chair.

Caleb pulled a face at her, and she jabbed him in the side with her foot again until Hazel coughed to gather their attention.

"That's near impossible, she'll go even if I don't, she likes talking to strangers. I've been dodging her calls all day. I have to go in case anything happens."

"Hazel, we can't do that. You haven't got full control yet. There will be too many people," Caleb said, giving her an apologetic look.

"Plus, our mum would probably kill us," Ophelia added with a little raise of her hand.

Caleb tilted his head toward his sister in agreement.

Hazel stared between them, squinting, and then spun around, pulling out her phone. "I'm not letting her go without me. I can handle it. You both want to find the bitten anyway," she said, typing a quick message to Amber without looking up. "Either way, I'm going, so come with me, or stay in here arguing about it until one of you strangles the other."

The Thorns looked at each other in silent debate, then reluctantly agreed.

Hazel grinned to herself and placed her phone back into her jeans pocket. "We've got five more hours to practise control before we go out," she said enthusiastically, clapping her hands together.

Ophelia shook her head violently and stood up. "You two can do that on your own, I'm going to get my hair done."

CHAPTER TWELVE
Moroi Fundamentals

Hazel threw a punch at Caleb, but he sped out of the way, catching her fist and spinning her around.

"Try again, use your instincts, think less boxing match and more life or death," he said into her ear. Hazel pushed out of his grasp, turning to grab him, only to be met with a gust of wind.

She glanced around as he snuck up behind her again and grabbed her shoulders, pretending to bite her neck.

"*Vlah, vlah, vlah,* and you're dead," Caleb joked with a Transylvanian accent.

Hazel playfully shoved him away, raising her eyebrows. "Dracula, really?"

"Yeah, he's kinda iconic," Caleb quipped, folding her fists and lifting them up. "With all the movies and the plays, he's very mainstream. It gives us a bit of a bad reputation, though, with all the—" He pulled his lips back and lifted his hands, springing them forward like claws.

Hazel smiled, knitting her brows together and accidentally falling out of the formation he'd placed her into.

He lifted her fists up again. "Did you know there's apparently a Dracula musical now?" Caleb said, nudging her ankle and motioning for her to shift her weight evenly.

"Really? Wonder how he'd feel about that?" Hazel mused, following his lead. "The Prince of Darkness belting show tunes?" she said, watching uncertainly as Caleb lifted her chin, balling her hands into fists like a video game loading screen. She felt a little silly, but he'd been adamant this was important.

"I mean, he is quite dramatic, maybe he'd like it?" He shrugged, taking a step back to look over her, before gently sweeping at the back of her ankle. Hazel gasped, but he caught her, placing his hands around her lower back and motioning for her to use the angle to hit him in the chin.

Hazel did so, gently, a few times to practise and then he sped away, causing the wind to rustle through her hair and blow dark, wavy strands into her face. When she felt him sweep at her ankle again, she swiped up with her fist. Of course, Caleb had expected it, so he swerved at the last second but still smiled proudly.

"He's also not real, right?" she asked, grabbing onto his shoulders with a squeak as she stumbled from the momentum of her swing.

Caleb snickered, straightening her before tapping the side of his nose. "You never know, he could be standing right in front of you, *vlah, vlah, vlah!*"

Hazel pushed at his chest with a snort and he winked, letting himself fall back onto the grass and landing on his elbows smoothly.

She shook her head with a condescending smile. "Yeah, because why wouldn't Count Dracula be in the British countryside disguising himself as an over energetic teenage boy."

"Oi, this over energetic teenage boy still got you, you're dead," he teased, smirking as she dropped down beside him.

Hazel rolled her eyes. They'd been out in the back gardens of Thorn Manor for over an hour, going over *the basics of vampirism.* They'd gone through control, amplified hearing,

,, drifting – a euphemism for supernatural speed – and about a million other things that Hazel still couldn't comprehend.

Hazel picked at the grass, threading it through her fingers. "I'm not getting the hang of this, am I?"

Beside her, Caleb lifted his head, looking up at her with an encouraging look. "You will. It just takes time."

Hazel furrowed her brows crossly. "If this were a game of Mario Kart or something, I would beat you so hard you'd be crying."

"I wouldn't be so cocky if I were you," he snickered. "I can do a mean corner drift."

She pressed her face into her knees and groaned. "Don't mention drifting, it's too soon, and my leg still hurts."

"I've never seen anyone hit the floor that fast. It was kind of impressive."

She sighed loudly. "Yeah, it's called being accident prone, I'm the world's worst vampire."

Caleb bit his lip, holding back a snicker. "Nah, not yet. Give it a couple of weeks and if nothing's changed, I'll buy you a 'world's worst vampire' mug to make it official."

She looked up at him, tilting her head. "Thanks. I'll get you one that says, 'massive wanker'."

A snort slipped from Caleb as he leaned back on his elbows, looking up at the sky.

The sunlight peered down, shining through cracks in the grey clouds. Hazel realised she couldn't really feel the nipping chill in the air. She knew it was there, she could see the trees rocking with the breeze, but it didn't bother her like it had before. That got her thinking, what else had changed?

"So," Hazel began with a hum, grabbing Caleb's attention. "Yesterday, Ophelia mentioned us having abilities, *fire* abilities."

The blond boy arched an eyebrow. "You can barely throw

a punch, do you think adding mind control into this is a good idea? Never mind the dark fire."

Hazel widened her eyes. "Mind control? *Dark* Fire? Why is it dark?"

"I don't know," Caleb replied, looking toward a pile of logs near the greenhouse. "Just what we call it, maybe it's a metaphor for something, creatures of the night and all."

From what Hazel had gathered, vampires were deemed as nocturnal by default, like bats, but maybe it wasn't so farfetched. Hazel had always been more of a night owl. She wondered if that was the same for Caleb. He had the energy of a morning person, but he'd told her while they were driving that he's always up late.

Or maybe he was just saying that so she wouldn't feel bad about messaging him when she couldn't sleep.

As Hazel focused on his face, thinking back to their car ride, a burning smell drifted toward them. She turned to see smoke rising from the logs, before the whole thing burst into flames.

Hazel jumped back, tripping over with excitement as she covered her mouth with her hand. "You have to show me how to do that!"

Caleb broke eye contact with the logs to give her a grin and the fire stopped as the red faded from his irises. "We probably shouldn't overdo it, might be a bit much all at once."

She sighed in agreement and slumped onto her side.

"You never answered my question last night," Caleb said as the smoke dissipated.

"I didn't?"

"I asked you to tell me something I didn't already know about you, then we went off on that tangent about stars. I still want to know more about you."

Hazel looked out across the yard and wrinkled her nose in thought.

"I can speak Spanish."

Caleb glanced toward her. "Like, fluently? Or you just watched a lot of Dora growing up?"

She smiled to herself, fiddling with the grass. "I'm half Puerto Rican, from my dad's side. Even though I don't know any of his family, I guess I wanted to feel at least some sort of connection to them."

"You taught yourself?" The words came out whispered as Caleb practically gaped at her.

"I tried," Hazel said, chuckling bashfully. "It was a lot of online classes and stupid apps, my Spanish probably isn't perfect, but, you know… I know enough."

He furrowed his brow, lightly biting down on his lip. "Don't sell yourself short, it's not easy learning another language. I couldn't have done it by myself.""

Hazel tilted her head to the side. "You speak another language?"

"Romanian. It's where my family's descended from."

The sound of the water fountain buzzed in the background of their conversation, and Hazel hummed in realisation. "So the writing on the water fountain in the driveway is Romanian?"

"'*Frumuse ea trandafirului, ascu imea spinului, îngropat în sol, dar g zduindu-se la soare*'," Caleb recited. The accent came through perfectly, swirling around his tongue with every letter.

"What does that mean?" she asked.

He glanced down to the ink on his forearm. "'*Beauty of the rose, sharpness of the thorn, buried in the soil, but basking in the sun,*" he said in a mocking tone. "It's the family motto."

"You guys take that Thorn stuff pretty seriously," Hazel said, motioning to the tattoo.

He hummed in agreement and pulled his sleeve up further. "Got it on my seventeenth birthday. It's a family tradition, looks cool at least. Just glad my name isn't Caleb Turd."

She smiled up at him, reaching out to brush her fingers across the stem of the rose. "I don't know, that name kinda suits you." Hazel skimmed over one of his handmade bangles as he flashed her a playful grin. "You made these yourself?"

"Yeah, when I was six," he said. "Lia got a friendship bracelet kit for Christmas one year. The three of us sat around making them all night."

She smiled softly. "I like it."

He peered down at her. "Yeah? There're probably some beads left over. I could make you one?"

"No, thanks."

Caleb chuckled, watching as her fingers brushed over his wrist. She almost expected there to be no pulse. Vampires were supposed to be undead, just empty vessels to feed from the living, or so that's how they were perceived in the media, but beneath the feather-light touch of her fingertips she could feel a steady beat.

Maybe they weren't even *undead,* they were more like a different species.

Caleb had mentioned how, after they are first turned, it takes a little while for them to fully come into their immortality. Their life essence lingers, human blood still flowing around the body. That's why vampires turned in their teenage years don't reach full immortality until at least their late twenties. It must take a few years for their hearts to truly stop beating, *if* they stopped beating, that was.

Hazel let her touch slip back to the tattoo. A tangle of

thorns wrapped around the flower. They looked sharp, and she traced around the thorns carefully, almost expecting them to cut her fingertips.

Caleb's shoulders moved with amusement as he watched and Hazel peered up to see him smirking. Could he read her mind? He had mentioned mind control before, briefly, but they'd passed over it in favour of the fire-like abilities.

She peered up at him sceptically, searching his eyes. *If you can read my mind right now, then you better tell me.*

Caleb bit his lip and stared back at her with a puzzled grin.

"Can you read my mind?" Hazel whispered, wrinkling her nose suspiciously.

He studied her for a second, eyes raised with perplexity before his lips grew wide and he erupted with laughter.

"You said mind control!" Hazel grumbled, waiting for him to get it all out of his system. It took a while. "So, no, then?"

Caleb shook his head. "Nope, your mind is safe. I say mind control, but really, it's something to do with our natural *allure*, I think. It's more like a power of persuasion. We can't control minds, but we can sort of charm people into doing things for us, people who are attracted to us. It doesn't always work, it depends on the person," he said, pulling a face. "I don't use it, anyway. Doesn't feel right."

That gave her a sense of ease. Vampires weren't monsters, even if they had the ability to be. Especially not Caleb Thorn.

She placed her head onto the top of her knees, pursing her lip at the thought for a moment. "Can vampires have visions?"

"You mean see the future?" he asked.

Hazel shook her head. "No, I mean visions or, well... I don't know. If it is the future, then I'm screwed either way," she mumbled, staring off into the forest.

Caleb rolled on his side to face her, softening his expression. "What do you mean?" he asked, waiting patiently as she stumbled for an answer.

"Remember when we were in your car, and I said I couldn't sleep because of a dream?" she said, and he nodded for her to continue.

"Well, it's been the same dream for the last four months. Basically, I'm running through the woods, then I stop, look up, and a guy in a hoodie stabs me with a dagger. A grumpy-looking, dark-haired guy, with brown eyes."

Caleb furrowed his brow. "Lucas?" he asked.

Hazel pulled her leather sleeve into her mouth for a second, chewing on it. "Maybe. I don't know for sure. In the dream, I'm standing in front of… here." She gestured to the manor sheepishly. "He throws the dagger at me and then yells my name, but it's not my name, well, it used to be, but…"

As she rambled nervously, Caleb placed his hand on the grass, casually brushing his fingertips against hers.

She took a deep breath. "Lucas shouts Dominique Valdez, which is my old name. Then I wake up or, well, that's how it usually went, until…"

"Until?" Caleb asked.

Hazel cringed. "Until my last dream, where I'm pretty sure *I* killed *him*. He was drained of blood, and I was covered in it."

Caleb placed his hand over hers, causing her to look up and meet his gaze as he squeezed it. "You're not a killer, Hazel. I don't think it's a prediction, we're not psychics. We can't see into the future."

She pulled a face. "Like I said, though, I've been having these dreams long before all this happened."

"Maybe it's something to do with your father?" he offered.

"Vampires can't send mind messages or anything like that, but there are other ways. He could have got someone to manipulate your dreams. Maybe he wanted you to see this?"

Hazel shook her head. "I've never really met him. He left when I was a baby. Why would he be trying to communicate with me now? We don't even know if he's a vampire in the first place," she grumbled, creasing her forehead.

"If it's not your mum with the vampire gene, then it has to be your dad. If I'm honest, the name 'Valdez' kind of sounds familiar. There's definitely a vampiric ring to it," Caleb murmured, tilting his head in thought.

Hazel widened her eyes. "Do you know anything about them?"

He shrugged his shoulders, giving her an apologetic smile. "I'm not too sure, I just feel like I've heard it before."

Hazel nodded, brushing a hand through the grass again distractedly. "If it is my father, then what would he be trying to tell me?"

Caleb just looked at her. "I have a disturbing idea..."
She nodded. "I think he wants me to kill Lucas."

CHAPTER THIRTEEN

Night Fever

The cool November air swept down the high street as Caleb's car pulled up on the road.

Outside the stretch of bars, a group of girls huddled together, shivering in their heels. Hazel watched them, remembering Caleb's advice to try to pretend the weather affected her. It wasn't hard – she felt a little uncomfortable in the clothes Ophelia had lent her – so she happily pulled her jacket closed. She missed her band T-shirts and fishnet tights, especially as she looked down at the shimmery mini skirt she'd borrowed, which probably cost more than her phone. It was one Ophelia said she was going to throw out anyway.

At least it was black.

Amber was standing outside one of the bars, giggling with the group of girls as if they were old mates. She looked up once she heard the car approach and widened her eyes, both in relief and bewilderment. When Hazel had messaged, Amber had been surprised that the Thorns were joining them, if not *incredibly* confused.

When Hazel stepped out of the car, she almost tumbled backwards at the force of her friend pulling her into a vice-like hug.

"I've been worried about you! Your mum called me before, said she hadn't been able to reach you since you texted her last night," Amber said, accusingly. "She asked if you were planning on sleeping over at mine, *again*. I had to lie to Nina! Are you sure you're not on drugs?"

Hazel shook her head, frowning as Amber peered into her mouth. "I'm sorry," she mumbled.

There was a tingle under Hazel's gums, matching the pulsing of the vein on the side of her friend's neck.

She stared down at it, before the sound of Caleb clearing his throat broke her out of her trance. "That's my fault," he said, raising a hand as he stepped out of the driver's seat of his car. "She was with me. We went on a drive and crashed at my house. Hazel told her mum she was at yours so it didn't seem seedy."

Amber subtly raised an eyebrow at Hazel, in a *we'll be discussing this later* kind of way before turning towards Caleb enthusiastically. "Oh, right! Well, in that case I'm happy to assist," she said, clapping her hands together. "Shall we do this thing, then?"

Hazel tugged at her leather jacket, fixing it with a small nod as Ophelia joined them huffing. "God, I'm going to need a drink to get through this."

Caleb turned to Amber with a sheepish smile as the blonde walked away, heels clicking against the cobblestone. "Don't mind her, she's just a little…" he trailed off.

"Hostile?" Amber offered, watching as Ophelia barged past the bouncer at the door.

"Yep."

The bar was mostly empty, seeing as it was still quite early. When they got inside, Ophelia was sitting on one of the barstools, knocking back a drink as the bartender waited patiently.

Caleb leaned on the bar beside his seventeen-year-old sister and squinted suspiciously. "How did you get served?"

"I'm very persuasive," Ophelia murmured.

She leant forward on the counter and snapped her fingers. The bartender refilled her empty glass instantly. Hazel saw Amber frown as they sat on the other stools.

Caleb sighed, resting on his elbows as he looked toward the bartender, catching his gaze and blocking Ophelia from his sight. The bartender's expression cleared, causing him to blink in confusion. "I'll just have a coke, please, mate," Caleb asked politely, reaching into his pocket for his wallet. "And whatever they're having."

Hazel tried to stop him, but Caleb simply smiled and shook his head. Meanwhile, Amber grinned. "Cheers, I'll get the next round," she said, glancing down at the menu.

As the barkeep moved along to make the drinks Ophelia glared at her older brother. "Boring."

"Well, I'm driving, so unless you want to walk home?"

She rolled her eyes. "You know I'm not just talking about the alcohol."

"Unfortunately."

She chugged back the remainder of her drink with a sadistic grin as the bartender came back with their drinks.

Amber accepted hers gratefully and turned to the blonde, lifting her drink in a cheers motion. "Yeah, that's the attitude I'm after!"

Ophelia moved away from the bar.

Hazel exhaled slowly, reaching for her own glass and clinking it to Amber's with a forced smile.

It wasn't long before the club began to fill with people, all talking over each other and crowding the dance floor. Hazel pulled a face and stared into her drink, trying not to think about the dozen heartbeats blending into the loud music.

They'd managed to get a booth in the corner. Amber was chatting away to a stranger at the table next to them and Ophelia was yelling something into her phone, leaving Hazel to dwell on the dull ache rising in her throat.

Caleb returned to the table with a tray full of drinks and slipped into the space beside her. He placed a hand onto her knee. "Are you okay? If you want to leave, we can leave."

Hazel hesitated, then shook her head. Caleb nodded, giving her knee a reassuring squeeze before reaching for his glass.

"Hey Caleb, nice watch. Very sharp. Rolex?" Amber asked from across the table.

He smiled, running his fingers along the watch face. "Yeah, thanks, it was a gift from my parents. I got it for my sixteenth."

Ophelia snickered to herself from the other side of him, still staring down at her phone. "Not the only sharp thing you got for your sixteenth," she murmured.

He glanced toward her discreetly and let out a small, humoured breath.

"My dad got me a watch once. I mean, it was pink, and the hands were part of a cat's whiskers, but it got me through some pretty tough times," Amber said. She had a bright orange cocktail in her hand and twirled the straw around as she spoke.

"Oh, yeah?" Caleb hummed sweetly.

Amber nodded and placed the straw into her mouth to take a few gulps. "Mostly nine…"

Hazel glanced up. Amber didn't speak much about her life before Aramoor Bridge. When her mother had died, she had only been thirteen. Still, from what she'd mentioned, her life before then had been pretty decent.

"What happened when you were nine?" Hazel asked, confused.

She shrugged, grinning into her cocktail. "Nothing. I meant nine in the morning. That was the toughest time because it's when school started."

Caleb laughed. "I like that, I'm going to use that one!" he said. "Might change the number to two-thirty, though."

Amber glanced up, pointing her soggy straw in his direction. "Because you hate the dentist? You need help getting through 'tooth hurty'."

Caleb picked up his glass of coke and raised it toward her. "Exactly," he snickered, turning to grin at Hazel. "I like this one, she's funny."

Amber raised her glass and clinked it against his.

As the drinks connected, a high-pitched sound echoed through the air and Hazel clenched her eyes shut. She swallowed thickly, barely paying attention to the rest of the conversation until Ophelia grumbled in her direction. "Great, now there's two of them, look what you've done."

"Just because *we've* actually got a sense of humour." Caleb looked over at his sister and Ophelia kicked him in the shin, the force of the blow prompting her to knock into one of the table legs, sending a few of the drinks tumbling everywhere.

Hazel stood up shakily, staring down at her cocktail-splattered jacket, the spilt liquid, and then over at the shattered glass on the table. All it would take was one tiny cut…

She closed her eyes, squeezing her fists as the pounding in her head got heavier.

A hand grabbed her arm and Hazel jumped.

"It's okay, just a couple of spilled drinks, no harm done," Caleb whispered, studying her gently. He'd piled up most of the broken glass on his side of the table, covering it before anyone else could touch it.

"I just need a minute… to dry off," Hazel explained, attempting to control her breathing.

"Want me to come with you?" Amber asked, using a tissue to clean up the spill.

"No, I'm fine," Hazel replied, making her way to the bathroom.

Hazel splashed a handful of water on her face, using the hand dryer to dry her jacket. She gripped the sink, willing herself not to have a breakdown, before stepping back into the overwhelming buzz of the club.

It was a tight squeeze between bodies as she stumbled back to the table. Hazel held her breath, clamping a hand to her mouth, as her heightened senses began to overwhelm her.

A guy bumped into her from the side and apologised, leaning in so she could hear him over the blaring music. Black hair was slick against his forehead with sweat, and as he moved closer, Hazel couldn't help but notice the flush of blood rise into his cheeks from the alcohol. Unintentionally, her hand slipped from her mouth, and a burning sensation fluttered down the back of her throat. She could smell the blood coursing through his veins, see it as he swayed, and with every beat of the music, her own heart pounded louder against her chest.

Hazel pushed past him, dropping her phone from her pocket as she did so. It fell to the ground with a crash, and as she reached to pick it up again, a foot came down on it.

An unintelligible sound slipped from her lips as heat rose through her stomach, burning her insides with an acidic feeling. She stood up and whimpered at the connection of another body. Only this time, it was gentler, tugging her forward with a tender grip and enveloping her senses with cedarwood and a hint of caramel, mixing into the thick odour of sweat and blood.

"Hey, you're okay," Caleb whispered, twirling her around to face him. "Your phone isn't, but that's not important right now."

Her head was spinning. The alcohol probably didn't help. She'd only had two drinks, but it made his words sound distant.

"Hazel?" Caleb whispered, whisking her away from the crowd as best he could, but there were people everywhere now.

She could feel her eyes shift. It was a funny feeling, like an itch she couldn't scratch. Caleb must have noticed too, because he quickly grabbed onto her shoulders and steered her towards the exit.

The door was blocked by a bunch of smokers and Caleb swore under his breath. Hazel winced, accidentally biting her lip. Her mouth filled up with a metallic taste, one that made her want to gag. Caleb peered down and carefully brushed his thumb over it, wiping the blood away before glancing around the club. It was so crowded. People were drunkenly throwing their bodies around to the blaring music, hardly paying attention to their surroundings. Caleb tilted his head to the side in consideration, before mixing them both into the crowd. As they reached the middle of the dance floor, he lifted her quivering chin so he could see her face, and gave her an encouraging look.

"You can do this. Concentrate on something."

Strangers bumped into them, swaying and jumping to the music, and she swallowed hungrily as she watched sweat pour down the sides of their necks.

"Don't look at them, just close your eyes."

A high-pitched laugh beside her had Hazel's head pivoting again, but Caleb's grip on her chin tightened, forcing her to keep her eyes on him.

"Close your eyes," he said, a little more sternly this time.

Hazel closed her eyes.

The music rang in her ears, reverberating as the warmth of a dozen bodies radiated around them. Hazel shook her head. "It's too much," she grumbled.

Caleb placed her arm on his shoulder, pulling her closer so they were pressed against each other, like everyone else. He leaned in, brushing his lips past her ear. "Find something to focus on."

Hazel took a deep breath, homing in on the music, the smell of alcohol in the air, and the feeling of Caleb's fingers against her bare skin. His hand sat on her waist, just below the fabric of her shirt, filling her with a buzzing electricity that burned beneath his touch. The more she focused on it, the more her breathing steadied and the unconscious hunger faded into the background of her overbearing thoughts.

One touch, and it was as if she'd been hit with a beam of solar energy.

That static feeling gnawed at the back of her throat, trying to rush back to the surface, but Hazel pushed it down, focusing solely on the feeling of Caleb's fingers caressing her skin. She melted into his touch, leaning into it, and let her head drop onto his shoulder.

Caleb pulled her in tighter with both hands, causing a rippling blaze to erupt within her, burying the hunger deeper until it was just a bearable itch.

She lifted her head to see a series of flashing lights bouncing off his face, casting him in a euphoric glow as he grinned at her.

It was as if, for that moment, it was just them in the room.

She didn't care about anything else going on or who was watching them as the blinking lights illuminated their faces, painting them both in an array of colour. Hazel's lips tilted upwards and she moved both of her arms around Caleb's neck, pulling him impossibly close as he smiled like an idiot.

It was the most normal she'd felt since all this had begun, or ever, really.

Whereas she was usually so reluctant, too uncertain to really let go, there was just something about Caleb, this vibrant energy that surrounded him. It shone down on him, casting him out from everyone else in a way she'd never really noticed before.

Now that she was looking at him, really looking at him, she didn't understand how she'd never seen it.

It was magnetic, how he could just light everything up around him. How he could fill her with that same energy so easily and make her forget about their problems for even a mere moment.

It felt like time had slowed down, and the moment could be infinite.

Though nothing ever is, apart from the stars.

Soon enough, Hazel felt another pair of arms rip her away from Caleb.

"What's your problem, Ophelia?" she grunted, yanking her arm free from the blonde's grip. The girl had stepped between them, appearing from seemingly nowhere to pull them apart.

Caleb frowned at his sister. "Really? Got bored, did you?"

She rolled her eyes. "Sorry to interrupt whatever the hell is happening, but if you paid attention to your surroundings, you'd see we have an issue, and it's heading through the door."

Over by the club entrance, a boy was blending through the crowd. The luminescent colours poured over him as he took down his hood, revealing his face.

Lucas.

CHAPTER FOURTEEN

Tear You Apart

"Maybe we should just go," Caleb suggested, following his sister who had started to storm back towards their table.

"No way, I'm not afraid of him and his little butterknife," Ophelia hissed, eying the hunter suspiciously. Caleb sighed and looked back at Hazel for help, only to be disappointed.

"She's got a point, leaving just makes him think we're intimidated, plus, the best way for him to not find out about me is to act normal," she muttered as she sat down at their table.

Amber's head perked up at her return and she moved closer to greet her. Hazel half expected the closeness to bring her unease, but thankfully the hunger had settled into the pit of her stomach, manageable for now.

Ophelia shoved past Caleb to take a seat, and he rubbed at the back of his neck, glancing around apprehensively before following suit.

"Hey, isn't that Lucas from school?" Amber asked. "Hey, Lucas! Come sit with us!"

Caleb and Ophelia turned to look at Hazel with different levels of condemnation as she avoided their eyes, tugging at her jacket sleeves.

When Lucas glanced over, a dark glint ran through his eyes. He sauntered toward them. "Hey." He coughed awkwardly.

"What are you doing out on your own?" Amber asked.

Lucas shrugged, watching the Thorns closely as he replied. "Just checking out the… *nightlife.*"

Caleb snorted and Lucas glared at him as Amber continued. "Well, why don't you take a seat. The *nightlife* is definitely better with friends."

Somehow, Hazel's necklace found its way into her mouth. She chewed on it as she watched Amber pull the boy down into the spot between herself and Ophelia. Lucas let out a befuddled croak at the abruptness of it, then coughed again to rid his voice of the tension, sending a quick greeting nod in Hazel's direction. "Uh, great, thanks… but I don't think I've been properly introduced to these two," Lucas said, staring between the Thorns.

Caleb smiled and offered out his hand. "Hey, mate, I'm Caleb." Lucas didn't take his hand, just looked down at it with disgust. The blue-eyed boy let out a breathy chuckle and brushed his empty palm through his hair. "Right, well, it's a pleasure to meet you too."

Ignoring him, Lucas steered his attention towards Ophelia, who remained silent, watching him with narrow eyes.

"You seem friendly," he mumbled provocatively, peering over her before piquing a brow. "What's your name?" Lucas stuck his hand out toward her and Caleb raised his eyes at the gesture, looking at Hazel with mock offence.

She bit back a nervous laugh.

Ophelia slowly pushed the hunter's hand away with her forefinger and smiled dangerously. "You don't need to know my name. We'll probably never speak again."

"Okay," Lucas grumbled as they locked into a weird sort of staring competition. "I'd *probably* forget it anyway."

Amber raised an eyebrow at the pair then stood from the table. "Right, well, I'll go grab us some more drinks. Haze?"

She gestured toward the bar and Hazel nodded, happily jumping to her feet.

As soon as the girls stepped away, Lucas's lips twisted downward. "We can laugh and act like we're friends, but we both know the truth. You two should stay away from those girls."

Ophelia scoffed. "No one's laughing, saddo. Don't come over to us and start making demands. Especially when you don't even know what you're talking about."

With a glare, Lucas ignored her and glanced toward Caleb instead, who, after the initial rudeness of their greeting, had resorted to ignoring him. He was paying more attention to the coaster he was flicking around, seeing how fast he could make it spin.

"I saw you two dancing, you seem pretty close," Lucas accused, gesturing to Hazel.

"So what? Not breaking any laws, am I?" Caleb mused, raising a brow as the coaster moved through his fingers.

"Not yet, but you know what happens to you if anything bitey happens to her, right? If it hasn't happened already."

Caleb let go of the spinning coaster, slamming his hand onto it and letting it fall back onto the alcohol smeared wood. "Nothing is going to happen to her, or anyone. We've been living in this town for years. *We* aren't the issue here." He spoke through gritted teeth.

Lucas pulled his dagger out just far enough for them to see. "I don't care how long you've been here, fifty years, a hundred…"

"I'm literally eighteen years old," Caleb said, raising a

brow in amusement.

"I don't care," Lucas spat, raising his voice. "Just stay off my radar, that's it. You don't cause trouble for me, and I won't make any for you." He stared at them for a moment, then stood from the table and walked towards the girls at the bar.

Caleb snickered under his breath, flipping the coaster up again while Ophelia let out an irritated huff, attempting to grab it off him.

"Are we really going to let him threaten us like that?" she hissed.

He glanced up at her, taking in her frustrated face and sighed. "He's all talk. Wouldn't worry too much about it."

"So, Lucas, what brings you to town?" Amber asked as he approached them, handing him a freshly made drink. Hazel had politely declined one of her own, deciding it best not to drink any more, especially after overhearing the disaster of the other three interacting alone.

At least her amplified hearing was somewhat working, whether she intended it to or not.

"Adopted family moved here. I'm just along for the ride." Lucas shrugged, his attention remaining on the Thorns.

Hazel swallowed, noticing his sharp eyes. She tried to think of a conversation starter to steer his attention away from the siblings – anything that wasn't along the lines of who the hell are you and why are you haunting my dreams.

"I like your T-shirt," she blurted out as soon as she noticed it peeking out under his hoodie. His attention turned toward her and her mind flared with victory.

"You like Cityscape Casual?" he breathed.

She nodded enthusiastically. "Yeah, absolutely. I've got that same T-shirt at home."

Something shifted behind his gaze at that, his expression softening for a split second.

"We went to see them last year, they're amazing live," Amber added from between them. "I've got some clips on my phone."

As she pulled the device out, Lucas threw a glance towards the booth again before peering down, failing to hide the excitement on his face. "I've always wanted to see them live," he whispered, glancing up at Hazel with a shy smile.

She smiled back, bemused, then peered over at Caleb and Ophelia as the blonde stood up, arguing with her brother.

The climax of the thumping music began to throw Hazel's enhanced hearing on and off, but whatever Ophelia was saying, she was clearly irate. Her eyes were a fiery red. She started to make her way to the DJ booth, ignoring Caleb's protestations.

Mildly alarmed and still focusing all her attention on trying to stay in control, Hazel trailed back over to the table, sliding into the seat beside Caleb as he dropped his face into his hands. "What's she doing?" she asked.

He groaned loudly. "I don't know, but it can't be good."

Ophelia strutted up to the DJ and demanded he hand her the microphone. Of course, he refused, until she gripped his shoulder and whispered something to him.

Hazel glanced at Caleb, who still had his face in his hands. "Mind control?" she asked. He nodded sadly.

The music stopped, and the crowd booed.

"Shut up and listen!" Ophelia yelled, before smiling sweetly. She nodded at the DJ and raised the microphone to her lips as music blurred through the speakers again.

"Cold-blooded, my lips sting with a touch of venom. I'm in your head, got that wild animal magnetism."

Red light shone down on Ophelia as she sang, stepping towards a helpless stranger.

"I can send you to heaven, like a dream from above."

She touched the boy's cheek, caressing it, then her eyes darkened and she grabbed his chin.

"I can make you my weapon, pull the strings of your love."

Her hands stayed on the stranger's body, resting on his shoulder as she peered toward the bar and locked eyes with Lucas.

"I'm only gonna bring you down, so run from me or wait it out. Can you wait it out?"

Amber slid into the seat next to Hazel, giving her a wildly entertained look. "Oh, sick, dibs next," she cheered, taking a sip of her drink. "Since when did this place do karaoke?"

"I'm gonna chase you down, my crime is an art."

Hazel gulped. "It doesn't."

"Don't you know that I'll, that I'll eat your heart?"

There was a thud, and Hazel turned to see Caleb drop his head down on the table with a muffled groan.

"I thrive on the pain, so I'll play the part for your love, your love."

At the bar, Lucas put his drink to his lips and sipped it, not once taking his eyes off Ophelia as she spun around and danced into the arms of a stranger.

"Can't go back, you're running blind in the dark."

Ophelia let the guy spin her around, holding the microphone to her lips.

"And if you'd like, you can have a head start."

She tapped the stranger's cheek, then detached herself from his arms.

"Baby, you can't hide, it's far too late for you."

Just before she reached the stage again, she turned, sending a pointed smile in the hunter's direction.

"'Cos I'm gonna tear you apart."

Hazel cringed, glancing over at Lucas to see his eyes were narrow and dark as Ophelia sauntered over to the bar.

His free hand was tucked into his hoodie pocket, probably getting ready to toss his dagger in the blonde's direction. Hazel almost didn't blame him – this was excruciating to watch.

"Why does this seem so rehearsed?" Amber asked. Hazel shrugged, biting so hard on the inside of her cheek that the same vile, acid taste filled her mouth again.

Ophelia carried on, getting through another chorus before stopping before Lucas.

"I'm gonna tear you apart," she sang, grabbing his chin and singing directly to him.

He peered up at her coldly, forcefully pulling away from her touch, and she turned toward the crowd again.

"I'm gonna tear you apart. I'm gonna tear you apart."

Lucas dropped his drink on the counter, wiping his face where her fingertips had touched with a disgusted look as she turned to face him one last time.

"It's far too late for you."

The hunter pushed past her, glancing briefly at Caleb and Hazel before he stormed away.

The crowd cheered, yelling out intoxicated, incoherent nonsense as Ophelia threw the mic back to the DJ and took a bow, looking quite pleased with herself. She jumped from the stage, appreciating the praise from drunken strangers, before her brother grabbed her by the arm and pulled her away.

"What the hell was that?"

Ophelia grinned, crossing her arms. "That was me

teaching him a lesson.”

Caleb blinked. An exasperated expression painted his features, and he scoffed, biting the corner of his lip. “That was you causing a scene, you just couldn’t help yourself, could you?”

“Are you joking? He threatened us, Cal. I was just having a little fun with him. Calm down, you know I study drama. I thought you would be used to it by now,” she muttered, stepping past him, but he stopped her, pulling her back with a frustrated look.

“So you threaten him back? He was just testing us,” Caleb hissed, throwing his arms up. “Now, thanks to you, he’s not gonna let us out of his sight. He’s going to be watching us, meaning he’ll be watching *her*.” He gestured to their table, where Hazel was pretending she couldn’t hear them, and Ophelia rolled her eyes.

Caleb stepped back, brushing a hand over his disappointed face. “Like always, you had to bring all the attention to yourself. You’re so selfish sometimes.”

Ophelia glanced behind his shoulder, locking eyes with Hazel, and her expression hardened. “I’m going to go get some air.”

Hazel peered down at the table.

The crowd rippled as Ophelia moved toward the exit, leaving Caleb standing alone. The muscles in his arms tensed and he cursed under his breath, brushing a hand through his hair.

Hazel pursed her lips. “One sec,” she said to her friend. “I think we might be heading home.”

Disappointed, Amber’s brow furrowed. “You’ve hardly been here an hour.”

Hazel picked at her fading nail varnish. “I know, but it’s

getting late, and… can you just trust me on this? I'll make it up to you."

Amber huffed, glancing down into her almost empty drink. Her cheeks were quite flushed from the alcohol and she spoke a little slower than usual, frowning. "I don't know what's going on with you lately, Haze. First you disappear, then turn up with the Thorns of all people, and now you're ditching me for them."

Hazel scrunched her nose. "No, it's not like that, trust me. Come with us, we'll drop you off at home."

"I guess, but can we just—"

Over on the other side of the room, Caleb's back suddenly straightened, and he moved toward the door.

Hazel stood up before Amber could finish her sentence. "Sorry, one sec, just wait here. I'll be back in one minute," she promised, rushing toward the exit.

Outside the club, Ophelia had stormed off into an alleyway. She leaned onto the cold brick wall, letting her head flush against it with a tiresome breath.

She knew she could be selfish, she knew she could drive her brother up the wall, and vice versa, but they never took it too far, that's just the way they were. She bit and he brushed it off with a joke. They'd argue, then a few minutes later he'd say something stupid and they'd both laugh.

Ophelia had never seen him so disappointed in her before, and for what, her ex-best friend? Ever since Rosemary left, Ophelia had been Caleb's best friend, the one he went to when he was lonely, the one she went to when she was insecure. They had each other, and that had always been enough.

Now she was going to be second choice again.

She grunted, pulling a hand-held mirror from her clutch bag. Her mascara was smudged slightly. As she rubbed at it, the mirror was swept from her hand and two arms came down onto the wall at either side of her head. Ophelia looked up to see sturdy brown eyes staring into her own, dark and dangerous, like an eclipse.

Lucas dropped an arm from the wall and let the coolness of his dagger run along her cheek.

"My mirror!" she hissed, pulling her knee up to kick him in the crotch.

Lucas pivoted to the right and dodged the hit, then he pushed her against the rough brick again, placing his dagger over her throat this time.

The hand that held the dagger lingered around her throat, while the other pressed against her torso firmly, keeping her in place.

Though nothing blocked her Louboutins.

Ophelia slammed her foot down onto his, making him release her with a wince. Then she moved away before his blade could find a way back to her neck.

"Okay. If that's how you wanna do it," he spat, lifting his dagger.

Ophelia bared her teeth and rushed forward, ready to pin him against the wall. Unfortunately, that's what he'd been expecting, and he promptly kicked her in the shin, knocking her to the ground and forcing her to bang her head against the pavement.

With a grunt, Ophelia sat up, pressing a hand to her head as she glanced at the hunter, irritated.

Lucas bent down beside her. "That little show in there didn't scare me. It amused me, definitely, but I've dealt with your kind before," he mumbled, twirling his blade around his fingers.

Ophelia watched him for a second, then pushed up and swung her legs out. He leaned back to avoid it, which caused him to lose balance. With a smirk, she jumped to her feet, swiping at his elbow as he tumbled backwards onto the cobblestone.

"Well, my family and I are different, and you need to understand that. Don't come into our territory and make threats and demands, it won't work." Ophelia pouted provokingly, pressing a hand to his chest before turning and heading for the alley exit.

Lucas grunted and staggered to his feet, moving for her again only to be shoved backwards by Caleb.

"Back off," he warned, opening his mouth to reveal the sharpness of his teeth.

Ophelia turned around, standing behind her brother with her arms crossed as Lucas glared between them. She could see Hazel stepping around the corner into the alley but motioned for her to stay put.

"We'll finish this later, killer," Lucas growled through his teeth.

Caleb tried to step forward, but Ophelia grabbed onto his arm, holding him back. "Trust me, you wouldn't want that. Shouldn't you be off looking for the bitten?" she asked, looking the hunter up and down. Lucas pulled a face and Ophelia grinned sarcastically, pushing her brother out of the alleyway. "Goodbye, psycho."

Lucas had to resist the urge to slam his fist into the rough brick wall as he stormed towards the main road. He gritted his teeth together, grinding them so hard he could feel the tension tugging at his jaw.

"Lucas?"

At the sound of his name, he glanced up to see Amber hugging her arms as she waited in the empty taxi bay. She motioned for him to come over and he hesitated for a second before he did so.

"Are you walking home?" she asked.

"I don't live too far away from here." He shrugged, looking off to the side, and she nodded, seeming to notice his reluctance for conversation.

Amber's attention was diverted toward her phone screen and he peered at her, curious as to why she was alone.

"Are you okay?" Lucas asked after a minute, noticing the tears on her face.

She wiped at her cheek. "Yeah, I just… it's nothing, just a silly little thing with Hazel. I'm fine. I won't keep you if you want to get home."

Lucas looked around. It was pitch black out and there wasn't a single person in sight. He couldn't leave her alone, not with the bitten on the loose… or the Thorns.

"No, it's fine, I'll wait with you till your taxi comes. Have you booked one?" he asked, and she nodded, showing him her phone. There was a little car icon showing the taxi's location. She went to click on it but accidentally swiped up, pulling up her home screen. At the sight of the photo of herself and Hazel, Amber let out a high-pitched sniffle.

Lucas looked up in alarm. "Wanna talk about it?" he mumbled, uncomfortably tapping her on the shoulder.

The girl let out a soft chuckle and rubbed at her cheeks

again. "It's probably just the alcohol. Vodka makes me cry sometimes."

Lucas tried his best to soften his expression. "No, really, it's okay. What's wrong?" he asked.

Amber smiled gently, looking up at him. "Okay, well, it's always been me and Hazel, right? We were fifteen when we met, when I moved to town, and we've been inseparable since," she breathed, taking a minute to stifle her tears. "But before I came along, she was friends with Ophelia, which is absurd on so many levels."

Lucas knitted his brow.

"They did everything together until Ophelia decided she didn't want to be friends anymore," Amber continued.

Lucas hadn't expected an insider source, but at least he wasn't going home empty-handed. Plus, now that Amber was talking, the tears seemed to stop, and her smile was a lot nicer to look at.

"Over the last couple days, she and Ophelia seem to have become friends again, which is weird because I thought they hated each other. I'm sure it's got something to do with Caleb. He's always been nicer than his sister, but I don't know, something feels weird. Hazel's acting different, and maybe I'm being selfish, but it seems like she's pushing me away. She said she'd be right back, but it's been like fifteen minutes, so I guess she forgot." As Amber finished ranting, she looked up at Lucas and smiled apologetically. "Sorry, I'm rambling, I do that a lot. Taxi's almost here, you can leave if you want."

Lucas shook his head. "Nah, I wanted some fresh air anyway, I can wait. For the record, I don't think you're being selfish. The Thorns... they seem strange. They keep to themselves a lot," he said, trying to keep the accusatory tone out of his voice.

Amber looked up at him with a nod. "Yeah, well, it's always been that way. Their parents are super rich and live in a mansion in the middle of the forest, so maybe they're just not used to human interaction." She chuckled, and Lucas held back a snide laugh.

A car pulled up on the side of the road and rolled its window down. "Here's my ride." Amber smiled, clutching her little floral, green bag. Lucas helped her inside, holding the door open as her phone started to ring. She pulled it from her bag and let out a confused hum, answering it. "Caleb?"

Just as he was about to close the car door, Lucas subtly pulled it open again. "Oh, Hazel. Why are you using Caleb's phone? I've left, I'm in a taxi now… It's fine. Look, I'll see you tomorrow."

There was a muffled voice on the other side and Amber looked at Lucas, shaking her head. "Study group for our exams, I signed us up, remember?"

Lucas gave her a comforting smile and leaned against the door as Amber ended the call.

"Sorry about that," she said. "Are you coming tomorrow? It's an extra class for English catch up. They're every Sunday now, and seeing as you just started, I thought maybe you'd be at them to… well, catch up."

Lucas thought for a second. There was something about Hazel, Lucas wasn't sure what, but he felt a dawning obligation to figure it out.

It was probably a coincidence that the strange girl in his dream just also happened to be a brunette with tawny eyes.

"Yeah, I'll be there."

CHAPTER FIFTEEN

Extra Credit

"No, absolutely not!" Ophelia exclaimed, storming up to the giant oak door of Thorn Manor.

Caleb followed after her, rambling continuously.

They'd argued practically the entire way home, stopping briefly to go to a fast-food drive through. Much to Hazel's bemusement, the siblings had even shared some fries before going straight back into their fight.

"You have to, you are in that class! I'm not even in your year. It's harder for me to blend in," Caleb complained, catching the front door as Ophelia swung it open carelessly. She sipped her diet coke and strolled inside as he frowned at her, holding the door open.

Hazel ducked under the boy's arm and wandered into the hallway, wrapping her arms around herself.

"It's a Sunday, Caleb! I've already given away my Saturday for her! I'm not sacrificing my entire weekend! I have things to do," Ophelia huffed, heading towards the stairs only to be stopped by her brother, who appeared in front of her with a jaunty grin.

"What things? Looking into your mirror and practising insults?"

She narrowed her eyes, though before she could muster a comeback, Hazel strolled past both of them. "I don't need a babysitter."

Ophelia scoffed, taking a pointed gulp of her drink while Caleb followed Hazel upstairs, running his fingers through his tangled hair. "I didn't mean that... Well, I kinda did," he admitted, and she turned to face him halfway up the staircase with a frown. "You don't understand how hard it will be to stay in control this early in your transition, especially in stressful situations. You've stormed out of class on many occasions, and that was before you had to hold back any... killing instincts."

Hazel scrunched her nose. "I stayed in control tonight," she argued, turning back around to climb the stairs. "I'm fine."

Caleb caught up with her as she reached the top of the landing. "Every day is different, what if you can't anchor yourself tomorrow? If you lose control, then..."

"I could hurt someone, I know, but I can do it. I have to go. I can't let Amber go alone. She's only going to this class for me in the first place."

Hazel clutched the handrail, startled, as Ophelia drifted past her and suddenly appeared in front of her, sipping her drink. "Don't do that!"

The blonde pulled the cup away from her lips. "If you lose control, then that bastard from tonight will be onto you, meaning he'll be onto us." She paused for a second, rolling her eyes. "Fine, I'll go. I'll make sure you don't mess this up, but you owe me. Both of you."

"Lucas won't even be there, it's a Sunday."

"He might be. He's new, he'll need the extra help. Either way, it's a risk."

"He won't find out about me," Hazel muttered, swivelling around with a frown as Ophelia scoffed. They caught eyes and glared at each other.

Caleb stepped between them. "I agree, but only if we work together."

Ophelia snarled at him. "I'm gonna vomit. Oh, *teamwork*. Oh yes, let's all work together like perfect little angels, make mother proud. You disgust me," she spat, giving him a detested look before storming towards her bedroom.

Hazel sighed exasperatedly, then smiled at Caleb once Ophelia was out of sight. "So, you're coming?"

"Of course I am. Just because I can't be in the classroom with you guys doesn't mean I can't lurk in the shadows. I'm pretty good at that, actually."

Hazel let out a stifled snort as Caleb winked at her, then he gestured down the hallway, walking her to her room.

"What class is this for, anyway?" Ophelia asked, aggressively ripping apart a bagel as they drove towards the school.

Hazel was in the backseat. Ophelia had almost knocked her over in an effort to get to the passenger side door first, but she didn't mind. She could still see out the window, and she wasn't subject to Ophelia's nasty glares this way.

"Mr Hardington's class," she explained as she glanced around for a blue, egg-shaped car. It wasn't long before she spotted it, parallel parked on the pavement. Amber was leaning against it, pulling her knitted jumper closer as she flipped through her copy of *Macbeth*.

"I can't believe I'm wasting my Sunday in that miserable classroom because of you," Ophelia grumbled as Caleb parked his car. "Can you smell that?" she asked, stepping out of the car and looking towards the dark brick building with a look of disgust. On the other side of the Jaguar, Caleb nodded, curving his brow.

"Nightshade… Lucas is definitely here," he uttered, glancing over at his sister. "Stay together, I'll stay within earshot. I'm gonna scope this little bastard out." His gaze trailed toward Hazel, lingering for a few seconds, before he smiled softly and disappeared with the breeze.

After a long inhale, she looked away, heading over to Amber, who waved upon noticing her. She didn't seem angry, or even irritated, just concerned if anything, especially when she spotted Ophelia reluctantly trailing behind Hazel.

"She wanted help with her exams, she's falling behind. I told Caleb I'd give her some pointers," Hazel sheepishly explained once she'd reached her friend. Ophelia stopped beside her, rolling her eyes with an unenthusiastic nod.

Amber glanced between them both questionably, pulling a face. "But you're failing that class, why would you give anyone pointers? Do you even know what book we're working on?"

As Hazel floundered for a response, Amber tutted and steered her attention toward Ophelia.

"I've never seen you at school out of hours. In fact, I've never seen you as much as I've seen you in the last couple of days. Why are you suddenly interested in Hazel?" she asked, half-accusingly. "Is this some sort of *Mean Girls* method acting for your drama class?"

Ophelia laughed shrilly, crossing her arms as she looked the girl up and down. "I prefer *Heathers*." She turned on her heel and walked towards the school building with a snarl.

"We're working on our differences." Hazel sighed as Amber raised an eyebrow.

The other girl hummed, unconvinced, and linked their arms together, moving towards the building. "Okay, fine. I'm sure it has *nothing* to do with her incredibly attractive brother who you *spent the night with.*"

Hazel widened her eyes. "It's not like that, I stayed in their spare room," she whispered, glancing up at the school to make sure both Thorns were out of earshot. She leaned in closer, gesturing for Amber to talk more quietly. "We're just friends," Hazel mumbled, sulking at the scoff she got in return. "No, really. It'd be weird, anyway, because of the whole me and Ophelia being friends when we were little thing. She'd probably skin me."

Amber did not, in fact, take the hint and carried on speaking at an unreasonable volume. "Haze, come on, don't chat rubbish to me. I saw the way you two were dancing last night. You guys might as well have just started ripping each other's clothes off right in the middle of the dance floor. The way he looks at you sometimes, I don't know if you've noticed, but it's like he can't take his eyes off you. It's really sweet actually, and god, Haze, he's well fit, like inhumanly fit. I wouldn't even blame you for trying. It would be worth Ophelia's wrath for just one night—"

"Okay, yeah he's… he's attractive, let's just stop now before we get ahead of ourselves, yeah?" Hazel pleaded, throwing her hands up over her eyes as blood rose into her cheeks.

"God, that family has good genes," Amber continued, and by this point Hazel could only hope it would end soon, either the conversation or the world, she didn't care, she just wanted it to stop. "I mean, have you seen their father? Sometimes I go to Thorn Antiques just to stare."

Somewhere down the hallway, there was an amused chuckle. Hazel peered over into the dark corridor with a frown, then dragged her friend into the classroom.

"Miss Surley, Miss Bridget, both on time for once. Next time, let's aim to do that during actual school hours."

Hazel blinked, barely able to step through the door before Mr Hardington's sour tone stopped her in her tracks. She frowned at the man, then, as he adjusted his glasses, changed her expression into a strained smile and stepped past him, glancing around the room.

Some students had opted for the class for actual revision, and some seemed to be there solely for moral support, boredly flicking through the pages of their books.

Then Hazel spotted Lucas.

The hunter had deliberately chosen to sit behind Ophelia, watching her carefully as he rocked a black thermos back and forth.

Hazel gulped and moved to take the seat beside Amber in front of the board, but a book slammed on the desk before she could.

"Sit at the table behind, I'm not having you two delinquents conversing through this whole thing," Hardington huffed, peering at the girls down the bridge of his nose.

With a frown, Hazel stepped past Amber's desk, dropping her stuff on the floor at her new table, next to Ophelia.

"And if you dare turn around to face each other…" the teacher grumbled, letting his sharp eyes finish the sentence.

As Hardington muttered irritably and handed out paperwork, Ophelia snapped her head up, tilting it to the side ever so slightly. She glanced down at the desk again moments later. "Hold your breath," she whispered.

Hazel gave her a perplexed look before the metallicness of blood filled her senses. It wasn't the same as before. It didn't give her that mind-numbing sensation the blood bags in the forest had, nor was it as overbearing, but she didn't hesitate to suck in a breath.

Subtly glancing over her shoulder, Hazel watched Lucas

slip a small blade back into his hoodie, looking slightly uncomfortable at the fresh cut on his thumb. He let it sit at the edge of the table, avoiding looking at it as blood dripped onto the floor like a tiny leak from a tap. She fixated on it, her mind filling more with bewilderment than hunger.

Out of nowhere, Ophelia kicked Hazel in the shin and she whirled back around as the other girl gave her a pointed look.

"Can you smell it?" Hazel breathed. "The blood, his blood… it's not the same…"

Ophelia leaned over, picking up a worksheet from the brunette's side of the table deliberately. "Because it's warm, fresh. Hold your breath, that's what I'm doing. I can't even smell it," she said through gritted teeth. "I just heard his bloody knife clatter against something in his pocket and knew he was up to something."

Hazel met her gaze and swallowed deeply. "No. You don't get it…"

Ophelia pushed back to her own side of the table with a sigh, interrupting her. "You're new to this, sometimes this stuff can be confusing at first… but just stop staring. It's creeping me out."

"Got something you want to share with the class?" Hardington spat suddenly, stopping at the end of their shared desk.

"Just discussing the syllabus, Sir," Ophelia replied innocently, playing with her hair. The English teacher peered at her for a second, then turned back to the class, leaving Hazel to scrunch her nose as Ophelia smiled smugly.

"So, what can you tell me about Macbeth? What are his motives? His understanding of social expectations and appearances? Is it fair to say Lady Macbeth uses these things to manipulate him?"

Amber's hand shot up first, and Hardington gestured for her to speak. "I actually thought Lady Macbeth was the more interesting character."

Hardington narrowed his eyes, sitting down on a desk as he motioned for her to continue.

"She's supposed to be the epitome of evil, but really she's arguably the most powerful female character in literature," Amber said, smiling proudly. "She's the only one willing to take things into her own hands. Lady Macbeth retains the ability to control her emotions and her sanity for way longer than her husband. She's strong-willed, persuasive, ruthless, but in the end, she can't reject her sense of humanity, as well as her feelings of remorse and guilt." Amber flipped through the pages of the book as she spoke. Hers looked a little more worn than everyone else's, filled with annotations in the margins of the pages. "She was never truly evil, she just fell victim to something deeper inside, her ambition turned her into something else."

As Hardington turned to write notes on the board, Ophelia let out a quiet hiss. Hazel glanced over to see Lucas had his feet up on the table, and was digging them into her back, studying her reaction.

After a minute, Mr Hardington walked past, knocking the boy's feet off the desk with a warning look and Lucas shrugged, grabbing his metal flask with both hands.

Hazel turned around, not wanting to know what he was up to. She picked up her pen, tapping it against the side of the page. She had no idea where to even start with the work, not with the ticking time bomb sitting behind her. She popped her pen into her mouth and chewed aggressively as she heard Lucas's flask opening.

Hazel let out a small, croaked noise, barely audible, as a

heavy scent drifted over her.

Ophelia must have also smelled it this time, because she suddenly leaned over and gripped Hazel's wrist. "Push it away, or he's going to find out. Hold your breath."

Involuntarily, Hazel reached up to rub at her throat, exhaling slowly. "Too late."

Behind them, the hunter let out a small gasp, and Hazel's heart sank. Both girls turned to see him peer down at the plug socket below him suspiciously. There was a slight plume of smoke rising from it, as if it had suddenly overheated.

Hazel and Ophelia glanced at each other accusingly, but it was obvious it had been neither of them. As their questioning looks subsided, they both turned to see a rush of movement behind the window in the door. Lucas must have noticed it too, because he sat up, narrowing his eyes.

The scent of blood was still thick in the air, emanating from the table behind them. It made Hazel's throat tighten, a throbbing pressure building in the back of her mind as she tried not to think about the flask behind her.

In that moment, Lucas's chair creaked as he leaned away from the plug socket, and Hazel heard a gasp as he accidentally spilled the contents of his flask over his hands in the process.

With a croak, she clamped a hand to her mouth, trying to keep her focus forward. No one else seemed to realise anything was wrong – except Ophelia, who kept sending her wary looks – but it felt like the walls were closing in on her.

She clamped her eyes closed.

"Keep her head down. I'll try to draw him out here," Caleb whispered from somewhere out in the hallway, loud enough that only students with amplified hearing would hear.

Ophelia rolled her eyes. "Yes, must protect the chosen one at all costs," she mumbled back, pushing Hazel's head down, forcefully.

Hazel opened her eyes. "Get off me," she hissed, trying to pull away from the blonde's hold until a splash of red landed on the page in front of them.

"Shit." Ophelia rubbed it away, only for another to land directly on Hazel's hand.

She swallowed thickly, staring down at the liquid as it pooled over her fingertips. Ophelia reached over to rub the blood away with the sleeve of her shirt.

"Just listen to the sounds," she whispered, frowning at her now stained blouse.

Hazel exhaled restlessly, feeling a familiar tingle behind her irises. "What sounds?"

"I don't know! It's just what Caleb says!"

Hardington had put on a video now, using a pointer to aggressively tap at the screen every now and then. There was no need for how loud it was playing, although Hazel wasn't sure if it was too loud for everyone else or just her.

A few seconds passed by before there was a slight bubbling sound from behind them, like the sound of liquid boiling, followed by an aggressive cry of pain from Lucas.

Another shadow passed by the door. This time moving slower, with a flicker of crimson eyes and dirty blonde hair.

Lucas stood abruptly, pushing away his flask, which had steam rising from the top. "I'm going to throw up," he announced, not taking his eyes off the doorway.

As whispers spread around the room, he stalked forward and flung the door open with such force it swung violently and slammed shut behind him. A number of amused eyes watched him go before turning toward Hardington, who stormed to his desk.

"I'm writing him up, that's *not* a reasonable excuse to leave my classroom."

Out in the corridor, Lucas stormed forward, clutching the dagger he'd pulled from his belt. He usually carried at least three blades on him, all sheathed onto holster straps which were hidden by his hoodie. It was sort of like a utility belt, only for weapons and not tools.

"I know you're here, Thorn," he snarled, twirling the blade around his fingers. The door to the stairway shook as something fast moved past it, and Lucas followed without hesitation.

As he got to the empty second floor corridor, the lights above him flickered. Smoke rose from the bulbs, draining them as Lucas let out a bitter grumble, holding his dagger out in front of him. "Is that all you can do? Put on a pretty little light show?"

The lights flickered off completely, leaving Lucas in the dark. There was a creak of movement above as something crawled past on the ceiling. As Lucas narrowed his eyes, aiming upward, Caleb jumped down and kicked him in the back. Lucas dropped his dagger and stuck out his hands to break his fall, staggering to his feet as the lights flickered again, the dim light glimmering on the vampire's face, illuminating his daunting red eyes.

Lucas snarled, wiping at his brow with his now weapon-less hand as Caleb grinned, licking his tongue around pointed teeth.

"Hey, mate, think you dropped your toy," he chuckled, pointing to the blade that sat on the floor between them.

Lucas shot forward, sending a harsh punch toward Caleb's jaw. Unfortunately, the boy dodged the hit, speeding away and shoving Lucas into the wall from the side.

His back hit the slab of concrete and he groaned, barely having time to adjust before Caleb swung forward, his fist hitting the empty wall as Lucas ducked.

CHAPTER SIXTEEN

Earthquake

The concrete floor shook above the classroom, sending particles of dust falling down like rain. Ophelia peered up at it and coughed as confused voices spread around her.

Mr Hardington put his hand up to silence everyone, pausing the videoclips of *Macbeth*. "It's an old building, it's going to creak sometimes. Everyone focus on the board."

As the other students quietened down, Ophelia wafted at the dust and relaxed into her seat. "What a pair of absolute idiots," she whispered to Hazel. "He was supposed to just distract the stupid hunter, not the entire class. Right, okay, here's what we'll do. You pretend to be sick, and I'll volunteer to take you home."

Hazel nodded, moving her head in slow, hypnotic-like movements. She picked up her book, pretending to read it as her shoulder twitched. Ophelia pulled a face, closing her eyes, before sticking her hand in the air. However, before she could get Hardington's attention, a thud from above shook the ceiling again, rattling the tables and knocking Lucas's flask of blood forward on the desk. Ophelia felt the rest of the hot liquid splash against the back of her head.

And she wasn't the only one it had hit.

A few small drops started to drip down from Hazel's hair, landing on the page in front of her. Her breath hitched and she stared at the blood with wide, uneasy eyes, her staggered

177

breathing quickly turning into tiny growls as her head hung low. Ophelia gulped, looking upwards again as more rumbling and crashing came from the ceiling.

Muffled voices started to rise up again, and this time, Hardington didn't bother to stop them, confusion crossing his own face as he moved with intention towards the door.

Ophelia stared after him. She couldn't just let him go investigating either, if he stumbled upon her brother and Lucas's pathetic cat fight then it would definitely raise some flags.

With a huff, she rushed over and slammed the door shut, standing in front of it before Hardington could open it.

His eyes narrowed, a furious look appearing on his face before the ceiling shook again.

Ophelia had to fight the urge to grin at the innovative idea that came to her. "Earthquake! Everyone get under your desks!" she bellowed, watching with amusement as everyone complied. Or, well, mostly everyone.

From the table closest to the board, Hazel's annoyingly vigilant friend, *Amber*, remained standing. "We don't get earthquakes like this in England," she said accusingly.

"It must be global warming!" Ophelia responded, glaring at the girl with a sarcastic smile. "Get. Under. Your. Desk!"

The wall cracked beneath the vampire's fist and Lucas rolled out of the way, snatching his dagger from the floor.

When he jumped up again, looking at Caleb's turned back, he kicked forward, but the vampire drifted out of the way, as if he'd expected it. In fact, the next three swipes that Lucas threw at him he dodged easily, barely retaliating. Even when he'd punched the wall, his aim had been off, giving Lucas the room to slide out of the way.

Either Caleb was just really bad at this, or he was only trying to cause a distraction, but either way, Lucas kept aiming for him, grabbing at his shoulders and forcing him to the ground with a thud.

"Nightshade blade?" Caleb asked, scrunching his nose as he looked up at the weapon inches from his face.

The hunter nodded, trying to push the dagger down. With a hum, Caleb kicked upwards, sending Lucas flying back into the opposing wall.

"Thought so. That's a nasty plant, you know, and hard to keep. Maybe you should try something else," Caleb mused, making a smoking gesture. "You could use something to mellow you out, if you get what I mean?"

Instead of responding, Lucas jumped to his feet and plunged his blade forward, only for Caleb to grab his wrist, stopping it from reaching him.

They fumbled for a second as the dagger slipped from Lucas's grip. He kneed Caleb in the stomach and caught the blade in his free hand. Without a second to adjust, he swiped again for the groaning vampire, who jumped back from the knife's sharp edge.

With a long-winded breath, Caleb paused. "Stop… swiping… You know the rules, the Arcane Council says you can't touch us. Not if we've done nothing wrong."

Lucas raised an eyebrow, throwing his blade to the ground and reaching into his inside pocket. The blue-eyed boy watched him apprehensively as he pulled out a pointed stake.

"I know the rules. I can't kill you, but there's nothing that says I can't hurt you."

Caleb peered at the weapon and then let out a wild,

amused laugh. "A stake? Really? Have you got some holy water in there as well?"

Lucas narrowed his eyes, then flung the stake out, unfolding it to reveal a full-sized spear.

The humour fell from the vampire's face.

"Get off me!" Hardington spat as Ophelia forced him under one of the desks. Her gaze was settled on the fire alarm in the corridor as she tried to steer his attention from the rumbling upstairs.

"But the earthquake, Sir. Gotta protect the elderly," she said in a falsely sweet tone as he struggled against her, his freckled face turning flush with anger.

The other students were whispering to each other or watching the *earthquake*, but Ophelia looked up to see that Amber's gaze was strictly on Hazel, her eyebrows furrowing with confusion.

Ophelia swallowed back a breath, peering between the two. They were only a desk width apart, but with the way Hazel had her head down, breathing raggedly, it seemed like she was miles away.

"Haze?" Amber tried, stepping towards her friend with a gentle look. "Are you okay?"

Ophelia sucked in a breath, hearing another low growl from the brunette. Amber clearly hadn't spotted the spilled blood – yet, anyway. But she looked determined to get closer, so before she could, Ophelia bolted into the corridor and quickly pulled the fire alarm.

There was chaos as the alarm blared deafeningly. Amber barely had a moment to register what was happening before

Ophelia had grabbed Hazel by the shoulders and dragged her from the classroom.

The vampire jumped over the spear before it had time to reach him and kicked off from the wall, flipping out of the way. Then he kicked Lucas in the stomach, sending him stumbling backwards, but the hunter was fast with the spear, twisting it and barrelling the nightshade-dipped, pointed end towards Caleb's face.

As the spear came towards him, the vampire clutched the metal, wincing slightly as he came in contact with the poison. He looked up at Lucas with a grin, before flinging the weapon back and knocking the hunter's balance long enough to jump up onto the window ledge. He smiled, and the tips of his sharp teeth sat against his mouth, mockingly.

"Okay spider-boy, come on down, let's chat," Lucas huffed, throwing the weapon to the ground.

Caleb shrugged his shoulders casually. "As fun as this was, it's pointless, mate. You can physically hurt us, yeah, but you don't need to. *We're* not the threat here, you know that. Truce?"

Lucas's face twisted with disgust. "Truce? what do you think this is? A game?"

Caleb softened his expression, shaking his head. "I'm just trying to keep my family safe. I know that's what you're doing, too. We're not so different."

Before Lucas could retaliate, the blue-eyed boy jumped out of the window with such ease that a groan slipped from the hunter's lips. He rushed forward and grabbed onto the window ledge as the vampire landed softly on the ground below. Caleb looked back up at Lucas and waved before vanishing with the wind, leaving the hunter to huff in frustration.

After a second of silent cursing, his phone started to ring. Lucas stared out the window, narrowing his eyes as he answered. "What?"

"*Lucas!*" It was Miles, his words muffled and rushed, as if he was trying not to be overheard. "*We're out by the park, the bitten got by us. It's heading further up the high street. We need backup! Jamie's hurt!*"

"*No, I'm not! It barely got me, I'm fine. We don't need help. Miles, get off the phone!*" Jamie whined somewhere in the background.

Lucas grunted under his breath as the call cut out, grabbing the spear, collapsing it, and slotting it back into his belt.

Ophelia flung the car door open, throwing Hazel in the back, and then rushed around to the driver's seat, looking for the keys her brother had purposely left in the car *for emergencies.*

Hazel attempted to reach for the door handle, but before she could, Ophelia clambered into the back seat, grabbing her arms, and strapping the seat belt around her torso.

"Get off!" Hazel growled, which only made Ophelia pull the belt tighter in retaliation.

"You move any more, and I will knock you out," she warned.

Hazel scoffed and attempted to free herself, panting as her movements grew more frantic.

A blast of wind hit Ophelia in the face, and she glanced over her shoulder to see Caleb opening the door.

"Drive, I've got her!" he said, climbing into the seat beside them and grabbing the makeshift restraints Ophelia had created.

"You're lucky. I was this close to putting her to sleep. *This close*," she grunted, pinching her fingers dramatically before drifting to the driver's seat.

Hazel pushed against the seatbelt, growling up at Caleb. He placed his hands onto her forearms and pushed her back down against the leather seats, glancing over at his sister. "Start the car!"

With all the wrestling in the back seat and the determination to get as far from the school as possible, Ophelia barely gave a second thought to the small, blue car pulling out of the car park behind them.

Two of Hazel's teeth had sharpened into points, inching towards Caleb's neck. With her newfound strength, the makeshift seatbelt prison had ripped apart and she lunged forward immediately, ready to attack. Hazel knocked Caleb back against the seats and wrapped her legs around his waist, snarling down at him.

Ophelia glanced over her shoulder and cringed, before looking back at the road. "How are you holding up?" she exhaled.

Caleb snickered breathlessly in response. "I'm managing."

Hazel wrapped her fingers around his palms and pushed both his hands above his head, keeping them there as she bared her teeth.

"Hurry up," Caleb said through gritted teeth.

Ophelia peered back at him through the rear-view mirror and pulled her lips in with a disgusted expression, swinging the steering wheel to the right.

As the car swerved, Caleb freed one of his hands, wrapping

it around Hazel's hip and twisting it, so that he was now straddling her instead of the other way around. She let out a puff of air, disgruntled, and he stuck his tongue out at her.

"Where are we going? Home?" Ophelia asked, pressing her foot on the accelerator.

Caleb shook his head, trying to get a grip on the brunette's wandering palms. "We won't make it there in time, she's getting more aggressive. Go to Dad's shop, it's closer."

Hazel suddenly kicked her knee up into Caleb's stomach and he winced, cursing under his breath.

"Hurry up, Ophelia, before she kicks somewhere else and I'm rendered useless," he grumbled, using his own knee to push her back down against the leather.

Ophelia pulled a face at him through the mirror and swerved the wheel to the left, following the road towards the town centre.

As Caleb pushed against Hazel's shoulders, his gaze fell on the crimson trickle knotting up her hair.

"Is that blood?" He grabbed a handful of dark, wavy curls and pulled them towards his nose. "Why is she covered in blood?"

"Lucas's *test* splashed onto her when you two idiots started fighting upstairs. What were you doing, anyway? It sounded like you were going to fall through the ceiling," Ophelia said, sharply turning onto another road.

"He's stronger than I thought he would be. Kid can throw a punch."

"Sounded like he was throwing more than a punch."

After around ten more minutes of driving, Ophelia pulled the car into a quiet alleyway on the high street and turned off the engine, glancing around to see her brother just about holding Hazel together, the girl was still growling at him, but she no longer had use of her arms as Caleb was holding them down by her sides, resting his head against the window tiredly.

Ophelia jumped out of the car and swung the door open for her brother, helping him drag the frenzied brunette towards the back door of the antique shop. Caleb always kept a spare key to the store on his car keys.

"It's the black one, Lia," Caleb said as Ophelia looked at the selection of keys, both of his arms occupied around Hazel's torso as she thrashed about like a wild animal.

"I've got it, thank you," Ophelia hissed in response, shoving the oldest looking key into the lock and twisting. She stepped into the shop and held the door for Caleb, enjoying watching him struggle with the new vampire.

Antiques filled every inch and corner of the shop, from two-hundred-year-old porcelain dolls to seven-foot-tall grandfather clocks that creaked as the hands moved.

Ophelia coughed at the damp smell and crept further inside, motioning with her hand for Caleb to stay back as she turned the corner towards the public part of the shop. Luckily there were no customers pottering about.

"Daddy?" she called, stepping through an old, bejewelled curtain, and Alexander looked up from where he'd been crouched on the floor and creased his brow.

He'd been fiddling with some old wooden rocking chair, fixing one of its dented legs. As Ophelia glided through the room, he stood up, abandoning his tools to rush towards her.

He placed a hand on the side of her face, looking over at what she presumed was the matted blood in her hair. "Oh dear, what now?"

Ophelia let out a sigh. "I need you to promise not to tell Mum." She smiled overly sweetly.

Alexander shook his head, backing up and moving to pack away his tools. "No, none of that, that doesn't get you out of trouble anymore."

Ophelia looked over at him with a pout, and he stared sternly for a second, before releasing a deflated breath. "Okay, fine, but I'm not promising anything. Just because you don't want to get in trouble with Mum doesn't mean I want to either," he mused, smiling at the grin that fell onto her lips.

They stepped into the back of the antique store, where the waiting room for the blood bank sat. Brown sofas lined one wall whilst charity posters covered the other, with a small TV in the corner playing *The Antiques Roadshow*.

As soon as Alexander's eyes fell on Hazel, who was baring her teeth, he sighed deeply. "Don't let go of her," he told Caleb, shaking his head tiredly as he turned toward a closed metal door, fumbling with a set of keys. "Lia, come with me, give me a hand," he called out as he stepped down to the basement.

Ophelia glanced back at her brother, letting her head fall against the metal door. "He's *so* gonna tell Mum," she exhaled sadly.

Once Lucas saw the park, he knew there'd been a bad scuffle. Blood lingered on the grass not far from the cutoff point to the main street. He turned his head, looking over at the gate, and heard narrow breathing. Lucas spun around, lifting his dagger and accidentally slicing his finger with the blade in the process.

He hissed, lifting it to his mouth and frowning as he glanced up just in time to see a shadow rushing towards him.

In one swift motion, Lucas threw his now bloodied dagger forward, cutting through the stale air as the figure sped past. A gag-like sound echoed through the wind, but when he spun around to see who it had come from, the gate connecting the park to the street rustled with movement, clinking together as if someone had just slammed it shut.

Lucas sighed, dropping his defensive stance, only to be tackled to the ground a second later. He flicked his body upwards, tugging onto the grass beneath for support as he wrapped his legs around his attacker and flipped them over, peering down into Jamie Chandra's frustratingly egotistical face.

"Lucas, what are you doing?" Jamie yelled, standing up to scan the area before kicking at the dirt. Miles and Hollie ran into sight behind him, weapons raised, only to lower them when they spotted Lucas.

"Miles said you were hurt! I came to help," Lucas scoffed, picking himself up from the ground.

Jamie turned around with an irritated expression, brushing the dirt from his T-shirt. "Well, I told him not to call," he replied. "You've only gone and scared it off, you wanker. I was just about to get the jump on it, too. It was lingering back here."

"Yeah, probably to finish the job," Lucas spat, scanning over the other boy's frame. His hair was falling into his half-lidded eyes, and the top of his shirt was torn on the right side of his shoulder. The boy was wincing in pain, jamming a fist into his mouth, and there was a loose bandage around his neck too, covered in blood

Clearly, he'd been bitten.

It mustn't have been that deep, but the bacteria would be affecting him soon enough. It couldn't turn him on its own – he would need to be infected with vampire blood for that – but it could still make him ill if they didn't treat it soon enough.

"I almost had it. Why do you always have to get in the way?" Jamie grumbled arrogantly, looking off toward the high street. "Chris is going to be pissed. This is all your fault."

"Oh, shut up, you'd have got yourself killed. Just be glad I turned up," Lucas said, reaching out to steady him, but the taller boy pulled back, almost tripping over himself.

"Why do you always have to be the one to get them? I had it!" Jamie stumbled again, his words slurring as the other three exchanged a nervous expression.

"Come on, we should get back to camp," Hollie huffed, grabbing Jamie's other arm.

He shook his head, refusing to move as they forcefully pulled him away. "Three seconds and I'd have got it. *Three seconds.*"

"Yeah, I know, bud, you'll get it next time."

Lucas stayed put, his eyes trailing the line of blood on the floor, leading out toward the high street.

"You coming?" Miles called, glancing toward him as Jamie grumbled into Hollie's shoulder.

"Nah," Lucas said. "I'll go after it."

Miles let out a disgruntled noise, muttering something about it being dangerous alone, but Hollie dragged him away, pulling him and Jamie toward the treeline.

"He won't find it. It's gone now. Come on," she mumbled, thinking he couldn't hear as they walked away. Lucas rolled his eyes, reaching into his pocket for his dagger.

CHAPTER SEVENTEEN

Spider's Web

Caleb guided Hazel onto a couch. She snapped and growled at him, wanting to swivel around, but he leaned back against the sofa, resting his head on the wall as he wrapped his arms tighter around her.

"I'm sorry. I should have been more careful. I know it hurts, but it'll get easier, I promise. Think of it like… like a game. The more experience you get, the better you get at playing," he explained as he glanced down at her. "You're at a beginner level now, but you've already got so much further than you realise, you're like your very own cheat code."

Clumps of blood were matted at the back of Hazel's hair, which she could feel becoming more tangled as she pressed and writhed against his shoulder, scanning the windowless room.

There had to be some way to get out. The room they were in felt very stuffy, hot, and so did the body behind her. Although, that wasn't entirely a bad thing. Pushing aside the burning in her throat, Hazel quite liked the feeling of Caleb's lean, strong arms wrapped around her, tugging her to his chest.

Admittedly she'd like it better if he wasn't trying to hold her back. She didn't want to be held back. *She wanted blood.*

"Listen to the clock," Caleb said, motioning to an old, weathered grandfather clock across from them. "It's a bit warped because of how old and battered it is, but it still works the same. See how the rhythm of it matches a heartbeat?" He tilted her around so she was facing him, ignoring how her hands immediately moved for his throat, and gripped one of her palms tenderly, prompting her to raise her head and meet his determined gaze. Caleb lifted her hand over his chest, placing it onto the thin fabric of his T-shirt as he let out a steady breath. Hazel stiffened beneath his touch, blinking up at him.

"See, my heartbeat matches the timing of the clock when I focus on it. Do the same," he whispered, placing his hand on top of hers and trailing the tip of his forefinger over her thumb.

A shiver ran down her spine at his touch.

Hazel forced her eyes to close, letting the ticking of the clock infiltrate her senses. With every beat, she matched it to her own breathing, and gradually, the crimson bled out of her irises, blurring back to their usual warm brown colour.

As she focused on the sound and the feeling of Caleb's heart beating beneath her palm, Hazel glanced down, watching as his chest rose and fell in a sturdy rhythm until something suddenly hit the side of her head.

"Eat up," Ophelia snapped, monitoring the pair with narrowed eyes.

Hazel's gaze dropped to the blood bag that had landed on her lap. She grabbed it and practically poured it down her throat.

Alexander Thorn leaned against the metal doorway, shaking his head at his children. "What happened? Where have you been?"

Ophelia shook her head, but Caleb's eyes turned guilty. She widened her eyes, motioning for him to stay quiet, but he bit the side of his lip, and then turned back to their father. "We were at the school," he said. Ophelia groaned and looked away.

Their father raised an eyebrow. "It's a Sunday. Correct me if I'm wrong, but don't normal kids tend to stay away from school on the weekend?"

"It was a revision class, only for certain students. We thought it'd be safe."

Alexander pulled a disappointed face, pushing off from the doorway. "That doesn't matter, Caleb, she could have hurt someone… killed someone. You risked that for what? Extra credit? We trusted you."

Hazel finished her blood bag, finally able to think a little more coherently. She could feel Caleb tense beside her. He dropped his gaze down to the floor, rubbing at his knuckles sheepishly.

"It's not his fault… it's mine, I asked them to come," she wheezed, still a little twitchy as she grabbed onto her hand to stop it from fidgeting in her lap.

Alexander softened his expression, letting out a small sigh. "Doesn't matter, he still knew better than to let you go."

Ophelia pursed her lips, crossing her arms over her stomach. "Dad, Caleb can… no, he *has* handled this. He created a distraction and got *him* out of there before he found out about…" Her words fizzled out into nothing as she watched her brother close his eyes with a groan.

"Got who out of there?" Alexander asked, turning to face his daughter apprehensively.

Ophelia whimpered, settling back into the settee. "Him… self?"

"The hunter boy, he was testing us." Caleb sighed, rubbing a hand over his face.

Alexander's eyes lit up with a mixture of frustration and alarm as he blinked at his son. "Stay here, we'll discuss this later," he said scornfully, turning toward the front of the shop.

Caleb drifted from his spot on the sofa, blocking his path. "He didn't find out anything, I lured him away. He doesn't know about Hazel. They're here for the bitten, not for her."

The older man shook his head and stepped past him, wandering back through the bejewelled curtain. "Stay here!"

After a couple more blood bags and a bit of time to come back to herself, Hazel was handed an old, almost bristleless brush to help clear the blood from her mattered hair.

She glanced down at it, then back at Ophelia, who'd grabbed it off a random shelf. "Thanks?"

Ophelia rolled her eyes, pointing an accusing finger. "Stay here."

Hazel slumped back on the sofa defeatedly as the snarky girl disappeared into the antique store after her brother. She tried not to eavesdrop into their conversation, she really did, but she couldn't help picking up on pieces of it.

"He's gone to call Mum, thinks it's gone too far with the hunters," Caleb murmured.

"Guess we should start packing."

Hazel widened her eyes.

"She wouldn't make us leave," Caleb replied after a second of silence. "She said she'd protect Hazel and she wouldn't come with us. I know you're sceptical, but I trust Mum."

"Whatever you say, golden boy," Ophelia huffed.

After a moment, there was a small shuffling sound followed by a heavy thud. Hazel stood up, widening her eyes as she moved towards the corridor.

The door ahead of her had closed, a metallic shutter slamming to the ground, cutting her off from Caleb and Ophelia who were on the other side. Hazel swallowed nervously, blinking up at the hard metal as the sound of a motor echoed in the distance, followed by a feral groan which she could only guess was Ophelia.

"A bit extreme," the blonde girl hissed through the door.

Caleb grumbled in agreement. "We should have kept our mouths shut."

"You spoke first, hypocrite."

"Caleb?" Hazel breathed, stepping closer. There was a slight pause before the door jolted with movement, but despite the force on the other side, it didn't budge.

"One sec, our dad has locked us in here. He went to get my mum. He thinks he's keeping us all safe. Just… I'll try to get it open, wait there," Caleb replied, his voice muffled by the metal door.

Hazel nodded despite the fact he couldn't see her and took a few anxious steps back, wrapping her arms around herself as she settled into the darkness of the hallway. It was quite creepy on her own, with the dusty, beady-eyed antiques watching her like some sort of ancient surveillance system.

As she stood there, listening to the muffled voices on the other side of the door, an excruciating screech echoed through the back halls of the building.

"Hazel?!" Caleb called, shoving into the metal again, still it wouldn't budge.

She let out a croak, turning toward the direction of the scream. "Still here," she exhaled shakily.

"Oh god," Ophelia whispered. "Amber… I think she might have followed us."

Hazel's head shot up, backing away from the door as another scream filled the space behind her. She focused on the scream, the familiarity of it, the pain that tore through the vocal cords. Ophelia was right.

Ignoring Caleb's voice calling after her, Hazel turned towards the hallway. The back of the store was mostly covered in darkness, apart from the splatter of fading sunlight creeping in under the wooden door at the end of the corridor. It was older-looking than the rest of them and not metal like the shutters blocking the main parts of the store, but it was still locked. The door had a mechanical frame around the edges, which was no doubt part of Alexander's intricate security system.

Hazel pressed her hand against the wood. Every nerve ending seemed to be running on adrenaline as her eyes blurred, watering anxiously. She pushed at the door. It didn't open. With a grunt she dropped her head against it, then took a breath.

Her fingers felt static, almost numb. It was a strange sensation, she could feel it running up the veins in her arms.

Slower this time, she pressed her hands to the door, pushing. The wood creaked under her grip, seeming to bend to her will the more pressure she applied. Her new strength had its perks. She pushed, until the hinges bent in on themselves, forcing the door to open. Hazel rushed through it, peering into the alleyway.

There was a pool of liquid shimmering under the light of the sunset a few metres ahead. Hazel gulped and moved towards it. A piece of fabric was sitting in the puddle. She picked it up, recognising the rapidly deteriorating light green colour.

"Amber!" Hazel called out, looking around in a panic. Her

gaze followed droplets of blood leading out of the alleyway, to the road that led to the forest.

Hazel stumbled over branches, roaming the woods blindly with only the scent of blood to follow, her *best friend's blood.*

There was fog in her mind still, elevated with the dizziness of trying to stay in control. The blood didn't help that, but at the same time it propelled her forward, giving her something to focus on. Hazel felt like passing out, vomiting, and crying all at once. She'd been trying so hard to protect Amber and had somehow thrown her right into the middle of everything. Now she wasn't even sure if she was still breathing.

Hazel's own breath strained at the thought, and she grabbed onto a tree trunk for support. It was dark out in the forest, with the overhead trees masking the dim sunlight. Every now and then a glimpse of light would seep through the leaves, but it didn't do much to clear the fog Hazel was battling with, mentally *and* physically.

Blinking back tears, she pulled back from the tree and forced her fist into it, letting out a frustrated grunt. Wood splintered off in different directions, her fist carving a dent in the trunk. She pulled it back with a wince and stared down at her bruising knuckles with wide eyes as they began to heal right in front of her.

Things weren't looking good. She could still track the blood which meant her friend was bleeding out somewhere, but the longer it took to work out a direction, the less chance Hazel had of saving her.

Caleb and Ophelia would have handled this better. They'd probably track Amber with their bloodhound senses and take the bitten down easily, but no, they were trapped in the antique store and Hazel was alone. She wondered whether she should have tried to break the Thorns out first, or speak to Caleb before she left, at least. He'd have known what to do, he always seemed to know what to do. Hazel just hadn't considered that in the moment – she'd heard Amber's voice, scared and in pain, and ran towards it blindly.

Hazel clutched the green, floral bag in her hand and carried on through the tangling trees.

The sun bled in through gaps in the leaves, blurring her vision ever so slightly as she stepped into a particularly bright spot in the woods. She squinted, holding a hand up to block the glare, then clamped a hand over her mouth as her eyes adjusted to the light.

Three dead bodies were wrapped in the trees ahead, slotted between branches like flies stuck in a spider's web. Hazel gulped, feeling her throat tighten. She kept her hand plastered to her mouth, forcing back tears as she tried not to focus on the blood coating the forest floor. She could hear Caleb's voice in the back of her mind.

Feel the earth around you, let it pull you back. Listen to the sounds, the different smells, anything you can find to focus on.

Her attention flickered toward the wind, how it blew through her hair, kicking up leaves around her feet. How sounds moved through it, each different one passing through the forest like a train of thought. Hazel focused on the breeze, closing her eyes as she heard it drift around her. Within the lively sounds of the forest was a lighter noise, a soft, rustled croak, like the sound of breathing. Snapping her eyes open, she followed the sound, letting it guide her deeper through the woods until she caught sight of dark, curly hair sticking out from behind one of the trees.

"Amber!"

Hazel sped forward, crouching down in front of her friend. She was unconscious, with a bloodied gash on the side of her neck, but she was breathing. She was alive.

Hazel held her breath as she tore at the hem of the girl's paisley shirt, pressing the fabric to her neck. Liquid spread across her hands, spilling over her fingers. Hazel closed her eyes again, trying to avoid looking at all the red as her mind buzzed from the feeling. It nauseated her just as much as it pulled her in.

As she focused on the soft sounds of Amber's scattered breaths, a twig snapped behind them. Hazel spun around to see the rough-looking man from the alleyway, glaring at her with the same cold, animalistic eyes.

"She's mine!" he growled.

Hazel gulped. The bitten was more dishevelled than the last time she'd seen him. Torn clothes, mouth stained red, cuts and bruises up his arms and torso. His canines were still as sharp as ever.

Without taking her eyes off the man, she pulled at the fabric in her hands, wrapping it around her friend's neck in a makeshift bandage, like her mother had shown her once. The bitten watched her carefully, his bright red eyes glistening. Hazel glared back at him. She wanted him, no, *needed* him to know that he wasn't going to be getting anywhere near her friend.

He snarled, crouching into a defensive stance, ready to pounce, only to be thrown to the side and knocked into the stump of an oak tree by a blur of movement.

Hazel blinked, watching as the blur swivelled around. It looked like he'd been running, his hair was a mess and his cheeks were flushed. Despite that, she hadn't heard him coming, or smelled him.

It was as if he was a ghost.

"Keep applying pressure to her neck," Lucas ordered, holding out a hand as if telling her to stay back.

He flicked his wrist out and unsheathed his dagger. The bitten ran for him, snarling, but Lucas ducked out of the way swiftly, grabbing the vampire by the arm and flipping him onto his back. The vampire jumped up with a snarl and the hunter sent a swift kick to his left leg, knocking him backwards into a ditch. The bitten were ruthless creatures, fast, unhinged, and aggressive, but so was Lucas by the looks of it.

He fought back effortlessly. Every time the vampire would glance Hazel's way, Lucas would throw himself into its line of sight.

Sharp nails cut across his arm and Hazel winced, clutching Amber tightly. Soon enough, the girl began to stir, coughing through reddened lips as she glanced around her. Hazel furrowed her eyebrows and grabbed onto the girl's arms, steadying her trembling body as she woke up.

"What's going on?" Amber gasped. Her voice caught the attention of the other two.

Hazel glanced over as Lucas was shoved to the ground. The bitten was staring right at them, saliva dripping from his razor-sharp canines. He growled, taking a step towards them before a pained gasp slipped from his lips. Lucas had stabbed the man from behind, right in the middle of his back. He pulled the blade out and narrowed his eyes tauntingly, backing into the trees. The vampire followed after him.

Hazel stood, her gaze lingering after them as Amber moved to grab her arm, letting out a wince.

"Where are you going? I thought you were getting

kidnapped. Did I get kidnapped? Huh? Are you kidnapping me from the kidnapper? That's far too much kidnapping for one day," Amber trailed off, her eyes hazy.

Hazel gripped the girl's hands with a tender look and pulled them up to her neck, wrapping them around the makeshift bandage to hold pressure to it. "I have to help Lucas, just stay here. I'll be right back."

Lucas led the bitten through the trees, trying to lure it away from the girls, and it worked.

Behind him, leaves flew into the air as the vampire drifted forward. Fading sunlight flickered through the trees like a running zoetrope as Lucas trailed across the rough forest ground, blocking the glare from his eyes with his armed hand. He glanced back mid-run and threw his dagger, piercing the snarling man in the chest before he could get too close.

With a hiss, the vampire pulled the blade from its skin, gripping the handle as if he intended to use it as Lucas reached for the other dagger on his belt – the nightshade-infused one.

The vampire growled, launching at him and, using the hilt of the stolen dagger, whacked the hunter across the face. Lucas staggered backwards, dropping his blade in the process, and wiped a hand over the fresh cut on his cheek. He dropped to the forest floor as quickly as he could, rummaging around in the mossy leaves for his dagger, the one that could land the killing blow. As he searched, he heard the wind move behind him and let out a grumbled breath, spinning around.

The bitten kicked him in the stomach, forcing him down into the pile of leaves. He tumbled over onto his back with a grunt, and the monster roared into his face, fresh blood dripping from its mouth as it pushed him further into the mud.

It takes time for the bitten to realise their speed and agility which makes them easy to hunt down, but this one seemed to know what he was doing. Maybe he wasn't so freshly turned as the hunters thought he was.

All vampires were tricksters. They were known to lie and deceive. If Lucas had to guess, he would have said this one had probably been roaming around for at least a few dozen years. The lone ones always were more dangerous for some reason. Probably because they had nothing to lose.

Sharp teeth trailed along Lucas's neck, making him thrash about as the vampire grinned above him. It was toying with him, building an appetite. He creased his brow, feeling his blood boil as he reached into the leaves below him, his hand searching for the icy metal.

An animalistic snicker fell through the vampire's lips, vibrating against Lucas's neck in a way that made his jaw clench. As his fingers trickled over the hardness of a handle, the bitten all of a sudden jumped backwards.

No, not jumped. He was dragged.

Lucas shot up to see Hazel holding the man down – or at least trying to. She seemed to be struggling as he flailed about in a frenzy.

"Shit, shit, shit," she whimpered under her breath, repeatedly whacking the bitten in the head with her elbow as it thrashed beneath her.

Lucas stared for a second, wondering how she'd managed to pull the vampire away, until she finally glanced at him, face scrunched up with effort. "Can you help, please?"

As their eyes met, he let out a gasp. Fire burned in her irises, bright red and crimson faded. "You're one of them," he whispered, pulling the blade free from the leaves and holding it out before him.

Hazel blinked at him, widening her expression as a baffled noise slipped from her lips. She peered down at the monster in her grip, then back up at Lucas. "Can you just... you know!" Hazel squealed, motioning to the vampire as her voice strained. "Please!"

Lucas stared at her, at those red, demonic eyes. The sense of humanity he'd felt looking at them before began to fade away just as quickly as the beating of her heart.

"Lucas!" Hazel called out, yelping as the bitten gripped onto the back of her arms and clawed its nails into her skin.

Her wound healed before Lucas's eyes and his throat filled with bile. The world around him seemed to quieten as a deadly rage grew in his chest.

He was too late to save her, *always too late.*

He looked down at the purple laced dagger in his hand. Lucas hadn't known Hazel for very long, but that didn't matter, he'd still *known* her, and he'd never killed one he knew before. Even if she hadn't been so friendly at first, Hazel didn't seem so bad, in fact, given more time, he probably could have come to like her.

How could he kill her without seeing her face every time he closed his eyes?

He scanned over her, avoiding her face, and peered down at her hands instead, at the blood that covered them. Amber's blood, a girl that *could* be saved. It was his job to protect people, no matter who he was protecting them from.

"Lucas!" Hazel screeched again, pulling him from his thoughts as the vampire began to wrestle free from her grasp, and just as he got the upper hand, Lucas sprung forward.

Hazel jumped out of the way, avoiding the blade as it

found its place in the back of the bitten's neck. The vampire grunted in pain and snapped his head backwards, falling to his knees and then to the floor, lifeless.

Lucas turned to the sound of heavy breathing behind him and glanced up to see Hazel, her hand stiff, as if she was still holding the dagger. The red melted out of her irises and she let out a strained sound, glancing back in the direction of Amber.

Without another word, she turned to walk away, but Lucas jumped to his feet first, grabbing the purple-edged dagger from the bitten's body and holding it out at her.

She hesitated for a second, then slowly began backtracking the way she'd come, holding her arms up. "I've got to get back to her—"

"You're not going anywhere," Lucas warned. She frowned, glancing down at the dagger as Lucas stormed towards her. "You're with them, aren't you? The Thorns? They turned you."

Hazel took in a sharp breath, shaking her head as he pressed the blade against her chest. "They didn't turn me... I'm just like this. Can you help me with Amber?" she exhaled, motioning toward the part of the forest they'd left her friend.

Lucas studied her. "Are you going to kill her?"

"I'd never hurt her."

"It's inevitable, one way or another. You always end up hurting someone," he replied, pressing the blade closer. Hazel's eyes were watering now, probably the effects of the nightshade residue.

She glanced back toward the trees. "If you're not going to help, at least let me go to her." She breathed hoarsely. "You like her, it's hard not to, don't let her die."

Lucas narrowed his eyes at the emotion on the vampire's

face. They usually didn't care about the living, whether they knew them or not, unless it was to feed.

Keeping his dagger aimed, he turned Hazel around, guiding her through the trees until they reached Amber again. Her head lolled against one of the trees and the ripped material on the side of her neck was growing darker.

Hazel let out a choked sob and tried to move forward, but Lucas sent her a warning look.

"Stay where you are."

She nodded with tears trickling down her face, watching intensely as Lucas grabbed a handful of gauze from his pocket. He lifted Amber, placing her onto his knee, and she opened her eyes, blinking.

"Lucas…" she whispered.

"Don't speak, you need to save your energy," he replied gently, wrapping the gauze around her neck. Amber rested against him as he placed the end of the dressing in his mouth and pulled, making sure he kept his eyes on Hazel the whole time.

"That'll stop the bleeding. I'll take her back with me and get her to the—"

"No!" Hazel cut in frantically. "She needs medical attention now. I can get her there faster!"

Lucas glanced up, frowning dangerously, and she shut her mouth. "How do I know you aren't going to kill her, or turn her?"

Hazel looked down to the ground, avoiding his eyes as she let out a quiet sob. "She's my best friend, I love her. Let me save her."

When she looked up again, he couldn't help but look into her familiar brown eyes, light and vibrant, like the sunlight that shone down on them through the cracks in the trees.

"I'll kill you. If she… if she turns… if she dies… I'll kill you," he said.

Hazel nodded, pulling at the sleeves of her leather jacket. "Okay… just let me save her."

Their eyes stayed glued to one another for what seemed like a lifetime before Lucas sighed and carefully moved the girl from his lap. Hazel rushed over instantly, placing her hands onto her friend's cheeks as Amber blinked in and out of consciousness.

Above them, Lucas clutched his dagger, glancing down at Hazel's undefended back.

She turned around to look at him. "Thank you."

"Don't thank me, I'm not doing this for you."

A visible lump formed in Hazel's throat and her gaze fell from his face to the sharp blade in his hand.

"Hazel!" A male voice cut through the air, warm and soft like honey, but full of caution. *Thorn*, Lucas thought, grunting in the back of his throat.

"No second chances," he mumbled.

Hazel glanced up at him, studying his features closely and pulling his focus to the soulful look hidden within her eyes. It was a mirror, he could see his reflection so clearly, standing above her with the dagger shimmering in his hand.

He sighed, and then, with nothing else to say, sprinted into the woods, blending in through the trees without looking back.

CHAPTER EIGHTEEN

Callouses

The journey from the edge of the forest to the hospital wasn't long by car, but it had felt endless.

Hazel watched as paramedics put her best friend on a stretcher – an animal attack they'd called it, a feral badger or fox that she'd unfortunately wandered across.

As for the other bodies Hazel had found in the woods, there were apparently people equipped to handle this stuff in the Arcane Council. Ophelia had dealt with it. After making several comments about dead Uncle Ernie, she let her parents know where to find them, both the vampire and the lifeless bodies. The sight of them scattered in the trees would forever be seared into Hazel's memory.

She had called Amber's father, who was hysterical. He'd already lost his wife; he couldn't lose his daughter too.

Hazel felt awful. Amber wouldn't have followed them if it weren't for her, if she hadn't lost control. She couldn't stop thinking about it, the confused and pained look on her best friend's face as she struggled to stay awake. She knew Amber was safe now she was at hospital, with her dad on his way, still she found it hard to leave her. But they couldn't stay, not now that Lucas knew about her.

The car ride back to Thorn Manor was mostly silent, apart from Ophelia, of course. Hazel ignored her rambling, choosing to look out of the window at the passing trees instead. They were duller now, coated with a thickness of mist and fog.

"*Lucas* is a cocky little shit, isn't he? We should prepare for a fight. From what he said, he is not going to stay away," Ophelia ranted, kicking her feet up on the dashboard.

Caleb gave her a deadpan stare, then swivelled around slightly, offering Hazel a sweet smile. "We won't let anyone hurt you, okay? You'll be safe. He's not going to touch you."

Hazel sighed and wiped at the tears that had started to cling to her cheeks, hoping he hadn't seen. There was a deep feeling of dread crawling under her skin. "Amber definitely won't turn into one of those things, right? Not if she didn't ingest his blood?"

Ophelia clicked her fingernails against the side of the car dismissively. "No, obviously, otherwise half of the country would be full of those parasites."

"Then why call them the *bitten*? It's a bit misleading, don't you think?"

"Well, they still get bitten first, and it's not like the person who invented the nickname was in the right state of creativity after probably being gorged on by the freaks!"

"Lia," Caleb groaned, pulling the girl's attention as they turned into the driveway of the manor, where their parents were already waiting for them.

Julianna Thorn's mouth was twisted into a frown, one that seemed to tighten into her cheekbones. Her husband sat beside her on the steps leading up to the door. His face was in his hands, pushing his glasses up on top of his forehead. Caleb had mentioned briefly how he and Ophelia had escaped the antique store, something involving an old porcelain piggy bank and melting door hinges. He had looked quite proud as he recited the story, leaving Hazel to guess that it had been a terrible plan, and they had got lucky.

The couple were in the midst of an argument. Hazel just about made out Julianna hissing the phrase 'target on our backs' as she watched Caleb rub a hand over his face, also clearly listening to his parents bicker from across the driveway. He peered through the gap in his fingers at the sound of Ophelia clearing her throat. She was fixing her hair, ready to put on an act of feign innocence.

Caleb locked the passenger side door. "Let me do the talking," he pleaded. "We don't want to piss them off any more than we already have."

Ophelia scoffed. "Mum's about to burst a blood vessel. We're going down anyway. Might as well try to butter them up a bit."

Caleb let his head drop forward onto the steering wheel with a groan as Ophelia stepped out, clicking her heeled boots against the cobblestoned pathway.

"We can explain, Mum. It's not our fault, those sword boys just can't play nice," Ophelia whined through an Oscar-worthy pout. Julianna sent her daggers, ignoring the rambling that began to spew from her mouth, and instead turning her expectant glare to Caleb, who was still peering over from the driver's seat.

"Can you stay in the car?" he whispered softly, glancing at Hazel through the rear-view mirror. She nodded, too tired to argue, furrowing her brows at his narrowing optimistic look as he stepped out of the car.

Caleb moved past the whirring fountain and stopped next to his sister, placing his hands in his pockets. As she watched them from the slightly open window, Hazel thought the siblings looked like seven-year-olds who'd just broken a priceless family heirloom.

"I don't know what Lia told you on the phone, but it's not that bad. We can fix this," Caleb said, rocking back on his heels.

His father stood up with a look full of disappointment painted on his face. "I thought I told you to stay put."

"Well, you also told me to protect Hazel, and you locked her out on her own with a feral bitten on the loose. So, technically, I was doing what you'd asked…" Caleb replied, opting for an overly charming smile.

Ophelia muttered a quick "hypocrite," under her breath.

Alexander's forehead creased, and he looked away, likely to avoid the furious expression on his wife's face as she tilted her head toward him. "I thought she was with you," he whined in defence. "I didn't realise Hazel had been separated. Look, we know about your little scuffle in the school, and your spontaneous and might I remind you *underaged* trip to the club." He glanced briefly at his daughter. "Where you apparently threatened one of them," Alexander continued, moving swiftly along.

Ophelia let out an outrageous cackle. "Come on! It was hardly even directed toward him, like, if you really focused, maybe there was a bit of meaning in the words, but it was barely readable."

Caleb snorted, covering it up with a cough as his mother's eyes narrowed even deeper.

"I mean, it was just a song, not my fault if he gets all whimpery about it," Ophelia huffed. The other three stared at her until she sighed loudly and made a zip motion over her lips, gesturing for them to continue.

"The head of the boy's group found your father's phone number from one of our store ads."

The leader of the warriors had just… called them. The

idea of it would have almost been funny if it wasn't for what Julianna said next.

"They think Hazel is a freshly transitioned bitten, and won't be convinced otherwise. There's no evidence that she comes from pure blood, they think one of us turned her," Julianna explained. "And as you know, unless they have proof of vampirism from a blood relative, we have no say," she spat, letting the words come out thick and condescending.

Caleb closed his eyes with a huff, chewing at the corner of his lip, while Ophelia let out a loud, tiresome whine. "Well, there must be something we can do!"

"They offered us an ultimatum," Julianna added, folding her arms over herself as she studied her children, watching their reactions carefully. Beside her, Alexander stiffened, giving her a strange look. Julianna narrowed her eyes. "They said if we give her to them by tomorrow night, they'll leave us out of it and leave our territory."

Inside the car, Hazel's stomach tied itself in knots. She pulled her knees up into herself, playing with the fraying hems of her ripped jeans as she listened apprehensively.

Caleb's eyebrows furrowed, and he stepped towards his mother, a little hesitant, but his expression was determined. "We are not giving her to them," he said, clenching the muscles in his jaw.

Beside him, Ophelia stood up a little straighter, giving him a wild, almost proud look before crossing her arms with a nod.

"Sometimes you have to make difficult choices," Julianna said, studying them for a second. "You can't be serious?" Ophelia muttered, barely audible, but she shut her mouth as her mother glanced at her. Hazel was a little surprised that she hadn't clapped yet, surely Ophelia would be excited with the idea of handing her over.

Caleb stood firm, breathing out slowly as he repeated himself. "We. Are. Not. Giving. Her. To. Them."

Alexander stepped between them with a tired look as the two stared each other down. "You're right, we're not giving her up, we're not animals. Hazel's one of us now, and we have vouched to protect her," he explained, looking from Julianna to Caleb, who took a step back with a huff. The older man's lips lifted at the corners, and his head swivelled toward the silver Jaguar in the driveway.

Ophelia scoffed in disbelief. "Then why act like we were throwing her to the wolves?"

Julianna tapped her fingernails against the sides of her jacket. "I wanted to see how you would react, especially with something so sensitive. I had to see how you'd handle it, and I can't help but say that I'm proud."

A soft look fell onto Ophelia's face, but quickly dropped at her mother's next words.

"Caleb, especially. It takes a natural born leader to step up to your head of clan like that, especially when it's your mother, good job, son," she praised, stepping closer to cup a hand to his cheek. Caleb unintentionally relaxed into it, his features softening but still filled with mild concern as he raised a bewildered eyebrow.

Ophelia tensed and clenched her jaw.

"Well, what are we going to do, then? They'll find us soon enough, we need a plan," Alexander asked, moving the conversation along with a tentative expression.

Caleb placed a hand onto the man's shoulder and grinned, looking around his family enthusiastically. "Okay, I have an idea."

Ophelia sighed dramatically. "Dear god, we're all doomed."

A couple of hours later, Hazel was sitting on the bed in the guest room. It almost seemed less showcase display now and more of a lived-in space, with her leather jacket over the desk chair, the unmade bed sheets, and the pillows that still scattered the floor from where she and Caleb had sat watching the stars a few nights ago.

She wished she could go back to that moment, before the world had turned on its axis. The Thorns still hadn't fully decided what they were going to do, but Caleb was very keen on his idea. Instead of waiting for the hunters to find them, he had suggested they take the conflict right to them. There was more opportunity in the forest, whether for a quick getaway or a full-blown brawl. He'd made it quite obvious that he was willing to fight, but he stressed that he wanted to talk things through first, try to convince the hunters to at least take the matter up with the council before jumping to conclusions.

If they managed an agreement with the hunters, then they could prove to the council that Hazel was of pure blood – which was hard to do with no living vampiric relatives, but not impossible.

There was something that could be traced in their blood, it took a while to process and was hard to decipher between born and bitten vampires, but it was there. It took a medical professional, a lot of time, and a whole lot of paperwork to sort through it and the Nosferatu Warriors had *a duty to serve*. They lived by a code and were permitted to hunt any creature they presumed dangerous, and they were certainly not patient by any means.

A council appeal could take up to a month, and that

was even with Alexander's brother, Edmund Thorn, holding one of the superior chairs. It was up to chance, really, the possibility that the warriors would actually listen to them.

Caleb was optimistic despite it all.

As Hazel was pondering the possible futility of his plan and whether she could ever find and match his optimism, there was a knock at the door and Ophelia let herself in without waiting for Hazel to answer, followed by Caleb. He held a few blood bags, one for each of them. The thought of blood still made Hazel feel a little dizzy, but with every other sense either numbing or spiralling around her, she needed something to help her think more clearly.

She considered Caleb's plan again and what the outcome might be if the hunters weren't willing to talk. She couldn't imagine him harming anyone, but then again, she'd seen how he'd looked at Lucas after he'd tried to attack his sister in the alleyway.

Caleb was sweet, and instinctively protective. He'd probably take a bullet for someone he cared about, but Hazel decided then and there that she wouldn't let it come to that.

He offered her a cheery smile, along with a blood bag, and her heart jumped in her chest. She glanced at Ophelia, who had popped a hole into the bag and was drinking the contents with a straw. Caleb stood in front of Hazel and ripped the plastic open with the tip of one of his fangs, motioning with his eyes for her to do the same.

She took a breath and before she could think about it too much, Hazel ripped the bag open and wolfed the contents down. When she finally came back to her senses, she shyly wiped her mouth and threw the empty packet on the bed next to her.

Caleb grinned as he did the same, sitting down beside her.

"That's the good stuff, the non-animal kind." He winked.

Hazel looked closer at the bag. There was a little sticker with the words *'thanks for your donation'* on the side. She scrunched up her nose. "I almost thought you were joking about the blood bank, until we went there today and I realised the fake charity thing was actually… real."

"Not everything I say is bollocks, surprisingly." Caleb grinned. "And for the record, we pay people for the blood."

Hazel made a face in disagreement and he laughed. "I'm surprised you even remember the blood bank, anyway. You seemed pretty preoccupied trying to bite my head off."

Hazel sniffled in amusement and grabbed a pillow, hitting him with it playfully.

Ophelia let out a disgusted huff. "Keep the PDA at a minimum, please," she groaned, drifting out of the room.

While Hazel felt her cheeks flush with heat, Caleb ignored the comment and tapped her knee, which only made her face feel hotter. "Try to get some sleep, okay? You're going to need it."

She looked down at her hands, now clean, but she couldn't get the image of them covered in blood, *Amber's blood*, out of her mind.

Almost as if he'd read her thoughts, Caleb grabbed her hands and pushed them out of sight. "It's not your fault. Amber's going to be okay, she might pester you for information when she gets out, but she'll do it in full health," he said. "Don't worry about the warriors, either. Lucas, he's a little shit, but we can handle him."

A comfortable silence washed over them as he moved closer, clearly testing the waters. Hazel smiled shyly. She could feel the tension leave her shoulders as he rubbed his thumb over her fingers.

After a moment, he stood up to leave, but she gripped his palm tighter. "Can you stay?" she whispered.

Caleb nodded with a soft smile and moved back toward the bed. She glanced away, dropping down against the pillow. He was definitely going to get in trouble for this, but from the look on his face, he didn't seem to care, and she really didn't want to be alone.

She felt the mattress dip as he lay down beside her, mirroring her position only inches away as they both stared up at the ceiling.

In the warm orange light of the room, Caleb turned to look at her. He looked so gentle in the ivory sheets, his sandy hair curling ever so slightly at the top of his head as his watercolour eyes studied her features.

Hazel averted her gaze, continuing to stare up at the ceiling. Without saying a word, she placed her hand over his again and held it there. Her black painted nails stood out in perfect contrast to his pale skin as he wrapped his fingers with hers.

For some reason, Caleb had a way of making her feel at ease, even if they were just lying in silence.

"Tell me something about you that I don't already know," Hazel asked.

Caleb grinned then leaned backwards, brushing his fingers over the curve of her palm. "That's my line."

Hazel scoffed and grabbed a pillow, placing it between them to prop her head up. "Just answer the question," she whispered.

He chuckled and leaned forward on the same pillow. "I can play the piano. And not just a little bit, I'm *really* good."

"Oh, right. So, you can play the *Mario* soundtrack, then? Anything else?" Hazel muttered.

"Harsh. I mean, you're absolutely right, I know that soundtrack by heart, but I play a mean *Moonlight Sonata*," Caleb replied. "Oh, and you should hear my rendition of Piano Sonata no. 16. I always add my own spin on it, and it drives my mum insane."

Hazel leaned up on her elbow to face him, squinting. "You're being serious, aren't you?"

He nodded, turning to look up at the ceiling. "Deadly."

"You're into classical music?"

Caleb tilted his head as his gaze met hers again. "No, that's just what my parents wanted me to learn. I've been forced into playing since I was six, another Thorn family legacy thing." He rolled his eyes. "I hated it until my dad gave me a Bowie sheet music book on one of my birthdays. Once I was playing stuff I enjoyed, I realised how much I actually loved it."

Hazel squeezed his hand a little, looking down as his thumb brushed over her skin. "What do you like to play?" she asked.

His eyes crinkled and he shuffled closer, sticking his tongue between his teeth in thought. "Fleetwood Mac, definitely… a bit of Harry Styles. Oh, I love The Smiths as well, and Arctic Monkeys."

Hazel smiled softly, leaning her head against the pillow. "I love Fleetwood Mac," she whispered.

"Yeah?" he breathed, and she nodded.

"Do you play anything?" Caleb asked, picking her hand up and threading his fingers back through it, glancing down at where they intertwined.

"Bit of guitar, a bit of bass. Oh, the ukulele as well," Hazel replied, frowning a little. She hadn't thought about how much she missed her guitar, which was silly, it had only been a few days, but sometimes it felt like an extended part of her.

"I kinda guessed you could play guitar," Caleb said, with a small, mischievous smile as he brushed over her calloused fingertips. "You just have this whole tortured soul thing going on."

She raised a brow, smiling softly. "Of course, because that's all guitarists. I had to sign a contract actually, that said I'd keep it moody and gloomy for as long as the strings touched my fingers."

"You're doing a great job."

Hazel scoffed and buried her head into the pillow.

"You have calluses on your fingertips," Caleb said, re-linking his hand with hers with less hesitation this time. "Sharp eyes, remember?"

She glanced up, letting out a bated breath as he turned her palm around, trailing over her fingertips.

"Nothing gets by you, does it?"

"I pay attention to detail."

"Must be hard with the attention span of a toddler," she whispered, playfully.

He grinned in response. "You been playing long?"

Hazel nodded, glancing up from the pillow with a hum. "Ever since I was seven. My mum bought me an old guitar one Christmas. She always says music helps everything make more sense. She used to sing to me instead of reading stories, and as stupid as it sounds, it works."

"I get that," Caleb replied, nodding. "It helps you think when it gets too quiet."

"Yeah, I don't really like the quiet so much, it's always a bit… loud," she muttered, cringing at her own cliché.

Caleb laughed, looking down at his fidgeting fingertips. Despite his usual calm and confident demeanour, Hazel had noticed he could never really keep still. He was always moving in some way, bouncing his knee, shifting his weight from foot to foot, chewing on his lip. He did that last one a lot and in such a way that she could almost decipher what each one meant by now.

She buried herself into the pillow, trying to hide the withering expression on her face, she didn't want to bring the mood back down when he'd tried so hard to raise it. However, as quietness slid back into the room, the sound of her heart pounding was heavy, unmissable, rising and falling with every shivery breath.

Caleb dropped her palm and she looked up instantly, almost offended at the disconnection as he drifted to the window, pulling the curtains back to reveal the night sky.

Her expression brightened as soon as she saw it, smiling at Caleb's 'ta-dah' motion as she sat up and looked out toward the stars. He slid back onto the bed then and rested on his arm, brushing his fingertips over her hand again.

Her gaze fixated on the window, watching the sky darken. She could feel his eyes on her, could sense the strain in them. There was a wariness in the room, something unspoken, until he decided to speak it.

"I'm not going to let anyone hurt you, you know? I mean, none of us are. You're with us now, you get that right? My mum, she's going to do everything she can," he whispered.

Hazel glanced up at him, her bottom lip between her teeth as she focused on not letting it tremble. "This isn't her fight, though, or yours. I don't want you putting yourself in danger for me. It's not fair."

Caleb furrowed his brow, sitting up from the headboard to face her, but she quickly glanced down at the sheets. "Hazel," he began, frowning as her hand suddenly disconnected from his.

"I don't want to put any of you in danger. No one else should get hurt because of me." She rolled into the sheets, covering her face with the silky material to hide the tears that were threatening to fall.

Caleb reached out to touch her cheek, gently turning her face toward him. He brushed under her eye with his thumb, rubbing away a tear. "No one's going to get hurt.""

She glanced up, watery eyes burning as they met his gaze, and he smiled, brushing a hand through her hair, pushing it out of her face.

"But—"

In an attempt to shut her up, Caleb pressed his palm over her mouth.

Her eyes widened and she tilted her head, trying to wrestle free. "Caleb," she mumbled, creasing her brow with a tiny laugh, which was muffled through his hand. "*Let go.*"

He shook his head. "I'll let go when you stop trying to handle everything alone."

She peered up and frowned, gently biting down on his hand after he let out a snort at her stubborn expression. Caleb pulled his hand back with a surprised laugh and she smirked, satisfied with herself until he pounced, tackling her into the mattress.

"There's no way I'm letting you go now."

CHAPTER NINETEEN

Golden

"Hey, I've been shouting—"

Ophelia's voice woke Hazel up abruptly, especially the screech that came after it.

The blonde was standing at the door, her jaw wide open as her eyes fell on Hazel and Caleb, or more specifically, the lack of space between them.

With an awkward croak, Hazel glanced down to see she'd been nestled into Caleb's side, his hand sitting in the middle of her back.

"Why are you yelling?" Caleb grumbled, carefully pulling away from Hazel to rub at his eyes and sit up against the headboard.

Ophelia lifted her nose in disgust. "Why am I yelling? Why do you think I'm yelling?" she said, taking a second to gag theatrically.

Hazel pulled the sheets up around herself, clinging to them tightly as she wished they'd absorb her and spit her out somewhere else, *anywhere* else.

A sigh left Caleb's throat, and he wordlessly rolled onto his side, avoiding his sister's glare until her hostile eyes turned to Hazel instead, full of accusation.

She fiddled with the blanket. "Well... You could have knocked."

A look appeared on the blonde's face, so past fury that a

blue vein popped out at the top of her forehead.

Caleb chuckled into his pillow, the sleepy sound muffled through the fabric and Hazel felt her cheeks heat up. She looked up at Ophelia and played with the hem of the quilt, wrapping it around her fingers. "We were just—"

Ophelia held her hand up, stopping her from talking. "Please spare me the details. We don't have time to unpack this right now."

"Unpack what?" Hazel asked, giving the angry girl a perplexed look. "We... this isn't... We fell asleep, we weren't..."

The other girl blinked at her, clenching her jaw so tight Hazel was sure some tendons were about to snap. "I'm not doing this right now! We're putting a pin in it until later! Just get up! And you!" she spat, pointing an accusing finger at her brother – who stopped chuckling and grabbed the pillow he was leaning on, holding it over his face. "Get back to your own room before Mum finds out you're in here and has you fixed like a dog. You disgusting, vile..." Her insults trailed off as she left the room, shaking her shoulders with a shudder before the door slammed closed behind her.

"Is she gone yet?" Caleb asked, his face still pressed into the pillow.

Hazel nodded, pressing her chin into the quilt. "Yeah, you're safe... for now, at least."

Caleb turned to face her with a shy grin and leaned on his arm. "Morning," he mumbled, smiling idiotically.

Hazel chuckled softly, still toying with the fabric of the quilt. "Morning."

"Don't mind her. She tends to jump to conclusions. I'll talk to her, don't worry about it."

"Right, yeah."

"I should go before someone else walks in, or Lia comes back with a weapon or something," he yawned, sitting up with a stretch.

"Caleb?" Hazel called, pulling the blanket tighter around her frame. "Thanks, for staying with me. I know your mum would kill you if she found out you slept here last night."

"It was worth the risk."

After changing, Caleb was on his way downstairs when he was waylaid in the corridor by his sister. He blinked hard, head still heavy with sleep.

"Nothing happened," he started, "I just stayed with her because—"

"I don't want to talk about you sleeping with my worst enemy."

Caleb placed a hand on the wall and leaned into it with a sigh. "She's not an enemy, she never was, and I didn't sleep with her. Nothing happened."

"Don't say it, it's worse when you say it." Ophelia shuddered. "And don't lie, Caleb. I'm not stupid! I know what was going on. I wish I didn't though. I kind of want to gouge my eyes out."

An irritated huff fell from Caleb's lips, and he pushed past her, making his way down the stairs into the entranceway. "*You* brought it up and I. Didn't. Sleep. With. Her. Can we just focus on what's important, please?"

Ophelia twisted her lips with disgust but after a moment she nodded and followed him. "That little rat is still out there, we should go and find him... and feed him to some snakes."

"Almost!" he said, cheerfully sarcastic. "Take out the snake part and I'm in. We should definitely try to find him."

"No, Caleb, you want to go *talk* to him. He's preparing for a fight and not one where everyone walks away. This is stupid, you can't just talk to a hunter, they don't talk, they *hunt*. This is borderline idiotic, no — not even borderline, *it's just idiotic*."

An enthusiastic grin lit up his face as he stuck his hands in his pockets. "Good thing I'm the best at doing idiotic things then, isn't it?"

Ophelia sharpened her expression.

"Look, I know what I'm doing, okay? Even if I go alone. If I can just talk to him, talk to all of them, we can come to some sort of agreement, then maybe this can all be avoided," Caleb said, shrugging. "If people talked through things instead of just going straight for each other's throats all the time, then there would be a whole lot less death and maiming in the world."

"You don't know that! Talking turns to arguing, which turns into aggression. It's full circle. You can't escape it."

"Not with that attitude," Caleb said, playfully arching an eyebrow at her unimpressed expression. "I'm fully prepared to knock some sense into him if I have to, but if I can talk it into him first or at least buy us some time, then it's worth giving it a go, isn't it?"

A muffled noise of defiance fell from Ophelia's lips. "Fine, but I'm coming with you."

Caleb smirked. "I thought this idea was borderline idiotic?"

"It is," she scowled, rolling her eyes. "And so are you. But I'm not letting you go alone."

"You gonna let me do the talking?" he mused, lifting a brow. She pulled a face full of false consideration.

"Unlikely."

Caleb grinned, making way for the front door, when a loud throat clearing sound stopped him.

They both turned to find their mother standing behind them, her face stony and arms crossed.

Ophelia turned to her brother with a questioning expression, and he returned the look with a little nod and placed his hand on the door handle. Julianna narrowed her eyes, thinning them into slits, like a cat's.

"Trust me, okay?" Caleb smiled charmingly, keeping his gaze on his mother. "You want me to lead this family, let's start here." He yanked the front door open, only to be met with his father's disapproving face on the other side.

"We don't want you to just lead this family, Caleb," his mother said, "we want you to be a leader, to balance the supernatural world as a council member, just like your uncle. Until you learn the importance of that, and what it takes to fill that role, then you'll still live by my rules."

"I do respect you. I always have… but he let her go, Mum, that means there's hope. We can get through to him if we try. Let me try," he pleaded, slackening his jaw.

Julianna Thorn tapped her fingertips against her arms, tightening her icy glare. "No, this isn't a risk I'm willing to take, not on our lives."

"Then just risk it on mine. Lucas is bound to show up at the hospital to check on Amber. I'll find him alone, in public, somewhere he wouldn't attack. I'll take him for a bloody coffee, just… I can get through to him. He's just a kid, and you agreed last night you'd think my plan over. Go to them instead of them coming for us? If I find Lucas on his own first, maybe we don't even have to do that. What's the harm in me trying to prevent it in the first place?"

Julianna's expression changed for a second, her gaze fading over to her husband who appeared from another room, having heard the exchange. He looked guilty. Caleb turned to him questioningly.

Alexander let out a solemn breath, looking down to the ground as Julianna straightened out her features.

"You didn't need to think it over, did you?" Ophelia breathed, knitting her eyebrows together. "You'd already decided." Her mother met her eyes, neither confirming nor denying her accusation, instead, she just lifted her head higher.

The younger Thorn leaned back against the curve of the door and chuckled dryly. "I told you."

Caleb's brows furrowed, the look on his face hardening at the expression on his mother's.

"It's too dangerous. I've called your uncle, we're going to be spending the next few days with him while he tries to get us a council summons. And if he can't get one soon enough, I'm booking us flights to New York. We'll stay with your Aunt Annalise for a bit. We'll be safer there until this mess is all sorted out."

"But you said!" Caleb widened his eyes as his mother brushed her palms together, quite literally cleaning her hands of it. He gave her a look of disbelief. "You said you'd think about it!"

"I've changed my mind…" she said and he knew she was lying. Julianna Thorn never changed her mind, just her doubts. "There's nothing we can do, not without proof. She can come with us—"

Caleb growled, cutting his mother off as he brushed a hand through his sandy hair. "But she won't go all that way. I don't think she's even left the country before, never mind all the way to New York. Her mother is here. Her best friend is in the hospital. Hazel's not going to go anywhere without them." He could feel the tingle of his eyes changing colour and closed them, wiping a hand over his face. "You just don't care," he muttered angrily.

Julianna scoffed, but it faded into the background as Alexander pushed through the archway of the living room, looking up the stairway subtly. "Of course we care, son. That's why we're doing this. The Council is the best chance Hazel has."

"Not if she's already dead," Ophelia chimed in, picking at her nails.

Alexander gave her a disappointed look, then shifted his gaze towards Caleb. "Talk to her, convince her to come with us," Alexander tried, placing his hands on Caleb's shoulders, but he shook them off, peering between his parents.

"No."

"No?" Julianna repeated.

The other two watched with different levels of anticipation as Caleb stepped towards his mother, narrowing his eyes. "No, she won't come, not that far and for who knows how long. I know she won't and I'm not leaving her," he said, glancing up the staircase before looking back at his mother's surprised expression. "Run if you have to, if you're so scared, but that won't change anything. I'm staying. I'm going to change their minds, and if I can't, then I'm going to make sure they can't touch her."

"Don't be absurd," Julianna replied, her forehead creasing.

Caleb shrugged his shoulders. They wanted him to step up, to be a leader, but the second he takes initiative, she knocks him back down again. Ophelia was right, it didn't matter what they did, they could never please her.

"I'm sorry, Mum, but I can't stand behind you on this one, not this time."

Something stirred in Julianna's demanding eyes and she reached forward, moving to caress his cheek, but Caleb brushed past her, darting away from her touch and drifting upstairs without another word.

She glanced over at her husband, widening her eyes at the knowing look on his face.

Ophelia coughed to break the tension. "Guess your golden boy's not so golden." She smirked, standing up and stepping past her unamused parents with a skip in her step.

Hazel was getting sick of training. Caleb had knocked the intensity of it up a notch, and she was struggling to keep up.

At first, he'd been a little quieter than normal. Something was obviously bothering him, but he'd eventually returned to his usual dopey self. Now, he had her pressed against a tree, and before she could even calculate what was happening, she was being tied in place.

With an impatient exhale, she struggled against the thick rope, but it wouldn't budge.

Caleb drifted off and landed on the edge of the fountain a few feet away, leaning back onto it as he watched her struggle.

"Really? *Really!*" Hazel yelled, pulling against the restraints.

He smirked at her and shrugged. "You should be able to break out quite easily if you focus enough."

She pulled at the rope, but it seemed to only grow firmer in retaliation. "Just unwrap me, let's do the combat again. I reckon I'd be pretty good at punching you right now," Hazel grumbled, wrestling against the tree as it almost mocked her with its stillness.

Caleb glanced down with a grin. "I'm sure you would, but you need to learn this. Strength is a natural part of our abilities. You could pull that tree apart if you tried hard enough."

She glared at him. "If you don't untie me right now, I'll tear *you* apart."

He let out a laugh in response, peering up again with an infuriatingly buoyant expression. "Is that a threat or a promise?"

Hazel let out a furious squeal.

Caleb sat up and dashed to her side, positioning himself a hair's breadth away as he assessed the grumpy shape of her lips. "That's good, be angry at me, you can use that."

She glanced up at the sudden movement and her breath caught in her throat before she forced it out again with a grouchy sigh.

"Focus all that frustration into your arms, feel it under your skin like a heavy weight," Caleb carried on, laying an arm against the tree so his face was inches away from hers. "Punch me," he whispered with a wink. Hazel let out a scoff and jutted her lip.

"Don't know if you've noticed, but my arms are behind my back."

"Free them, then," he enthused. "Focus your energy into your arms, imagine yourself breaking free, and when you do, I'll give you one free hit, right here." He trailed his fingertips across the edge of his chiselled jawline. "This is your chance to absolutely knock the crap out of me, don't waste it."

Hazel's shoulders slumped and she dropped her head back against the tree trunk with a frustrated grumble. "Can you just untie me? I can't do it," she sighed, kicking at the dirt around her feet.

Caleb glanced toward her again, chewing his lip. "Just try, please. I want you to break out at least once."

"Then you shouldn't have tied the rope this friggin' tight."

That only seemed to amuse him. Caleb smirked and inched closer to her. "Relax your muscles, cut out the tension, and then let it move through you. Anger works, but it can be unpredictable. There are better things to rely on."

She glanced down as he traced his fingertips over the skin of her arm, leaving a trail of goosebumps that made her want to move forward and reciprocate the touch – either through a punch to his jaw or a returned brush of the arm.

"You can do it, break out."

Hazel blew out a slow, tantalising breath, watching him, until a loud, bitter voice cut through the air behind them.

"Mum wants to speak to you!" Ophelia called out, narrowing her eyes from the back door.

A small sigh left Caleb's lips and he stepped back, placing his hands in his pockets and acting as though he'd never heard her.

Hazel pulled a face, glancing over his shoulder at Ophelia, who rolled her eyes so hard it must have hurt, and then picked up a small pebble.

Before Hazel even got the chance to warn him, Ophelia threw the stone, aiming for the back of Caleb's head. Instinctively he dodged it, and the pebble bounced right off Hazel's forehead.

"Ow!" she shouted, staring blankly at Ophelia as the girl snickered loudly, clapping her hands together. Caleb widened his eyes and drifted to Hazel's side, apologising profusely as he gently rubbed at her forehead.

"I'm fine, it was just a pebble," Hazel whispered as he

continued to fuss. "Maybe you should go see what they want before she gets ambitious and has a go with the fire logs."

He closed his eyes with a sigh, chewing on the corner of his lip before nodding.

It wasn't until he'd walked away that Hazel realised she was still tied to the tree. "Caleb, no wait! Caleb!" she called after him.

At the sound of his name, he turned to face her, but the blonde backstabber grabbed his arm, smiling sweetly at him. "I'm on your side, just so you know… I'll keep going with training, you go talk to Mum."

He gripped her arm lovingly before moving toward the house.

Hazel let her head fall back against the tree, sighing before she let out a startled noise as Ophelia suddenly appeared in front of her. She stared, wordlessly, crossing her arms as an increasingly alarming grin spread on her lips.

Hazel blinked at her, feeling heavily uncomfortable. "What? Why are you looking at me like that?"

The blonde kept staring, tapping her perfect pink nails against her arm. "I'm just taking a minute to enjoy this."

Hazel frowned, opening her mouth to speak again, but Ophelia held her hand up. "I'm not done yet."

With a quiet grumble, Hazel placed her palms flat against the tree, pressing them against it. The rope strained against her midsection, holding her in place tightly. She focused on her arms, on pulling them free and snapping the rope clean off. There was a slight tingle at her fingertips, spreading up her arms as if moving through her veins.

The rope strained further, growing firmer for a second before loosening, allowing her to pull it over herself.

Hazel looked down at her now free hands and let out a

surprised laugh, glancing up at Ophelia excitedly.

The other girl didn't look so impressed.

"And it's ruined."

With a small shake of her head, Hazel sat down on the grass, still smiling at her victory.

Ophelia moved towards her, taking her jacket off before neatly placing it on the ground and sitting on it. "Clearly it wasn't tied properly, I wouldn't celebrate yet. You were supposed to *break* free, not shimmy free."

Hazel shrugged, picking at the grass. "I still got out, maybe I'm not useless at this after all."

"Doubt that," Ophelia scoffed, blocking the glare from the sun with her hand as she looked up at the sky. "Time will tell, I guess."

The way they sat – Ophelia staring at the clouds whilst Hazel picked at the daisies below her fingertips – was like a glimpse of the past, something so familiar yet now so odd. It filled Hazel with a downcast nostalgia.

"When we were younger, you used to say you were scared of change. Was this the change? Being a vampire?" she asked hesitantly.

"Not entirely."

"What was it?" Hazel waited for a response. Ophelia lay back on the grass, turning away from the conversation, and Hazel furrowed her brow. "Fine, we'll just sit here in silence," she mumbled, tearing apart the daisies in her palm.

After a few painful seconds of silence, Ophelia sighed. "I looked forward to being a vampire, always had, but it can get lonely, especially when your annoying older brother is your only real friend. Don't get me wrong, I love that idiot, but he's a guy, you know?"

Hazel stared for a second, sceptically. "You've got plenty of friends, like those girls you hang around with in school, the other evil ones."

The blonde shrugged. "Doesn't mean I like any of them. Even if I did, I can't get too close. My mother thought it best that way, she never encouraged us to make friends. One way or another, humans always get hurt in our world."

Hazel swallowed, feeling a sudden tension in her throat, because, well, Julianna was right. It had been barely two days since her world changed and already her best friend was in the hospital.

"That's why Caleb doesn't get too close to anyone," Hazel said.

Ophelia nodded. "Yeah, he always listens to Mum, but it's not my fault I'm burdened with being popular," she replied, holding a hand to her forehead dramatically.

Hazel wanted to pick up the stone that had dented her forehead earlier and return the favour, but she decided against it as Ophelia continued. "Anyway. With the whole… well, you know, I knew I'd have to stop being friends with you…"

So that was why. That was the reason they were no longer friends, because it wasn't *safe*. Ophelia had abandoned her, lied to her, and turned them both against each other, and it had all been for nothing in the end, because Hazel had ended up in her world anyway.

She understood to an extent. Maybe in some messed up way Ophelia was trying to protect her, but by breaking her heart and making them hate each other? Hazel would never put Amber through that, even if it wasn't safe for her friend in this world, she'd find a way to make it safe before she cast her aside.

They sat in further silence for a couple of seconds, only this time it was extremely uncomfortable. Ophelia sighed loudly to break the awkwardness. "I'm perfectly fine with it now. I can't stand you or your constant nagging most days."

"*My* constant nagging?" Hazel complained, but she was interrupted with a scowl.

"And your weird *thing* with my brother repulses me."

Hazel stared down at the grass, huffing under her breath. Part of her felt guilty for how everything had gone down when they were younger, especially now knowing the truth, but there was still an irritated feeling that sat in her chest, a pang of hatred that she couldn't push away. There was just so much distance between them now.

After wrestling with what to say for far too long, Hazel threaded the strands of grass through her fingertips. "There's nothing weird going on with me and Caleb," she replied awkwardly, and Ophelia released a short breath before humming suspiciously in response.

Caleb wandered into the living room to find his mother sitting on the couch, looking up at him calmly. Her mouth was set in a thin line, and her posture was stiff, but her eyes were soft, regretful even, as he took a seat on the armchair in the corner of the room.

Julianna leaned forward, crossing her fingers together. "You know I'd do anything to keep you and your sister safe, I'd tear the world in two if anything tried to take you from me—"

"Mum," Caleb interrupted, chewing on his lip.

She narrowed her eyes and he let out an exasperated breath, rolling back in his seat.

"There are too many of them and only five of us. If we

stick around, we're only setting ourselves up for failure. Do you understand that?"

Caleb brushed a hand over his face. "You don't know that. We haven't even tried. You raised me to always face my problems head on and not to run, so why are you running?"

"A mother's job is the hardest out there, harder than any position of leadership. I'm not just trying to shape you for a role, love, I'm trying to shape you for a future." She sighed breathlessly, taking a minute to compose herself with her eyes closed before resting them on him. "You're already so brave, noble, and sometimes that scares me, because what makes my job so hard is that I don't want you to leave, I don't want you to fight. I want to keep you safe."

There was fear on her face, an emotion so alien on her sharp features. Caleb sighed and stood up, taking a seat on the edge of the couch she was sitting on.

"That's a little contradictory considering you've been setting me up for this my whole life. I thought you wanted me to be a leader?" he asked, the words coming out light and with the tiniest hint of humour in them.

Julianna almost smiled. She reached up with a sniffle and caressed the side of his cheek. "I want you to be on the Council. There's no fighting involved in that – they save that for their guards."

He furrowed his brow playfully. "Well, Ophelia is far more equipped for arguing than me, she enjoys it, actually. Don't you think she'd be better suited for that role?"

"Your sister is a natural born fighter, you're right. She knows when to strike, but she's also hot-headed and unpredictable. You're strategic, a leader. Ever since you were a little boy, you've always been empathetic. You'd sacrifice yourself before anyone else, and I hate that, but it's what makes you so valuable. You should be on that table, keeping the peace, that's what you're good at."

Caleb swallowed, looking out towards the fireplace, watching the flames dance. "You know, if we leave now, we're just proving to them that we're guilty, even if we're not."

"We'll leave a message to explain."

"It won't matter, they'll see it as us running away. They'll follow us, they'll keep following us. They'll kill her, Mum, then they'll line us up in front of the Council and force them to punish us, too."

"No, your uncle—"

"Uncle Edmund can't do anything, not if we look guilty. You said yourself there's no way to prove her blood status by tomorrow, so instead, we prove her innocence. We go there and show we have nothing to hide, that we simply want to talk."

Julianna shook her head, her expression becoming firmer. "They'll kill her on sight."

"She won't be there," Caleb replied, turning to face her with a tentative expression. "She'll be here until they agree to listen."

"You can't be in two places at once, you can't protect her here if you're out there with us."

"I know," Caleb agreed, clicking his knuckles together. "But she'll be safe here, they don't know where the manor is. It's not ideal, but this is the only option we have, unless you'd rather run? You know I'd always prefer to have you on my side, but I'm going to do this with or without you," he said, smiling sheepishly as his mother let out an exasperated breath.

"And if it doesn't work? Not everyone is open to discussion, Caleb. I'll be surprised if you can get barely three words in before they start pulling out their weapons."

"Then we fight."

CHAPTER TWENTY

Into the Labyrinth

After tea, Caleb had said he'd needed to grab something. He'd given Hazel a look, clearly asking her to join him, and, of course, Ophelia trailed after them with a suspicious look in her eye.

"Come on, we can't do that to Dad. You know what these things mean to him. He isn't going to like it," Ophelia complained, crossing her arms as she followed her brother.

They stopped outside of a door, a normal oak door, with a heavy padlock on the front.

"We'll get them back. It's an offering, to show we're up to reasoning," Caleb replied, a little guiltily, reaching up to the top of the doorframe where he grabbed a key out from a little indent.

Ophelia scoffed. "Dad will offer *you* up when he finds out."

With a sarcastic smile, Caleb pushed the door open, and Hazel stared in bewilderment at the odd, dimly lit room inside.

"One of Dad's rooms. We keep this one locked, though. Some of the things in here are a little... um, hazardous," Caleb explained, lifting a fancy-looking sword off the wall. It was tinted black and had a golden, ritualistic carving on the handle.

Ophelia brushed her fingers along a wall of weapons, all

decorated with intricate patterns or fancy colours. "Yeah, try not to touch anything, and if you do, don't come crying to me when you cut your finger off."

Hazel gulped at the sight, the walls were dark red, lined with stacks of swords and bows, weapons of varying sorts and sizes. It was what she imagined a torture room would look like. There was even a box full of vintage pennies in the corner. The antique store may have been a ruse for the blood drive, but Alexander clearly still had a passion for timely things.

Outside the manor, the Thorns were waiting for their children when Caleb came out, tossing his father a crossbow filled with metallic red arrows, and holding the same sword he had taken from the wall.

Alexander caught the bow and looked down at it with a strain in his eyes as Caleb swung the sword over his shoulder excitedly. He shook his head, sticking the bow under his arm and then moved forward to grab the sword. "No, no, no, absolutely not."

Caleb glanced up at his mother, who sighed and grabbed onto her husband's shoulders, caressing them as he frowned deeply. "Listen, Alex. I hate this idea too, but at least this way we'll have weapons on us," she said sympathetically as he turned to her with a sad look, before checking over the sword's carvings.

"They're more likely to hear us out if we bring an offering," Caleb enthused. "And what better than some fancy weapons?"

"A pasta bake or something, probably," Ophelia mused, stepping out of the doorway and spinning a pair of small knives in either hand. Alexander let out a faint choked noise.

Hazel stepped out behind them, still in shock from the sight of the weapons room. She wrapped her jacket tight around her torso, fiddling with the loose buttons.

Caleb smiled at his father apologetically. "It gives us a better chance," he insisted. "I want to prove to them that we are willing to talk, and that there doesn't need to be a fight."

"By showing up on their doorstep with a handful of weapons…" Ophelia added, giving him a doubtful look.

A heavy sigh fell from the blue-eyed boy's lips and he brushed a hand through his hair, purposely letting his middle finger stick out to her.

Alexander let out another sad grumble. "Does it have to be these?"

"Yes," Caleb and Julianna both confirmed at the same time, though Mrs Thorn's tone was a lot harsher than her son's.

"It's okay, though," Ophelia said. "We're going to get them back, aren't we, *Caleb?*" She shot her brother a sharp look, and he nodded, pointing at her enthusiastically.

"Exactly, I'm going to distract them while Ophelia swipes the weapons back as soon as we can."

Alexander's lips were settled in a grouchy frown, though they relaxed ever so slightly when Hazel shyly stuck her hand up. "He's actually really good at distractions." The boy in question smirked at her and she pulled at the lacy T-shirt thread lining her stomach. "Plus, with Ophelia's ability to sneak up on people, it's a pretty good plan."

Mr Thorn sighed. "Okay. I'll take your word for it." He smiled at Hazel, then his expression turned sterner as he looked to his son, hesitantly handing the sword back. "But no damage."

Caleb clapped a hand to his shoulder, flashing a brief but

cunning smile in Hazel's direction.

"So, are we walking, or do you guys have some sort of Victorian style hearse stashed somewhere?" she whispered to Caleb a few moments later as everyone was getting ready to leave.

"We're drifting. You are staying here and locking the doors," Caleb explained somewhat hesitantly, avoiding Hazel's eyes as he pulled on his denim jacket.

She jutted her lip in response, opening her mouth to retaliate, but her words were cut short by Julianna, who brushed past her on the doorstep.

"He's right, dear, you need to stay here. Having you there will only put you in more danger, and if we are protecting you, we cannot efficiently fight them," she said, looking at Caleb pointedly as he angled his head toward her.

"If it comes to a fight."

Julianna rolled her eyes at her son's words, handing out small brown bags to everyone.

Ophelia sighed in disappointment as she accepted hers, flicking a dagger up in the air and catching it. "And I was *so* hoping to squish Lucas like the foul, disgusting bug that he is."

Her father tutted, catching the blade in mid-air as he drifted past her. "Lia, we do not wish for a fight," he cooed softly, turning to stroke her hair. "Squish him in other ways, angel, there's nothing like taking a man's dignity and pride, at least that way he gets to keep his head." He tapped her on the nose, and Ophelia grinned brightly.

Caleb gave Hazel an embarrassed look. "Yeah… ignore that… We're a sane, normal family, I promise."

Hazel looked back at him sceptically as his mother handed them both a *packed lunch*. It consisted of a blood bag, a packet of crisps, and a small bottle of water.

Caleb bit his lip, looking up at Hazel with a small laugh, before taking her arm and guiding her away from his family. "Can I have a word?"

She nodded and he led her back into the house to one of the many sitting rooms. One that Hazel hadn't been in before. It had the same feeling as the rest of the place, the same stylish décor, but this room had a grand piano sitting in the corner. Caleb sat down on the small seat accompanying it and gave her a charming grin, tapping the space beside him.

Hazel remained where she was, giving him a stubborn look. "I'm coming with you."

Caleb exhaled slowly and glanced down at the piano, beginning to play a sombre, melodic tune.

"What was the point of training me to fight if you're just going to leave me here? I can help," Hazel pleaded, leaning against the door.

Caleb continued playing, speeding up the melody. Hazel wondered if he'd started playing to hide their conversation from his family's enhanced ears.

"You've only been training a couple days," he tried, looking up at her. The tune never faltered, not even as he leaned back, gesturing for her to sit down.

Hazel looked up at him with wide, frustrated eyes, trailing over to him and slumping onto the chair with an empty breath. "You just expect me to sit here, twiddling my thumbs?"

Caleb grinned to himself, reaching for one of her hands and pulling it over to the keys. He carefully threaded his fingers through hers and guided her hand to play, focusing mostly on her thumb.

She gave him an unenthusiastic look, and he bit his lip with a chuckle, releasing her hand, but continuing to play.

"No, but I'm asking you to. Hopefully it won't come to a fight, but if they see you there, they might not hold back. It's just for now, until we know it's safe," he explained quietly, pausing the melody to give her a delicate look. "Give it a couple of hours, okay?" Caleb said, pivoting his body to face her. "These guys are dangerous. Plus, usually one of us stays behind anyway, in case we need backup later."

Hazel frowned again, letting her hand drop down onto the keys to play a sour note. "If you're gone more than two hours, I'm coming after you."

"Do I have to lock you in here?"

Hazel smirked at that. "It may not end well for you if you did."

He gave her a mischievous smile, playing a 'dun, dun, dun,' sound that made her laugh, before reaching out to grab a book from a shelf nearby.

It was sheet music for beginners. He opened it to the first page and laid it out on the piano's music rack. "Lock the doors."

Hazel nodded reluctantly, feeling her mouth go dry. "Don't die," she whispered playfully, but was sure Caleb would be able to hear the worry in her voice.

Caleb laughed, standing up. "Don't worry, I'm indestructible," he joked, before stepping out of the room.

"So, what's going on with you and Hazel? You like her?" Ophelia blurted out, watching her older brother suspiciously as she twirled blades around her fingertips. Their parents were ahead of them, glancing around the trees carefully.

Caleb stopped in his tracks. He'd been walking backwards,

whistling under his breath. "Huh? No, what are you on about?" he stuttered, frowning at her condescending look. "Nothing is going on between us, we're just friends… She could do with some good ones, seeing as she hasn't had much luck with them in the past."

She scoffed. "Is that supposed to be a dig at me? Oh, you are pathetic sometimes, it makes me sad."

They began to bicker, ignoring the shushing from their parents, until another voice crept around them.

"Your children have no respect, Mr Thorn," someone called out through the trees. Caleb couldn't tell where the voice was coming from, only that it was up ahead. The thick trail of nightshade in the air must have been messing with their senses.

"We're here to talk about the girl, about your accusations. We want to come to some sort of understanding, a peaceful one," Julianna said, stepping forward and standing tall. Her sharp eyes darted around the dark for danger.

A man stepped out of the shadows. He had the dusty, greying hair of a man beyond his years, years that had clearly not been kind to him.

"We don't tend to meet your kind like this – there's usually one of us covered in the other's blood – so excuse me if I take a little extra caution." He snaked around the trees, looking up every so often.

Caleb could sense them now, the snipers, armed with large metallic bows high up in the branches. He eyed them wearily.

"I'm Christopher," the man said, holding a hand out toward Caleb's father, completely brushing past his mother.

Alexander frowned over the top of his glasses and directed his hand toward his wife. "She's the one in charge. I just do whatever she asks."

Christopher pulled his hand back, frowning in judgement as Julianna stepped in front of her husband, subtly smiling at him before offering her hand out to the hunter. "We hope to keep this evening blood-free."

The man hummed as more hunters appeared on either side of him. Without looking at them, Christopher directed the hunters to the Thorns, twisting his lip. "Take their weapons."

Before Julianna could say anything, Caleb suddenly inched forward, slipping past his parents and holding out the vintage sword in his hand with a kind, and very forced, smile. "Well, these are actually a gift… for you."

A small whimper fell from Alexander's lips in the dead silence of the forest.

The Nosferatu Warrior held his hand up, stopping his hunters in their step as his face curled with curiosity. He stepped forward, snatching the sword from Caleb's hand, and making a point of slicing the sharp end against his cheek.

There was a stinging sensation left behind by the metal but Caleb didn't react to it, instead, he kept his head held high, staring at the hunter until Julianna tugged him backward.

"Nice. Decent weight to it, actually," Christopher remarked, turning the blade in his hands before using it to gesture toward the other weapons. "Take the rest of them."

Alexander wrinkled his face, gripping the gold-plated bow in his hand tighter until Julianna grabbed onto his shoulder. "Darling, just do it…"

A frown fell over Alexander's face, but he reluctantly handed over the weapon. "Careful with that!" he warned as one of the warriors flung the bow over her back carelessly and gave him a judgemental look. "It's an antique…"

Julianna gave him a soft expression, squeezing his shoulder, before jolting forward as a sparrow-faced woman yanked the quiver of arrows from her back. Alexander hissed, his teeth sharpening into points, but his wife gave him a pacifying look. She turned around and made a point of taking the quill off, then slammed them into the hunter's arms. The sparrow-faced woman quickly turned the bow around and placed one of the arrows into it, aiming it up at Julianna.

Ophelia growled from behind them and the woman spun around, ready to strike. Before either of them could, Caleb grabbed the hunting knives from his sister's hand and passed them to the hunter, watching her carefully.

"That's all of it."

Christopher smiled, clamping his hands together eagerly. "Great, who's up for a cuppa?"

Hazel was tired of the piano. It didn't sound the same when Caleb wasn't playing; she couldn't get the melody right. It wasn't the same as playing the guitar, and it filled her with an unreasonable rage each time she couldn't play a tune properly.

She slammed the book closed and sat up. It also stressed her out that she didn't have a phone on her. Since hers was broken, Hazel had been using Caleb's to sign into her social media accounts and check on Amber and her mother.

The urge to talk to her mum was overwhelming. She hadn't in so long, and she had so many questions. Did her mother know her father was a vampire? Nina had always said her father was demon-spawn. Did she mean that literally?

She hadn't eaten the packed lunch Julianna had prepared, so she decided to go find it.

Hazel stalked across the room and pulled the door open, peering into the empty hallway. It was eerily quiet without anyone here – creepy. Extremely creepy, she thought, when her eyes landed on the four-foot-tall stone woman standing guard in the hallway.

Besides the unsettling statue, there was something else off with the entranceway as well, something that took a moment for her to notice. When she did, her blood ran cold.

The door was wide open.

The Nosferatu Warrior camp centred around a clearing in the woods, not too far from the hill that led to a series of small, grassy cliffsides overlooking the town.

Four large cargo trucks acted as a gate around the main perimeter, shielding the tents inside. There was a makeshift medical tent in the far corner that was covered with a large sheer curtain. A man inside glared at Caleb, who waved at him before the curtain promptly slammed shut. Next-door was a shower block with portable toilets and a lingering smell.

Despite the questionable layout of the camp, Caleb quite liked the canteen. It was huge, it reminded him of a circus, with open curtains all around its empty plastic benches, so any insects or animals could waltz right in and steal the cold baked beans and fruit cans that were stacked up in the centre.

Caleb couldn't help but think it was all rather sad. It wasn't like a circus at all – except maybe for the clowns. Speaking of which…

His attention quickly snapped back to the camp leader, Christopher, who led them into the centre in front of an unlit fire pit. He motioned for them all to take a seat on the flimsy, dingy looking deck chairs they had lying around, but unsurprisingly, they each declined.

Christopher shrugged and took a seat, causing a layer of dust to float around him as he slumped down. Ophelia coughed, wafting the air.

"Sandy, light the fire for our guests," Christopher said, not taking his eerie eyes off of the Thorns.

A tall woman with a buzzcut wearing a sleeveless jacket stepped forward towards the firepit, eyeing Caleb and his family warily.

"That's okay, I'll do it," Julianna replied, turning to face the unlit fire. Suddenly, the flames came to life, creating shadows and patterns on everything they touched. The black mass waved forward, coating the side of Christopher's face in darkness as he thanked her in a flat voice.

"So, what brings you to us? The girl?" he asked, giving them a strange, unwelcoming smile as he picked up a broken bow from the floor and started to re-wrap its strings.

Caleb raised his hand in an attempted cheerful manner, giving his mother a reassuring look as he spoke. "Her name's Hazel. She's born, not bitten. We've been helping her adjust, and I give you my word, she is not a threat—"

The warrior leader tutted, interrupting him with a shake of his head. "*Your word* means nothing," he said, tightening the wire on the bow until it snapped.

The friendly expression on Caleb's face faltered at the sudden change in the man's demeanour. "What?"

"She is not part of your family. Are there any other known immortals sharing her blood?"

"Well, not exactly… But—"

"Then it is out of your hands. You can't just take in a rat from the street and decide to keep it. Go get a dog, lad, it'll be a lot less hassle."

Before he could stop himself, Caleb growled, the sound

low and gravelly in the back of his throat. A few warriors sat up from their chairs and armed themselves, but Christopher held them back with a raise of his hand, poising an almost delighted eyebrow.

Julianna sternly grabbed her son's shoulder and stepped in front of him.

A familiar tingle flared behind his irises, until Ophelia gave him a purposeful look. "Get it together, this was your plan," she muttered.

"Excuse my son," Julianna said.

With a long, frustrated breath, Caleb licked his tongue around his teeth and forced another polite smile, relaxing his shoulders.

"This is pointless," Christopher yawned, beckoning a few of his hunters to stand up. They staggered up from their deck chairs, leering dangerously.

Julianna cleared her throat. "You're right. We will be petitioning the Council. We might not be able to prove her status right this second, but we can be responsible for her until we can," she tried. "She has shown great control in only a matter of days, she can learn to be one of us. She's only just turned eighteen. Give her a chance."

The leader laughed, looking around at his group, who all began to join in stiffly until the humoured look suddenly disappeared from Christopher's face and he turned back to Julianna, expressionless. "In nature, no one gets a chance. If you are not willing to stand out of the way, then, by all means, give it your best shot."

Christopher put his arms out, gesturing for his followers to move forward. The hunters gripped their weapons, loading their bows with arrows and swiping at the air with daggers.

Julianna and Alexander nodded at each other and turned

towards their children. "Get ready to run," Julianna whispered, in a voice so small only those with enhanced hearing would hear.

In an instant, flames roared from the campfire, rising upwards and billowing around the hunters, blocking them behind a burning wall. Caleb glanced up as the smoke engulfed them, pulling Ophelia back from the heat that cut them off from the Nosferatu Warriors. Smoke billowed and sparks flew in different directions, some landing in Ophelia's hair, and she jolted back with a yelp, furiously brushing it out.

"Sorry," Alexander whispered. His focus was steady, not leaving the fire as it danced circles around the clearing, covering everything in its fiery wake.

The hunters retracted, leaving their chairs to burn as they rushed to safety. Some raised their weapons up at the fire, unsure what to do.

Christopher's eyes were strained, angry, as he surged towards the engulfing red glare, throwing a dagger through it with a frustrated roar. He stopped before the heat could grab him, but his blade shot through the air, nearly missing Alexander's forehead. "Get them!" he bellowed.

Most of the hunters gave the leader a perplexed expression. They were completely blocked off and would have to go through the fire to do as he was asking.

"Wait, where's Lucas?" Ophelia suddenly demanded, slipping out of Caleb's hold and shimmying between her parents.

The hunters ignored her, trying to find a way through the fire. Caleb watched as a tiny path arched through the labyrinth of flames, clearing a space in front of her and forcing them to look her way.

"Okay, blade boy, come out!" she yelled, crossing her arms

as the wind blew ash through the open space.

Julianna grumbled. "Ophelia!" she shouted, reaching for the girl, but she stalked forward, putting herself between the flames. They didn't touch her directly, despite the smell of smouldering bleach-blonde hair.

Alexander's expression became strained, focused on making sure the fire wouldn't hurt his daughter.

"Shouldn't he have a say in this?" Ophelia yelled, shielding her eyes from the glare. "Where are his parents? They should know that without her, he could have been killed! She helped him! What sort of bitten vampire would help a hunter?" She stepped forward again, narrowing her eyes. "Are you all so incompetent you can't figure this out for yourselves? You're all idiots!"

Amid Ophelia's raging outburst, someone ran up and grabbed her arm. It was the woman with the buzzcut. She hissed, pressing her blade against Ophelia's chest. "He doesn't have parents, kid. They're dead, like you."

Something faltered in Ophelia's face, her eyes unreadable as the hunter pulled back the dagger and brought it down with immense force.

As soon as he saw what was about to happen, Caleb drifted across the clearing, gripped Sandy's wrist, and shoved her backwards, pulling Ophelia through the withering flames, which rose at least another ten feet in height around them, coating the area like a maze.

The path Ophelia had created when she'd rushed forward remained partly clear, luring Nosferatu Warriors right into the blaze.

They couldn't see much through the fire, only the shadows of hunters trailing after them at every angle.

CHAPTER TWENTY-ONE

Déjà vu

The sound of arrows being fired in the near distance bargained with the flames. The blaze melted most of them, though some charred ones still found their way through.

Caleb ducked out of the way, pulling Ophelia down with him as one came barrelling straight for them. Another zipped past at such velocity it would have gone straight through him had he not twisted his body.

"Where's Lucas?" Ophelia exhaled, glancing out over the wall of fire.

Raising a hand over his eyes, Caleb jumped onto a bench, hopping across to a less severely scorched one to see over the flames. "I don't know."

"He's got to be here somewhere," Ophelia grumbled, before turning to glare in the other direction. "Here's your chance, Butter Knife! Come get me!"

"Lia," Caleb warned, twisting his eyebrows.

She snarled at him. "I know what you're thinking."

Caleb sighed. "I'm not thinking anything."

Ophelia huffed, her voice cracking as she kicked a loose tin can. "You're thinking this is my fault! That we could have got away, but then I had to open my big mouth and get us into trouble again."

"I'm not thinking that."

"No, you are. I know you are and I know Mum and Dad

will be, too. They'll give me that look, the same one they always give me."

"Lia," he breathed, lifting his hand from his eyes and freezing, though she didn't notice, too busy ranting.

"They always look at me like that, and—"

"Ophelia!" Caleb cried, his voice higher than before as he leaped from the bench.

"Oh, you know what!" she growled, her face seething as she spun at the sound of a harsh swoosh in the air.

"Frigging hell!" Caleb said, his voice filled with relief as he slunk down, sitting on the edge of the bench. There was an inky black arrow in Ophelia's palm, the sharp end of it inches away from piercing her stomach.

She stammered for an answer, staring down at the arrow she'd just caught, before dropping it with a wince. "We need to get out of here."

Caleb didn't argue. As they darted through the fire, he could just about see his parents a couple of yards away. His father was too focused on trying to keep the dark fire steady to notice them, but his mother was desperately staring into the blaze.

A red tinted arrow came barrelling out from the darkness and Julianna ducked out of the way, snarling. She pulled it from the tree it had landed in, and threw it back. After a few seconds, the trees stilled, and she turned around, brushing her hands together nonchalantly.

Alexander's face lit up when he caught sight of his children rushing towards them, and Caleb watched as Ophelia instantly moved to their father, who was leaning against a tree, looking a little worse for wear.

He stayed back, chewing his lip as he met his mother's unamused gaze.

As Caleb opened his mouth to speak, a whistle cut him off. He spun around and grunted, looking over at the hunters who were getting closer through the withering smoke. Lucas wasn't with them.

He wasn't here, and if he wasn't here…

A multitude of weapons started to fly. Arrows with purple-tinted ends barely missed them, axes and rusted hammers rushed past their heads. A dagger landed in the tree beside Alexander and he closed his eyes, cutting off the flames completely.

"Caleb!" Julianna yelled. "We have to go, now!"

His father was panting, crouching down while Ophelia patted his back. Julianna stood in front of them, a strange sort of desperation in her eyes.

"Caleb!"

He glanced over at his family and cursed under his breath, one woman had a sword aimed right up at his mother's head, yelling at her, though her glare remained vigorous. They were circling them, herding them into the centre like wild animals. Caleb peered up, locking eyes with Christopher, who had stepped out from the crowd with two hunters by his side.

Caleb gritted his now pointed teeth. "Where's Lucas?" he asked.

In response, one of the hunters raised an axe. As he came rushing forward, Caleb caught the hilt of the weapon, stopping it before it could come down. He pushed the hunter backwards, using the force of the swing to send him tumbling off to the side, only for the other guy to then block his path.

"Well, he's not here!" Christopher laughed, watching the scene unfold from where he stood. "I'll let you put two and two together."

"He's gone after her," Caleb said, looking up with a

strained expression. He pushed forward, but the other hunter stood in his way. "Hasn't he?"

The warrior leader did nothing but smirk.

As he stared incredulously, the hunter beside him plunged a dagger forward. Caleb ducked and grabbed the man's shoulder, shoving him away, but not before receiving a whack to the face with the back end of the dagger.

"Don't matter. Either way, she'll be dead before you can do anything," the man hummed, before instant regret filled his features as he looked up into Caleb's glowing red eyes.

Caleb grabbed the hunter and thrust him into a nearby tree, holding him in place with one arm as he pivoted around to face the few dozen warriors rounding up behind him.

"Don't let their weapons slice you. They're covered in nightshade!" Ophelia yelled out as she jumped on the back of one of them, flipping them to the ground. She stood up and turned around, narrowing her eyes as a dipped arrow flew towards her father. With a furious grunt, Ophelia leaped forward and caught it, snapping it in half and pulling a face at the burning sensation on her fingertips.

Alexander drifted past her with a thankful smile. He looked tired, it would have taken a lot of focus to maintain the extent of flames, but nevertheless, he grabbed two warriors that were moving for Caleb and held them up by their necks.

There were two more on the opposite side, bows aimed up at Caleb as he flipped another warrior onto their back, pressing down on the man's chest with the flat of his palm. Caleb snapped his head up at the sound of bow strings being pulled, but before any arrows could fly, Ophelia barrelled into the warriors holding them.

One of the hunters she'd knocked over grabbed an arrow from the ground. He pivoted around to aim it, but the blonde was too fast, slamming down on his arm with her heeled boot. The other one, a short, narrow-nosed girl, grabbed a dagger from a pouch on her stomach and moved towards Ophelia, grunting ferociously.

Another hunter raised a metal pole in the air, spinning it in his hands before running at Caleb, who kicked at the man and yanked the pole from his hands. Turning, Caleb threw the pole towards the narrow-nosed warrior, knocking her balance before she could reach his sister.

He glanced up then, looking for his mother. She seemed to be scanning the area. The Nosferatu Warrior leader had miraculously disappeared. "Mum!" he called, catching her attention as a dagger was thrown her way.

She swiftly dodged the attack and leapt at whoever had thrown it.

Her heart in her throat, Hazel turned and made for the stairs and the safety of her room, but before she even took one step, someone grabbed her from behind.

Hazel swung an elbow carelessly, and the figure staggered backwards. She twirled around to see Lucas snarling up at her.

Before she could even attempt to drift away, he pulled hard on her arm, forcing her back into him and grabbing her neck. His muscular arms barely tensed as she clawed at them, trying to pull them away from her throat until she felt icy metal pressing against her skin.

"Move, and we'll see if you can heal without a head," Lucas hissed.

Hazel went limp. Lucas didn't sound like he was exaggerating.

"Don't fight it. I have to kill you. I don't have a choice. You'll hurt people, even if you don't want to, it's just who you are now," he continued, almost sounding regretful.

"Lucas! Please!"

"You may not be yet, but soon you'll be out of control. It's inevitable, and you're not the first bitten to be good at mind games, so I'm not going to fall for any more tricks."

"You don't have to do this," she pleaded, her voice straining from the pressure on her vocal cords.

Lucas brought the knife closer to her throat, and the sensation stung her skin. "Yes I do. It's my job. I have to kill you… and them. Amber, too, if she isn't already dead. Is she here somewhere? In transition?"

Hazel gulped, her eyes were stinging, either from the nightshade or the intimate fear of death. "Amber isn't involved in any of this, don't hurt her, please. I'm not like the other ones, I was born, not bitten."

Lucas didn't budge, but she could hear his heartbeat thudding faster against his chest.

"You think I'm lying? I understand that. People are scum, I know that better than anyone. They lie, cheat, but I'm not…" Hazel breathed, her voice hoarse, cutting out before she could finish her sentence.

"You're not a person," Lucas replied in a harsh breath.

Hazel scrunched up her features. "Well, I mean, I am…"

He shook his head. "No, you're something else."

"I'm still a person!" she complained.

"No, you're not!"

"If I wasn't, I wouldn't be standing here, would I? I wouldn't be talking to you, trying to get you to listen to me. I wouldn't be feeling this bloody knife pressed against my throat," she croaked. "I'm a *person*, I may be a little different now, but I'm still me!"

Lucas closed his eyes, his hands were trembling slightly, but the weapon stayed attached to her throat. "Shut up! This whole conversation is ridiculous. I know you're just trying to distract me."

Hazel flinched as the hunter pressed his blade into her throat harder, his hands stiffening yet again. She let out a yelp as the dagger began to pierce her skin, then panicked, glancing around the hallway. The stone statue was staring right at her, her smiling face almost mocking. Hazel frowned and let out a whimper, tilting her head until her gaze fell onto the statue's bony finger, still pointing toward the open front door and the leaves sitting on the carpet.

Hazel stared at the leaves, breathing in slowly. If there was time for self-doubt, it wasn't now. Caleb hadn't shown her how to do this, but she'd watched him do it. She focused on the leaves, imagining them starting to burn, picturing smoke rising from them and building into thick, raging flames.

The leaves blew into the hallway, the wind moving them in waves as they covered the ground. A faint iridescent sage colour wormed its way through them like veins on the marbled flooring, but there were still no flames.

Hazel closed her eyes with a grunt and slammed her head back in frustration, unintentionally ramming it into Lucas's nose.

He winced and toppled backwards, fumbling with his balance for a second, before slipping on the pile of leaves and losing his footing.

Hazel didn't waste another second. She dashed up the stairs, staggering into the closest room she could find.

There was a giant bathtub sitting on a fluffy white mat in the centre of the room. On either side of it sat two potted palm trees that were so big they almost blocked the huge open window behind them. Hazel rushed toward it, looking down into the dark green and red rose bushes below. She delved into the possibility of the bush being full of thorns – given the fact she was at the Thorn residence and they were a family that clearly prided themselves on name play – but she'd rather take her chances out there in the dark, unpredictable forest than here with the maniac from her nightmares. Closing her eyes, she sucked in a breath and pushed off from the ledge.

She'd expected the jump to hurt, or at least sting a little, but surprisingly, she landed crouched on her feet like a cat. After picking rose petals and a few stinging thorns from her jeans, she stood up and turned the corner towards the driveway, hoping to find the gate open.

Instead, she found Lucas, standing in front of her with his hood covering his face and the moonlight glimmering off his vine-covered dagger. The manor stood stiff and stalwart behind him, its extravagant lighting illuminating his figure in the darkness. It was like she was in one of her dreams.

Hazel started to pace backwards, not liking the image in front of her or the unforgiving look on the boy's face.

This could only go one of two ways.

CHAPTER TWENTY-TWO

Unakite

The Nosferatu warriors started to surround the Thorns, separating them.

Ophelia darted through the gaps of hunters, looking for her family, but pinpointing them through the crowd was getting harder.

Someone grabbed her. It was an older woman with pale grey hair and a sharp-tipped spear. She had lines under her eyes and her fingers shook slightly with age. Ophelia pulled back, holding her arms up reluctantly. She was a bitch when she wanted to be, but this was a frail old lady – she wasn't entirely heartless.

As she let down her guard, the woman's fingers stopped shaking and she smiled. In one quick motion, she flung the spear down.

Ophelia hit the ground with a harsh thud and clutched her waist, looking down to see a bloodied gash seeping through her white jumper. Her eyes widened with rage, and she looked up at the elderly lady, gritting her teeth. "This is premium wool!"

She was met with a breathy cackle and the sound of metal swiping through the air. This time the woman was aiming for her head. She rolled out of the way just in time for the spear to come back down and hit her in the ankle. Ophelia yelped and yanked at the weapon, it toppled to the floor with a clang, and she kicked it out of the woman's reach.

The hunter grimaced, reaching for something on her belt, but was knocked down from behind before she could get it.

"Don't you dare touch my daughter," Julianna hissed, yanking the blade from the woman's hand.

She stepped over the hunter, helping Ophelia to her feet and inspecting the partially healing wound on the curve of her waist. Ophelia could feel it throbbing, the blood was sticking to her jumper, making her wince when her mother pulled the material up.

Julianna's head pivoted in the hunter's direction, sneering before pulling her daughter towards the blanket of trees. "It wasn't laced with nightshade, so you'll be okay," she said, once sure of their safety. Her voice was gentler now as she gazed over the wound again. "Does it hurt much?"

Ophelia peered at her wound with a shake of her head, avoiding her mother's gaze. She was still half expecting to be scolded for her little outburst earlier.

"Can we get out of here now? We need to get back to the manor."

Her mother nodded, glancing over her shoulder to peer at their surroundings.

"Where's Dad? Caleb?" Ophelia asked, placing a hand over her bloodied waist and pulling at the material to stop it from stinging. As she let out a wince, Julianna's head snapped in her direction and she reached down to tie the top of the jumper together so it wouldn't stick to the wound.

"I don't know…"

Suddenly, the sound of struggling brought their attention to the treeline ahead. Ophelia moved forward, following the noise, and gasped when she saw what was unfolding in front of her.

Just ahead, her father was throwing a hunter backwards, while another crept up behind him with an axe.

Without hesitation, Julianna shot forward and jumped on the woman, yanking the axe from her hand. It fell, and the hunter reached for it, but Julianna caught it first, swiping the weapon from the air and using its handle to win the fight. She drew back with a restless breath and dropped the axe, glancing at her husband.

Alexander was watching her with an amazed expression, his lips peeking up at the corners as he elbowed his other attacker in the neck. "You've always been the jealous type," he quipped, his dopey smile creasing his eyes as he stepped toward her.

Julianna met him with a huff, but her face softened as he reached for her, kissing her lips.

Ophelia gagged and glanced away from them, searching around the small clearing for her brother.

Caleb knocked a hunter against a tree as the whoosh of an arrow swung over his head.

He turned around and drifted forward, flinging his right fist into the stomach of the person who had shot it, and their bow fell to the floor. Two more hunters ran for him, but Caleb sped out of sight. The Nosferatu Warriors peered at each other, panning around the now-empty space before Caleb reappeared beside one of the trees, leaning against it with a teasing grin.

One of the men dashed forward, dagger aimed, only for the light-haired boy to grab it by the hilt. He threw it somewhere behind himself then gripped the hunter by the shoulder and pushed him into the man behind.

After waiting for them to fall, Caleb bent down to pick up the dropped bow. At the sound of crunching leaves, his head snapped up, aiming the bow up at a girl who was watching him.

She was around his age, with long auburn hair that was braided into two plaits and decorated with beads and multicoloured flowers. No weapon was in her hand, which was odd, given the circumstances.

Slowly, the girl raised her hands in a calm, almost whimsical manner, and smiled sweetly at Caleb, who raised an eyebrow. "I've heard you were looking for Lucas?"

Her voice was curious, there was no malice or warning in her tone, but there was an accent, one Caleb couldn't quite place. Northern, perhaps.

"I can help you, as long as you don't hurt him," she continued, lowering her hands but keeping them visible.

Caleb narrowed his eyes. She was clearly different from the other hunters. "If he doesn't hurt Hazel, I won't hurt him," he replied, letting the bow drop to his side.

The girl nodded, gesturing for him to follow her through the trees.

It was thick with smoke in the woods, but the flames had stopped. It didn't linger like normal flames, it didn't spread. If you could control it, dark fire could be contained as easily as running water. When you were done with it, you just turned off the *tap*.

If Caleb were less trusting, he'd have probably thought the girl was tricking him into some sort of trap, but something about the genuine concern on her face when she'd mentioned Lucas's name kept him striving forward. They both had someone they wanted to protect, to fight for, and he admired that.

Once they reached the outskirts of the camp the girl motioned for him to stay back while she crept out of the tree line.

Caleb rolled back on his heels, fidgeting with a loose branch on a tree. The wind rustled over his shoulders as he waited. He often missed the feeling of it, or more what came after it: warming his hands at the fireplace while his mother wrapped him and his sisters in a fluffy blanket, their father bringing them some almost scorching soup to warm them up.

It was a weird thing to miss, the cold, but it was mundane and ordinary, and Caleb couldn't help but feel nostalgic about it. Maybe it was more the memories he missed rather than the cold itself, but he still felt the longing in his chest.

As his thoughts trailed off, his senses awakened, bringing him out of his daze in the form of a burly stranger who had appeared from somewhere in the mist.

The bearded man grumbled unpleasantly and launched forward, grabbing onto the worn silver bow as they both tumbled to the ground.

He pushed on Caleb's shoulders with one hand, grabbing onto the weapon's hilt with the other. Instead of trying to pull it away, Caleb clutched the bow and pushed upwards, whacking the hunter in the face.

He stumbled back, falling into a thick patch of mud with a grunt.

Even with the limp from landing on his ankle, when he stood again, he was double the size of Caleb, towering over him. His face was angrier now too, especially with the bloodied cut on his cheek from where he'd been whacked with the bow.

Caleb brushed a hand through the back of his hair, which was coated in mud. He grimaced at the dirt, shaking his head like a dog to get rid of it.

"Oh, sorry, mate. You got a bit, just there," he said playfully, motioning to the mud that had splattered on the hunter's face.

That was enough for the man to lose it. With a growl he shot forward, only to be struck down by something long and sturdy.

Caleb peered up to see the auburn-haired hunter standing above the bearded man with a long metallic spear.

She met his gaze and shrugged her shoulders, placing the spear back into the ground and leaning over it. "Pete's an arse, stole my bag of granola bars and lied about it, been wanting to do that for a while."

"Screw Pete, I guess," Caleb laughed.

She led him into one of the tents, which was actually more reasonably sized inside than he'd expected, though he still had to duck on the way in. There were two camp beds on opposing sides of the tent, one was covered in books, all neatly piled in a corner, while the other was cluttered with gemstones. Caleb furrowed his brow and picked one up, turning it in his hand as the girl pulled the tent shut behind her.

"Ah, lapis lazuli," she said, pointing to the little blue gem. "Funny you picked that one up."

Caleb watched her as she slumped down onto one of the beds, picking up a drawing of a toad in an umbrella hat. He'd have chuckled at that if he weren't still slightly on edge.

"Um, why?" He blinked at her, placing the gem back

down with a cautious expression and wiping his hands on his dirty jeans.

The ginger girl laughed. "It's good, don't worry. Lapis lazuli is the universal symbol for truth and wisdom. You picking that up tells me a multitude of things: you're honest, for one, open to communication even in the face of conflict, and you have some information to share, hopefully for the benefit of us both," she explained, sitting cross-legged. "Or you just like the colour blue."

Caleb laughed then, leaning against a bedside table. "Is Lucas here?" he asked, glancing around the tent. "I mean, he's quite short, so it wouldn't surprise me if he just happened to pop out from somewhere, but I'm pretty sure there would be a knife in my back by now. Is he in one of the other tents?"

Caleb watched the girl move to the table next to him apprehensively, tightening the grip on the bow in his hand, but he released it when she reached for another crystal, one from a different trinket box. This gem was green with tiny orange specs, the colour of guacamole.

"Unakite." She smiled, offering it out to him. With an unsure look, Caleb opened his palm, letting her drop the gem into it. She placed her hands over his and wrapped it around the stone, giving him a gentle look. "For resolving conflict, it's the stone of balance."

Caleb exhaled slowly, letting the bow fall from his shoulder. He placed it against the table and looked up with a smile, one that she returned.

"I'm Farah, Lucas's friend."

A small, amused noise fell through Caleb's lips at the word 'friend'. He was convinced Lucas didn't have any of those.

"I'm Caleb. Why are you helping me?"

"Because I believe you, Caleb. I don't think your friend is

a threat, neither do I think you or your family are," she said, shrugging her shoulders. There was a gem around her neck, a bright purple pyramid-shaped crystal. Her fingers trailed up to it as she spoke.

"Then why don't your cultish friends out there think the same?"

The girl shrugged her shoulders. "Lucas told them otherwise."

Caleb's eyebrows furrowed, and he placed the gem back on the table. "That little brat," he spat. "You know Hazel helped him, right? She saved him, they fought the bitten off together. A bitten vampire, a *dangerous* vampire, wouldn't help a human, never mind a Nosferatu Warrior."

Farah nodded in agreement, looking a little downhearted that he'd put down the unakite. "I know. He told me his version of the story, and I called him out on it immediately, but he wouldn't see reason. He was brought here when he was only a baby. He's been raised to think your kind are the enemy, all of your kind, not just the… unsociable ones." She sighed. "He's a little bit brainwashed, you see, but he's a good guy, honest. I've been trying to talk sense into him, but he's stubborn, too, and doesn't like being told anything."

"Why aren't you brainwashed?" Caleb asked, almost suspicious despite the slightly amused expression on his face.

Farah laughed a little in return. "I haven't been here as long as Lucas has. I was with another group. We worked with your kind. I had friends, a girlfriend, that were born vampires, but there was a raid from a small army of bitten. She saved me and brought me here, and, um… the details aren't important right now. Look, I think you could reach Lucas, show him that you're not a threat."

She patted the empty space beside her. Caleb sighed and

wandered over, sitting down as Farah reached for a book on the pillow.

"He writes down everything, always has… he's a little… paranoid."

"A little?" Caleb mused, watching as Farah opened a notebook and laid it on her lap.

She smiled at him tenderly. "But you can tell from his words that he knows deep down, *very* deep down, that you guys aren't a threat."

Caleb gave her a sceptical look as she handed over the book. He glanced down at it cautiously, biting the corner of his lip.

The newest entry was about Ophelia. At first glance, it was a warning profile, studying her flaws and fighting techniques, but below that were more thorough observations. Lucas thought she had a sweet voice for an evil bloodsucker and suggested it was a technique used to lure men to their deaths, like a siren. He had noted down little quips and jokes Ophelia had made during their interactions in the club, marking it as a defensive technique. However, it was obvious he'd found Ophelia intriguing and wanted to know more about her. He used the word *fascinating*.

"He's a good guy. He just needs a little guidance. He thinks what he's doing is right. He doesn't understand that he's wrong yet, but he will," Farah said quietly.

Caleb let out a breath and closed the book. "We don't have time for him to battle his own moral compass. Hazel's alone, and he's after her, isn't he? Like that lunatic hinted. He isn't here?"

She shook her head guiltily, and he cursed under his breath, standing up from the bed and brushing a hand through his blonde hair.

"Does he know where the manor is?"

The redhead frowned, avoiding the question, and reached for the book that had fallen from Caleb's lap. "We can convince him, if he sees you guys aren't the bad ones, then—"

"How are we supposed to convince him? He's out there trying to kill her. Look, I appreciate that you don't want to murder me, it's really nice, actually, but I have to go."

Farah closed the notebook and held it flat against her chest, following as he started to leave. "Caleb, if we don't figure out a way to work together, where does it end? When we're all dead? How many times do we have to go back and forth, turning on each other, when the real enemy is out there poisoning all their minds… Chris, he's the evil one here, not Lucas."

Sighing, Caleb spun around to face her. "I agree. That's the reason I came here in the first place, but—"

His words fizzled out as his gaze landed on the notebook, or more specifically, the name on the front of it. It was Lucas's, of course, written in his own cursive handwriting. Caleb read the name, then read it again, and his eyes nearly popped out of his head in shock as he stared at the words.

Lucas Valdez.

Caleb and Farah looked over the rest of Lucas's books, trying to piece everything together, until Caleb's back suddenly stiffened and he stood up, peering at the doorway.

Farah followed his gaze. She stalked toward the tent door, reaching for her spear as Caleb twisted his head, sniffing the air.

"Wait, it's just my—" he began to say, but the words went

unheard as Ophelia pounced through the door and jumped onto the redhead's shoulders.

They wrestled for a second, tumbling to the ground before the ginger girl quickly rolled out of the vampire's grasp and hopped onto her knees. She held a hand out. "I'm not a threat."

Ophelia hissed, glaring up with red eyes. "I'll decide that for myself."

She shot forward, teeth bared, but Caleb grabbed onto her, holding her back as he stepped between them both.

"Seriously? I came to save you. Now you're standing with the enemy?" Ophelia yelled, motioning to Farah, who lit up a lilac floral incense stick, wafting it around the tent and filling it with the scent of lavender.

"This should calm her down," she murmured.

Ophelia widened her eyes murderously and glared at her brother.

"Farah's helping us!" Caleb tried, but she just scoffed loudly in response.

"Oh, now it has a name!"

He groaned and shoved the notebook into her arms, causing her to huff dramatically until he sighed and pointed to the cover. "Valdez is Ha–"

"Hazel's father's surname," she interrupted. He gave her a bewildered look. Ophelia shrugged. "I remember her telling me when we were younger, but that doesn't mean anything. Weird coincidence, yes, but…"

Caleb grabbed the book from her and placed it on the bed with the rest of the notebooks, all with the same surname plastered over them. "Think about it, they have the same eyes, same hair colour, same stubbornness."

"Again, doesn't mean anything. You and I haven't got the

same hair colour, and we are *actually* related, unfortunately."

"Same eyes, though," Caleb added, pointing a finger between them. Ophelia scoffed, rolling her eyes as he continued. "And if you didn't drown your hair in bleach all the time, it would be practically the same shade."

"Oh, I'll drown you in bleach."

They started to bicker, almost forgetting where they were. "You guys have quite the resemblance, actually, from an outsider's point of view. Same cheekbones, same *act first, think later* mindset." Farah commented, raising a hand to get their attention. They both turned to her with a dubious look, and she let her hand fall down with a light chuckle. "Besides, apart from the obvious, there's more. They're the same age."

Ophelia folded her arms over her stomach. "So?"

"They were both born on the fourteenth of October, same year, same birthday, same last name," Caleb said.

Farah smiled and stepped closer but Ophelia straightened her back defensively. The redhead sighed and took out a dagger from her sleeve, offering it out. "Take it."

Ophelia reluctantly reached for the blade, eyeing the girl warily.

"Lucas was brought here when he was a baby, the same time Hazel's father left, by the sound of it," she explained, gesturing to Caleb, who nodded. Farah looked back at Ophelia and gave her a hopeful look. "I know this sounds crazy, but we're pretty certain. See, Lucas has this photograph of himself as a baby with his mother, and the photo has his father's name written on the back."

Ophelia let out a breath. "Alden Valdez?"

At the name, Farah and Caleb glanced at each other excitedly.

"We need to tell him," Farah said. "If Lucas knows Hazel's

his sister, he'll stop all of this, I know it."

Caleb nodded. "If we can get them both back here, get that photograph from Lucas, then maybe we can prove that Hazel's not bitten. If we can prove they're related, then we can test his blood and we'll be able to tell if he carries the gene."

With a grin, Farah stood up, grabbing something from one of the bedside tables. She placed it in Caleb's palm, and he looked down, wrapping his hand around the unakite.

"That's a rock," Ophelia said, bringing both of their attention toward her as she stared at them with a bewildered look. "An ugly one at that. You two are insane."

Farah frowned a little at the insult but Caleb smiled at her, clutching the stone between his fingers. Across the room, Ophelia rolled her head back onto her shoulders.

"Okay, fine. Say they are related. That still doesn't help the fact that he's off trying to murder her with the better end of a butter knife, and we're stuck here trying not to get killed! How are we getting out there?"

Farah squeezed Caleb's shoulder, giving him a crafty look. "I can get us out. I sneak out of this place all the time."

"Okay, but I'm not listening to you two giggling like schoolgirls the whole way," Ophelia said boredly, moving toward the door.

She pulled back the curtain to reveal a group of hunters, five young hunters to be exact, standing on the other side and waiting for them to come out.

Ophelia froze, slowly closing the curtain and turning to face her brother with a frenzied look.

CHAPTER TWENTY-THREE

Parallel Lines

"Lucas, listen to me," Hazel begged, raising her arms, "I'm not going to hurt anyone. I'd never hurt anyone. I wouldn't even hurt you, not purposely."

"What, and I'm just supposed to take your word for it?" Lucas raised the dagger, pointing it at her from across the driveway as he started to snake closer. "There's no other way. Are you going to fight or are you going to run? Make your mind up. I've not got all day."

"There's always another way," Hazel replied, gulping as Lucas shook his head, his eyes growing dark under the shelter of the manor.

He sprung forwards, aiming the blade right for her, and she yelped, pivoting out of the way just in time. It lodged in the arm of her leather jacket. She pulled it out and stared at the blade in shock.

The mirror image of her dream filled her with dread, and almost instinctively, Hazel threw the dagger behind her, into the forest.

Lucas pulled a face, wrinkling his nose in judgement. "Really?" he spat.

"I didn't even mean to do that. It was just instinct… I—"

"Are you being serious? Oh my god."

"I don't know what I'm doing," Hazel winced, almost tripping over as she back-stepped closer to the forest. Lucas followed closely.

"Clearly," he mumbled, reaching down to pick up his dagger from the ground.

Hazel bumped into a tree, gripping onto the branches with a restless breath as she struggled to slow down the rapid beating of her heart. "I can't even run like them, I'm not... I didn't choose this, Lucas... I don't want this!"

He flicked the handle of his blade into the air before twisting it and flinging it straight at her. It landed in the wood above her head, forcing her to duck.

Hazel opened her eyes again and Lucas was right in front of her. She attempted to drift but it didn't work. He grabbed her arm and swung her into a different tree, bashing her head hard.

She groaned, reaching up to cradle her skull, but there wasn't enough time to dwell on it. Lucas ripped the dagger from the tree and jabbed it in her direction. From this angle, Hazel could see the moon's reflection in the blade. Its pointed end was pushing against her chest, not yet piercing skin, but even through her jacket, she could feel a burning sensation, sending a hot, sickly feeling into her stomach.

"You've really got nothing else to say? Nothing at all?" he asked.

Hazel didn't reply, instead, she looked up, studying his face. There had to be a chance he wouldn't go through with killing her, he let her save Amber, they'd worked together to fight off the bitten. He was a protector, a hunter, surely, he could distinguish the bad vampires from the good.

Something was flickering in his temperamental gaze, a silent debate, a short burst of reluctance before he pushed the blade closer, cutting another hole into her jacket.

Or maybe he would go through with it.

He wasn't just going to stop with her, Hazel thought. No, he'd already said the Thorns were next, whether they were guilty or not. Caleb was strong, and definitely skilled, but he was also kind. Would he take down Lucas if he had to? If the hunter threatened his family, maybe, but what if he got to Caleb alone first? He'd try to find another way, and Lucas would take advantage of that.

There was no doubt in Hazel's mind that Ophelia would take Lucas down if she wanted to, but if he'd got to Caleb first… if her brother were… She'd be broken. She wouldn't be thinking properly. He could easily get the upper hand.

Would Julianna and Alexander even try to fight if their children had been taken down? As cold as Julianna could be, it was painfully clear that her children were everything to her, her husband, too, and Hazel was sure Alexander would never outright harm anyone, whether Lucas was a killer or not.

Then it would be Amber's turn. Hazel didn't even want to think about how easy it would be for Lucas to get to her friend. She wouldn't even see it coming.

It wasn't fair, it wasn't their fight. None of them should be at risk because of her, because she'd somehow managed to bring her nightmares to life.

Hazel thought for a moment. Her dream had two parts, and she wasn't the only one who could lose. She'd never thought of herself as capable of anything so violent, but if Lucas wasn't going to back down, why should she?

"No?" Lucas sighed, tightening his hold on the dagger as his expression strained. "Okay, then, say hi to the devil for me." It seemed like a joke, but there was no humour in his words. He pulled the blade back, working up momentum, and Hazel took the opportunity. She sucked in a breath and struck the hunter, kneeing him in the stomach at full pelt.

Lucas grunted and stumbled backwards, holding his stomach.

Hazel staggered away, letting her now ripped jacket fall from her shoulders. She frowned at the shredded material and fixed the sleeves of her maroon hoodie. "Don't tell me he's real, too."

Lucas pulled a face, straightening his back as his grip found his dagger again. He shot forward, swiping with his left hand. Hazel ducked, grabbing his shoulder from behind and pushing him away, using strength she hadn't realised she had. She glanced down at her hands in awe as Lucas tumbled forwards, then looked back up at him, dark red eyes gleaming under the moonlight.

A dagger slashed through the tent fabric, cutting it in half, and Ophelia jumped back to avoid being punctured.

The wind blew the tent the rest of the way open, and one of the closer hunters, a handsome but arrogant-looking boy with a bandage around his neck grabbed onto her wrists, twirling her around and holding her against his chest.

Caleb's eyes lit up crimson red in response, and he took a step towards the group with bared teeth.

The bandaged hunter held him back, twisting Ophelia to the side to show the short, purple-tipped sword resting against her skin. "Stay where you are," the hunter warned, letting the blade trickle down the side of Ophelia's body. She hissed, but he shushed her, peering up at Caleb with an expectant look.

He bit back a growl, but it was Farah who reacted first. She picked up the staff leaning against her bed and struck out with the hilt of it, whacking the hunter across the hand and releasing Ophelia.

The others turned to give her a series of treacherous looks as Caleb pulled Ophelia behind him, standing in front of her while she rolled her eyes and shoved him away.

"You're siding with them?" a wild-eyed girl hissed, gripping a hammer. She was fiery, buzzing with energy as she stood in front of a younger teenage boy who looked like he didn't want to be there.

"I'm siding with the ones who don't want anyone to die," Farah replied, twisting the pointed end of the spear towards them.

"They're vampires... disgusting, blood-sucking monsters," a darker-haired girl with piercings in her nose and eyebrows snarled.

"Vampires, yes. Monsters, no," Farah replied calmly.

The oldest looking of the group, the one who'd initially grabbed Ophelia, shook his head. "She's off in fantasy land again. Grab her before she gets herself killed, too."

"Jamie," Farah began, eyeing him precariously before letting out a shallow breath at the hardened look on his face. "You can learn to get along with them, all of you. I'll teach you."

"Oh, shut it, Hippy," Jamie spat, wrapping his hands around his sword.

Two warriors moved to grab Farah, but she knocked them back with the edge of her spear, twirling it around skilfully.

Caleb swiftly ducked under the metal pole and pushed back a boy whose bow was tipped up at Farah. He gripped the bow and swung to the side, smiling roguishly at the sound of string snapping. The hunter swallowed nervously and pushed forward, pinning him up against a makeshift plastic wardrobe. He pushed at Caleb's shoulders, struggling to hold him down until the sound of a pained gasp made him turn his head. Ophelia had kicked one of the hunters in the stomach with the heel of her boot.

The hunter kept his attention on the other two and Caleb chuckled under his breath. "You like her, don't you?" he whispered, and the hunter whipped his head back with wide eyes. He shook his head briskly, and Caleb smiled, glancing at the dark-haired girl. She was slashing a dagger at Ophelia now, moving forward with deadly precision as the blonde dodged every hit.

"You should take your chance. Here, I'll even let you get one swing in, make you look all powerful and that. She'll be drawn to you, then, I promise," Caleb said, winking.

The guy scrunched his face eagerly, before balling his fist. He aimed for Caleb's perfect teeth, but Caleb used that to his advantage, dodging the blow and letting his swing break through the plastic doors of the cabinet.

"Sorry about that. In all honesty, just talk to her, mate. Be open with her. I'm sure it'll all work out."

The hunter tried to pull his hand free from the splintering wardrobe, but it was stuck. "You think?"

"Yeah, definitely." Caleb ducked under his arm, shoving the hunter into the broken frame. "Sorry about that, too, you seem like a nice bloke."

He watched as Ophelia stuck her leg out and tripped the snarky-looking girl over. The hunter crumpled to the floor and Ophelia stepped over her with a disgusted snarl, only to be grabbed by the leg. She hit the ground with a thud and peered over, watching as the hunter girl smirked down at her.

She rolled her body to avoid the blade crashing towards her before diving forward and knocking the weapon from the warrior's hand, kneeing her in the forehead as she did so.

Caleb held his hand out, helping Ophelia up and then glanced around the tent.

The hammer-wielding hunter was lying on one of the beds, unconscious – she'd lunged for Farah and found herself meeting the dull end of a staff. So now there was just one hunter standing in their way: the one Farah called Jamie. He gave the youngest hunter, who really wasn't a threat to anyone, a nod to stay back, then raised his sword, aiming it at Caleb.

Caleb smirked and pivoted to the side, dodging the weapon swiftly. "Almost," he taunted, with a toothy grin.

The hunter grumbled and dived forward, wrestling the vampire to the ground.

They hit the floor, Caleb pushing up against Jamie as the hunter tilted his blade down, forcing the pointed end across the ground. It cut through the floor of the tent, carving a line in the mud before narrowly missing Caleb's neck as he twisted, flipping the hunter onto his back, winding him.

The sword dropped from Jamie's hand, and he covered his eyes, a low whine coming from his throat.

Caleb knitted his brows together, frowning, as he sat back on his knees to catch a breath.

After a second, the hunter reluctantly removed his hands from his eyes and peered up expectantly. "Are you not gonna…?"

A look of perplexity and mild horror took over Caleb's features as he staggered to his feet and offered his hand out to the boy, shaking his head. "Course not, mate. You just stood in our way, got places to be, you know?"

Jamie stared at the vampire's hand, flabbergasted. His attention flickered over to Farah, who was placing pillows under the other unconscious hunters' heads.

Ophelia moved over to the slashed open doorway and

peered around it. "Caleb, I can hear more of them coming."

Caleb bit his lip and sighed, still holding his hand out to the hunter with a gentle smile. "We're just trying to get back home and save our friend. I came here to talk, not to fight."

The hunter boy peered up at Farah again, furrowing his brow, and she smiled calmly. "Chris turned this into a fight, not them."

Jamie looked down, his eyebrows knitted in deep thought. "He wanted us to go into the fire. He pushed Liam… the kid's only thirteen, and Chris yelled like he didn't care if he got burned. Liam almost went, too, if it weren't for Claudia and Miles pulling him back, then…" His gaze snaked around the room, over his friends' sleeping figures, no real injuries covered them, only a few scrapes and bruises. The young boy in question, Liam, was looking down, fumbling with his partially burned fingertips as Farah wrapped a blanket around him.

Jamie sighed. "In the Barracks, before I came here, before Chris, the trainers said we'd come across good and bad ones, and that we had to decipher between them because the good ones would help if we asked." He looked back up at Caleb, studying him sceptically before accepting his hand and letting the vampire pull him up.

Caleb grabbed his shoulder, steadying him, and then smiled warmly. "We would."

Jamie nodded, letting out a debated hum as he looked over at Farah.

"Okay… fine, get them out of here."

Hazel ducked as Lucas threw another dagger, which flew past her. He grunted in frustration as he moved across and pulled it from the tree it had landed in.

Once his blade was free, he began to circle Hazel again, swiping the dagger with a smooth flick of his fingers. She sighed and mirrored his movements, letting out a tired breath. For an allegedly skilled hunter, he was missing more times than he was used to.

"Oh, am I boring you?" Lucas scoffed, pouncing forward. He went for her ankles, pushing his foot out to knock her off balance, but as the air moved around them, her fist came up instinctively, connecting hard with his jaw – much to his surprise.

"Ow!" he exclaimed, cupping his chin with an exasperated look.

Hazel smiled impishly, pulling her fists into a defensive position.

Lucas almost snickered before he reciprocated her hit with a sharp jab to the shoulder. She grunted as he rocked back and grabbed her arms from behind.

He struck her leg, causing her to drop down to her knees with a gasp. Then he kicked her, pushing her onto her back and slamming his foot hard against her chest.

Hazel peered up at him. "You don't need to do this," she tried, catching his gaze. Lucas lingered for a second, looking down into the brown eyes that sat below him, they were swirling with warmth, golden like the rings of Saturn. Her eyes were so human without that ugly red glare.

"I have to," Lucas replied monotonously, kneeling beside her. If he didn't, he didn't know what would happen, who would get hurt because of him, who would die… or what Chris would do.

Hazel closed her eyes and finally stopped struggling, letting out a small, barely audible breath. "Don't hurt them…

if you have to hurt me, just hurt me. Leave the others alone," she pleaded. "Caleb and Ophelia, they've done nothing wrong. They didn't turn me, they helped me, and Amber isn't involved in the slightest. She's in the hospital. It's just me. No one else. Just kill me."

Lucas flinched and lowered his blade briefly, staring at her with uncertainty. The monsters he'd fought before usually pleaded for their own lives, they didn't give themselves up voluntarily to save others.

"I'm supposed to do this. This is what I have to do," he conceded, gripping his dagger as he shook the thought out of his mind.

Her hands moved up to his blade. At first, he thought she was trying to pull it away, to wrestle for the dagger, but instead, she slowly placed her hands over his. "No, it's not… but if it stops you from hurting them, then just do it," she whispered, her voice cracking.

Lucas stammered. His eyes were wide and a bit blurred. He was holding his blade, the purple tip turned down toward her chest, ready to drain the life from her, as she would from the lives of many if he spared her, but it felt… wrong.

Shelley had always told Lucas they weren't really hunters, they were protectors, for whoever needed their help. *Because sometimes people hate those that they don't understand.*

He'd pushed her words aside because she'd died the same day she'd said them, and so it had meant nothing in the end.

However, there Lucas was, with the dagger Shelley had given him, his first dagger, aimed and ready to kill one of them, like he had many times before, and yet, the thought was making his stomach ache. Hazel didn't seem like a threat, but he knew what she was capable of. He just didn't know if she'd live up to it or not, and that made him fear her.

Fear quickly turns into hate.

Lucas knew hate, hate had been his only company for the better part of his life, up until Farah, who never hated anyone, not even Jamie. No, like Shelley, she vouched for things she shouldn't, because why hate when you can understand?

If Chris were here right now, he'd grab Lucas's arm and bring it down before he could even decide to do it for himself. Hate infects, poisons, and spreads like wildfire. It manifests inside the very core of a soul and warps it into something else entirely, into the very monsters they're trained to hate.

But warriors don't kill without reason, Lucas thought. They fight for a cause, for a solution, until they end up paying for it. Peace has a price, like everything. He trusted Eli, and because of it Shelley died, Farah's family died, and she almost died herself because she wouldn't kill the very things that eventually tore her loved ones apart. If he didn't kill Hazel now, then who would pay the price later? Amber? Farah? Maybe some innocent person who just found themselves in the wrong place at the wrong time.

His hands shook as his fingers curved over the tree vine carvings on his dagger.

Yes, protectors protect, but hunters…

Hunters kill.

With a heavy breath, he brought the blade, cutting with the wind as it slashed right for Hazel's chest.

Hazel squinted and blinked, her eyes growing wide at the sight of the dagger pierced into the ground beside her, inches away from her face.

She heard a barely audible mumble and peered up,

catching sight of Lucas on his knees above her, staring down at his empty hands. A bruise was forming on his fingers, and he didn't look like he knew whether to be happy about it or not.

There was a girl standing above him, with flowers in her long red hair. She looked like she lived in the forest, with her crochet jacket and flared leggings flowing in the wind. Hazel watched as she jammed her spear back into the ground. Maybe she was a nymph, or some woodland spirit… or maybe Hazel's head was still spinning.

As she debated her mental state, a flutter of motion caught her attention, and she looked up to see Lucas being tackled backwards. Sharp teeth snapped at him and a cashmere coated body straddled his torso, wrestling him into place until he stopped thrashing around.

It took Hazel a moment to realise it was Ophelia.

She pulled the boy to his feet, clamping his hands behind his back, and growled in his ear as he tried his luck at escaping again. Lucas glared up into her icy blue eyes, and Ophelia snarled, pushing his head in the opposite direction.

Hazel turned her head as a sudden whoosh of air blew her hair across her face. She looked up to see Caleb rushing towards her. "You're alive," he chirped, smiling stupidly as he crouched beside her, his hands resting on her arms.

Releasing a breathy noise, Hazel nodded, snaking her eyes over him. His hair was tousled and slightly charred, and there was a strong smoky smell coming from his clothes. He was also caked in mud, from his jeans to the white top beneath his chequered shirt.

She gave him a bewildered look, and he bit his lip, holding back a laugh.

"Yeah, don't ask questions you don't want the answer to,"

he mused. "Are you okay?" Caleb tenderly rubbed his finger over a cut on her neck.

Hazel frowned, the cut should've started to heal by now, but she swallowed the pain and nodded, opening her mouth to reply, but was interrupted by Lucas.

"What the hell is going on here? Farah!"

With a sigh, the ginger girl dropped the spear she'd been leaning on and reached for the bag on her back. It was woven and covered in an array of flowers. She pulled a small, scruffy-looking notebook out of it and gave the dark-haired boy a cheery grin. "You're not gonna believe this."

Lucas's gaze travelled down to the book, and then his eyes darkened. "Oh, try me. I'm hoping the angrier you make me, the stronger I'll get, and then I can break free from this—"

His words were cut short as Ophelia jabbed him in the ribs, causing him to grunt and bend over himself, looking up with an even more vicious expression – if that was even possible.

"Just listen, please, Lucas. This is going to be good for the both of you, for all of us," Farah replied, holding the notebook against her chest.

Hazel peered up with a disorientated expression and Caleb gestured for her to listen to what the girl had to say.

"Lucas, you were brought to the Nosferatu Warriors when you were a baby, right? Your mother and father were supposedly killed," she stated. Lucas pulled a face at the abruptness of the question and pushed against Ophelia with a grunt, nodding gruffly.

Farah grinned, which seemed highly insensitive given the question she'd just asked, then looked over at Hazel, who gulped.

"Your mother raised you, yes? You took her surname

instead of your father's when he left, when you were just a baby?"

Hazel reluctantly nodded. "What's that got to do with anything?"

"You two share a connection," Farah continued.

Hazel swallowed, blinking over at the brown-eyed boy in Ophelia's grasp, the one that heavily resembled the same guy from her dreams, who she seemingly couldn't escape from, however hard she tried.

Yes, they had a connection, that was for sure.

"You have the same birthday, you know? The same colour eyes. Ain't that weird?" The redhead trailed off, looking between them before raising a brow at the dazzled, confounded looks she received in return. Farah leaned against her spear and pointed at Lucas, holding the book close to her chest with her other hand. "The photograph you have," she began, and his eyes bore into hers grumpily. "I'm pretty sure Hazel would recognise the woman in the photo."

The trees rustled around them, and the eerie sound of the wind in the leaves was the only noise.

After an excruciating few seconds, Ophelia groaned. "God, seriously, just get to the point, will you? You two are the same age, share the same last name, and share a mother. You're related. More than that, you're twins."

Lucas stared. His eyes were brimming with a strange, unreadable tension that seemed to seep into his bones as he struggled beneath the blonde's hold, wrestling to get free.

Farah motioned for Ophelia to release the hunter. The blonde hesitantly let go, and Lucas pushed away, giving the vampire a cold, demented look before storming towards Farah.

Lucas snatched the notebook from her hands. "This is

private," he muttered, attempting to walk away, but Farah grabbed his arm.

"Lucas…" she began.

"No! You're full of crap!" he yelled, shrugging her off.

Hazel could feel Caleb studying her, tightening his grip on her shoulders as if he was afraid she might fall, or vomit, or something. She swallowed and rubbed at the bags under her eyes, keeping her focus on the swaying trees. "He's… my brother."

Caleb nodded, slinking one hand around her waist to steady her. He was right, actually, she probably would vomit if she could move.

"Twin brother. You guys can wear matching outfits like in *The Shining*," Ophelia chimed in with a hint of false enthusiasm, glancing over at Caleb, who shook his head light-heartedly. Hazel blinked between them both.

Lucas brushed off Farah's attempts at calming him down and stormed over to Hazel and Caleb with a burning fury in his eyes. "No! We're not twins! I'm not your brother. My family is dead! They're gone!" he raged.

Caleb gently pushed Hazel behind him, letting his irises turn vermilion in warning. Lucas scoffed in response and stepped closer, lifting his head in what appeared to be an attempt to look taller than the older boy.

With a snide chuckle, Caleb knitted his brows together, flicking his tongue around sharpened teeth. "Don't do anything stupid. We're only trying to help, you little bastard."

Lucas's eyes went wide at the other boy's words. He pushed on the taller boy's chest harshly, clearly wanting some confrontation, and before Caleb could give it to him – by the way his fists clenched, Hazel could tell he was debating just giving it to him – she stepped between them.

A strangled noise fell from Caleb's lips, but she gave him a pleading look, sliding her hand into his, before pushing in front of him. He whined slightly, but remained where he was, and she was thankful for that. She had to do this alone.

Hazel stepped towards Lucas, whose chest was still rising and falling. Come to think of it, their eyes *were* a similar shade, and so was their skin. Although, even if they were related, that didn't immediately make the situation better. Lucas wasn't even looking at her. It was almost like he couldn't.

A tight feeling wound into her chest as her voice came out shakily. "My… my father's name is Alden Valdez…"

The hunter's eyes closed. "No… No, no, no, no, no." He breathed in strange, disordered spurts, turning around and dropping his head into his hands.

Hazel sucked in a breath, studying him. Her mother had got rid of all the photos of her father after he left, but she had secretly found one a few years ago that she had seared onto her memory. Clearly there was still some small connection in Nina to the man she had once loved and she couldn't bring herself to eradicate all memories of him, and so she had kept just one picture. In it, the two of them looked young, carefree, still in love. He wore a fashionably dishevelled leather jacket over a lithe and muscular frame, so like Lucas's, she realised. Even their hair was the same – dark hair, curled up at the top of his head. The most notable similarity, of course, was his eyes, a rich brown, like sunlit tree bark.

From the second Hazel had locked eyes with Lucas, back in the corridors of her sixth form, she couldn't push away this strange feeling of familiarity, the sense that somehow, in the back of her mind, she knew him. That she'd seen him before.

She understood why now. He looked just like their father.

Lucas slowly reached for something in his pocket. Not a

dagger, much to her relief, but a photograph. Hazel stared at it with a jolt: the woman in the picture was absolutely Hazel's mother, with her gentle green irises and long brown hair she'd since cut short. She was younger, of course, and had less stress-induced wrinkles around her eyes, but there was no denying that it was Nina Bridget.

"Lucas, look at me, please," Hazel said breathlessly.

He reluctantly raised his head, looking up with a painfully unreadable expression.

"That woman in the photo is my mother. She's… alive… I think she'd want to meet you. Lucas, this is good. Weird, definitely weird, but I…" Hazel exhaled, keeping her gaze steady and looking for any sign that he was listening to her.

Hazel reached over, ready to place a comforting hand on his shoulder, but as she did, Lucas let out a choked noise, and she peered down to see that he was staring at the pendant dangling down from her necklace.

He inched away from her and Hazel glanced up to see him pull at a chain around his own neck. It had been hidden before, beneath his hoodie the whole time. But now that she could see it, she couldn't help but reach out to get a closer look.

The pendant was a golden tangle of leaves, staggered in a line, a perfect mirrored image of her own necklace. In fact, it was precisely the same in all ways but one, the leaves on her one faced the right, while his looked left.

Parallel lines.

They were parallel lines in every sense of the word. On two sides of the same coin, never facing each other.

They were so similar in such ways that didn't just stop at their looks. Both had a brutal stubbornness and reluctance to trust, to believe, but with that came a stern, protective nature if they ever did let anyone in. But circumstances of their upbringings had created stark differences, too. Hazel was kind, gentle, she wouldn't hurt anyone, not without reason, whereas Lucas was accustomed to having weapons fit into his grip, like he was born for it. His instincts were to attack, and she had the blood of the very creature he was drawn to kill.

They were on separate sides of an ancient war. Their worlds were never meant to meet, because if they did, they would surely crash and burn. They almost did, and he'd been the one to bring down the blade.

Lucas released a shaky breath and stepped away from Hazel, stumbling over as he did so. She reached out to steady him, but he backed away, barely able to look at her. He turned his back so quickly that a hollow noise fell from her lips.

"I can't do this," he heaved, dropping the photograph onto the floor and staggering into the woods, picking up his dagger on the way.

Farah glanced over at Hazel with an apologetic look and then went after him.

CHAPTER TWENTY-FOUR

On Edge

Hazel slunk down to the ground, picking up the photograph abandoned on the floor.

A flicker of movement caught her attention and she glanced up to see Ophelia standing over her. "We need to go," she said, staring off into the woods. "The others are probably after us by now, that includes you, so if you're quite done—"

"Lia!" Caleb scowled, stepping past her and crouching down beside Hazel, placing a hand on her shoulder.

"How could… how could she not tell me I had a brother?" Hazel choked as she looked down at her mother's smiling face. The photograph was a little torn at the edges: well-worn, well-loved. It made Hazel nauseous to think about how much he must have stared at it.

Hazel didn't know how to feel. She had a brother, someone out there who shared her blood, had once shared a womb with her, and they hardly even knew each other. Her own twin had tried to kill her, and almost did. If Farah had got there a couple of seconds too late…

Would knowing the truth have prevented everything? If Hazel had known she'd once had a twin, then perhaps she could have found him. Hazel had gotten to grow up with a normal, easy childhood, but Lucas, well, it hurt to think of the childhood he must have had. Some force out there somewhere had been pulling them together for some reason, maybe this was why.

What else was her mother hiding?

"Why didn't she tell me?"

Caleb's face grew soft as he opened his arms and pulled Hazel into his side, tracing his fingers along her back. She fell forward and let herself crash into him, burying her face in the crook of his neck as she let out a sob.

After a few minutes, Ophelia broke the pair apart. She was right. They needed to go back into the woods and sort everything out.

Julianna and Alexander were still in the camp, and now, with Lucas, a living blood relative, they had a chance to prove that Hazel was a born vampire.

As long as Farah could convince him to join them.

As they neared the Nosferatu Warrior's camp, there was an eerie silence lingering in the air.

"They should've realised we were gone by now. Maybe they're looking for us," Ophelia whispered, stepping over a burnt deck chair.

"Or hiding in the trees, waiting to pounce," Hazel added.

"That's optimistic," the blonde replied, sighing. Caleb turned around and shushed her. The wind drifted through his golden hair and Hazel couldn't help noting how outrageously beautiful he was, even with mud splattered on his cheeks.

The Thorn family really was blessed with the best genes. She wondered if it was a vampiric thing, the natural *allure* they carried, or if it was just a Thorn thing.

"Some of them are still here somewhere," Caleb whispered, glancing up into the empty window of a truck that stood like a gate outside the campsite. Hazel gulped, fixated on a handprint mixed into the dust, the outline of it covered in some sort of lilac powder.

They'd told her about the dark fire, how it burned at least ten feet tall, cascading through the surrounding woods in a misty inferno. It was hard to imagine that now, with how calm everything looked, disregarding the burned grass and melted tents. The only flames left were from the original campfire, and even that was almost burnt out.

It was quiet, a bit too quiet. A few birds, or maybe they were bats with the way their inky eyes glistened, either way they were perched on the trees beside the burnt-out fire pit, dropping down to pick at empty tin cans until Ophelia started kicking around the rubble, scaring them off. She pierced through faded fabric tents and kicked at woven hammocks, pulling at them aggressively.

Caleb walked over to her, stopping her from slamming her foot through a table. "What? What's wrong? We're going to find them. Don't break things."

Ophelia pulled back and pointed a sharp acrylic nail at a pile of burning weapons on top of the campfire. A set of knives with Victorian-style carvings and dark red metallic arrows with gold tips were disintegrating in the flames. Caleb's eyes lit up. Wordlessly, the siblings sped from one side of the campsite to the other, dipping in and out of different charcoaled tents.

Hazel sat down on a log, patting it first to see if it was still hot. Her mind kept drifting off to Lucas. He must hate her, she'd gotten everything he'd never had, everything he *should* have had.

There was a blur of motion as Ophelia sped into sight again. "No one's here, Caleb. There's no sign of anyone anywhere… Oi, dickhead, are you listening?"

Caleb was a few metres ahead, glancing at something in the distance. There was a nervous feeling bubbling in Hazel's stomach at how alert he'd grown.

The trees rustled, and a girl around their age, with long, fine black hair and piercings in her nose and eyebrow appeared. She had a dagger in her hand.

Ophelia let out a dramatic groan that seemed to catch the girl's attention. The hunter narrowed her eyes and pulled the dagger back as if she were going to throw it, but someone grabbed her arm before she could. It was an older boy, with a mop of curly brown hair and a bandage around his neck. He was wearing a bright green hoodie with a brown harness over his chest, pocketed with different weapons.

"Oh, thank god," Caleb said as Ophelia grumbled beside him. Hazel sat up from the log, standing behind them. She peered up at Caleb with an alarmed expression, but it relaxed as his smile brightened.

"That's Jamie. He's alright. I'm pretty sure we can trust him, like Farah," he muttered over his shoulder, keeping his eyes on the hunters.

Jamie waved at the trio before pushing the angry girl's hand down, giving her a stern expression. "Hollie, c'mon, we talked about this," he said. "You're embarrassing me. We help them and they help us. So just suck it up and back me up, yeah? I'm confident about this."

Hollie scoffed, still looking as if she was planning on attacking them but she let him take her blade nonetheless. "You're confident about everything."

"And I'm always right. That's why I'm in charge," Jamie replied, stuffing the weapon into his harness.

Three more kids crept out of the woods behind them,

glancing at Jamie sceptically.

Caleb moved forward, shaking the bandaged hunter's hand with a kind smile, while actively avoiding the looks he was receiving from the others.

"I see you found your friend," Jamie mused, waving at Hazel, who was still partially hiding behind Caleb. She waved awkwardly, Jamie let out a strange hum. "Don't look feral to me."

An amused sound left Caleb's throat, and he tilted his head to give her a humoured look. Hazel chewed her lip.

"Yeah, I, eh, I'm not…"

The other girl, Hollie, kept sending over threatening glares. She had a venomous air about her as she glanced over from her conversation with the stubble faced guy which only intensified when she finally spotted Hazel behind Caleb's back. She grabbed a bow and stormed forward, aiming it at her. "She's the one! The bitten one!" she shrieked.

Hazel gulped, stumbling back a little as Caleb stepped in front of her.

"She's not bitten," he warned. His voice was lower than usual, grittier. The sound of the bowstring strained through Hazel's ears and she flinched, grabbing onto Caleb's arm.

Hollie narrowed her eyes, pulling back on the string, still aiming at Hazel. A younger boy stepped in front of her, frowning. Her face fell.

"Liam? What are you doing? Move," she tried.

He shook his head. "No, Jay's right… They're nice, we shouldn't hurt them."

"Didn't look so nice when they were knocking us all on our arses earlier," Hollie muttered under her breath murderously.

Caleb laughed and he tilted his head toward Ophelia, raising his hand ever so slightly by his side. Subtly they bumped fists. Hazel wanted to strangle them both.

"I mean, they'd have probably attacked us by now if they were going to," the stubbled guy exhaled.

Hollie's head snapped toward him, her lips puckering in disappointment. "Miles? You're supposed to be on my side."

Miles peered up at Caleb then, almost grinning, and the blue-eyed boy stuck his thumb up.

"Right, let's all just take it down a notch," Jamie ordered, his voice was stern. "Trust me on this," he pleaded. "These guys could've killed me earlier, but they chose not to. That's not why they're here! I know it's absurd, but you all saw what happened out there with Chris. He's finally lost it. Hippy was right. We're fighting the wrong battle here."

"Hippy?" Hazel whispered.

Ophelia peered over in her direction and rolled her eyes. "That ginger friend of Lucas's, with the flares and obnoxious rings, obviously," she mumbled.

Hollie sighed deeply, shaking her head as she brought the bow down ever so slightly, but keeping her eyes on Hazel.

Hazel didn't feel afraid, not really. The situation wasn't exactly ideal, but she could see the girl was starting to come around, or was at least trying to listen to her friend. Hazel couldn't blame her exactly, if she'd been told there was a bloodthirsty maniac on the loose, she'd probably be on edge, too.

As Hollie lowered her weapon to the ground, the bushes behind her began to rustle again. Everyone turned to see a burly man appear.

He was older and more worn compared to the others, covered in scrapes and scars, giving him a rugged and violent appearance. He also sported a long, stringy beard that was coated in mud, just like the rest of him.

Hazel blinked, watching anxiously as more sleazy-looking men followed him from the forest.

The first man stepped forward, peering over at the vampires – or, more specifically, at Caleb. Hazel felt him tense. He cursed under his breath.

The hunter marched over with a wide, grimy smile, clamping a hand down on Jamie's shoulder. "Ah, you found them. Well done, kids."

Lucas could hear Farah running after him, but he didn't slow down.

He glanced back, watching the forest move behind him. He'd always been fast, faster than most of the people he'd trained with, but it had never really clicked as to why until now.

She'd only track his footprints, anyway, not that she'd need too. She'd know where to find him. He always found peace sitting at the cliffside, looking over the town.

Slinking down, Lucas pulled his knees into his stomach as he stared out, not really looking at anything at all. He cleared his throat, attempting to hold back tears as he pulled his body in as tight as he could.

"Lucas?" Farah called out, approaching him cautiously. She sat down beside him, letting her legs hang off the cliffside. "It's fine if you don't feel okay yet. It was sprung at you all at once, and it's a lot to take in, but Lucas, she is your sister. She's your blood."

Instead of responding, Lucas picked up a stone and threw it off the cliff, watching as it disappeared into the camouflage of trees below.

"I didn't believe you, not at first. I thought it was just, I don't know, a desperate attempt to change my mind," he said.

Farah frowned, peering down into the darkness, the shine of the moon reflected on top of some of the taller trees. Lucas had always been able to see well in the dark, full moon or not.

He had a set of torch gloves, they didn't work so well, but that had never really been an issue – which, looking back, is another thing he should have questioned more.

"Then… I saw her necklace," he continued, moving his hand toward his neck. "It looked like the earrings from the photograph. The pendant is the same as mine. Well, not exactly the same. It's a parallel line… a parallel life. She got a home, a mother, everything, and all I got was a load of crap. A giant, shit-shaped burden. How is that fair?"

"It's not," Farah whispered, keeping her eyes on Lucas, even as he turned to stare out towards the open air. The cliff top went on for miles, overlooking the whole town.

Lucas's gaze was dead set on it, on the houses, the high street, the school. He couldn't look away.

"Why did she get everything, while I got nothing?"

Farah wrapped her arm around his back, pulling him into her. His head fell against her chest and he buried himself into her side, holding onto her as if he was already falling from the cliff.

"I don't know. I'm sorry. You have a family now, though, they're out there. You can have everything you've ever wanted."

Lucas let out a sob, masking it with a small grunt as he rubbed his eyes. "I'm sorry. I'm sorry I didn't listen to you… You were right… my head's been so messed up. I almost… *I almost…*"

Farah shushed him softly. "It's okay. At least you know now. I always knew you'd come around eventually, as stubborn as you are." She chuckled.

"A couple more seconds and I would have killed her, Farah. I had the dagger right there, and I was going to kill her. I… I wanted to," he whispered. "I kept hearing Chris's voice in my head. How we need to destroy them, how we have to hate them. She wasn't fighting back like they usually do, she just laid there, looking at me. I was going to kill my own sister."

"Chris poisoned you, manipulated you. It isn't your fault," Farah tried.

Lucas shook his head, scoffing as he kicked a few loose stones over the side of the cliff. "She wasn't fighting back, and I still had the dagger aimed. If you hadn't…"

"You still wouldn't have done it," Farah interrupted. "Before I reached you, I could see you hesitating. Lucas, I honestly believe if I wasn't there, that dagger would have still ended up in the ground. You would have done what's right. You may be a stubborn arse sometimes, but you have a good heart." She smiled, tapping him in the chest. "A really good heart."

Lucas sucked in a breath, clamping his eyes closed. "I don't want to hate her because she got a better life, or got to have a mother… a proper childhood… none of that is her fault, but she's still one of them." He trailed off, unable to stop the malice that entered his tone.

Farah sat up on her knees. "You don't have to hate that about her either, you know that now, and for the record, I don't think you do hate her. I think you're afraid."

Lucas glanced away, rolling his eyes ever so slightly as he picked up another stone, tossing it into the abyss. "In all the stories I've read, nothing ever goes right in the end. Theseus was still exiled, even after he killed the Minotaur. Achilles lost Patroclus and was never the same again. Bellerophon never found his Pegasus. Even Hercules didn't make it out alive in the end. Love always gets destroyed one way or another. I've seen it happen," he said, watching the pebble disappear. He turned to face her, hardening his expression. "I don't want to go through it again."

Farah reached up and toyed with the gem around her neck. "You can't know what's going to happen. Nothing that is already written can't be adjusted to change. That just means you have to love more freely while you can. You let me in, and look how well that turned out for you."

Lucas let out a breathy chuckle and she pulled him in closer. They sat there for a little while, watching the trees silently.

He fumbled with the knife in his fingers, looking at it like it was a foreign object. "Farah?" Lucas asked. She hummed questionably. "If Hazel… if she really is a born vampire… and biologically shares the same blood as me, that means…" Lucas stared down, choking on the words as they fizzled out.

Farah grabbed his hand and squeezed it. "It doesn't change anything. If you want to stay human, you can. It's a choice."

"It's a curse," he mumbled under his breath, feeling his shoulders tense as he stared at his blade. He slid it into his pocket with a shiver and glanced up. "What happens now?"

Farah smiled at him. "We go meet your sister, *properly*, then your mother, and go from there, I guess."

Lucas swallowed back a croaked noise as he sat up. Farah stayed on the ground for a second, picking up a stone and tossing it over the cliff with a hopeful look.

It flew out further than Lucas's did and she grinned. Her smile subsided however, when she saw the look of horror on Lucas' face.

He brushed a strained hand over his forehead and pulled

her up, dragging her towards the forest as she widened her eyes questionably.

"Chris. He's going to kill Hazel if he finds her."

CHAPTER TWENTY-FIVE

Friendly Fatality

Caleb glanced over his shoulder at Hazel, raising his eyebrows. A silent question. She nodded, letting him know she was okay, or at least only mildly terrified. He reached behind him and subtly clasped their hands together.

Jamie and his friends were only a few metres ahead, walking stiffly. With the others next to them for comparison, Hazel realised they stuck out against the other hunters like sore thumbs. They were like the runts of the pack. They weren't as harsh or aggressive-looking as the others – not even Hollie, who was watching the older men warily, clutching her bow.

There were six of them in total, the older hunters. All men with sleazy smiles and unforgiving stares. The axe-wielding warrior beside Caleb was sending his bald friend next to him – the one holding a dagger to Ophelia's back – watchful looks every now and then. Clearly they had orders to keep the two siblings separated.

Hazel wasn't exactly sure how they were going to get out of this situation, or if their new friends were about to turn on them or not, but something about the gentle squeeze Caleb gave her hand calmed her nerves a little. She peered up to see the familiar tug at his lips, there was no worry or fear on his face, just a breezy determination.

"We're going to get out of this," he mouthed, squeezing

her hand again. Hazel chewed on her lip and furrowed her eyebrows.

"Oi, biter, turn back around!" the axeman yelled. He was at least a foot or so shorter than Caleb, with a dirty bucket hat on his head, looking as though he belonged on the floor of a muddy festival. He whacked Caleb in the ribs with the blunt end of his axe, forcing his hand to disconnect from Hazel's.

Caleb winced as he turned to face his attacker.

The festival goer laughed snidely, bouncing the hilt of the axe into his other hand. "I'll do worse than that if you turn around again, no scheming!"

"We weren't— okay, woah, never mind!" Hazel closed her mouth as the crooked-toothed man beside her pointed a dagger in her face. The blade was caked with purple powder that made her want to sneeze.

At the stagger in her words, Caleb attempted to twist his head around, only to be struck in the side again, this time with the sharp end of the axe. He gasped in pain as it tore through his denim jacket, marking his skin with a thin line.

There wasn't any purple powder on the axe, but it still must have hurt. Caleb cursed under his breath. "Frigging hell… You really don't hold back on your threats, ay?"

The wound stitched itself back together, leaving only a light layer of blood around the edge of the ripped denim. "Disgusting," the bucket hat man gagged, looking away to spit.

Caleb furrowed his brow at that, glancing over his shoulder to Hazel with an almost comical look.

"What did I just say!" the hunter bellowed.

He raised the axe again, though before it could come down, Ophelia hissed. She grabbed the weapon by its hilt and twisted the man's arm to the side, forcing him to drop the axe and knocking his dingy bucket hat right off his sweaty head.

Immediately, a variety of weapons were pointed in their direction. Hazel noticed that the bald hunter, who'd been behind Ophelia, was now clutching his stomach.

As the hunter leading them, a guy called Pete, grumbled from the front of the line, Jamie turned around, pushing through the other hunters with a stress ridden expression plastered on his face. "Woah, woah. I thought we were taking them to Chris?" he said, peering around the group.

"Shut up," Pete uttered, stepping past the boy furiously.

Caleb quickly kicked the axe a few feet away and grabbed the moaning hunter by the shoulder, steadying him on his feet. "Hey! No harm done here, let's just keep moving," he said, patting the snarling man on the chest before reaching down to pick up his bucket hat.

The hunter snatched it from him and slinked away, cradling his arm with a sickly expression. He turned back to look at Ophelia, almost stumbling over himself as she glared at him, her eyes a dangerous ruby.

The rest of the hunters took that as their cue to encircle the vampires.

Caleb sighed. "Let's just go to *Chris* and work it all out there. No one else needs to get hurt." His expression was sterner now, a little more warning in his voice.

Ophelia snorted. "Yeah, I'm sure that creep has a lot more creative ideas to kill us with than you dimwits. Might as well save yourselves the headache."

Hazel shot the girl a wild look. "Are you trying to get us killed?" she grumbled, almost stumbling over a branch.

"Looks like you're perfectly fine at doing that yourself," Ophelia retorted.

Caleb glanced over his shoulder at Hazel. "I'll distract

them, and when you see an opening—"

"No," Hazel interrupted. "I'm not leaving you."

A dagger swung down toward them and Ophelia redirected it, kicking the perpetrator. "Well, personally, I think we should all leave! So if you two can stop coddling each other for two seconds, I suggest we get the hell out of here!" she yelled, grunting as a tracksuit-clad warrior swung for her.

Hazel peered over at Caleb, who was trying to avoid the swipe of another dagger. He caught it between his palms and pulled upwards, throwing it into the air before catching it and tossing it into the darkening forest.

Hazel swallowed thickly. There were only eleven hunters altogether, and five of them were *maybe* on their side, so they had a fair chance. Ophelia had already injured one, who was standing off to the side, cradling his now broken arm and hurling into his bucket hat, and the younger hunters had grouped together by the trees, whispering amongst themselves. So really, there were only five hunters threatening them.

Hazel couldn't fight, not like the Thorns could, but she felt useless just standing there. She slowly side-stepped, falling out of the sandwiched formation the siblings had wordlessly placed her in, and attempted to blend into the fight.

Ophelia and Caleb both snapped their heads in her direction. "No!" they shouted simultaneously, pulling her back between them.

Pete came barrelling through the crowd, axe aimed at Caleb's throat, and the boy turned to face him, letting his fangs jut out onto his lip. However, before the axe collided, something knocked the older man back. He hit the ground with a thud and winced, grabbing his foot.

Just above his ankle was a small line of red, an incision

made by a blade.

Hazel strained her expression as the hunter stumbled upwards again, towering over the small boy who'd stepped in-front of the vampires with both blades in hand.

"Liam!" one of the younger hunters bawled, muffled behind the size of the bearded man.

"You little traitor!" the man snapped.

Liam's shoulders trembled ever so slightly, but he held his daggers up, ready to fight the grizzly bear of a man almost three sizes bigger than him. Before he could, Caleb placed a hand on the younger boy's shoulder and pulled him away, peering at the hunter cautiously.

The other hunters lowered their weapons, turning to look at the older man. One had a busted lip, holding onto his arm with a wince. "Well… what now? Should we get him, too?"

The bearded man cleared his throat, gripping his axe tighter as he locked eyes with Caleb, who stood still, catching his gaze steadily.

"Take them all," Pete said in a low voice. "We don't stand for traitors."

"No!" the young hunter yelled, breaking out from her friends who were trying to hold her back. She ran forward, whacking one tracksuit-wearing man over the head with her hammer before swinging for another one. It hit him square in the chest and he staggered backwards, only for the first guy to grab her by the back of her arm and slam her into a nearby tree trunk.

"Claudia!" Jamie rushed forward, sword held up over his head.

Pete pulled out a dagger and grabbed Claudia, holding the blade over her throat. "One more move," he warned, peering at Jamie, who let the sword fall to the ground hopelessly, releasing a bated breath.

From the other side of the stand-off, Liam's jaw slackened. He gripped his blades so tight that Hazel could smell blood pooling.

Ophelia grabbed his arm, stopping the small boy from rushing forward. "Stop wriggling—"

"They're hurting her!"

She sighed, softening her tone. "It's okay. She's gonna be okay, as long as no one acts *irrationally.*" She looked up at that, sneering at the older hunters.

Pete tutted. "What is this? You all made friends while we weren't looking?" He laughed, the sound echoed by his followers. One of the hunters placed a hand against the side of Claudia's cheek, taunting her. She tried to push away from him, but Pete tightened his hold on the dagger.

"Let her go," Jamie pleaded, holding his hands up in surrender. His face was full of panic, wincing every time Claudia gasped. "Just let her go."

"And what? Where do we go from there? You go back to helping them? Those bloodsuckers?" Pete gagged, growling as he looked at the vampires. Hazel felt her throat go dry as his dark grimy eyes fell over her.

From the right of her, Liam pushed forward, still trying desperately to move, but Ophelia held him back.

Caleb sighed. "It's us you want, not them, Pete. Let her go."

The man grumbled under his breath, practically barking as he turned away in disgust. "I don't want to hear my name coming out of your filthy mouth."

"Okay. Hey, dickhead, take your hands off her, yeah?" Caleb said, gesturing at the hunter. "Better?"

Pete narrowed his eyes furiously.

"You did tell him not to use your name," Ophelia hummed. Caleb raised a hand toward her in agreement and Hazel dropped her head to the floor, closing her eyes with a heavy breath. She had a strong feeling they were all about to die.

Pete scowled at the pair, then turned to Jamie, changing the angle of the dagger and drawing blood. Claudia groaned, straining her neck to avoid the blade.

"Grab them," Pete said impatiently, motioning to the vampires.

Bad breath wafted in Hazel's direction and she turned to face the crooked-toothed hunter. The torchlight from the camp broke through the cracks in his teeth as he raised his knife. Hazel didn't fight back, there was no point. Instead, she held her breath, trying not to gag at his toxic smell as he pulled her into his chest.

Ophelia released Liam as the bald hunter grabbed her arm from behind, surprising her. The small boy drew his daggers out, while Caleb lowered his fangs, inclining his head and bouncing a little on his feet in preparation as the hunters approached them, though they stopped when Pete held his hand up.

Everyone glanced at the bearded man, watching as he dragged Claudia towards Jamie, who was still frozen in place. "You have to make a choice. You can't be with us and with them."

From the corner of her eye, Hazel spotted Hollie drawing her bow.

"Jamie…" Claudia winced, her voice hoarse as Pete pressed the blade against her throat.

"Chris was wrong," Jamie uttered, holding his hands up. "He doesn't care about us. He wanted us to go into the fire.

We're just a means to an end for him."

"They told you that, did they? With their mind control? I thought you were stronger than that, boy."

"We aren't the ones controlling minds here," Caleb retorted.

Pete ignored him. "Him or her? Make your choice."

Jamie stuttered for an answer, his eyes watering as Claudia cried out in pain. Hazel watched as his gaze briefly drifted over to Caleb.

"Him or her?"

The dark-haired hunter closed his eyes, holding onto the harness around his chest for support. When he looked up again, his eyes were focused on Claudia. Only Claudia.

There was a lump in Hazel's throat. It sank down to her very core, swirling around her stomach with static energy that she was sure would burn her up from the inside out. She could feel it surging through her veins, stinging her fingertips, and she instinctively closed her fists, looking up at the hunter holding her. For a split second, something stirred in his eyes, and he started, dropping her arm as if he'd been burned by the look she'd given him.

Hazel took the opportunity to swivel towards Caleb, calling his name as she moved, but almost as quickly as she did so, the crooked-toothed hunter grabbed her again, aiming his dagger for the middle of her back to keep her still.

She could feel his toxic breath against her neck as he held her in place, making her shiver. Nevertheless, her attention remained on Caleb, holding her breath as his head turned.

He chewed at his lip, softening his features to smile at Hazel, with that same optimistic expression as he opened his mouth to speak. However, nothing but a pained grunt left his lips.

The blue-eyed boy glanced down to see a purple laced arrow sticking out from his shoulder, only a few centimetres away from his chest. He let out a choked noise and gripped it, soaking his hands in his own blood while Hazel could only watch in horror.

"Caleb!" Ophelia screeched, grabbing everyone's attention. They'd been too busy staring at Jamie and Pete, waiting for an answer, to even notice that the decision had already been made.

Everyone froze as Caleb staggered backwards, looking uneasy on his feet. The colour was draining from his face fast, almost as fast as the purple powder sinking into his skin, spreading around his wound and causing him to scrunch his face together in pain.

Liam quickly clapped a hand to the vampire's back, holding him up, though his expression was dire when he peered down at the arrow.

Pete turned to Hollie, smiling brightly as she stood, bow still aimed at Caleb. The bearded man dropped the blade from Claudia's neck and shoved past Jamie, giving him a disgusted look.

Jamie ran to Claudia, grabbing onto her shoulders to steady her as she called out to Liam, who was still looking down at Caleb in shock.

Blood was falling from his mouth now, painting his chin a dark red as Liam struggled to keep him upright.

Hazel wanted to scream. She could hear Ophelia's staggered breathing beside her, whimpering as a dagger sliced at her back every time she tried to move.

Opposite them, by the far trees, the other young hunter, Miles, held a hand over his mouth. He brushed it over his face nervously as Pete moved towards them, holding his hand out to Hollie with a gritty smile.

He placed a hand on her shoulder, muttering something along the lines of 'that's a good girl.' Hollie quickly raised her head and struck him in the face with the bow.

Pete's yell distracted the other older hunters long enough for Ophelia to slam her knee up into the stomach of the man holding her and drift out of his reach. She rushed to her older brother, taking him from Liam's shaking arms.

"Cal, look at me. Keep your eyes on me," Ophelia whispered shakily, lowering him to the floor. Her hands were already coated in his blood.

The crooked-toothed man holding Hazel faltered, watching as Hollie slammed into Pete for a second time with her bow, knocking one of his teeth right from his gums.

Swallowing, she glanced up at the man's disconcerted face and tilted her head, deciding to test her luck. Hazel elbowed him in the face, right in his already cracked teeth, and he yelped out in pain, stumbling backwards.

She breathed out in shock, almost smiling, but her face fell as he looked up at her furiously, holding his bruising face. Hazel cringed, stepping back, but before the man could pounce, Jamie swung his fist from behind, whacking him over the head.

He fell down in front of Hazel, landing at her feet. She widened her eyes, glancing upwards as Jamie nodded, then he ran to Liam and Claudia, who were fighting off the other hunters together.

Hazel rushed to Caleb's side, kneeling beside him as Ophelia pulled at the arrow. He winced in pain, twisting his body until she dropped it again. It was buried deep.

"Stay still, idiot," Ophelia spat. Caleb groaned and leaned his head back on the grass, covering his already mud-filled hair with more dirt. He could almost pass for a brunette now.

"Hey, look at me, keep your eyes open."

Ahead of them, Liam let out a yelp as a dagger cut through his arm. Caleb lifted his head at the sound but grumbled in pain the second he did.

"Stop moving! I need to take the arrow out," Ophelia screeched as he tried to sit up again. "Caleb!"

Blood was sticking to the top of his forehead. Hazel didn't even know how it got there. There was just so much blood. She cradled his face, pushing the damp hair from his skin, before laying the back of her palm on his head. He was burning up. A staggered breath slipped from her lips and she looked down at his shoulder. His blood was darkening as it mixed with the purple substance.

Ophelia must have noticed too, because she suddenly gripped the arrow again.

"Should we really be taking that out?" Hazel asked, grimacing as Caleb cried out in pain with every little movement. Ophelia let go of the arrow, grunting under her breath, and the blue-eyed boy fell back against the grass.

"He can't heal with it in. We need to get the nightshade out before it seeps into his bloodstream."

Hazel gulped. "He's gonna bleed out!"

At the crack in her words Caleb glanced up, a pained smile forming on his face. "It's okay. I... I... like... blood..."

Ophelia gritted her teeth together, exhaling shakily, and then glanced at Hazel, her eyes sharp. "It's not the blood I'm worried about. Hold his hand."

Caleb's hand was on his stomach, covered in red. Hazel gripped it without a second thought, lacing their fingers together. The nightshade stung at her nose, making her eyes water, she couldn't imagine how much it burned Caleb from the inside.

"Okay, hold your breath," Ophelia instructed, sitting up on her knees and peering over her brother with glossy eyes.

With one quick tug, she pulled the arrow upwards.

Caleb's head fell back with a groan as the sharp end pierced upwards through his shoulder, tearing more flesh open on its way out. He curved his spine, grunting through his teeth, and Hazel squeezed his palm, holding his body down with her other hand.

As soon as the arrow was ripped out, Ophelia threw it behind her and abruptly tugged Hazel's hoodie off, pulling it over her shoulders and holding it down to her brother's wound, applying pressure using both hands. Caleb's breathing began to even out, and his eyes fluttered closed.

Hazel leaned down, tapping his cheek. "Caleb?"

He didn't reply at first, and so in a panic, she began to tap him frantically. After a second, Caleb let out a small hum, his head lolling to the side. "M'okay... just... catching my breath."

Hazel let out a sigh of relief and dropped her head down onto Caleb's uninjured shoulder, not caring about the blood staining her T-shirt. His hand came up to rest in her hair, pulling her closer as she let out a shaky breath.

"S'all good," he mumbled. "Not dead yet... told you. I'm invincible."

Hazel let out a small chuckle as Ophelia dropped her head back and flicked her attention toward the group of adolescent hunters. They'd knocked down all the older warriors and had begun to tie them onto a tree.

A bloody rage flamed in Ophelia's eyes and she staggered to her feet, staring at Hollie, who was busy helping Miles lift one of the unconscious men. The wind whistled as she drifted over and grabbed the girl by the throat, holding her up in the air.

"Ophelia, put her down!" Hazel tried as Hollie was pulled higher off the ground. She was ignored of course.

"I... had... to," Hollie croaked through a scowl, and Hazel watched as Claudia and Miles discreetly reached for their weapons.

"You had to?" Ophelia yelled venomously, tightening her hold. "You *had* to shoot my brother?"

Jamie glanced up, quickly tying the rope he had in his hands before rushing over. "Pete wasn't going to back down. He'd have killed them both," he explained, sending pointed looks to his friends as he walked over. Claudia lowered her hammer with a disappointed grunt as Jamie frowned at her. He did the same to Miles, who hesitated, glancing at Hollie with nervous eyes.

"Go help him, I've got this," Jamie whispered to the boy.

Ophelia chuckled coldly, sharpening her expression. "So you were just going to kill him? Instead of fighting back, you'd rather take the easy option?"

Hollie struggled in Ophelia's grasp. "I did what I had to."

"Oh, I'll tear your head from your body, you insufferable cow."

Caleb groaned as he tried to sit up. He held onto his bleeding shoulder, wrapping an arm around Hazel's back for support as she and Miles helped him. He peered over at his sister and let out a breathless wince. "Lia... I'm fine... really, look."

Ophelia's head snapped towards him. "You could have died," she hissed.

Caleb chuckled through the pain and nodded. "Yeah, but... I'm still breathing, aren't I? Now drop her, come on...

drop her," he said, elongating the words lazily, as if speaking to a dog.

He seemed a little out of it, Hazel thought, looking at him with slight amusement. His pupils were dilated and unfocused as he leaned into her side, chuckling obscenely at his badly timed joke.

Ophelia grumbled, muttering incoherently under her breath as she dropped Hollie. The two girls glared at each other.

Miles was bending over Caleb, grabbing some spare bandages Liam was passing to him. He'd pulled the denim jacket off too, tearing away most of the blood drenched t-shirt with a dagger, leaving Caleb's collarbone bare whilst he wrapped his shoulder up. He worked with gentle care and Hazel watched him carefully, appreciatively.

"Right," she started breathlessly, looking around the little group, "we have to get him home as soon as he can be moved. Where are your parents?"

Ophelia sucked in an angry breath, turning to Jamie. "Where *are* my parents?"

"They surrendered. I didn't get a chance to explain before, but Chris took them further into the camp, I think he'd told them that he'd caught you guys," he explained, sheepishly.

"Took them where?" Ophelia asked.

"Where we were taking you. Where we... put out the waste."

"Lovely," Hazel breathed, side-eyeing Ophelia cautiously. She looked like she was about to burst a blood vessel.

"Where you put out the waste!"

Jamie sighed. "We call it the *pit*. It's a cliff edge with a big drop... Chris wants to fill you all with daggers and then throw you off it once he catches you all... he has a flair for the dramatic." He shrugged. "They'll be holding your parents there until they find the rest of you."

Ophelia scowled. "Take me to them."

"Are you mental, love? They're surrounded. We step in there and you become target number one, especially now that there's just you two. We got lucky here, but we can't take them all on," Jamie said, pointing between the two girls.

Hazel chewed on her lip, looking up at Ophelia's face. The girl tapped her acrylic nails against her crossed arms.

"I don't care if there's a bleeding tank waiting for me, *love*. You take me there. Now!"

Jamie exhaled harshly, stroking a hand down his face before nodding reluctantly. He turned around and started barking orders to his friends, rounding them up as he leant down to pick up his sword.

Hazel pulled Ophelia aside. "We have to get him back first," she whispered, gesturing over to Caleb. He was still sitting up with Liam's help, leaning back to let the younger boy wash away the rest of the nightshade with some water. He flinched as it washed over him, but the look melted away when he caught Hazel's gaze and smiled stupidly, lifting his uninjured arm to wave at her. She couldn't help but shake her head fondly.

"You know how to get to the manor, right?" Ophelia asked.

"I think so… You are *not* going alone?" Hazel muttered, incredulous.

Ophelia shrugged, bringing her still somehow perfectly curled hair onto her shoulder. "I'm not alone. Got my new mates, haven't I?" she said snidely.

Hazel scrunched up her nose. "You know what I mean, just wait and—"

"I can't. Mum and Dad need help and Caleb needs to get out of here. He won't survive another run in; any more nightshade and he's done for. He needs to heal. You have to get him out of here." Ophelia paused and looked Hazel in the eyes. "Please," she whispered. There wasn't the usual snark or hatred in her expression, just a tired desperation.

Hazel nodded. There was a flicker of something on Ophelia's face (gratitude maybe?) before she turned to her brother, helping him stand up. "I'm going to get Mum and Dad. Hazel's gonna take you home, okay?" she told him, as if speaking to a child.

He didn't respond until Ophelia flicked him on the forehead, a little too aggressively. "Did you hear me?"

Caleb nodded and flopped his head forward, almost tumbling over until Ophelia grabbed his shoulders.

She sucked in a frustrated breath and placed a hand over her eyes. "Just… don't let him fall asleep, okay? Keep him awake until all the nightshade leaves his system. It'll make him a little loopy for a while."

Hazel nodded, snaking her arm around the boy's back to steady him. "I've got him," she said, holding Caleb upright as he wobbled slightly, giggling under his breath.

Ophelia sighed, closing her eyes. Then she nodded decisively and turned toward the hunters, who were standing by the trees, waiting for her.

Hazel watched her go, before grabbing onto Caleb's arm, hoisting it over her shoulder.

CHAPTER TWENTY-SIX

Cliffhanger

After a few minutes of silent walking, Hazel dipped her head down to face Caleb, tapping his cheek to make sure he hadn't dozed off.

He hummed dopily, burying his face further into the crook of her neck and letting out a small laugh.

Hazel knitted her brows together in amusement. "What?"

"Missed my heart by an inch." Caleb's voice was muffled by her hair as he turned to face her with a bloodied grin.

She sighed, scrunching her nose. "Why are you laughing at that?"

He chuckled to himself giddily, glancing down at his wound. "It's just funny."

Hazel stopped walking, pulling the bandage back to see that the bleeding had slowed down a lot. She tugged it back in place and then placed a hand on his forehead, shaking her head as he grinned. His temperature was back to normal now, or at least as normal as it probably could be for a vampire.

"You *must* be delusional, because it most definitely is not funny," she whispered, eyeing Caleb with a forced frown. Though her lips turned upward at the corners ever so slightly as he giggled again.

Caleb reached his hand up to her face, unintentionally smearing his blood on her cheek as he carved out the shape of her dimples. "Then why are you smiling?" he asked, following the curve of her lips with his fingertips.

A small chuckle left her throat, and she glanced around to make sure she was moving in the right direction. "Because you're an idiot."

Nightshade tugged at Ophelia's nose, stinging her eyes as they got closer to the cliffside.

Once the gaps in the trees got smaller, Jamie stopped walking and reached into his pocket, pulling out some rope. She frowned.

"I suggest you put that away right now, pretty boy. Unless you want some very bad things to happen to you."

"It's just—"

"Very. Bad. Things."

"You can trust him," Liam said from beside her. "Jamie knows what he's doing."

A deeply rooted sigh left Ophelia's throat, coming out as more of a grunt as she placed her hands on her hips. Liam had been the only one to voluntarily walk beside her. The others kept their distance a little, as Jamie led the way. But not Liam. He reminded her a little of her younger cousin, they were around the same age, only Liam was less cheeky.

Jamie grinned and took another step forward, holding the rope. "Thank you, bud," he said, swallowing as Ophelia looked at him with sharp eyes. "It's just for show, so they think we're still on their side. I'll tie them loosely, so you'll be able to break free when you need to."

Jamie pulled on the rope suddenly, making a snapping sound that had Ophelia glancing up at him with a snarl.

"Nightshade free," he chimed. She huffed and offered her

arms out, letting him tie it around her wrists.

Once it was secure, he peered up with a flirtatious smile. "So, blondie. Are you single?" Ophelia bit back a laugh, raising her eyebrows as Jamie pulled his lips back with a shrug. "What? You called me pretty boy, was worth a try."

There was a sharp croak from up ahead. As Claudia stormed away, Hollie smacked her leg into the underside of Jamie's knee, causing him to stumble.

"What was that for?" he whined.

"You know what it was for."

Liam let out an amused snort. Hollie marched past, shoving into him.

"Come on, let's get this over with," she spat, grabbing onto Ophelia's ropes and tugging her forward.

Trees hung over the dark cliffside, their branches leaning toward the harsh drop below. In the distance, the town lights were shimmering like mini torch fires, and Ophelia felt like she was about to be burned at the stake for witchcraft or sacrificed on some creepy altar.

A dozen hunters were waiting for them, dotted around the open space in clumps, watching the teenagers with eerie, eager eyes. Ophelia bit her tongue, holding back a few choice words at the force Hollie was using to pull her forward, before pouting her lip to emphasise her act of being afraid.

A few of the hunters pat Jamie on the back with whoops and whistles as he led the way through the crowd, reciprocating their enthusiasm.

The hunters waiting for them moved aside, revealing a trio of authoritative-looking figures. Ophelia recognised the one in the middle straight away – the same stony-faced woman with the buzz-cut from the camp. *Sandy.* She had a set of rings on her fingers, spiked into points, like fancy knuckle dusters.

Ophelia scanned the area for her parents, and it didn't take long for her to find them once the crowd had cleared. She locked eyes with her mother, who had been bound to a tree overhanging the cliff edge. Her father was tied to the neighbouring trunk.

The only reason they'd let themselves be captured in the first place is because they'd been told their children had already been taken, that's what Jamie had said, and Ophelia didn't find it very hard to believe. Her mother had grown up in the Carden family, who were known as strategists and guards, her grandfather, Oliver Carden, had been a general in the first and the second world war, so there was no way Julianna Thorn would give herself up so easily. As for her father, he was a peaceful man yes, but he'd been around long enough now to know how to handle hunters.

Ophelia swallowed thickly and raised her eyebrows, setting her lips in a thin line, a secret gesture, one that told her parents she had a plan. Julianna's expression widened with concern.

"Chris isn't here," Jamie whispered, pulling Ophelia's attention back to the task at hand. He was walking on the right side of her with his sword hanging by his side.

Hollie shushed him under her breath and pulled at Ophelia's ropes, keeping her eyes forward.

Just over a dozen hunters were surrounding them now. There were a few in the back who looked a little unsure, hesitant even, though they were mostly looking down at the ground. The so-called warrior leader, Chris, wasn't beside Sandy at the head of the group, nor was he anywhere amid the crowd, who seemed to get closer with every step they took, cornering them.

Sandy didn't say anything, she simply watched with narrow eyes as Jamie pointed up to one of the overhanging trees and directed Hollie to it.

Hollie threw a handful of rope to Claudia, gesturing for her to help tie the blonde in place. As she threw the rope, however, another hunter caught it. A narrow-nosed woman with singed hair.

"I'll take it from here," the woman said, grabbing the rope and pushing Ophelia against the tree with her hands pulled behind her back. The tree overlooked the edge, giving her a perfect view of the lethal drop below, straight into the forest of spiky trees.

"Where's the other one?" Sandy demanded, narrowing her eyes.

Ophelia could feel her parents' eyes on her, but she couldn't bring herself to look up at them, she didn't want to give the hunters any indication that Caleb was still out there.

"He got away," Jamie lied.

A few grunts of disapproval spread around the clearing followed by the sound of weapons being unsheathed. Jamie cleared his throat, eyes growing wide as the woman signalled for her hunters to manoeuvre through the kids, separating them.

"But not before being shot with a nightshade arrow," Hollie added quickly, pushing through the hunters.

Jamie nodded enthusiastically. "He's not leaving these woods alive, that's for sure."

Ophelia didn't have to look up to feel the absolute horror radiating from her parents.

"Oh, that's good to hear," Sandy said, monotonously.

The self-assured boy grinned at his friends over his shoulder, but as he turned back to face Sandy, she punched him across the jaw, splattering blood over her rings.

Before it had even started, their rescue plan had fallen through the cracks. Jamie was knocked back, spitting blood as he fell into the unwelcoming arms of another warrior.

Hollie reached for an arrow, loading it into her bow. Unfortunately, she wasn't quick enough. Someone else crept up behind her, grabbing her wrists and forcing her to drop the weapon.

In the near distance, Liam slashed his daggers to the side, only to be kicked in the stomach, while Claudia was restrained beside him.

Ophelia blinked, creasing her brow as she watched it all unfold, rather quickly at that.

Mixed in through the crowd was a guy with a broken arm. The same guy from the clearing, only he'd left his bucket hat behind. He must have slipped away during the fight.

With a grunt, Ophelia dropped her head against the tree trunk.

"Sandy. Please, you have to listen," Jamie tried, staggering to his feet. His hands were now bound behind his back.

She gripped him by his harness. "You're with them. You took down men on our side. Your own people for these monsters," she scorned, snaking her eyes over to the Thorns. "You've let yourself get corrupted. Stupid boy."

Jamie shook his head, scrunching his eyes shut as the woman's grip tightened.

"No, I haven't. They've not done anything to me, they had the chance to hurt me, hurt my friends, but they didn't," he coughed, cringing as Sandy's ringed hand came up to his left cheek. "Once we stopped attacking and just spoke to them, they were no longer a threat. We are the ones coming into their home and trying to tear them apart!"

She frowned, a sternness resting in the crease on her forehead. "We're balancing nature. Chris—"

"Doesn't care about us… any of us, he wanted us to go into the fire. He tried to push some of us in, but did he try to go in himself?"

An awkward tension rose in the air. The hunters near the edge of the forest started to whisper amongst themselves, filling the air with speculating voices.

Sandy narrowed her eyes. "You've got no respect," she hissed, pulling at the collar of his hoodie. Jamie croaked as she ran one of her pointed rings down the scar on his neck.

"He's not even here!" Miles suddenly yelled from across the clearing, making everyone turn their heads. No one had bothered to restrain him, and he looked quite pissed off over it, although as the attention turned to him, he coughed, and self-consciously brushed a hand on his sweater.

A guttural growl left Sandy's throat, but Jamie tugged on his restraints to bring her attention back to him. "Why are we even here? Why are we not in Manchester looking for that wild pack, or in Ireland searching for whatever killed those kids from that secondary school last month? The bitten is dead. He's gone, so why are we wasting our time here?"

There was silence for a second, followed by more whispers that crept around the mountain edge.

"This is for the greater good!" Sandy shook her head. "Round the young ones up over there. We'll deal with them later. You lot." She pointed to a few of the hunters. "Go back into the forest and track the other two, they should be easy enough to find if the male really is hurt."

The hunters ignored her, and a handful near the back

seemed to be caught in a deep discussion, eyeing her suspiciously.

Sandy frowned. "What is it?"

One hunter swallowed. "I'm part of the research team," he began, looking a little flushed as she turned to face him with an outraged look. "The Thorn family are actually well respected in the community, one of them is on the Arcane Council. Up until now, they've had no history of violence, Chris told me to keep looking into them anyway… until I found something that gave us reason to go after them… I never found anything."

Ophelia widened her eyes, staring blankly. Her gaze landed on her parents, who looked just as shocked as she did.

The whispers of the crowd got louder, all eyes turning to Sandy, who kept her expression stern, putting her hand out to stop the conversation from continuing. When that didn't work, she pulled one of her sharp rings off and threw it through the air, pinning one of the speaker's sleeves to a tree.

With her attention diverted, Jamie backed away from the commotion and pulled his sword out of its holster, swinging diagonally with his hands still bound behind him and cutting at the rope that had been tied behind Hollie's back.

She freed her wrists and jolted upwards, knocking into the chin of her attacker and sending him stumbling to the floor.

Sandy swirled around at the noise, grunting, before motioning for someone to grab the teenagers. Two of her men moved instantly, but the remaining hunters simply stared, breaking out into another weighted debate.

"They're just kids."

"Yeah, I'm not hurting them. Let's just handle the vampires and take the kids back to the Barracks, they'll know how to handle them there."

"Have the Thorns even done anything incriminating? What are we hunting them for? The council says we don't kill the born ones."

"They turned that girl."

"I didn't bloody turn her," Ophelia grumbled.

"But she's a vampire. A new vampire, too. That can't be a coincidence," the narrow-nosed hunter sneered, smirking as if she'd just caught her in a lie.

Ophelia rolled her eyes. "She's of pure blood, like the rest of us. Trust me, it was a shock to me too. Girl's got no coordination at all."

"There's been no reported attacks since the bitten was taken down."

"It's only been a day."

"Still, most bitten vampires are messy, they leave trails. If there's really no threat now that the bitten is dead, then we don't need to be here."

"What? You're just gonna take her word for it?"

"We have proof," Ophelia replied. "She has a brother, a blood relative, someone that shares the vampire gene, we can test it. You might know him, actually. Short, grumpy, never speaks above a mumble."

"Lucas?" Jamie spat, contorting his expression in at least five different ways as he turned to gawk at Ophelia.

"What? Did we not tell you guys that? Oh, yeah. Apparently, those two are related, matching necklaces and everything… crazy."

"Would have been nice to know that going into this," Hollie mumbled, keeping her eyes on Sandy's unreadable expression.

"Yeah, well, surprise."

The narrow-nosed hunter smacked the tree beside Ophelia,

aiming her dagger at her face. "The sad writer boy…? He can't be! He's one of us!"

"He's been here since he was a baby. There's no way. If he had the gene we'd have known," another hunter said.

A third one hummed. "Would we? It's kind of unrecognisable unless you undergo certain tests, and even then, we'd have to at least have some suspicions first."

"He is faster than most of us," Miles said in his nasally voice, stepping through the crowd to get closer to his friends. No one stopped him. "And stronger. He's our best fighter."

The crowd broke out into more whispers, each hunter looking more confused than the next as they wrapped their heads around the facts.

One of them rubbed at their forehead. "They're just kids… Lucas is a kid. We can't hurt them without reason. What if they're right?"

"They aren't! The bloodsucker's lying. The Barracks wouldn't take in a tainted blood orphan," Sandy fumed, clutching her remaining rings in defiance.

There was a sudden blur of movement and Ophelia glanced over to see her mother pull against her rope, tilting her head toward the hunters condescendingly. "Would you kill him, if he was like us?" she asked.

Some of the hunters stammered, looking at each other uncomfortably.

Sandy stepped towards Julianna, snarling. "You can't prove they're related… and if the girl was bitten, we have every right to—"

"This is a legal issue, right?" Ophelia interrupted, ignoring the dangerous scowl sent her way. "My uncle is on the Council, we can have this sorted before any more blood is spilt. Right, Daddy?"

Alexander nodded. "I'll call my brother. We can have someone test their blood, if it turns out they're related, then we have proof. We can do this the right way," he said.

"And then maybe, *just maybe,* we won't sue you for destruction of property," Ophelia added in taunt, smiling innocently.

The wind swept through the clearing, whistling around the small glow of torch light. Slowly, one of the hunters unwrapped the rope from Jamie's hands, causing the boy to grin victoriously.

"No, stop! That's an order!" Sandy yelled as the warriors began to lower their weapons, some of them stepped away, moving back towards the camp. "This is absurd."

One of the hunters stepped past her, gripping her shoulder. "The Council strives for peace, not this. We're supposed to protect people."

She narrowed her eyes, gritting her teeth together before storming forward and grabbing onto the closest person, Miles, who'd had his back turned to her, helping the rest of his friends out of their restraints. "You're *supposed* to follow my command."

He glanced back with a shocked breath as she pressed her pointed knuckles to the base of his skull.

"Woah, don't be irrational," Alexander tried, still tied to the oak tree a short distance away as Sandy dragged the boy backwards.

Jamie made an effort to rush forward, reaching for his sword, but one of Sandy's robot-like followers knocked it from his hand and held him back.

The hunter woman forced Miles toward the cliff edge, and everyone watched with unease as she spun him around, clutching his T-shirt in the palm of her hand as his feet bordered over the line between the earth and the air.

Miles closed his eyes, his breath trembling as Sandy turned to face the onlooking crowd.

"Turning against me is one thing, but to do it for these creatures… these monsters? They are not designed for peace. You're no better than them if you're willing to stand with them."

With one swift motion, she whisked around and pushed at Miles's chest. He lost his balance, trying to reach out for her, but she simply stepped away from the edge. "We might as well kill you, too."

"Miles!"

Hollie's scream echoed through the cliff-side as Sandy turned around, narrowing her eyes at her followers, who visibly tensed. "Get them, tie up anyone who resists! We don't tolerate traitors!"

As she spoke, everyone looked past her, focusing on the edge of the cliff. Sandy furrowed her brow and turned swiftly to see Julianna Thorn with her hand scrunched around the middle of Miles's T-shirt.

Her wrists were bloody and bruised, the rope once holding her now left behind at the base of the tree trunk. She steadied Miles, and then turned to face the other warriors with dark, dangerous eyes the colour of fresh blood.

With barely a second to adjust, Julianna pounced at Sandy, using the rings on the woman's own fingers to stab into her stomach.

Ophelia smirked up at her own captive and scoffed as the woman shot toward her with a dagger.

She pivoted out of the way, watching the blade stick into the harsh wood. Then, as the hunter struggled to pull it back out again, Ophelia jumped up and wrapped her legs around the woman's neck, twirling her body to force her to collide with the tree.

As Jamie grabbed his sword and raised it toward his own attacker, Hollie jumped onto the back of the other one pulling her bow over his neck. He tumbled to the ground and she jumped off him, allowing Liam to wrap the man's arms behind his back with rope.

The remaining guy raised his hands in surrender, dropping his weapon.

It was practically over after that.

After coming to some sort of legal agreement with Alexander, the rest of the hunters began to make their way back to camp – including Liam and Claudia, who dragged Sandy's unconscious body back with them.

Jamie glanced around, adjusting his harness with a cocky expression until he met Mrs Thorn's eyes.

"If my son really is out there bleeding out from a nightshade-laced weapon, then *you'll* be the one not leaving the woods alive," Julianna spat, grabbing the gulping boy.

In the near distance, Miles cut the rope from Alexander's hands. He rubbed at his wrists, thanking the boy, before instantly drifting to Ophelia, wrapping his arms around her.

"Caleb's okay… he was hit in the shoulder, but I got it out. He's with Hazel. They're on their way home," she whispered, glancing over her father's shoulder as Hollie raised a bow in her mother's direction, yelling for her to drop Jamie.

Alexander sighed into the hug, pulling back to kiss his daughter's forehead before spinning around and drifting to his wife's side.

Ophelia stepped in front of them, blocking Hollie's bow and eyeing her with a stern expression before gripping the end of it. "Won't hesitate this time," she murmured, locking eyes with the girl.

Hollie stared back before reluctantly lowering her weapon.

"He's all right, sweetheart, he's alive," Alexander whispered, tugging at Julianna's arm.

Julianna's eyes were a deep wine colour, and dark bags sat beneath them, blending with the tears dripping, but she finally dropped her hold on Jamie, letting him fall to the ground.

Miles swooped in to help him up, and after a further second of glaring, Ophelia stepped out of Hollie's path to let her do the same.

She turned toward her mother then, both of them eyeing the other warily. Ophelia wasn't sure what was running through the woman's mind. Maybe she was mad at Ophelia, for the outburst after the fire, or for running off to find Caleb and splitting them all up. Or even for messing up the rescue plan, really it could have been a multitude of things, and she was just waiting for that familiar disappointed look to fall onto her mother's face.

It never did.

Instead, the woman stepped forward, watching for a moment before she brushed a strand of Ophelia's hair out of her face. "It was very brave of you to walk in like that, to save us."

Ophelia blinked, glancing up wordlessly. Her father placed a hand on her shoulder, making her turn towards him. "And the legal issue," he chuckled. "Lia, that was brilliant."

"Yeah," Julianna added. "It *was* brilliant."

Ophelia let out a shaky laugh, unsure of what to say. It was rare her mother was actually proud of her. It felt nice.

"Let's go find Caleb and Hazel," Julianna stated after a second, squeezing Ophelia's arm attentively before stepping past her.

CHAPTER TWENTY-SEVEN

Static Energy

Hazel had never been more grateful for her *vampiric adjustments* than now. It was pitch-black in the forest, and she had no torch, but was making her way through the mist with no problem.

Caleb wasn't much help. Although he was leaning on her less now, and was spewing less nonsense each minute, he was still struggling a little, dragging his feet.

"Can we… stop for a second?" he winced, grabbing onto his wound and leaning back against a tree.

Hazel glanced around the area. There was nothing but trees ahead of them. The campsite was almost a mile back now, though she could still see the tiniest campfire glare in the distance.

Hazel stepped in front of Caleb, chewing on her lower lip as she looked over his pained face.

As if noticing her worried expression, he glanced up with a sweet smile. "Feels better," he assured her. She frowned in disbelief, and he chuckled, reaching up to his shoulder.

With a wince, he brushed his hand over the dried blood, revealing the slowly healing skin beneath. Dark purple bruises covered it, some of them fading into his veins but simmering out before they could reach his heart.

Hazel's eyes widened. She got closer, reaching out to his shoulder, but not quite touching.

Caleb chuckled under his breath, then dragged her wrist over, letting her fingertips brush against his bare skin. She could feel the sting from the nightshade residue as she traced one of the bruises.

He smiled, watching her, maybe still a little loopy with the way his tongue was stuck out between his teeth. He glanced back over at his bloodied shoulder and his cheeks flushed with a pretty rose shade. "See, almost all gone. I can barely feel it," he said, but Hazel could see the pain lingering behind his eyes.

She tugged at her T-shirt sleeves. "Caleb?"

"Yeah?" His eyes were glimmering in the light of the full moon. They were no longer dilated, and full of black, but more an outburst of baby blue, dripping with grey around the corners.

Hazel swallowed. "I'm sorry it didn't go to plan. I know you didn't really want to fight… I'm sorry for all of it."

Caleb creased his eyebrows together and pushed off from the tree trunk, placing his hands over hers, which were covered by her oversized sleeves. He pushed the fabric back, freeing her hands enough to link them with his own.

Hazel glanced up to meet his gaze. His eyes were darting back and forth, over the bloodied marks on her cheeks from where he'd cupped them, to the dimples lining her smile, then slowly down to her lips. She watched as his Adam's apple bobbed up and down a few times before he stumbled on his feet.

She reached out and gripped his shoulders, straightening him, and his hands instinctively found their way to her waist, to stop himself from falling. He moved them to her arms, looking up sheepishly, before biting his lip with a brazen grin.

Hazel chuckled, letting her hands slink down his arms and

linking their fingers back together as she gazed into the woods behind him. There was nothing but darkness for miles, just moonlight shining down on them from above, and the breeze blowing through the trees.

"I know how hard you tried to get through to them," Hazel added, her gaze falling onto his shoulder before one of her hands disconnected from his to brush over the purple veins on his skin.

Caleb shivered beneath her touch, and she flinched away, not wanting to hurt him, but then he frowned, tilting his head to the side. "I got through to some of them. That's enough. Now we can distinguish the ones willing to listen from the ones who just want us dead, at least."

Hazel felt herself swallow tightly, staring up at him. Dried blood still covered his chin and most of his collarbone. "I just wish none of it would have happened. Then you wouldn't have got hurt."

He shook his head, using his hand to push her chin up. His expression was soft and light, with the slightest hint of delusion in it from the poison. "I don't. I don't regret any of it."

Hazel felt her stomach twist, nerves spiralling up her spine as his fingers brushed against her cheek. It was magnetic, really, the way his fingers felt against her skin. It made her feel weightless as she let her thoughts wander somewhere else, focused entirely on him. His baby blue eyes, the warm smile on his face, the gentleness of his touch.

Even though he was the one injured, he held her like she was something sacred.

Caleb licked his lips, smiling as his hand reached up to trace patterns on her cheek, before something strange flickered on his face and he dropped back, glancing behind them.

Hazel pulled a face, reaching to steady him as he limped away. "What?"

"Someone's following us," Caleb said, a little too calmly for the seriousness of his statement.

Hazel widened her eyes and then pulled his arm around her shoulder. "Great, let's go then," she breathed, trying to tug him away, but he turned around and leaned forward onto a tree, staring off into the darkness as she stressfully chewed on her sleeve.

"I'll stop them," Caleb chimed breezily, propping himself up on the trunk. "I'll set the trees on fire, hold them off."

"Huh? No? What?!" Hazel said, the sleeve falling from her mouth.

He didn't reply, instead, he focused his attention on the forest, using the stability of the tree to hold himself up as Hazel wrapped her arms around his torso.

"Caleb!"

She could hear it now, the slight shuffling of feet getting closer. She tightened her grip around him and tugged, but he remained focused, his eyes burning crimson. As more energy was pulled from his body in the form of external flames, she could feel the hold around his arms loosen. Hazel let out a breath as she held onto him, not letting him fall.

An arrow came flying through the air, bursting with a bright violet undertone that lit up the woods as it went up in flames, hitting the ground and burning to ash right in front of them.

A wave of flames rose behind it, creating a walled inferno that shot up at least seven feet tall, glistening with intensity as Caleb gripped onto the tree for support. The hunters ran up to it, scowling at them from the other side before moving away, likely running off to find another way around.

Caleb let out a gasp as he closed his eyes, letting the flames burn out. He tumbled into Hazel's side, almost tripping over himself, but she caught him.

"Okay. We… can… leave now," he exhaled.

Lucas sprinted through the trees, using his blade to cut through some of the overhanging branches. Farah was behind him, her spear still in her right hand. There were trickles of light in the near distance, up by another cliff-top on the hill closest to the camp.

He stopped to catch his breath.

Farah stopped behind him, leaning forward on her spear for support as she let out a sharp exhale. "They could be up there," she wheezed, glancing up to the withering light in the distance.

Lucas pulled his lips back, chewing the corner of his cheek with an unsure expression.

"But the fire," he replied. At least ten minutes earlier, they'd felt a hot breeze and glanced over to see a giant wall of fire a few miles away, in the opposite direction to the torches. They were torn in the middle.

Lucas stabbed his dagger through another branch, letting it whack the ground below him as he let out a harsh breath. "We're losing time."

"The torches are closer, maybe we should keep following them."

"Could be anything, warriors still searching the woods, civilians in the forest, but that wall of fire wasn't a normal flame. It was crimson, dark fire. It's from them, and if we can see it, so can Chris," he said sombrely, glancing back the other way. "We should split up, you go to the cliff, I'll go toward the dark fire, so we can cover more ground."

Farah hummed, rubbing her forehead with the side of her metal cane. "We can't split up, not now. We don't even know who's on our side and who isn't."

"Anyone trying to kill you isn't on our side. They hit you, hit them back, hard, until they can't hit you again," he responded, yanking his hood up over his head.

As he started to move, Farah let out an uneasy sound. "Lucas…"

He stopped, inhaling slowly as the wind passed over him, threatening to blow the hood down from his face. "You said Jamie's with us now, for whatever reason. Find him, he's a good fighter, especially with the others. If we've got them on our side we've got a chance."

Farah nodded, looking down to the ground with a solemn smile. "That was very odd coming from your mouth."

"Yeah," he agreed. "Never tell Jamie I complimented him, he'll never let it go."

"Don't worry, I won't… Luke?" Farah asked, stopping him as he was about to leave. "Stay safe, okay?"

The corners of Lucas's lips rose as he twirled the dagger around his fingers, clutching the handle tightly.

"As if you have to ask."

The wind moved with Lucas as he continued through the forest, quickly, moving further away from camp.

About a mile away, he had passed a broken arrow, and a patch of blood left behind on the forest ground, infused with the unmistakable purple tint of nightshade powder. Lucas tracked the blood trail through the trees until it vanished. The more he moved, the more he felt like he was wandering in circles. Letting out a groan of frustration, he stopped, brushing his hands over his face as the cold wind blew the hood from his head. His eyes clenched shut in irritation – this was all useless. It didn't matter how fast he was running. He could be going the wrong way and it might already be too late. Chris could have found Hazel, hurt her already, and Lucas was too far away to get there in time. A prickling feeling ran through his fingertips, running down from his arms like pins and needles.

With a deep, pent-up grumble, he gripped his dagger in his left hand and thrust it forward, watching it tear through the air and splinter into wood.

The dagger lodged itself in a tree at a strange angle, sticking out like an arrow. He took a step forward and blinked as a sage colour fractured out from the blade, bleeding into the trunk like veins, before disappearing. Maybe it was his eyes playing tricks on him, but he could have sworn the wood shifted.

Lucas ran his fingers along the tree vine designs etched into the handle of his dagger before glancing up at its intended direction.

Up ahead was the sheer glow of torchlight in the distance, barely visible through the trees. He pulled at the dagger and sheathed it before following the light. As he got closer, he heard voices. Two, maybe three men were whispering, tracking something else through the woods. Lucas hid behind the trees, manoeuvring through them quietly to get a better look.

It was Chris. His slippery condescending voice was like a beacon in the dark, easy to pinpoint as he directed the other two hunters.

"He's injured, the amount of energy it would take for him to conjure up more dark fire would probably be enough to bring him down. Toy with him, get him to do it again, then we can take the girl," he muttered, motioning somewhere to the left. "Head up that way. We can split up and corner them. They won't stand a chance."

Lucas narrowed his eyes. His jaw clenched as he looked at the man who'd raised him. The moon's glow exposed a new perspective of him, emphasising the faded blood on his face. It painted the perfect mirror image of what Farah had been saying about him all these years. Only Lucas didn't see it until now.

There was malice in the leader's eyes as he spoke about what he would do when he found who he was looking for, how he was going to kill them, rip them apart.

While the other two men disappeared in different directions, Chris chose to stay in the middle, stepping through the trees. He moved forward, his back vulnerable, and Lucas, unable to resist, stepped out from the trees, wielding his dagger.

"What happened to my parents?" he demanded, hearing his own voice echo in the cold air.

Christopher slowly turned around, raising his hands cautiously as he examined the dagger he held, raising an eyebrow. "Lucas? You know what happened to your parents."

Lucas heard himself scoff before he'd even decided to. He shook his head, feeling his vision blur. "What *really* happened to my parents? My father?"

Chris's wary eyes showed a flicker of realisation as he dropped his hands, his face contorting. "You know what happened. Your parents were killed, Lucas, torn apart by those monsters your friend is trying to protect."

"Stop lying to me. I'm not a kid anymore. You can't keep telling me stories and expect me to believe them."

As Lucas's hands shook, Chris stepped forward and let the dagger tip hover inches away from his chest, maintaining eye contact.

"You were brought to my doorstep as a baby, if it weren't for me, you'd have been left out in the woods to die."

"No." Lucas shook his head, blinking hard. "You're wrong."

Chris took another step, letting the blade graze his own skin as he towered above the boy. "I took you in, I fed you, trained you. I gave you purpose! You're alive because of me, you're here because of me! Your family was killed, now stop moping and either stab me or come with me!" he barked. "We've been tracking two of them through the woods. Get your priorities straight boy, we have a job to do."

Lucas vigorously shook his head, stepping back and almost dropping his weapon as he raised his hand in exasperation. "No, you lied to me. They're not dead, my mother is not dead. My sister and my family are alive! You kept it from me!" he spat, peering up through a crumbling expression.

Apart from a flicker of interest and mild confusion on his face, Christopher remained unwavering. "What are you talking about, son?"

Lucas narrowed his eyes. "Don't call me son," he said. "Hazel, the girl you're trying to kill? She's my sister, my twin sister."

Christopher's expression changed, twisting with surprise as he glanced down in consideration.

"She's not bitten, she's born, and she's my blood, so you can't hurt her."

"Are you sure? She can't be, that's not possible…"

Lucas scoffed. "You want a bloody birth certificate? I'll probably have to get back to you on that when I speak to my dead mum who *isn't dead!*"

Christopher shook his head, glancing up with a cautious look. "She's your blood? You're certain?"

With a frustrated breath, Lucas nodded, watching the man's expression carefully. Chris's face was unreadable as he took in the information. Then, leaving no time to react, he suddenly lunged, swiping the dagger from Lucas's hand.

He looked up with a stunned expression and grunted as the dagger sliced across his upper arm.

"If she's your sister, and you share blood, then you're one of them!" Chris grimaced, gripping Lucas's shoulder harshly as he pulled the blade back. "And you know how we handle things here," he hissed, burying the dagger into Lucas's arm and shoving him backward.

Lucas hit the ground, clutching his bleeding arm as he looked up at the man who'd raised him, and the dagger dripping with blood. *His blood.*

"No exceptions."

As Chris moved forward, reaching for him again, Lucas grabbed a handful of dirt and threw it into his eyes. Christopher roared in anger and clawed at his face, giving Lucas a chance to sweep past him. He ran, creating some distance between them, before grabbing onto a tree for support. The pain in his arm was bordering on excruciating as he reached up to wipe at the blood.

"Come on, Lucas, there's no point in fighting it. You're going to turn, you'll be one of them, and I'll have to kill you. Wouldn't you rather me do it now? Save you from becoming one of those things," Christopher called out, following him through the trees. "I know you don't want to be like them."

Shielding his body behind a tree, Lucas huffed, gripping his arm. "I don't want to be like you either."

A feral laugh fell from Chris's lips as he drew forward, swiping at the spot Lucas had been, but it was now empty.

Lucas dropped his head back against a different tree, gripping it for support. As he pressed his palms against it, a mild prickling sensation ran through him, forcing him to let out an involuntary grumble.

Chris advanced, swinging his blade out blindly. With a rough kick to his torso, however, he lost his balance, staggering before propelling himself forward, blade in hand. Lucas grabbed the man's arm, stopping the dagger's path.

Using the injury to his advantage, Chris spun under Lucas's arm, twisting it and pushing him down. "It's a shame. You're a good fighter, you could have been useful to me," he said as Lucas dropped to the ground with a wince. "Suppose it's my own fault for letting that god-awful woman take care of you when you were younger. Should have known she would get in your head."

Lucas furrowed his brow. "Don't talk about Shelley… You should've helped her!"

A dark and unsettling laugh tumbled from the leader's lips, causing Lucas to raise an eyebrow and sit up, wincing as he held onto his arm. "That's not funny, you arse."

"No, it's hilarious," Chris replied, looming over him. "There's nothing I could have done. She set herself up for death, it was her own fault, going against me. I couldn't have her poisoning any more young minds."

Lucas blinked, feeling his mouth run dry. "You killed her?"

He felt like throwing up. Everything the warriors did was a calculated move, it always had been. It didn't matter who got hurt, or who paid the price, as long as it got Chris closer to some sort of destruction.

The dusty haired hunter shook his head, crouching down beside him. "Not personally, but she got what was coming to her, and the wolf still ended up dead. It was a win for everyone, really."

A ruptured sound escaped Lucas's lips as his eyes filled with animosity. Ignoring the pain in his arm, he firmly grasped the man's torso and yanked him down into the dirt with him, making him release the dagger. "I'm going to fucking kill you," he grumbled, using the momentum of the sudden movement to punch Chris across the face.

Chris laughed, swivelling his body around to avoid the next hit as Lucas pounced again. The older man quickly grabbed his shoulder and pushed his thumb into his wound.

With a yelp, Lucas rolled backwards and dropped his head in the grass. Suddenly, he felt the cool weight of a blade pressing into his neck as a faint, raspy voice resonated in the trees behind them.

"Lucas!"

Looking up, Lucas felt a sinking feeling in the pit of his stomach as he locked eyes with the same fiery, sun-kissed eyes as his own.

With her arm wrapped tightly around Caleb's shoulder, Lucas watched as Hazel staggered forward, eyes wide with concern. The pair looked like they'd been running through the forest for a while, with their mud-covered clothes and the orange leaves weaved into Hazel's ponytail.

Beside her, Caleb looked very worse for wear, covered in thick layers of blood with a battered bandage covering his shoulder. He was limping slightly, leaning into Hazel's side as she held him up.

Her blazing eyes were stuck on Lucas, and then, as they travelled up to the man hovering over him, he saw her swallow nervously.

Without looking, he could feel Chris smirking, could sense the glee on his face as he leaned forward and stabbed the knife into Lucas's wound once more, prompting a scream of agony.

Lucas's vision became hazy, the pain in his arm overwhelming as his head hit the ground. Although, the worst thing to hit him was the fear gripping Caleb's voice.

"Hazel, wait!"

He forced himself to glance up again, watching as the girl stalked closer, eyes burning red with fury. Caleb stumbled behind her, desperately trying to reach out, but Hazel had already slipped away from his grasp.

The woods stirred with movement, causing the vampire to turn around. Without much time to react, the two hunters from before grabbed Caleb, holding him back at Chris's request as the group leader stood up and moved towards Hazel.

As the Nosferatu Warrior advanced toward her, she sent a swift kick toward his crotch area, however her lack of expertise made her no match for the seasoned hunter. In a matter of seconds he'd managed to grab her and twist her around, holding her to his chest as he firmly grasped his blade.

"No, no wait!" Lucas shouted, struggling to stand. He felt dizzy immediately but pushed the feeling to the back of his mind, determined to get up.

With a firm grip on Hazel's shoulders, Chris glanced down at him, the blade digging into her skin, trailing a line of blood. Despite her efforts to appear stubborn and unaffected, the fear was evident on her face.

Behind them, Caleb was desperately trying to break free from his captors, but his efforts were in vain. He was too injured to put up a good fight.

Lucas stumbled, gripping his bleeding arm. "Don't… please! Wait! Let's talk about this." His words were staggered as his voice broke, coming out in breathless spurts that made the man ahead of him turn his lip up in disregard. "You raised me, Chris, you're the closest thing to a father I've ever had. Please don't do this."

The hunter's grip on the girl grew tighter, his unsettling face showing no concern as the brunette restlessly tried to break free.

"She's my sister, don't hurt her, please."

The corners of Hazel's lips tilted upward at his words, relaxing into the shape of her cheekbones.

In a display of disdain, Chris narrowed his eyes and snarled before plunging the dagger into her back.

Lucas's jaw dropped in horror as a screech of pain tumbled from Hazel's mouth.

"No!" Caleb cried, struggling against his captors. His eyes burned as he tried to rush over to her, but one of the hunters slammed him in the chest, holding him back.

With one quick tug, Christopher pulled the knife back, causing Hazel to cry out in pain as the blade flicked blood at Lucas, splattering it across his face.

Hazel stumbled forward, struggling to catch her breath, until Christopher kicked her to her knees with an eerie, exuberant expression.

Something inside Lucas ignited in that moment, transforming his shock into a fiery rage. He threw himself at Chris and knocked them both to the ground, pinning the man down and slamming his fists into his face. In one swift motion, he struck Chris's chin with the base of his knee, causing the man to cry out in agony.

Lucas glanced upward, fixing his gaze on Caleb. He was still trying to break free but the hunters held him back, each gripping an arm.

Chris used the distraction to his advantage. He clutched onto Lucas's arm, applying pressure to the wound yet again. The Nosferatu Warrior leader grabbed the dagger that had slipped from his grasp and stood up.

Lying on the ground a few metres ahead, Hazel exhaled softly. The blade she'd been struck with didn't have any more remnants of nightshade, Lucas had wiped it away earlier, though she was still struggling to get her breaths out.

Chris removed a vial from his pocket and emptied the contents onto the dagger in his hand, allowing the powder to cover the weapon.

Hazel's eyes widened as he lunged at her, targeting her chest.

In a rush of motion, Lucas knocked the hunter off her, wrapping his arms around the man and shoving him against the nearest tree before forcing him to the ground.

He could hear Caleb attempting to break free from his captors, but he didn't look up. The sound of someone yelling out in pain was quickly followed by the thud of their body hitting the ground, and then the crunch of another person hitting a tree.

As Lucas pushed Chris down into the mud, he stared up diligently, the corner of his lip tilted upward. Only then did Lucas become aware of the fact that Chris no longer held his dagger.

He quickly peered over his shoulder to see Caleb moving with unnatural speed towards Hazel. The vampire grunted in pain as he sank down beside her and pulled the girl onto his lap.

"No, no, no," he muttered frantically, pulling the blade from her chest. "You're okay… you're fine. Hazel, look at me. You're okay."

Lucas's gaze trailed over to her, and his breath caught in his throat when he spotted the blood coating her chest, soaking through her shirt and painting her a horrible mixture of red and purple.

Hazel tried to reply, but her voice came out slurred, the red on her lips causing her to stutter in trembling breaths.

Caleb brushed at the blood, wiping it away to no avail. "It's okay. Just… wait a minute. It'll start to heal," he whispered. There was a heaviness in his voice, raw and panicked, like the expression on his face. "You're okay… It just needs a second to heal."

Despite his words, the sickly colour of her skin only worsened. Thick black veins protruded from her skin, smoking with the purple haze of the nightshade.

A gasp came from the treeline and Lucas looked over to see Ophelia had appeared, her hand pressed against her mouth. There was an indescribable horror on her face, freezing her in place as her father brushed past and approached Caleb.

He peered up at his father, tears wetting his cheeks. "I pulled the blade out! Why isn't she healing? She should be healing."

Lost in a blur of thoughts, Lucas could barely perceive Caleb's cries, or the sound of trees rustling as more figures appeared. Even the birds above were void of their usual melodies, replaced instead by a vigilant and eerie silence.

The rise and fall of Hazel's chest was slowing down with every passing second. Lucas swallowed, feeling his own heart pulse in his chest. He felt disconnected from his body, hearing the rush of blood vibrate through his veins and the feeling disappear from his fingertips as he gazed at his sister's near lifeless body.

His own blade lay only inches away, having been the murder weapon.

An intense flame blazed within Lucas, compelling him to retrieve his spare dagger from his waistband. He locked eyes with Chris's bruised face as he extracted the weapon.

"Don't do it!" Farah said, appearing above him. She crouched down, reaching for the trembling knife in his grasp.

Lucas could feel his eyes stinging as he stumbled over his words. "But he… he…"

"I know," Farah replied sadly. "But it's not who you are. Go be with her, let me take care of him."

Lucas hesitated for a second, and Farah squeezed his hand. His eyes wavered between her, the dagger in his hand, and the manipulative bastard of a man below him.

"It's not who you are," Farah repeated. She must have noticed the gash on his arm, because she ripped some of the fabric from her shirt and wrapped it over the wound, creating a makeshift tourniquet.

With a loud thud, Mrs Thorn drifted over and used her knee to render Chris fully unconscious while Farah restrained him, looking up at Lucas and gesturing for him to go to his sister.

Lucas swallowed hard, nodding to them both, before dropping his dagger as he struggled to stand up.

With tears streaming down his face, Caleb was desperately pleading with Hazel to open her eyes. She lay on his lap, lifeless as the boy's father looked over her wound, wincing at the nightshade on his fingertips. The dagger had cut too close to her heart, allowing the deadly ash to puncture the artery almost immediately. There was no coming back from a wound like that.

Lucas sucked in a breath. Hazel looked so young, so innocent, even with the thick red stains covering her. Her face was rounded at the edges and reddened with blood, but the line of her dimples still stood out in her cheekbones.

Caleb pressed a hand to her cheek, swallowing back a sob as the colour continued to drain from her skin, turning her veins a sickly shade of lilac.

For a single moment, he'd had a sister. A living, breathing person with whom he shared a mother, a womb, a birthday, and the next minute, the life had been drained from her lungs as if that was the plan from the very start.

They were parallel lines, destined to follow the same path, but never to cross. Two worlds never meant to collide, because if they did, they would probably crash, and here they were, plummeting into the ground.

Lucas glanced away, unable to look at Hazel's painfully familiar face as a numbness spread over him, engulfing his whole body with a hazy feeling before being replaced by a strange buzz of energy.

It started at his fingertips, not so different from the prickling sensation he'd felt before back at the tree-stump and in the clearing. Looking down at his skin, Lucas felt only static until something grabbed his attention. Hazel's once purple veins were tingling with a faint sheer green tinge. He frowned and glanced at Caleb, who was too busy focusing on her face to notice.

Lucas extended his hand towards Hazel's arm, watching as a static current flowed from his skin to hers, pulsing through him with a rush of energy.

He let go of Hazel and stood up, slapping his arms as if trying to shake off some invisible force.

After a moment, Lucas peered at the bewildered faces before him and fixated on the shiny reflection in Mr Thorn's glasses. A pair of light green eyes shone in the dark. *His eyes.* The usual brown colour replaced by a startling, luminous green.

The blonde boy below let out a surprised grumble, causing Lucas to look back down. More of Hazel's veins were tinted in a more prominent sage green. It engulfed her, travelling up through her arms, all the way toward her face until, slowly, she opened her eyes.

There was a brief pause of silence while everyone watched in astonishment as Hazel gasped for breath.

She sat up with Caleb's help and glanced around, blinking as her once-red irises were consumed by a vibrant emerald hue, intertwining the two colours together – a perfect kaleidoscope of red and green.

"Ow," she croaked, rubbing at her head and glancing around slowly. "What's… what's wrong?"

Caleb gently lifted her hand, motioning down to her veins that were slowly starting to lose their green hue. She pulled a face, then looked up with a flabbergasted expression as she noticed the same thing in Lucas's arms.

Hazel reached out and grabbed his arm, watching as it faded away before looking up at him. "What the hell?"

He studied her with a laboured breath. She looked a little out of it, her eyes were sort of cloudy as she stared at him, as if searching for something familiar, then, with a strange croak, she wrapped her arms around him.

Lucas stiffened, before reciprocating the hug. "I'm sorry… I'm so sorry. I believe you. I promise I believe you," he whispered.

She tightened her hold in return, leaning up to look at the stars that shone above them.

352

CHAPTER TWENTY-EIGHT
The World's Not the Same

Murmuring voices, beeping, and indistinguishable hospital noises blurred in the background as Hazel wriggled in the sea-foam green chair, trying to find a comfortable position. She tried to focus on only one thing at a time, but it was practically impossible in such a busy place.

With a sigh, Hazel leaned back, rubbing at her forehead. The introduction of a trillion new senses was a lot to handle at once, and she wasn't so confident that she'd ever fully understand them.

There was a flutter of movement, followed by a yawn, and Amber sat up, rubbing at her eyes. "I thought you'd gone home," she said, tutting.

Hazel shuffled her chair along the floor, pulling it closer to the hospital bed as she let out a yawn of her own. "I did," she protested sleepily. "Then I came back."

Amber laughed, stretching her hand out to her neck, which was wrapped in a heavy bandage.

"How is it today? Do you want me to call someone to bring you some painkillers?" Hazel whispered.

"Nah, it's fine, Haze. I think they gave me some earlier, it doesn't hurt so bad," the other girl assured her, reaching over to pull the table of magazines and chocolate mousses over.

Hazel nodded sheepishly, moving to help her drag the table, though she was met with a look of protest.

"I've got full use of my hands, you know. I don't need you to do everything for me."

With a shrug, Hazel sat back in her chair, watching as Amber opened one of the mousse pots. She reached for a spoon, but before she could lean too far, Hazel quickly grabbed it, handing it to her with an awkward smile. "Yeah, but I will. Until you're out of this bed, I'm not letting you do any heavy lifting."

Amber jammed a spoonful of chocolate into her mouth. "Since when was a teaspoon classed as *heavy lifting?*"

"Shut up." Hazel grinned, grabbing a spoon and taking a mouthful for herself.

A sudden thunderous snore from the corner startled them both, prompting them to look up. Amber's father shifted uncomfortably in his chair, his nostrils flaring as another earth-shattering wheeze erupted from him.

The girls exchanged glances, struggling to contain their laughter.

"So..." Amber hummed after a few minutes, pulling Hazel's attention.

"No Lucas today? I thought you said you were gonna bring him in to see me. I've got about a million questions to ask that boy," Amber said, placing her half-eaten dessert on the table as she clamped her hands together.

Hazel lifted her legs onto the bed, straining her expression. "That's exactly why I haven't brought him in yet." Amber's lips tumbled into a frown and Hazel tilted her head with a tired look. "I don't want you to bombard him with questions. He's still adjusting."

"Aw, come on. I'm not gonna bombard him. I only want to know a few things," Amber enthused, pushing down on the bed to sit up further.

Hazel stood up to help. "Like what?" she asked, ignoring the unhappy look she received as she slipped a pillow behind the girl's back.

"Like, where the hell has he been all this time? How didn't you know he was your brother? Twin brother! Twin, Hazel. You guys shared a womb! You were *wombmates!*"

Hazel sighed, picking at the fraying edges of her nail varnish as she rested back in her chair. "I already told you. Neither of us knew anything… not until my mother got that letter from… from my grandmother, explaining everything."

"Explaining what, though? I'm terribly lost here," Amber said as she watched expectantly, awaiting an answer.

Hazel chewed her lip, fumbling to think of something believable, though all she could muster up in the end was a sheepish shrug.

As Amber scoffed, opening her mouth to retaliate, her eyes drifted upwards, catching sight of something behind Hazel, and she froze.

Hazel furrowed her brow and glanced over her shoulder, peering through the glass door. All she could see was the hospital corridor. There was a ward sign next to a portrait of two girls in old-fashioned clothing, sitting in a field of flowers.

She twisted back around and pulled a face at her friend. "What are you looking at?"

Amber glanced up. The glossiness of her eyes returning to normal. "Sorry, I thought I saw someone," she said, peering back up at the window for a second. "It was nothing."

"Okay," Hazel replied, eyebrows still raised as she grabbed the rest of her friend's dessert and held it out to her. "Eat, I think you're still a bit light-headed." Amber gave her an offended look, but Hazel pushed the mousse toward her, forcing the spoon into her hand. "Eat, or I'll call the nurse.

Or worse, I'll wake up Rob," she mused, motioning to the girl's sleeping father. Ever since the attack, he'd barely left her side.

Sighing, Amber accepted the cup, putting a spoonful into her mouth in defeat.

The smell of smoke and burning polyester lingered across camp as Lucas stepped over a few fallen tins of fruit.

He peered around, watching as a few hunters threw a bunch of burned furniture into a pile, adding to a large rubbish heap they'd made. In the centre of it, Claudia was rummaging through bits of scrap metal and fabric, with Liam behind her, arms outstretched as she piled things into them.

Farah made her way toward Lucas, smiling cheerfully as he kicked at another dented tin. "Hey, we're supposed to be cleaning up this mess, not playing with it. It's taking us long enough as it is," she teased, kicking it back to him.

He bent down to pick it up and threw it onto a nearby pile of rubbish. "Tell that to *her*, she's a second away from diving in,' he mused, pulling a face as Claudia plunged further into the useless crap.

Farah chuckled under her breath and grabbed his arm, pulling him into step beside her.

As they walked, other hunters stepped past, either smiling in their direction or nodding in greeting as they continued about their duties. Farah, of course, waved at every single one of them.

It was strange how mellow everyone had been in the past week. With Chris, Sandy, and the rest of their perilous little group locked up in the med tent, ready to be shipped off back to the Barracks and dealt with by the Council, everything had been a lot more peaceful. Friendly even.

The pair stepped into one of the larger tents in the main section of the camp, the one used for meetings. It was usually only occupied by Chris and his closest warriors, but now the curtains were wide open.

Jamie was sitting at the head of the table in the centre, peering down at a pile of letters. Investigation boards full of dangling red string and maps stood to the left of the table, with a whiteboard on the other side. Lucas could make out the faint message that had now been scrubbed off, '*sit still and become prey? or kill to fight another day?*'

It had always been a rhetorical question of course, and while it had never been all that motivational, now it just seemed arrogant and stupid. Never mind the fact it was an amateur rhyme.

Miles stood near the map, taking down the string that encircled the woods around Thorn estate.

Lucas grabbed one of the chairs, sitting down next to Jamie and reaching into the pile of letters. The older boy hastily snatched the letters back and Lucas scoffed, sitting up to forcefully grab another one. Before Jamie could retaliate, something hard slammed down against the circular table, snapping their attention to Farah, who was standing with her cane, shaking her head.

"Boys." She sighed, gliding the staff over to the pile of letters Jamie was holding and pushing them into the middle of the table. "Share."

Lucas sighed heavily as Farah smirked and walked away, clutching a yellow highlighter.

The table shifted as Jamie hesitantly pushed a letter toward the dark-haired boy. "It's from the Barracks," he said.

"They've been sending letters for months, asking for updates on the wolf pack that we were supposed to be tracking."

"The one in Manchester?" Lucas asked, reaching for the letter.

Jamie nodded. "Yep, we weren't even supposed to come here."

There were dozens of letters, all addressed to Chris, entailing the same instructions and information on the wolf pack. There were even a few letters that Chris hadn't sent back yet, detailing the progress of the case they hadn't even started.

"What about the bitten? Do any of them mention it? Maybe we had to go off course to track it."

Jamie shook his head, leaning back. His arms stroked the chair as if he was sitting on a throne. "No, nothing about that, either, but I found this." With a grin, he reached into a small hook on the chair's arm and pulled it back to reveal a hidden crevice stashed with cigars, a few wads of cash, and a notebook encircled with string.

Lucas grabbed the notebook and began scanning through the pages. The writings were mostly indecipherable murderous strategies, but there were parts that stuck out, like a series of last names. Vampiric last names. Some were crossed off in red pen, along with scribbled numbers on the sides. A few crosses down was the name 'Thorn' underlined in black.

Lucas placed the book down, creasing his forehead with an unsteady breath.

Jamie raised an eyebrow in agreement. "We tracked the bitten from the west, but only because we came across it on our path. If I hadn't found it that first night—"

"Eh, I found it," Lucas interrupted. "I was on watch when it drifted through camp *and I* tracked it to Henley Mar."

Jamie struck his hands down on the table, frowning

deeply. "No! We were both on watch! And I called it in," he huffed. Lucas sat up in his chair, glaring.

Slumping into one of the chairs beside them, Hollie sighed boredly. "Does it really matter?"

"Yes," both boys said, turning to look at her. She sneered at them.

"This is like that night in Cornwall all over again!" Jamie complained.

Lucas rolled his eyes. "Oh, shut up, just because I got to the cavern before you. Would you rather me have waited for your dead weight to catch up and let that rogue bitten get away?"

"Yes. Because then, Luco, I would have taken it down no problem without *almost* breaking my ankle."

"That cave was slippery and you know it!"

The end of Farah's spear landed on the table again, pulling their attention back up. She was standing by the whiteboard, fingers now stained with yellow ink.

Lucas dragged a hand over his face, groaning into it. "Fine. It doesn't matter who found it, even if it was me—"

"No—" Jamie started, but his words cut out as everyone turned to look at him. He lifted his arms in surrender and patted them back down on his throne.

"We were coming here either way, we just didn't know it…" Lucas said, holding the notebook up. "Chris can't be the only one not following the rules. I know for a fact Sandy has the same mindset as him, and they have forces all throughout the system."

"So, what now?" Miles asked, flicking his hand to free it of the string that had wrapped around it.

Farah peered at him with a kind smile and pointed her staff up at the whiteboard, using it as a pointer stick. In yellow highlighter ink were the words, '*In darkness, storms, or the break of day, subside your fears, and find a way.*'

She grinned as the group read over it, looking a little sceptical. "We won't let fear consume us. We'll protect those who need it, no matter who they are. This isn't a dictatorship, we have to stand together, decide *together*." She looked between Jamie and Lucas pointedly. "We do our jobs, go after the wolf pack or whatever else the barrack leaders have planned, but we also need to keep in mind that trust is scarce, especially now. Chris was willing to kill us just because of our association with the vampires, we don't know how people will react on the inside."

Her gaze fluttered over to Lucas and he felt his stomach turn, a nauseous feeling resonating in the pit of it. She hadn't said the words, but he'd known what she meant; because of his blood, the hidden gene in his DNA, he'd be a target now.

Lucas kept his head level, fixing his gaze on Farah as she swiftly moved on. "You can go back to the Barracks, find your own team if you want, make your own decisions, or even stay somewhere else for a while, but we have to agree, when the time comes, we can at least trust each other."

Lucas sighed. "She's right, as much as I hate to admit it. We have to trust each other," he grumbled. "Fight together or we die, picking at each other instead of the real enemy isn't helping us." He turned to Jamie, waiting for some sort of response.

The self-assured boy tilted his eyebrows in a false act of consideration before grinning. "Okay, mutant boy, because you asked so nicely, we'll fight together. If you really want to. I'll even lead the way."

Lucas rolled his eyes, and his hand flinched, itching to whack Jamie's smug look off his face.

"So who gets the honour of taking those arseholes back to the Barracks?"

"Yes, Ophelia's blood — I know. Look, Ed, we've been monitoring Hazel and I can assure you she's one of us, not bitten. Her brother has the gene, too. Julianna tested his blood and their mother confirmed the relation. I can send you what proof we have if the council requires…"

Julianna watched cautiously as her husband spoke into the phone. He nodded, swaying on the chair and she blinked at him, raising her arms questionably.

Alexander pulled the phone back, holding his hand over the speaker. "He says as long as we can get proof that Lucas and Hazel are related, then they should be in the clear, given Lucas has the gene."

She nodded and his attention turned back to the phone, his eyes widening in concern at the murmured voice on the other end. "Surname?" Alexander whispered, glancing at his wife unsurely.

She swallowed back a harsh breath and peered out of the doorway, looking around before slowly pulling the door closed.

Alexander rubbed his chin, clearing his throat. "Bridget, their surname is Bridget."

Books threatened to fall out of the open locker as Lucas pushed them, forcing them back inside with a grunt.

After realising that his time at Aramoor Academy was now

more than just a useless side-quest, he made the decision to utilise his locker space for practical purposes, such as storing books, weapons, and writing supplies. He'd even signed himself up for an English literature and writing class, not with Mr Hardington thankfully, it was more of an A level class. Farah had suggested he sign up for it, and at first, he protested, but, then he didn't really understand why he was protesting. Lucas was finally getting to stay in the same place for a while, he had the time on his hands and a passion for writing, there was no logical reason not to give it a go, and for the first time in his life, he was actually looking forward to something.

Lucas pushed the books into his locker, along with a couple of hoodies and a secret stash of weapons hidden discreetly inside a lunchbox.

Although he had taken a step back from his hunter duties to spend time with his newfound family, it was still in his nature to be armed at all times. He didn't know what was going to strike, or when, therefore he had to be prepared for anything.

A loose book slipped through the cracks in his arms, falling to the ground with a bounce. His fingers grazed the sage-encrusted spine, turning it around to read the front of the book, something about the stories and incantations of Hecate. As he lifted it, another book dropped from the heap, setting off a chain reaction. Lucas quickly grabbed them and shoved them into the locker, closing the door with such force he accidentally sliced his finger on the rough edge.

With a grimace, he glanced at his bleeding finger and a queasy feeling rose up in his stomach.

In that very blood resided the gene that had the power to transform him into something he once detested. A mere drop of blood could reshape his entire life. He knew that not all vampires were threats now, Hazel certainly wasn't, and he needed to overcome his preconceived notions if he wanted to remain with his sister, his family, yet, he couldn't ignore the uneasy feeling as he gazed down at the blood.

A sharp snapping sound brought him out of his thoughts and he glanced up, wiping his finger on the back of his jeans as his gaze fell on Ophelia.

She was strutting through the corridor, gripping a laminated poster in one hand and a stapler in the other. A few of the other students glanced her way, averting their gaze with a warning snap of her stapler.

Ophelia stopped in front of a notice board, opening the stapler with one swift flick and stabbing the poster into place, covering some sort of charity football match banner.

Students staggered past her, mumbling under their breaths as Lucas strode over, knitting his eyebrow in bewilderment.

"What?" Ophelia demanded as she flattened out the poster.

Lucas pulled a face. "*Tear You Apart, the performance?*" he asked, reaching up to tap the poster condescendingly.

She grabbed his wrist, turning to glare at him, then released his arm and resumed smiling at the wall.

A black background served as the canvas for the poster, and there was a white spotlight shining on Ophelia's million-dollar face. A blood-red dress draped her body and she held a sharp, gleaming dagger in her right hand.

It looked like an old murder mystery book cover.

"Well, the first one went so well, I thought I'd do it again, just not in a skanky little club this time, and with a dance routine." She gleamed, pulling out a sheet of paper from her designer bag and pressing it into his chest forcefully.

"What is this?"

With a snide smile, Ophelia tossed her hair over her shoulder, making sure he watched as she walked away. "A sign-up sheet, dickhead. I need someone to play the victim."

Lucas shook his head with a disconcerted expression. "You know, I've still got my daggers," he mumbled quietly, to avoid any unintended listeners.

As the words fell from his lips, drizzled in a threatening undertone, Ophelia spun around to face him, sporting a malevolent grin. "Bite me, blade boy." She smirked, spinning around and extending her middle finger towards him as she strolled away.

Caleb let out a yawn, putting his feet up on the cobalt bean bag next to his desk as he leaned back with his controller, waiting for his game to load.

He'd insisted he was fine, but his mother made him take the week off anyway, just to be safe. The nightshade was out of his system within a day, maybe, but even after a week, Julianna continued to constantly fuss over him, monitoring his consumption of vitamins, supplements, and blood intake to make sure he was building back his strength.

However, it did have a silver lining – he got to play games, watch classic movies, and spend time with Hazel. She'd also been sentenced to the same predicament by her own mother, though that was mainly to help her adjust to her new senses.

Thankfully, there was a loophole that allowed them to escape for a few hours to train in the forest – Alexander's idea. Caleb took full advantage of this loophole, savouring the passing time as he basked in the fleeting sunlight and watched

Hazel mostly stumble over her own feet. It was probably what he looked forward to most in the day. Despite her desire to learn and develop her newfound abilities, she also liked to talk. It didn't take long for him to realise that Hazel could talk for hours, about horror movies, bands, tattoos, stars, anything really.

For a girl that was always looking for a distraction, she was particularly good at keeping his attention.

After playing a few competitive levels of his game, Caleb reached for the fizzy sweets on his desk and glanced at the clock. A smile formed on his lips, he only had an hour to wait.

He cast a quick glance at his closed door and listened for any movement outside. When there wasn't any, his attention shifted to the computer screen, hesitating, before opening a new tab.

University courses for game design and animation.

As he looked into the different degrees, Ophelia burst through the door. He quickly closed the webpage and dropped a cherry gummy from his lips.

"I was, uh— a video game," Caleb stammered.

She held a hand up with a disgusted shake of her head and stepped into the room, letting the door close behind her.

Caleb picked up another sour cherry, stuffing it into his mouth with a cautious expression as she sat down on the end of his bed. "What now?" he asked, suspiciously. "I'm not being in your show thing."

Ophelia scoffed in return, crossing her legs. "Oh, please, like I'd even want you anywhere near it. I have a… proposal."

"No," he replied, turning back to face his computer.

With a half-offended noise, Ophelia rolled her eyes and slammed her hand on the azure blue sheets to regain his attention. "I didn't even say what it was yet!"

Caleb shrugged. "Yeah, but if I say no now, then maybe I can stop whatever twisted idea you have before it comes back to bite me."

Ophelia huffed and kicked at her brother, aiming for his shin. He twisted in his chair, dodging her attempts, and she frowned, snarling as he leaned back with a chuckle.

"Go on then, what is it?"

"I don't want to tell you now."

With a snort, Caleb bit into another brightly coloured sweet, tugging until it broke in half. "Come on, Lia, I'm just playing around."

She stood up, crossing her arms over her stomach sternly.

"If we are careful, if no one knows, and I mean no one! Maybe… *Maybe*, I will help you find Rose," she said, watching him carefully to interpret his expression. "I want to know where she is as well, I just think we should do it from a distance… it'll be safer for her that way."

Caleb looked down for a moment, glancing at the bangle on his wrist, then peered up at his little sister and wrapped his arms around her. She released a muffled squeal, snickering, as he relaxed his hold and peered down at her in astonishment.

"Really?"

Her breath wavered but she nodded. There was a slight nervous look in her eye as she brought him in for a hug again, squeezing tightly. It lasted for a good few seconds, before she pushed him away again, smoothing out her jumper.

"Right, that's enough sappiness. I'm off. Enjoy training. Who knows, maybe Hazel will electrocute you with her new *powers*," Ophelia pondered snidely.

"So, are you two friends again?"

Ophelia pulled a face. "Me and Hazel? God no," she said

with a sly smile that belied her words.

Caleb cocked an eyebrow, chuckling. "I'll tell her you said hi."

"Please don't," Ophelia shot back, and there was *almost* no malice in the tone.

As the door closed behind her, he beamed, settling back into his bean bag and chewing on his bottom lip with a hopeful smile.

The sound of a tree branch tapping at her window had Hazel clamping her eyes closed tighter. She was trying and failing to take a nap before she met up with Caleb.

Hazel grabbed her pillow and pulled it over her head, trying to drown out the noise, though it didn't seem to help much – those damned heightened senses.

With all the extra energy being used, she thought she'd find sleeping a lot easier, but even after almost losing her life, she had never felt more vitality coursing through her body. Although it did heavily affect her sleeping schedule, which was a shame because she loved sleep, especially when it didn't involve weirdly realistic dreams, which, fortunately, had stopped once her brother had come home.

Those first couple of hours after she'd woken up were a bit of a blur. Though she can recall being in the back of a car, and then all too soon she was staring at her front door, facing down the prospect of taking Lucas to talk to her – *their* – mum.

The sound of a car pulling away buzzed in Hazel's ears as she spun around to face the door, wrinkling her nose up.

As she unlocked the door and stepped inside, Lucas grew stiff, staying behind on the welcome mat.

"You coming?" Hazel croaked, rubbing at her chest. Although most of the wound had healed, it still ached and she still felt a little... not quite there.

Lucas stared down at the space between them. "Ahh... yeah, just give me a minute."

Hazel didn't want to wait for a whole minute. With a nod, she let her bag fall onto the countertop near the door and moved for the living room.

As soon as she saw her mother, the woman stood up and rushed forward. Hazel practically fell into her arms and Nina pulled her close, bringing her face into her hands and scanning over her features.

"What happened to you? Why are you covered in blood? Oh, god," she croaked, leading Hazel to the couch and sitting her down. She tried to open her mouth to speak, but her mother wouldn't let her get a word in. "We have to call an ambulance," she fretted, reaching for her phone.

"No," Hazel replied, sitting up and pressing a hand against her throbbing forehead. "We can't do that."

Nina crouched down to her level, softening her tone. "We have to. There's so much blood."

"It's mostly dried."

Her mother pulled a face. "That is an overwhelmingly uncomfortable statement."

Hazel pulled her shirt down a little to reveal the makeshift bandage that had been wrapped around her wound. "It's okay. I'm fine!"

"You're not fine, we have to go to the hospital!"

"Mum. We can't go to the hospital... It'll heal too fast," she whispered, looking up and locking eyes with her mother.

A few seconds passed before a realisation dawned on Nina's face and she slumped down onto the floor, clutching Hazel's hand. "How…?"

Hazel clutched her wound, swallowing hard as she thought about where to start, before a figure quietly entered the room behind them, looming anxiously.

"Doesn't matter, there's something more important you need to know right now."

Nina furrowed her brow, blinking, before her head swivelled around to Lucas, who rubbed at his arm awkwardly. "Who is that?" she asked, studying him.

"You know," Hazel mumbled.

An unsteady breath escaped Nina's lips as her face crumpled. Letting go of her daughter's hand, she stood to meet the boy. Silence lingered in the air for a moment as she took in his face.

At first, he glanced away, fidgeting uncomfortably. However, when Nina took a step towards him, Lucas's gaze instinctively shifted to her.

With a disbelieving look, Nina glanced over her shoulder and met her daughter's gaze. Hazel bit her lip, nodding, and her mother let out a sob, wrapping her arms around the boy.

It took a little while for Lucas to hug her back, but when he did, his eyes drifted up to Hazel, meeting her gaze with a small smile.

Nina had been eager to learn about everything that had transpired in the past few days, and in return, she had divulged some information of her own.

She confirmed for her children that their father, Alden, was a vampire. His family – and by extension, Hazel and Lucas's family – were very powerful, but also very dangerous.

The family had fallen into obscurity though Nina wouldn't tell them why, all she would say was that they should keep the name Valdez to themselves.

All these years, Nina had thought Lucas had died. Alden had taken him when he was a baby and came back empty-handed, covered in blood. That was why Hazel's mother left their father – not the other way around – and was the reason she'd brought them to Aramoor Bridge.

Nina hadn't wanted Hazel to know she'd ever had a brother, she wanted to spare her the heartache. Instead, it had caused the opposite effect; she felt more pain, betrayal even. If she'd have just *known*, maybe things could have turned out differently.

The more Hazel learned about her mother and the secrets she kept, the more disconnected she felt from her. It felt like everything she'd ever known had all been one giant illusion.

As for the mysterious matter of their green veins in the forest, Hazel and Lucas had both come to the same conclusion.

Their mother wasn't exactly human.

Hazel sat upright in her bed with a grumpy sigh, giving up on any hope of falling asleep. She moved to the end of her bed and stretched her arms out, getting up to get ready.

As she fixed her t-shirt, she caught sight of the pendant dangling down from her necklace and brushed her fingers over it, smoothing over the tiny formation of golden leaves. It was strange, really, that Lucas had the same one. Hazel didn't remember when she'd gotten it, only that it used to belong to her mother. In that photograph Lucas had, she'd worn them as earrings.

They'd been passed down from Nina, so what wasn't to say there weren't more. It could have been a family thing, like the Thorns with their tattoos. Maybe golden leaves were her family's tattoos?

She made her way over to her wardrobe, kicking at the pile of clothes pushed against it to pull it open. There was a trinket box tucked at the top, with a small stack of printed photos inside. Her mother's photos, mostly ones from when Hazel was growing up but there were a few from before then too.

There was one of Nina when she was younger, smiling with another green-eyed girl that Hazel didn't recognise. Whoever she was, it seemed they were close, just not close enough to still be in touch. For all Hazel knew, this could have been her auntie. Nina didn't talk much about her life before Hazel, or her family for that matter. It was always a touchy subject, and one that Nina always tried to avoid, which only made Hazel more curious.

She placed the photos on the floor with a sigh, sitting with her legs crossed. From the very few that were there, there were no signs of golden leaves, only in her mother's ears. What was she really looking for? More family heirlooms? More family? Clearly her mother didn't want to be a part of that family. So why would she even keep these photos? Hazel wasn't sure, but her eyes caught onto something else.

It was the picture of her father. He was smiling at the camera, a dangerous gleam in his eyes.

Hazel shifted a little, glancing down at the man. He was the image of her brother, complete with the same daunting expression.

"Who's that?"

A small croak left Hazel's throat as she turned around to

see Lucas leaning in the doorway, peering at the photograph.

He stepped into the room and let out a breath, holding his hands up apologetically. "Sorry, last time I swear."

"You say that and then appear out of nowhere and make me spill my cereal." Hazel frowned, scrunching up her lip.

Lucas shrugged. "I got you more cereal."

With a shake of her head, she glanced back at the photograph and stood up, handing it out to him. "It's our dad," she explained, swallowing back an awkward breath.

An uncomfortable look flickered in his amber eyes. "The vampire?"

"Yeah," Hazel confirmed, looking back down at the photograph. "If you got the chance, would you want to meet him?"

Lucas wrinkled his forehead. "Not really no."

She couldn't blame him, it was because of their father that Lucas had spent his entire life fighting, instead of being with his family. Still, she couldn't push away the strange feeling that wrapped around her as she stared at the photo. Hazel placed it back in the box and stood up.

"I was looking through old photographs for more golden leaves," she said, motioning to her necklace. "If mum gave us these ones. I thought, maybe it was a family thing or something…"

Lucas hummed, pulling his own necklace out of the confinements of his hoodie. "You think they have a deeper meaning?"

"Doesn't everything?"

"I don't know, some things are just that, *things*. Maybe they're just pieces of jewellery?"

Hazel fiddled with the golden leaves. "Maybe."

The sound of the doorbell interrupted them, and Hazel

glanced up, stepping past her brother as she moved toward the stairs.

She opened the front door to see Caleb, who was standing on the other side with his usual idiotic grin.

"Be back later!" Hazel yelled, turning back to the house as she stepped outside.

"Okay, remember not to let your back get exposed," Lucas replied, resting against the handrail of the stairs, before mumbling under his breath. "And keep an eye on the shadows *for that slippery—*"

"Thanks Lucas."

As Hazel stepped out of the door, pulling at the blonde boy's arm, he kept his gaze on the hunter, peering at him with a jaunty grin.

"I could always come with you?" Lucas offered, now standing in the doorway. "Teach you how to *really* fight."

Caleb leaned toward Hazel with a smirk. "Are you aware your brother is threatening me with a dagger right now?"

She turned around to see Lucas fumbling to hide his dagger and shook her head, leading Caleb toward his car.

Hazel brushed her hand through the trees as they walked through the woods. Every so often, she felt Caleb's gaze on her, watching her with a mischievous look.

They stopped in a small clearing not too far from the main road and he turned around, gesturing for her to attack him.

Hazel swept towards him, only to have him quickly grab her forearms and tug her forward. She spun around, wrinkling her nose in frustration as he disappeared from sight.

Caleb suddenly reappeared beside her and grabbed her

waist, leaning into her ear. "And now you're dead, *vlah, vlah, vlah.*" He smirked, making a quick move towards her. Hazel swiftly evaded it.

As she disappeared, Caleb glanced around, raising an eyebrow, before being tackled to the forest floor from behind.

"Got you! Now *you're* dead!" she exclaimed, clamping his hands together in the middle of his back.

He shuffled with an amused sniff, freeing himself from her grasp and rolling over to meet her gaze. "Is that so?" Caleb asked, giving her an infuriatingly smug smile. "We can't both be dead. How about we call it even and I'll give you a head start on the next one."

Hazel scrunched up her nose, pushing him back to the floor by his chest as he tried to sit up. "How about no?" she mused, raising a brow.

Caleb sank back to the ground with a chuckle. "How can I fight back if I can't use my arms?"

Hazel shuffled slightly, firming her grip. "Sounds like a you problem," she whispered, chewing the corner of her lip with a sly grin.

He blinked for a second, dazedly, before tilting his head upwards. "Oh, great, that's fine, then. I'll figure it out, no bother at all, even if your elbow is digging into my rib."

She moved her arm, giving him some leeway, and Caleb raised an eyebrow cheekily, grinning as he used his newfound freedom to clasp his arms around her and wrestle her to the ground.

A high-pitched titter fell from Hazel's lips as he pounced on her, covering her already dark hair in dirt while their laughter echoed through the surrounding trees.

Hazel wrapped her legs around him. His arms fell to either side of her head and she tightened her grip and reversed their positions, holding him down beneath her. Defeated, he let his arms fall and leaned back against the crumpled leaves as she let out a triumphant cheer.

After a second, Caleb raised his head and met her gaze again, his smile emitting a sense of warmth. Hazel stared down at him, her eyes lingering on his lips.

Her hands clutched his shoulders tighter while he held onto her waist, caressing her skin, and covering it in goosebumps.

The gap between them slowly began to bridge.

Their lips came within inches of each other, almost brushing, before Hazel suddenly felt a rush of heat coming from her left and her gaze shifted upwards. "Shit!" she shouted, grinning. "Caleb, I did it, I started a fire!"

He frowned at the sudden loss of connection and let her pull him up, sitting beside her to look at the flaming tree. "That's not usually a good thing," he said breathily, though there was a proud gleam in his face as his gaze drifted back towards her.

Hazel widened her eyes as the flames grew, fixating on them, but it wasn't long before they faded away. The crimson colour of her irises became mottled with a sage swirl before they dissolved back to their natural sunlit hue. She beamed back at him. "I think I'm getting the hang of this!"

Caleb leaned back on his elbows. "Hm, we'll see," he said, standing and offering out his hand to pull her up.

"Right, now, let's see if you can catch me." He winked, before drifting off into the trees.

"Caleb!" Hazel chuckled, taking a deep breath and exhaling it into the autumn air as she sped after him.